# Inferno

Justice/Vengeance

Volume 4

Erik Scott de Bie

# Other Lady Vengeance Stories

**The Justice/Vengeance Series**
*Libations for the Dead* (DefCon One Publishing, 2023)
*Public Enemy* (DefCon One Publishing, 2024)
*Fallen Angel* (DefCon One Publishing, 2025)

**Other Stories**
"Vengeance on the Layover," *Cobalt City Timeslip* (Timid Pirate Publishing, 2010)
"Angels of Mercy," *Triumph over Tragedy* (Terrene Press, 2013)
"The Curse of the Bambino," *This Mutant Life: Bad Company* (Kalamity Press, 2013)
"Queen of Demons," *Monster Hunter: The Good Fight* (Emby Press, 2015)
"Baggage," *Shadowed Souls* (Roc, 2016)
"Mother of Harlots," *Cobalt City Dragonstorm* (DefCon One Publishing, 2022)
*Eye for an Eye* (originally published as a part of *Cobalt City Double Feature*, 2012, Timid Pirate Publishing; reprinted 2018, DefCon One Publishing)
*Femmes Fatale*, with Amanda Cherry (DefCon One Publishing, 2022)
*Bad Intentions (Femmes Fatale 2)*, with Amanda Cherry (DefCon One Publishing, 2023)
*Pretty Hate Machine (Girl Vengeance 1)* (DefCon One Publishing, 2024)
*The Downward Spiral (Girl Vengeance 2)* (DefCon One Publishing, 2024)

# CONTENTS

---

*This one is for my father, who has spent his life fighting for justice that often seems elusive.*

# ACKNOWLEDGEMENTS

No surprise, but this book owes a lot to my many creative friends, including especially my co-writer Amanda "Killingsworth" Cherry, my editor Dawn "Dulcamara" Vogel, publisher Jeremy "Kensei" Zimmerman, my agent Gabrielle Harbowy, and my cheerleaders Alexandra "Shattered Phoenix" Pitchford, Kelsey Dawn "Wren" Scott, Jen "Savage Sparrow" Brazas, and the rest of the Cobalt City team: Rosemary "Electric Girl" Jones, James Do Hung Lee, and Catherine Warren. Without their constant love and support, this project would never have gotten off the ground.

# CHAPTER ONE: SHOT IN THE DARK

**December 2019**

"Will that be all, sir?" Maria asks over the intercom.

Antonio DeSantes idly taps his prosthetic eye, the way he often does when he's thinking. He knows the offer she's making, and he knows Henrietta is there waiting on his word, too. They love him, and he loves them too, in his way. But he's turned them down for months, and he knows they're curious at best, jealous at worst. He'll have to increase his management efforts.

"See that I'm not disturbed," he says coldly, then switches off the intercom.

DeSantes leans back in his chair, the half-dozen screens providing the only light in his penthouse office. His calendar, with his upcoming brain surgery, appears on one of the screens, but it's the only thing that's his. Every other inch of the screens is plastered with research studies, physics analyses, newspaper articles, and—importantly—field reports from his own private investigators. De la Vega had to go back to Cobalt City for one thing or another, but DeSantes has a dozen other detectives on the case. Some have powers, some don't, but all of them are well paid. So far, nothing, but he can't give up.

Angel needs him.

A bright flash illuminates his office, making him wince faintly, and he turns to the massive wall of windows. The storm over Valhalla, Colorado, is miraculously quiet, thanks to the soundproofed windows, but he still feels its ferocity. That glass is bulletproof to all but a concerted gunship assault or a nuclear blast, but the storm still makes the building vibrate.

He likes it. The storm. Or maybe "likes" is the wrong word. The storm is important. He recognizes it. He sees something in it. Something he needs to see. Always.

Sometimes, he sees the Raven in the storm. Sometimes, he sees the hammer. Sometimes, he sees the end of all things—the gods clash and the world trembles. But he always sees something.

Tonight, he sees the lightning. He sees the power and fury and knows it isn't spent.

DeSantes looks down at the phone in his hand. It's an old model, from two and a half years ago. Ordinarily, he would replace his technology every six months at a minimum, but he's held onto this phone ever since that day. It only has one number in it. One call log. He's erased everything else.

He's done everything he can to identify the caller. Trace the digital address. Isolate the signal. Voice recognition software. Decryption.

Everything except call her back.

He taps the number and holds the phone to his ear. It rings.

"Hello, Tony."

He didn't expect her to answer, so he didn't brace for and isn't ready for that vaguely familiar voice. It's older. Darker. Filtered through a veil, maybe. But it's undeniable.

"Nothing to say? After so many years?"

He sucks in breath between his teeth. "It was you. All of it. *You.*"

"Is that so."

Not a question.

"Energy cannot be destroyed. It can only be transferred from one form to another."

"Who says?"

"Thales of Miletus. Epicurus. Galileo. Newton. Noether. Poincaré. Einstein. Stevens. The first law of thermodynamics." DeSantes takes a breath. "All part of your plan. Right—Goddess?"

He can almost hear the familiar smile, with those too-white teeth.

"Goodbye, Tony. See you soon."

"Bet."

The phone goes dead. He knows that number won't go anywhere ever again.

He hangs up.

And immediately dials a new number.

The phone rings five times, which makes sense, as it *is* three in the morning on the East Coast. Finally, it connects, and a muffled voice, slurred slightly with sleep and probably several Bellinis, answers. "Arsho, I hope this is important. Need I remind you that your employment is—"

"It's me," DeSantes says. "I need your help."

A pause. "How are you in my phone? And under 'Arsho—Non-Emergency'?"

"I added my number while you were asleep," he says. "I reasoned you would never actually dial this number, because—"

"If I'm calling Arsho, it's an emergency, goddammit it." She sighs. "What do you want? This isn't some sort of booty call, is it? Because the answer's a decided *no*. No amount of blackmail—"

"As I said, I need your help."

"Tony, you're a billionaire," comes the annoyed response. "What can I do for you that you can't do for yourself? Other than that trick with my—"

"Magic, exactly. Oracular divination. Scrying. Demonic communion. Necromancy, maybe."

"What, you need help moving a body?" She laughs, that genuine guffaw he enjoys so much. "We're not that kind of friends. In fact, we're not friends at *all*."

"I need to find someone."

"A *dead* someone?"

"No," he says, flatly and definitively.

"Are you sure?"

"Conservation of energy."

"Is that supposed to mean something to me?"

It's too complicated to explain to someone who isn't a physicist, let alone over the phone. But if his calculations and suspicions are correct ...

"Ugh." Pillows shuffle around as she gets more comfortable. Probably perched on her elbows, red hair pushed back over her ear. "I'm supposed to believe you don't have your own scrying crystal? Magic mirror, perhaps? I could tell you how to read bones. Over a bottle of Dom Perignon 1959, delivered to my office, which you are not in, because normal people use Zoom."

*I need you*, he thinks but doesn't say. He pushes his own fantasies to the side for now. This isn't the time. "Please," he says.

A scoff. "I'm hanging up now."

"It's for Vivienne."

Silence.

DeSantes almost thinks she hung up, and he wouldn't blame her.

"Fine," Ruby Killingsworth says. "Exactly who am I looking for?"

# CHAPTER TWO: BLANK SPACE

---

**March 2020**

The phone buzz sets her teeth on edge, matching the rhythm in her pounding head.

At first, for an embarrassingly long time, she thinks it's part of her dream. A dream about gunships, firing hundreds and hundreds of anti-materiel rounds into the building where she and two of her favorite mistakes are beating the shit out of her body and her heart. And there's someone who's supposed to be there, saving her, but he's always out of reach. Whenever she touches his strong hand, he dissolves into ash, as though from a nuclear blast, and then her eyes snap open.

Vivienne Cain doesn't know where she is. She barely remembers her name.

But she remembers the dream in very distinct and very traumatic detail.

"Jesus, are you gonna get that?" comes a slurred voice, equally hungover to how she feels, and then she remembers she's not alone.

"For fuck's sake of *fuck*," she says, glancing over. "Ew."

One of the Chippendales dancers whose speedos she was stuffing bills down last night, the man is not. He's not even one of the muscular bouncers who rang her bell with a good punch last night. She loves a good two a.m. fistfight as much as the next hot mess of a semi-retired superhero. Hell, she would have taken one of the shrimpy dealers who was definitely cheating at cards—"no, you see, Mr. Bouncer, I'm psychic and I can *tell*"—who she would have happily fucked unconscious.

No, this guy is a casino manager: squat, hairy, and entirely too greasy. Worse, he's the douchebag who insisted the middle-aged goth who'd downed fifteen cocktails needed to be thrown out. And while Vivienne doesn't mind being demeaned and mistreated by *a* man from time to time—rather enjoys it sometimes—this guy is *the* man, and she has no love for The Man.

"Are you gonna answer that? Or maybe—" He puts one sweaty hand on her hip. "Ignore it?"

"Get out," she says.

"Huh? But it's *my* room—"

"Get out." Vivienne channels a little spark of fear energy into her face and voice, freaking him right the fuck out. "Now."

Not only does the douchebag fall out of bed and scramble to get away, but he soils his tighty-whities while doing so. Years from now, when his life has collapsed and he's telling his therapist about the she-devil he slept with that one time who gave him PTSD related to women, he'll probably omit the part about pissing himself. Which, well, maybe seeing a therapist earlier and being honest would have saved him all that suffering. Serves him fucking right, not taking care of his problems, just like Vivienne Cain definitely does every time.

Yeah, right.

"This is a no hypocrisy zone," she murmurs.

The phone keeps buzzing as Vivienne slumps back on the rumpled bed, breathes, and stares up at the crack and damp spot in the ceiling. The room is cheap and sleazy—she knows the sort, and that makes her hate the manager even more. Maybe she should have cursed him with subliminal urges to void his bowels whenever he gets excited about something. She's powerful enough to do something like that, right? Even without ...

"Call me or don't," a certain fire-haired sorceress billionaire media mogul with a killer ass said to her in the destroyed Valhalla tower, then marched right out of her life on five-figure heels.

Vivienne shuts her eyes to keep from thinking about Ruby. She's had some bad breakups (some that also involved white supremacist death squads, come to think of it) but that ...

She's been bouncing from hotel to hotel for about a month now, drinking and fucking herself mostly unconscious. The rickety desk is full of empty bottles and covered with white powder and other paraphernalia, and while she hopes she only attacked her *liver* all this time, she can't make any promises. Drugged-out sex and violence have always been her most reliable coping mechanisms, and this ... well, she wouldn't put it past herself.

Worst of all, as Vivienne lies there, she starts to feel all the feelings of the hotel and its guests: the desperation, the rage, the depression—oh fuck, the *depression*. It isn't just the down-on-their-luck gambling addicts, tweakers, exploited sex workers and the pimps who did the exploiting, but also the hotel itself. The place has stood here in old Vegas, off the glitzy strip, for decades now, and the dark, sad emotions of its many residents have built up in the walls and sunk into the foundations themselves. And when you're an empath like Vivienne? Not just an empathic person who gives a fuck about others, the way Millennials and Zoomers use the word, but an honest to goddess psychic *empath* ... Well, it's a *lot*.

The phone buzzes again. Half a dozen missed calls, all from the same number. This number.

This time she picks up. "Fucking *what?*"

"Viviana."

Nope. Nope nope nope, she's not going to put up with this.

She hangs up on Tony, then hurls the phone across the room, into the bathroom. It clatters against the wall and into the tub.

Ruby at least had a convenient portal to get away from that conversation. She left Vivienne there with an again-cursed Tony, and she was just supposed to *deal* with it. Well, not cursed, but *enchanted* not to be able to hurt Vivienne, and at least he wasn't still in love with Ruby fucking Killingsworth anymore. But regardless, Ruby left Tony and Vivienne alone in that destroyed tower, and somehow, they *weren't* supposed to fight? Because they did—oh hell yeah, they did. There were certain words exchanged. Certain bruises.

Tony fucking DeSantes. From engineer punk to violent vigilante to governor of a super advanced cyber state that stands in defiance against the white supremacist rule of the Bigot in Chief, Lyle Prather. In every sense except reality, he was her dream—the love of her life—the anti-fascist *god among men* with no superpowers but more grit and determination and ingenuity than anyone, who would cross any moral or ethical line to punch any Nazi in the face. They could have had a whole life together, but Vivienne had put a stop to that at the clinic twenty years ago. And ever since, however many times they reconnected, she has *consistently* fucked it up. Not always by fucking him or someone else, but often. Or used him as a tool to fuck up her other relationships. And she finally did that with Ruby, too, and now ...

In what world—in what universe—does that man have the audacity to contact her? Does he have zero sense where she's concerned? No, she doesn't have the space for that nonsense.

Fuck both of them. She doesn't need either of them. She doesn't need anyone or anything.

Except something to drink.

"*Vengeance,*" the old familiar voice says.

Vivienne paws through the small liquor store beside the bed, desperate for anything, and spills a good two shots of vodka before she can get the bottle to her lips. There's barely anything left, but at least it makes the feelings a little softer. Fuzzier.

"*It won't work.*" The demon's voice makes her teeth vibrate. "*You won't shut me out.*"

"Watch me," she says, and goes to the table. The cocaine is basically useless, but there's a half-full fifth of Stoli there, and that's what she needs. She chugs the bottle, parched and sore throat working, the liquor burning. As it gets to work inside her, she staggers over to the mirror and glares at her face smeared with black makeup, shrouded in greasy black hair. She looks like an angry oil slick.

Only her violet eyes aren't eyes. They're mouths of clacking teeth.

"*I'm watching,*" Azazel says through her eyes. "*I see me, Vengeance.*"

Before she can think better of it, Vivienne slams her forehead into the mirror, sending cracks splintering in all directions. The pounding pain makes her stagger back and fall into the bathtub, where she lies, staring at the spinning room, and wishes she'd thought better of it.

"*What do you have left, Vengeance?*" Azazel asks. "*What do you have left to protect?*"

The worst thing is that he's right.

He's evil, monstrous, and horrid, but he's *right.*

She'd been holding it together ... when Marcus was with them. He and Angel were happy—mostly—and they were helping each other, and Angel was even fixing things with her father. Fucking Tony. He spent the autumn ignoring Vivienne, yeah, but that was

12

because he was under Ruby's love curse,[1] so this was only partially his fault. Still ... she burned that bridge quite thoroughly, and now she and Ruby are on rocks so sharp they might as well be a bed of nails.

"*All those you love betray you,*" Azazel says. "*Everyone but me.*"

Andre called a few times, but she never returned those calls, and he gave up eventually. He's probably fine, in the house Ruby bought him in exchange for spying on her. Unless she's so spiteful she decided to take that back? Yes, yes, she is. Also? Ruby owns a not insubstantial part of the bar. If Vivienne goes back to Seattle, will she even have a home?

"*No one,*" Azazel says. "*You have no one.*"

Vivienne's options are incredibly limited. She can't call Jaccob, of course, for the same reason she can't go back to Seattle. She looked up Manny when she came southwest from Colorado and ended up in Vegas, but he had headed back east, probably doing something in Cobalt City. Not that he would have been all that helpful—she and Manny are just friends with very occasional benefits. Who's left? Wren? Ugh, Vivienne can't make herself do that to *Wren*. Not again.

She needs someone. Anyone.

But who does she have left?

"*Only me.*"

Her phone buzzes. She wouldn't answer if she had to move, but she's practically sitting on the phone. She fishes it from the trickle of stale water and checks out the screen, which resembles the ruined mirror, and the caller ID: "Nimue." That's a weird name. Is she supposed to—?

Oh.

Nimue, the Lady of the Lake, from Arthurian legend.

Our Lady of the Lake Catholic Church, in Maple Leaf, Seattle. Where she went to school as a kid.

Where her mother still goes to Mass every Sunday.

---

[1] This scene falls between round 7 and round 8 of *Femmes Fatale 2: Bad Intentions*; see that novel for more on Ruby Killingsworth's magical shenanigans. ~ Enchanter Vogel

The room seems to settle, and she becomes aware of her own breathing, which she has to force herself to do. In the reflection of the cracked phone screen, at least her eyes are her own again.

She touches the green call button. When she tries to speak, though, it's just a croak.

"Vivienne Cain?" asks a gentle, patient voice. "Viviana?"

"Sis—" She swallows despite her throat feeling like dusty death. "Sister Theresa."

"Viviana, it is you," the elderly nun says—she must be seventy by now. "I didn't know if this number still worked, but it's in your mother's file. You're her emergency contact."

Vivienne presses the phone to her chest, heedless of the broken screen cutting into her skin. She squeezes her eyes tight to stop the tears and bites her lip hard enough to draw blood.

"Viviana?" the nun asks.

"Yeah." Vivienne can barely talk. "What, uh—?"

"It's about your mother. She's—Vivianna, I'm so sorry. She passed away this morning."

Vivienne squeezes the phone so tight it snaps in half. Blood trickles down over the decades-old scars on her wrist. The pieces of the phone bite into her hand, creating new scars.

"*Vengeance*," the demon whispers. "*I am here for you—*"

"Shut up," she says, heart thundering in her head. She sees herself a dozen times in the shattered mirror, cowering in the bathtub. She's alone. Utterly, totally alone.

"*You can have her back. I can give her back.*"

"I said shut up."

"*You can have him back.*"

"Shut the fuck up, or I swear, I'll do it." She puts the sharp end of the phone to her throat. The glass against her skin is the most exquisite kiss.

Azazel says nothing more.

"That's right, you halitosis-ridden son of a bitch," she says. "I'm useless to you dead."

She has to go. Back to Seattle. Or somewhere. Just *go*.

Or maybe ...

With her foot, she reaches over and turns on the tap in the tub, which starts filling with warm water. The hotel is a shithole, but at least it has an actual tub. Doing something like this in the shower would defeat the purpose. As the water rises—she eventually

14

remembers to press down the plug—she considers the destroyed phone. That seems inefficient. Surely, she has something better.

When the tub is about half full, Vivienne opens her dimensional pocket and pulls out her sorcery focus: the silver Pentagonal Hex, the nightmare hate-child of Freddy Krueger's reaper glove and the Predator's claw, crafted of metals that rival space shuttle engines in hardness and heat resistance, and—most importantly—is extremely sharp. She spends a long time looking at it, scrutinizing its familiar joints and contours, the scuffs and dents it's picked up over too long in service to a doomed wielder.

Vivienne looks up at the broken mirror and sees a dozen pieces of her own face gazing back at her. Are those her eyes? Is that her face? She can feel the demon rustling around her head, angry but afraid. She likes him like that. She's a little worried he's not trying to stop her, but maybe that's reverse psychology. Or maybe he wants her to do it. She really doesn't care.

When the water is almost full, she slides the claw onto her hand. It doesn't feel comfortable and familiar. Instead, it's cold and alien, like something that isn't supposed to belong in this world.

"Well," she murmurs. "That's something we have in common."

Carefully, she sets the bladed fingers against her opposite wrist.

"*Don't.*"

It's another voice, one she's never heard in her head before, but it's so familiar it makes her eyes well with tears. For one drunken, reeling, fucked-up heartbeat, she thinks Orestes is sitting there, on the edge of the tub, looking down at her. It isn't embarrassing or awkward. It's just sad.

"Sorry, kid," she says. "I'm just about d—"

Which is when a fist pounds on the door, giving her pause.

Vivienne sits there in the tub for a long moment, frozen despite the warmth. Maybe she just imagined that, like with the kid. Who is, in point of fact, not sitting there. Which she knew. Of course not. He's fucking *dead*. She takes a deep breath and blows it out.

The fist knocks again, this time accompanied by a voice. A femme voice. "Ms. Cain? V?"

Vivienne sighs. She's such a fuckup, she can't even do this right.

"Well, can't be rude, I guess," she says.

Also, she gets the sense that her guest isn't just gonna leave. Especially not when she says, "the door's open—I'm coming in."

Fuck.

Climbing out of the tub is one of the hardest things she's ever done in her life. And not just because every muscle is sore, and she's exhausted and starving. Her body started to shut down prematurely, and now that she's demanding it start up again, the engine has to turn over a few times. Her bones creak, and her joints protest, but she manages it. She even grabs the ratty hotel robe just before the bathroom door opens. She realizes she still has the claw on, so she puts it behind her back.

"Rude, just bursting in like that," Vivienne says.

"Oh!" Yumi Kujikawa stands there, dressed head to toe in a very flattering black leather biker outfit. She gets an eyeful, then looks away, suddenly beet red. "I'm sorry! Um, I, uh—"

"It's fine." Vivienne adjusts the robe with her one hand. Not that she gets much accomplished, so she just leaves it as-is. "And don't apologize, kid. What's up?"

"You haven't been answering your phone, and I came to look for you, is all."

Vivienne tenses, curling the fingers of the claw. "Did Tony send you?"

"What? No, I'm totally over the whole Raven thing. I happened to be in town—"

"You just *happened* to be in Las Vegas. In the middle of March."

"Um, yeah. Felix and Manuel—well, mostly Manny—left me a message that you were in town."

Vivienne nods. It makes sense Manuel de la Vega would have some contacts left in the city, seeing as he'd been operating out of Las Vegas a few months ago. Maybe he *did* still care.

"Well," Vivienne says. "Here I am."

"Are you okay?" Yumi gestures around the room with one hand. The other is on the grip of her ancestral and highly magical katana, Muramasa. Would dying on that cursed steel be so bad? Probably. "Looks like there was a fight in here. Or a bomb went off."

"Both," Vivienne says, though from what little she can remember, that's way, way overstating the hotel manager's abilities. "Also, I'm never drinking again."

"Oh yeah?" Yumi smiles. "That's a very responsible decision, Ms. Cain. I'm proud of you."

Vivienne almost busts up laughing. What a ridiculous thing to say. So serious, too, for a twenty-something. But at the same time, it's strangely touching. Like, at least someone cares.

"Ms. Cain? Are you crying?"

"What? Oh, no. I was about to get in the shower." Vivienne wipes her face with the back of her unclawed hand. Her knuckles come away smeared with mascara. "And call me V, okay, kid?"

"Only if you call me Yumi."

"Deal." Vivienne's stomach growls, which she had started to assume was impossible. "I gotta get that shower. Then we can get out of here. I can tell you hate the place, rich girl."

"What?" Yumi, who has only continued looking uncomfortable in the dump of a hotel room, tries her best to look oblivious and fails utterly. "Okay, if you say so."

"See if you can find my clothes, huh? Also." Vivienne picks up the hotel phone and dials a number. "Hi, room service? I'd like one of everything, please. Yeah, charge it to the room."

"Are we eating?" Yumi asks. "I could eat. Though if the food is anything like the room, it's going to be worse than a truck stop grand slam combo."

"That, and the thought of eggs right at the moment makes my stomach want to wrestle with my liver for the first spot in line for the electric chair. But fuck that guy, and fuck his wallet."

"Evocative." Yumi pulls a face. "They probably don't have anything vegan anyway."

"Also, there might be mimosas."

Yumi brightens but narrows her eyes. "I thought you said you gave up drinking."

"Baby steps."

Also, something the demon said gave her an idea.

She closes her bleeding fist in determination. "I'm coming for you, kid—"

"Did you say something?" Yumi comes up from behind the couch with Vivienne's lacy black bra.

"I'll tell you later."

Vivienne hears the last of the water drain and heads for the shower. It's cold, because she used all the hot water, but that's okay. She can still feel Azazel's smug pleasure, but she tunes him out. She breathes deep and lets the smeared makeup wash away, along with the tears.

17

Baby steps.

"Wait for me, Marcus," she says.

# CHAPTER THREE: EDGE OF MIDNIGHT

"So let me get this straight," Yumi says as they take their seats on one of three Kujikawa family Cessna Citations. Unlike her stated intentions, she can't sit straight in her seat, but ends up with one leg flung over the side, head tucked back into the seam between the headrest and wrap-around side.

"Ms. Kujikawa," says the stern and ever-patient stewardess dressed in—is that a French maid uniform? "I really have to ask you to sit up straight and buckle your seatbelt for safety reasons during takeoff and landing."

"Yuriko," Yumi says. "You know I'm a superhero, right? The plane could *explode* on the tarmac, and I'd probably be fine."

"Ms. Kujikawa." The stewardess is all business, her body made of tightly coiled muscle. A faint scar traces from the edge of her left eye down her cheek, only noticeable when she's restraining her anger. Like now. "I must remind you, each time. These orders come from—"

"My father, yeah, yeah, of course. Thank you for your duty."

Yuriko bows slightly, simmering with murderous potential, then heads off.

"That woman," Vivienne says, "is not someone you should so casually piss off."

"What, Yuriko?" Yumi shrugs. "She's a trained assassin, but she's cool if you get to know her."

"What's with the uniform? It's very anime."

"Yuppers! It was my idea," Yumi says. "People always underestimate butlers and maids."

"So that butler guy outside is a highly trained assassin too?"

"That's Charles. He's a sniper."

"So you're, what, with the Factory now?" Vivienne asks. "I noticed your black card's working."

There's a pair of glasses and a ten-year-old bottle of Pappy Van Winkle, which might last until they're over the Midwest. Vivienne's trying to cut down.

"Guilty," Yumi says. "It ... it's not like I'm taking assassin jobs. It's a deal with my father, who's grooming me to take over. I'm trying to change things from the inside, you know?"

"Sure." Vivienne is still thinking about that bourbon, which is probably a thousand-dollar bottle. "And what's the girlfriend have to say? Lisa, right?"

"It's complicated," Yumi says, evading. "We're still together, but ... it's complicated."

Ordinarily, this would be exactly the sort of drama Vivienne would live for, but just now ... She's already opening the bottle of bourbon. Which has been inevitable.

What is she doing here? With this twenty-year-old and her private jet and the professional assassins waiting on them, and she didn't even snark about it? She must be *very* depressed.

Whatever Yumi was going to "get straight" seems to have gone entirely out of her head. But then, Yumi is a bundle of ADHD energy given form as an entirely too attractive young woman. She is a disaster. Reminds Vivienne of herself.

"So," Vivienne says, swirling her first glass slightly. "You've probably heard that Ruby and I broke up."

"What? No—" Yumi wouldn't be convincing even to someone who *couldn't* feel her emotions.

"I am entirely able to function without a rich sugar mama," Vivienne says. "I did just fine on my own, thank you very much."

"Of course," Yumi says. "Thank you for allowing me to support you."

"I could have stolen a motorcycle and made my way to Florida without your plane."

"No doubt. Thank you for allowing me to prevent your crime spree."

"I can also feed myself and buy my own supplies." She fills the second glass beside the first.

"Absolutely. Thank you for—"

"You're welcome, *sheesh*," Vivienne says. "And no, this one is for me too."

20

"I may be underage, but I *am* an adult, you know."

Vivienne rolls her eyes. "I'm literally twice your age."

"Aren't you forty-one?" Yumi asks. "That's *more* than twice my age."

Vivienne drinks both bourbons, one after the other.

"Ope." Yumi blushes a little. "Um, I thought bourbon was a sipping liquor."

"What do you care?" Vivienne fills up one of the glasses with what is at least a triple. "What were you going to ask me before?"

"Oh, right!" Yumi says, in a burst of ADHD energy. "Let me get this straight: you want to go to Angel's concert in Pepsi-Cola, because—?"

"Pensacola," Vivienne says. "And can't a doting aunt visit her beloved niece?"

"I heard you two weren't talking to each other."

"Where'd you hear that?"

"Oh. You know." Yumi waves her slick black phone around. "Word gets around."

Vivienne should have expected this. Yumi might carry an age-inappropriate torch for her, but she is, first and foremost, Angel's friend. She isn't sure how the rules of female friendships work these days, especially in the wake of an end-of-days split like hers with Angel. To be honest, she wasn't clear on the rules when she was their age, either. So fuck it.

"I know she's your BFF," Vivienne says.

Yumi looks confused. "Is that like a Boomer term?"

"Shit, you *know* how old I am, and I'm a burned-out Gen Xer, I'll have you know." Vivienne shakes her head. "Best friends forever—what do the kids say these days?"

"Bestie?" Yumi suggests. "Ride or die?"

Vivienne kind of likes that one. "You're best friends, right? Right?"

"Go on," Yumi says, evading the question.

"And I know you're being protective of your friend," Vivienne says. "If I were you, I wouldn't want her crazy medium-functioning alcoholic aunt anywhere near her, either."

"I've already commissioned a jet to take you there." Yumi leans forward, putting her elbows on the arms of her chair and steepling her fingers. "I just want to make sure you're not going to hurt her."

"Of course I won't," Vivienne says. "I just need her help with something."

"Something like—?"

"Marcus."

That strikes a chord with Yumi. Vivienne knows she had a thing with Marcus when they were both in high school back in Seattle. She isn't sure what their subsequent status is, er, *was*, but they always seemed friendly. Vivienne can feel a swelling darkness in Yumi—a ball of unresolved emotions—and starts to regret having said anything. Maybe she should have left it vague.

"Okay," Yumi says. "As long as you won't hurt her."

"I promise," Vivienne says. "Not *her*, anyway."

"Say what now?" Yumi asks.

"Huh?"

Shit. Did she say that out loud? She's been having trouble separating her inner monologue from her outer one. The bourbon probably doesn't help.

"What was that second thing?" Yumi asks. "Are we going to beat up some baddies?"

"Sure, kid." Vivienne sighs with relief. "Always."

Unfortunately, that just leads to more questions.

"Is there a threat against Angel?" Yumi asks. "Can you sense evil intent from this far away? That's like a thousand miles! More!"

Before Vivienne can think of a good lie, the door to the service section opens, and Yuriko appears again, her face furrowed with upset. "Apologies, Ms. Kujikawa, we're having some trouble with acquiring departure clearance."

"Oh?" Yumi asks. "What's up?"

But Vivienne already knows, even through the cheap mimosa and expensive bourbon haze. "ICE agents. Meal Team Six objects, apparently."

Yumi brightens. "That's amazing, you can sense the bad guys from inside the plane?"

In reply, Vivienne points out the window, at a couple of ICE vans that are even now approaching the plane across the tarmac.

"That works, too." Yumi's grin slips. "But why would ICE be here? Don't they know who I am? We're all American citizens on this plane. Yuriko's from Hawai'i. We're totally legit."

"That depends who you ask," Vivienne says. "Lyin' Lyle's been going hard on us Muslims recently. Even the cultural ones."

"Ugh. Can the fash *be* any more annoying?" Yumi summons Muramasa, making the sword dance and cut through the air to her hand. "I got this. Bad guys get the chop. Don't worry, I won't *kill* anyone."

Vivienne should really say something about this whole "good guys" and "bad guys" thing Yumi has going on, but she doesn't have the words. Also, though some of those agents probably mean well and are just stupid, she'll be damned before she defends fascist stooges of Lyle Prather. They were pigs when the *last* GOP administration created them in 2003, and they're even worse now. The only reason she doesn't let Yumi go terminate their little convoy with extreme prejudice is because they need to jet out of here as fast as possible. Time might be of the essence.

Also, though Yumi said she wasn't going to kill anyone, this avoids any possible bloodshed.

"I got this." Vivienne slips on her Pentagonal Hex from its dimensional pocket and rises to her feet. A little shakily, but that's part of her charm.

"You do?" Yumi's eyebrows rise. "Oh my gosh, oh my gosh, a Lady V special!"

"Something like that, kid."

"Hey." Yumi catches her arm, and their eyes meet. "I want you to call me Yumi. Please?"

"Yeah?"

"It means we're friends." Yumi bites her lip. "I want us to be friends. I wasn't sure before, and now it's awkward, and I just want to—"

"We're friends." Vivienne smiles slightly. "Yumi."

"Ah!" Yumi blushes. "I'm friends with Lady Vengeance! Squee!"

Leaving a very contented, rich, slightly crazy, ninja fangirl in her wake, Vivienne strides down the airstairs that haven't been rolled away. A steward in a similar uniform to Yuriko's has waved down the ICE vans, which skid to a halt close enough to be either spectacularly reckless driving or else intended to intimidate. If the latter is the case, it doesn't work—the steward doesn't so much as flinch, and not a hair is out of place under his black beret. That must be Charles.

"I got this, Charlie," Vivienne says, putting a hand on his shoulder.

He glances at her, but he must have sensed the fear energy coursing in her, because he makes no argument. The sniper butler steps aside, leaving Vivienne to face the swarming ICE agents.

There are eight of them, assault rifles trained on her, but Vivienne isn't bothered. She doesn't even raise her hands. They're carefully behind her back.

"Are you Vivienne Cain?" the captain demands. "Are you? Show me your hands!"

"You know any other hot goth capes my age?" she asks. "What, you wanna see my ID?"

With the unclawed hand, she reaches into her cleavage, making the circle of rifles twitch. Keeping their eyes off the Hex, with which she starts drawing a sigil in the air behind her back.

"Relax, boys." She pulls out her wallet and, with one hand, starts flicking cards out of it, scrutinizing each before she drops it fluttering to the tarmac. "I've got it here somewhere. Credit card. Club card. Sandwich punch card—ooh, two more and I get a free sub. Gotta remember to use this."

With a grunt of annoyance at the delay, the captain signals to his goons to lower their guns and steps forward, rifle still raised and ready. He, at least, moves with military precision. "Now, chiquita."

"A veteran. Nice. Didn't know Prather hired vets. Isn't he too busy cutting your healthcare?"

"ID." He sights his rifle between her eyes. "*Now.*"

"Gotta love a man who points his weapon at my face on the first date." She smiles slyly. "Can I thank you for your service later? *Privately?*"

He says nothing, but she can see his finger on the trigger. Terrible trigger discipline.

This is so stupid. She should have just armored up and kicked the crap out of these clowns. But now she's basically egging them on to shoot her. Is that what she wants? Just a hail of bullets, and all her worries are over? Maybe.

"Oh, here it is," she says, without even looking.

He leans in to get a better look. "Is that a ... library card?"

"Maybe." She reaches up with her clawed hand and grasps his arm, pushing the rifle past her shoulder. "Seattle has a great library system."

Then he's twisting over her shoulder, and she slams him to the ground. The rifles take aim again, expressions going wide with surprise, but it's too late. When she hits the ground, veteran ICE officer first, a wave of purple fear energy pulses from her, sweeping over the assembled agents. They stand stock-still for a minute, frozen first in shock, then in mounting terror. Some of them scream, some of them babble to someone she can't see, some turn tail and run as fast as their piggy little legs will carry them, but all of them are rendered utterly useless by her spell. At the epicenter of her discharge, the captain gets it the worst: her empathic projection leaves him staring catatonically at the sky. Trapped in a war flashback, maybe. Not that she cares.

A distant part of her reminds her that maybe she *should* care.

She gives the captain a little kiss on the forehead, recovers her fallen wallet and cards, then heads back to the Cessna Citation. "Clear for departure, Charlie," she says to the butler assassin.

"Safe flight, Miss Vengeance."

"That was sooo reckless," Yumi says, when she gets back inside. "And badass."

"Thanks." Vivienne settles in her chair and picks up the bottle. "Wake me up when we land."

# CHAPTER FOUR: APPLAUSE

Pensacola, Florida, was not a place Vivienne ever expected to visit. Because first of all, Florida, and secondly, she doesn't like to be anywhere hotter than Chicago, and that only under duress. Thirdly ...

"Um, this is Florida, right?" Vivienne asks, looking out the window at the white fields below them. "Did it snow or something? Is climate change real after all?"

"Yes, no, yes?" Yumi says, answering the questions rapidly. "That's not snow. It's sand. Party-Cola is known for its white sand beaches. And yes, climate change is definitely real, *God*."

"Sorry, I'm used to it being called global warming."

"Okay, Boomer."

"Hey."

To be fair, Yumi wasn't kidding. It's hot as *balls* outside: the sort of sweltering heat that instantly makes Vivienne regret her jeans and leather jacket, not to mention that it wreaks havoc on her hair.

Vivienne makes it to the bottom of the airstairs before she turns around. "I'm going back."

"We just have to make it to the hotel, V."

"But I'm melting."

"You're forty years old."

"Wah."

Vivienne doesn't usually feel like a cave troll, but decades of living in Seattle, where the climate is a little more conducive to human habitation, have severely reduced her tolerance for hot temperatures coupled with high humidity. It reminds her of the time she foolishly decided to visit Louisville in the summer, though at least there's a little breeze off the gulf. They haven't made it halfway to the waiting town car before she's soaking in sweat and reconsidering her decision to live.

By contrast, in her light, filmy sundress, Yumi only seems to glow with extra vibrancy in the heat. "Great, isn't it?" she asks, fanning herself with her sunhat.

"Blech."

"It's March. It's like seventy degrees, V."

"And what, three hundred percent humidity?" She practically lunges into the town car as Yuriko opens the door for them, then starts mainlining bottled water to replenish her body's diminished reserves. Honestly, the bourbon probably didn't help. "It's like a sauna."

"Lightweight."

As the town car lurches into motion, Yumi's phone buzzes, and Vivienne can see who it is from the screen. Her stomach turns over. "Tony, as in *my* Tony?"

"Antonio DeSantes, yes. But I thought you two weren't a thing anymore. Isn't that a thing?"

"Don't change the subject," Vivienne says hotly, both literally and figuratively. "Why does Tony have your number? I knew he liked 'em young, but this is a little—"

"Oh, ew, no," Yumi says. "We just wanted to keep in touch. After Vegas."

"Oh, it's *we*, is it?"

"I'm sure it's nothing important. Here." Yumi hits block caller on the phone. "There. No phone calls from bitter exes."

"I dunno, I have a lot of those."

"You literally snapped your phone in half."

"True."

After a couple of minutes with the AC on full blast and two waters down, Vivienne starts to feel like a human again. Yumi, by contrast, seems totally comfortable. She'd changed into her sundress on the plane and was apparently already wearing a black bikini underneath. She came prepared.

"You've been here before, I take it?" Vivienne asks.

"Occasionally." Yumi grins. "There's a whole Naval Air Station full of flight school boys here, of varying ages. So if you want to make some very bad decisions, that *is* an option."

"Pass." Aside from the aforementioned cave troll issue, Vivienne is trying to cut down on the totally irresponsible random sex, though considering her track record with the bourbon, the odds seem long. "Sounds like I should be more worried about you."

"Me? Why?"

"Well, as long as you have protection."

"I carry Muramasa with me everywhere I go."

"That's not what I—oh, I see. You're fucking with me."

"It *is* pretty funny."

"Ha ha."

Yuriko rolls down the window between the sections of the town car. The driver is also wearing a black beret, which flatters his dark skin very nicely. "Accommodations are acquired at the Hilton. Honeymoon suite was the best available. I know your preference for Oyster Bay, but—"

"Short notice, I understand." Yumi glances at Vivienne. "Honeymoon suite, honey."

Vivienne rolls her eyes and looks out the window as they make the short drive from Pensacola International to downtown. Yumi must be anxious, because she rattles off tourist trivia at a rapid pace, including that Pensacola was originally a Spanish presidio in the mid-sixteenth century and would go on to have four other ruling countries—France, England, America, then the Confederacy a.k.a. stupid America, then America again—hence its name as the "City of Five Flags." Why so many people would want to live in a city repeatedly decimated by hurricanes is beyond Vivienne, but then, she lives in Seattle, and the apocalyptic earthquake known as The Big One is supposed to come any day now.

Apparently, Pensacola also hosts the oldest Naval Air Station in the United States and is also the home of the Blue Angels flight-demonstration team. This random trivia has a visual aid, in the form of a good number of tight young men in tighter Navy outfits, which Yumi isn't shy about ogling as they cruise down the street parallel to the playa. Vivienne exercises enough self-control not to tell Yumi about that time Angel stabbed a malfunctioning Justice clone with a Blue Angel jet.[2]

It's weird being a cape.

"Every Blue Angel pilot trains here," Yumi says. "They're not in town, though—apparently, they're in Lancaster, California, this weekend. But they finish out their season with a show in Party-Cola every year, to really give back to their home community. We could come back in October—"

"Are you just reading a Wikipedia article?" Vivienne asks finally.

"No?" Yumi puts her phone in her lap.

Vivienne shrugs. "Can we just keep driving and head to New Orleans? We're as far west in Florida as you can get, right? Can't be that far to Bourbon Street."

Yumi looks it up on her phone. "Unfortunately, Alabama and Mississippi are both in the way."

"I will absolutely fight both of them."

The hotel is one of those big box affairs with what look like five thousand rooms, but it's right on the white sandy beach and the turbulent, wind-tossed waters of the gulf. Scenic, especially if one can enjoy it through a balcony window, and the honeymoon suite has just such a balcony with just such a view. The décor is extremely white and organic and involves a suspiciously high number of palm trees and palm tree paraphernalia. Whatever, she's too exhausted to care.

"Oh no, there's only one bed—" Yumi says.

"Uh huh." Vivienne collapses face-first into the bed, then looks over. "AC. Please."

"All right, well—" Smiling, Yumi shakes her head. Then she pulls out her phone. "Hey A, it's me. I'm in town, and I'll be at your concert. Can I snag you after? Okay. Okay. See you then—"

~

The trip to the Bay Center—which about half the locals call the Civic Center—is only a little bit of a zoo. The streets are packed

---

[2] She's remembering the explosive events of Angel's senior prom in *Public Enemy!* ~ High-Flyin' Vogel

with people pushing and clamoring their way to get into the concert hall. Vivienne wouldn't expect a town as relatively small as Pensacola to have a venue large enough for that many people, but Yumi—or more precisely, Yumi's phone—told her the Bay Center can accommodate up to ten thousand people. They even have hockey games there, as Pensacola has its own professional team. Which invites the question: who plays hockey in *Florida*?

Vivienne probably got about an hour or two to nap before Yumi woke her with some blaring anime hype music. "Goddess," she said into the pillow. "Couldn't you wake me up some other way?"

"Nope," Yumi said, "because I literally tried them all. Up and at 'em, V!"

Vivienne has probably slept more in the past twelve hours than in the previous twelve days, but that's only just now starting to pay back the sleep debt from a full month of cheap cocktails and demeaning debauchery.

"You know that's not a thing, right, V?" Marcus says to her, in her mind. "Sleep debts?"

"I've already got enough debts," she says in reply. "What's one more?"

For a second, it seems like he's sitting next to her in the car, smiling that goofy smile of his.

"What's that, V?" Yumi asks.

"Nothing," Vivienne says.

Marcus isn't there. He's dead. The flashing sign outside the arena proclaims the event the "I Don't Care" tour. Which, considering how shitty Vivienne has felt for months, seems apt. She's been struggling to hold onto something—anything—and she hasn't had the spoons or the self-awareness to think about how Angel might be doing. This is gonna suck.

"I'm really glad you wanted to reconnect with Angel," Yumi says, not looking up from her phone.

"Huh?"

"It gives me a chance to see her concert again. It's pretty fire."

Vivienne can tell there's more to it than that, but she lets it go. Yumi feels relieved, and also a bit trepidatious. She really wants this to go well and isn't sure she's done the necessary prep work for it to go that way. Despite her bravado, aggressive power set, and general manic pixie dream girl energy, Yumi's a solid friend and a good person. Vivienne just hopes she doesn't drag Yumi into her and Angel's inevitable shitstorm. She shouldn't have involved her at all, but time is short, and a Citation is faster than a stolen motorcycle. Not to mention the honeymoon suite at the Hilton.

The benefits of a rich fangirl.

The Civic Center or Bay Center or whatever is a sizeable sports arena, probably half the size of KeyArena in Seattle, but that's still saying something. There was some sort of opening act, but even if the two of them had arrived in time, they probably couldn't have pushed through to see it. Even the nosebleeds are sold out, but Yumi somehow managed to get tickets somewhere on the second level. The place is packed, and it's all the two of them can do to navigate the army of brightly dressed teens and tweens. Vivienne doesn't think she's ever seen this many sixteen-year-olds in one place, at least since she *was* sixteen. This is why she owns a bar, for fuck's sake.

"This is so not my scene," Vivienne says, as they push past yet another texting circle, where all the giggly girls involved are communicating via their phones despite being within literal arm's reach.

"Oh c'mon, not all of A's fans are Zoomers," Yumi says. "Well, most of us, but I'm sure there are some weirdo Millennials here too?"

"For the last time, I'm a cynical Gen Xer ... oh goddammit, I *do* know people here."

Specifically, she recognizes Eve and J. T., the superhero chasers (the battle kind, not the sex kind, though who really knows?) who she met back in August when she was searching for Angel. Apparently, based on the A-Girl merch they're wearing, and the number of checked off cities and dates on their "I DON'T CARE 2020" tour shirts, they've become massive fans of Vivienne's niece. Worse, they recognize Vivienne and wave frantically at her.

"I've changed my mind, I don't need A's help, let's just go—"

"V." Yumi takes her hands. "Just relax. I'll get us drinks. Go ahead and hide somewhere, if you need to. I'll find you."

Again, being handled by this barely adult is a little grating, but at the same time, Vivienne does appreciate how her emotions don't freak Yumi out. "You're twenty—they aren't gonna card you?"

"Chill out, V. It's Florida."

"What does that *mean?*"

Yumi heads off, and Vivienne takes cover in one of the dimly lit corners, where people's faces are distorted by the pink and purple light. Why is she so anxious? And what gives? She should be encouraging Yumi to drink and party and engage in reckless behavior. When did Vivienne stop being cool? Goddess, she's become her *mother.*

That triggers a fresh wave of despair and guilt—she went exactly the opposite direction from her responsibilities to her dead mother—but Vivienne stuffs it down. She's got a job to do.

She's spared from further doubts when a pulse of light makes everyone start cheering—a thunderous greeting for the main act coming out on the stage. Mist starts pouring around the stage, into which a good twenty dancers stream forward, wearing cropped white tracksuits obviously modeled on A-Girl's superhero outfit, but with a whole range of piping colors: some blue, some red, some green, some yellow. The flashing beams of light that cut through the mist pick up the color to create a scintillating rainbow effect. For a confirmed straight artist, it's pretty solid LGBTQ+ branding, but somehow it doesn't seem quite right to Vivienne. The dancers are mostly women but some men as well.

"Where's the band?" she asks, shouting over the roar of the crowd.

Yumi gives her a look like she's lost her mind. "No band, V—haven't you been to a pop concert?"

"Oh no."

Sure enough, a deep, resonant beat pounds through the arena, making the chairs vibrate and Vivienne's bones quake. She's been at some loud concerts before, but this is more than that. The light and sound show isn't just a show: there's powerful emotion laced into it all, and it rolls over Vivienne in a series of powerful waves, punctuated with drumbeats, each of a different color.

Seething red anger.

Purple disgust.

Green fear.

Crimson rage.

Deep blue grief.

Azure blue regret.

Blood red *rage*.

Each time the drum hits and a color flashes, a set of dancers crumples to the floor as though struck by that power. If that's what happened, they're the lucky ones, because Vivienne takes each shot right to the head and gut and keeps standing.

"V?" Yumi shouts at her. "Are you okay? What's wrong?"

She can't respond. It's beating in time with her heart, building up and through.

Golden ecstasy.

Vibrant aquamarine delirium.

A hint of pink hope.

Rage the color and texture of raw, burned flesh.

Indigo hatred.

Scarlet rage.

Viridian terror.

Boiling, volcanic *rage*.

Then she appears—A-Girl—floating down from the ceiling of the arena, like a star descending from the heavens, pulsing with that same red light. She's dressed all in black, including a black cape entirely too reminiscent of her father. Vivienne only knows it's her because she can *feel* Angel. And more than that, she can feel the intense rage churning inside, like a pot about to boil over—like a frozen turkey poised over a deep fryer and about to explode and napalm everything in a twenty-foot radius.

The arena falls silent as A-Girl descends, arms outstretched so the cape flutters around her. It mostly hides her body, but not the energy aura, which looks profoundly malevolent in the darkness of the arena. Then she touches down on the stage, among the supine dancers, and puts out her arms.

"This place," A-Girl says, her voice amplified by her own power and the speakers. It's eerie, promising, and threatening all at the same time. "This place about to *glow*."

The beat drops like thunder, and the music explodes in a cacophonous roar. The lights blast and strobe. A-Girl's energy explodes around her, dissolving her black cape in a flash of whirling ash to reveal her outfit: a black skin-tight suit, with bright red piping down her arms and lining the curves of her wiry frame. It reminds Vivienne of her A-Girl suit—the one most of her dancers are wearing—but the opposite. Like something The Raven would design. Her hair is a flashy red color that matches the power lines and the mood. She throws herself through powerful, strutting dance moves, emitting blasts of light and emotion with each thrust of her arm, hips, or her upraised hands.

The music has a Latin feel, but it's mostly just straight-up pop, and it's a back-alley knife-fight of a song, at that. There are lyrics—about beats and beating, about madness and being very, *very* mad—but the waves of emotion drown it all out. The audience just experiences it as high-energy dance pop, and they bounce and thrash with practically orgiastic fervor. Yumi seems to be taking it that way too, dancing even this far up in the stands. Vivienne knew Angel was upset after Vegas—who wouldn't be?—but this is a whole other level. And it leaves her shaken and raw.

"Hey!" Yumi touches her arm, and her crimson eyes gleam with concern. "You okay?"

It's all Vivienne can do to nod. Lying, per usual.

The second song is just as forceful as the first, dancers undulating and hurling themselves around seemingly with abandon. It reminds Vivienne a little of A-Girl's clumsy, uncoordinated fighting style, at least before all her training with Eiko "Silver Sakura" Kujikawa, Yumi's terrifying mother. She wonders if Angel's kept up with that. Somehow, she doubts it.

The next song is equally strong, but Vivienne has become adapted enough to the volume to hear some of the words this time. This must be the song the tour is named for, because the lyrics she can catch are things like "pull my hair, I don't care" or "strip me bare, I don't care" or "gimme a glare, I don't care." It's also a little more explicit than Vivienne was expecting, and one particular line about "dirty down there, I don't care" takes her by surprise. That, and the dark wave of perverse desire that flows out of Angel when she sings it. Vivienne may have become her mother, but it's like Angel has become *her.*

"Great Mother," she says under her breath.

The rest of her set blurs together, or maybe Vivienne's just overloaded. Angel performs "I'm Just A-Girl," but this version is a lot more explicit—a remix that makes the original sound like a chaste Disney Channel special. Vivienne has seen plenty of female artists go through this kind of phase—hell, she did something similar, but she was never clean-cut and blonde. Angel seems to be all-in on that aesthetic.

At length, Vivienne's sitting there, stunned, when Yumi shakes her arm. "V. Hey. You good?"

"Is it over?" Vivienne asks, voice rasping, and sure enough, it is. She wasn't keeping track of how long Angel performed, but it can't have been that long. Maybe twenty minutes? Thirty?

The crowd down below seems discontented. They mill around, caught somewhere between confusion and expectation that the show will continue. A chant of "encore" rises, and people start clapping and stomping.

Yumi looks at her phone. "Okay. That's her. Let's go."

"She's done?" Vivienne asks. "Not much of a concert."

Yumi is already heading back toward the stairs. "You coming or not, V?"

"She knows I'm here, right, Yumi?" Vivienne asks. "Yumi!"

# CHAPTER FIVE: I CAN DO IT WITH A BROKEN HEART

As it turns out, Angel "A-Girl" DeSantes did not, in fact, know Vivienne was here.

The door to the green room is closed, and a crowd of handsome boys and a few girls shooting their shot are lined up, clamoring to be let in. Several fill out crisp white Navy uniforms quite well, and Vivienne is starting to rethink denying Yumi's suggestion that they take a detour. No one can get past the bald, heavily tattooed, seven-foot bouncer with an earpiece, who seems vaguely familiar ...

"Pug?" Vivienne asks. "Is that you?"

"You know each other?" Yumi waves to the big bruiser.

"Miss K." The Pugilist looks at Vivienne like he's trying to place her. "Have we met, ma'am?"

"Ma'am?" Vivienne forces herself to grin at him. "Picture me blonde."

"Oh. *Oh.*" Pug's eyes go wide. "You can go in. Just don't tell anyone about—you know."

"Your thoroughly embarrassing fetish is safe with me."

The assembled groupies raise a stink when the Pugilist starts punching in the code to unlock the door for them, but a glare puts them back in their place. His thick fingers stumble over the code, delivering an angry red blare. He just sighs and tries again.

"Angel has a supervillain for a roadie?" Vivienne asks quietly.

"First, the Pugilist was a D-list henchman at worst, and he's turning over a new leaf," Yumi says. "And second, he's not a roadie—he was the opening act. Surprisingly soulful singer-songwriter."

"You're shitting me."

Pug doesn't seem to notice their conversation. He finally unlocks the door with a buzz, having fat-fingered the code three times. "You ladies have a good night now." He hits a button on his phone, and loud A-Girl pop music streams from his Bluetooth. He starts singing along—surprisingly well, at that.

Angel must have heard the door opening, or else she's just been pacing the room, because she's on her feet when they come in, her hands constantly moving. "Yumi!" Her heavily made-up face lifts as they enter, then her expression turns stormy when she sees Vivienne. "What. The fuck."

"Good to see you too, A," Vivienne says. "How you been?"

The state of the green room makes it pretty obvious. It's utterly trashed. And not just in the way that rockstars typically destroy rooms—such as empty beer bottles, unsavory spills, and at least one broken TV—but this green room also features half a dozen craters in the walls, every mirror in the place splintered, and about twenty mostly empty pizza boxes. A full spring collection of clothes lies strewn all over the place, like an actor's wardrobe exploded. All at the hands of one hurricane of destruction.

"Great," Angel says, eyes flashing. "Thanks for asking. Bye now."

"A," Yumi says, holding out her hands in a placating gesture. "V needs your help. Hear her out?"

Angel's still glaring at Vivienne. "Or what?"

"Or I pull funding for the next couple tour stops," Yumi says. "I'm the money, remember?"

Angel scowls. "Ooh, look at you, sugar mama."

"Hey, she isn't—" Vivienne looks to Yumi. "Wait, you're bankrolling her tour?"

"Guilty." Yumi shrugs. "I told you I wanted to catch one of the shows."

The heiress of the 2K Group paying the "I Don't Care" tour's bills explains a lot, actually. Like how Yumi got tickets at the last minute, got them backstage, knew all about Angel's henchman baddie turned crooning bouncer. And it's not like Angel would be *rolling* in money.

"Also, the show was fire, A," Yumi says. "A little short, but fire all the same."

At length, Angel rolls her eyes. "*Fiiine*. Come in."

She reaches up and pulls off her bright red wig, revealing her short-cropped blonde hair, buzzed on the sides and about three inches long on the top. That alone would explain it, as Yumi's a sucker for an undercut. Vivienne can relate to carrying a torch for a straight girl. The way Angel's moving: jittery, shifting from foot to foot, fingers constantly in motion, if Vivienne didn't know better, she'd think ...

"Are you high?" Vivienne asks. "How does that even work? With your metabolism—?"

"Ugh." Angel rolls her eyes. "What is this, an intervention or something?"

She tosses the wig behind the couch and tosses herself down on an armchair, which groans under the force. Vivienne remembers carrying her on more than one occasion, and she's real dense. She picks up a fifth of ... is that *Everclear*? She knocks back about half of it in one go, wipes her lips with the back of her hand—smearing her lipstick—and gestures with the bottle.

"They're shouting my name out there," Angel says, only slightly slurred. "You got one minute."

"Oh, don't let us keep you," Vivienne says, because she can't resist a little antagonism. "You look like you've figured out how to get drunk after all. Is that laced with something or just straight?"

"That piss you off, Aunt V?" she asks. "That I'm better at drinking than you?"

"Are you going to do another set?" Yumi asks, trying to defuse the confrontation. "Do you have more songs prepped?"

Angel shrugs. Vivienne recognizes the situation all too well: at this point in her music career, Angel is in her listless "I'm a star, we're running at zero margins, who gives a fuck" phase. She needs to buckle down and work harder if she wants to have staying power as an artist, otherwise she's already on the way out. But of course, the tour is called "I Don't Care," so ... seems pretty apt.

"Actually, I was going dancing after this—with a bunch of sailors," Angel says. "You saw the line? It's like that every night. So many hot boys just *begging* for it. And you're down to thirty seconds."

Vivienne suppresses a little twinge of concern and resists the urge to make a thoroughly hypocritical slut-shaming joke. Maybe she's grown. "I need your help," Vivienne says.

"That's what Y said. And the answer's a big fat fuck y—"

"To rescue Marcus."

There it was, and it took the air out of Angel as though Pug had come in, strutted up, and slugged her right in the stomach. Her words trail off, and she stares at Vivienne with a mixture of surprise and confusion. For a second, she's the old Angel, vulnerable and sad and daring to hope.

For a second. Then her face hardens, and her eyes narrow. "The fuck."

Yumi, who had no idea about any of this, gapes at Vivienne. "What? Did I hear right?"

"It's true," Vivienne says. "I know how we can—"

"Stop." Angel clutches the sides of her head. "Just stop."

"A," Yumi says. "Can't we—?"

"No." Angel looks up, eyes blazing. "No. Fuck you, V. You abandon me for six months and then you walk in and pull this shit? Get out."

"Mija—" Vivienne says. "Just listen—"

"Out!" Angel picks up the couch, the better to hurl it. "Get out! Get the *fuck* out!"

Vivienne ducks out the door, then leans back against it, totally ignoring the hallway crowded with speculative looks and questions. She can almost make out the words the two girls are exchanging in there—Angel shouting, Yumi a little more calm but still loud—and she lets out a sigh.

The only thing more humiliating than being so profoundly rejected by her niece is the pitying look the Pugilist gives her. Vivienne can't put up with that, so she staggers down the hall full of A-Girl groupies, using the opposite wall to keep herself up. They get the hell out of her way, but they regard her with sympathy, pity, or jealousy, each of them yet another little cut.

She needs a drink.

No, don't think about that.

Half of the groupies are dressed vaguely like A-Girl—with the typical pink piping aesthetic—and Vivienne wonders if Yumi has branched into selling official merch. She'd be crazy not to. Or maybe these fans are just so desperate they made their own A-Girl cosplay. It wouldn't be the first time a cape celebrity inspired such fierce parasocial devotion. Vivienne herself never had this many fans sublimating their own personas to hers. That's a relief.

"Ma'am?" says a dude in a white Navy uniform, probably in his early twenties. He looks a lot like Orestes, but with a buzz cut and no glasses. "Do you need help?"

At first, she wonders if she's hallucinating again. Then, when Marcus says, "you should take him up on that," right next to her, she *knows*.

"I'm fine," she says. "Leave me alone."

"Sorry, ma'am," the sailor says.

"Wasn't talking to you," she murmurs. "You're definitely her type. You'll be fine. I gotta go—"

Get out of here. Head to the parking lot. Find some teenagers drinking or smoking weed. She can't remember if it's legal in Florida, but then, it *is* Florida, and they have their own tyrannical, crassly materialistic Republican governor who claims to be a Christian (ha!) but is probably *also* in the thrall of some horrendous cosmic evil. Hastur, maybe? The Black Goat of the Woods? The Queen of the Black Sigh? Or maybe it's an entirely human evil, because Goddess knows we're capable. The encroaching unwashed micro-dick of fascism is just the *worst*.

She's already rocking enough power from the concert that she can go do something about it. She's a hero, right? Maybe Vivienne will get drunk, loaded, and/or stoned, and go punch the governor in the face. Like a hero. That would make her feel better. Right? Right?

Probably not. Nothing's going to make her feel better.

The door lock buzzes behind her, and Vivienne freezes even before Angel shouts after her. "V!"

Everyone goes silent, overawed by their idol's appearance. Angel is a total mess, though at least she threw on a coat with a hood to cover the worst of it. It gives her a very cool gothpunk vibe, what with the coat and the tights beneath, and the smeared makeup. Her attitude is anything but, though.

"Fine," Angel says, arms crossed. "Let's hear it."

~

As the air whips through their ears, Angel grumbles something Vivienne only vaguely hears through the mic. The flight helmet hides her face, so Vivienne can't see her expression, but she can easily feel the annoyance flowing out of her niece.

"What?" Vivienne shouts over the wind, which is silly, because she's still wearing the throat mic.

"I still say this is the stupidest thing I've ever heard," Angel says through the mic. "Marcus is trapped by your demon ex in this hell dimension, and we're just supposed to fly there?"

"Not ... my ex," Vivienne says, her teeth chattering. "And you'll just ... have to trust me."

"Whatever."

"Are you two okay?" Yumi asks, her transmission slightly garbled. "What's wrong?"

"Nothing," Vivienne and Angel say at the same time, in the same weary cadence.

This is Valhalla tech they're using—repurposed from the super suits Tony lent Vivienne and Yumi in the battle back in August[3]—and they have a pretty good signal, but Angel *is* flying really fast. The comms could probably use a tune-up, but it is what it is. Angel hasn't been in contact with her vigilante nutjob of a father, and like hell is Vivienne going to drop by his doorstep uninvited. Not after *last* time.[4]

Yumi's voice crackles in her ear. "You said the entrance was in the Bermuda Triangle? That's both weirdly specific and very vague. Can you narrow it down any further?"

"Nope," Vivienne says. "I'll know ... entrance ... when I see it."

"Watch for hypoxia. A's basically invulnerable, but you still need to breathe, V."

"I'm fine," Vivienne says, which is a buck-naked lie. They're cruising at eight thousand feet at least, and the air is even thinner than this ridiculous plan. Her chest already feels tight, but that might also have something to do with the *cold*. "Higher, A."

"Whatever you say, V." Angel climbs, and it gets even harder to

---

[3] See *Fallen Angel*. ~ Vigilante Vogel

[4] The brutal breakup in the second-to-last chapter of *Femmes Fatale 2: Bad Intentions!* Drama!

breathe.

Vivienne's pitch about rescuing Marcus worked well enough for Angel to give her twenty-four hours, and Yumi wasted no time loading them into the Citation to fly to Miami. She wanted to use the private plane to search for the promised entrance, but Vivienne insisted she needed Angel to carry her, instead. She needed direct access to the portal, and she was a practiced hand at being carried by superheroes. Ha ha ha, good joke.

It was partly true. She *did* need Angel to carry her. The rest ...

"Any sign of the entrance?" Yumi keeps filling the silence. She's nervous.

"Getting there."

Angel grumbles over the mic, but no words. Just annoyance.

She's funny, this darker version of Angel, though of course Vivienne would never say that to her. (Not sober, anyway.) For most of the kid's life, Vivienne has thought of Angel as fundamentally *Athena's* daughter, not really Tony's. She had a troubled childhood and was kind of a burn-out punk, but once she was discovered, she cultivated this image as beautiful, charismatic, beloved—basically the Platonic ideal of the girl next door prom queen with just enough allure to be universally loved without falling onto either side of the Madonna/Whore complex. Though of course, that didn't stop creepers online maintaining a countdown to her eighteenth birthday, because, well, *men*.

But the amazing, awesome, apex A-Girl was all a front. A careful persona that she built and wore for her entire life, until Marcus got fucking *disintegrated*, and the mask cracked, and Angel couldn't convincingly wear it anymore. She's spiraled from there, down and down and down, and now she's so much like Tony that she's *dressing* like him, too.

Maybe this isn't going to work. But Vivienne has to try.

"Are we almost there?" Angel asks. "I'm bored. And you stink."

"Just about."

They're high enough and far enough. Time to make it happen.

Vivienne concentrates, channeling all the fear energy she has absorbed over the last month and then some. She hasn't tried this in twenty years, but it has to work. If it doesn't, well ...

Angel's been around the block once or twice, and she knows the sensation of the fear powers spooling up. She tenses, which is almost enough to break Vivienne's comparatively frail body, despite all her time in the gym and high pain tolerance. "V? What are you doing? What—?"

Which is when Vivienne hits her with a fear blast.

Vivienne knows Angel's fear—loneliness, isolation, being forgotten—and it breaks her heart to take advantage of it. But she has no choice. Rending amethyst purple energy lances into Angel, filling her mind and heart and soul with her greatest terror. She fights it at first, obviously, but Vivienne came prepared. There's too much, and Angel's emotional state is too weak.

"No, I didn't ... I couldn't—" Angel cries. "I just left ... for two minutes—"

Fuck. She's seeing Marcus dying. Over and over again.

"What's going on?" Yumi asks. "What—?"

Vivienne pulls the earpiece out and flicks it away, partly to break off that communication, and partly so she doesn't have to listen to Angel breaking down. She's a coward—she knows that. But she has to see it through. Just a little more ...

One last spark of fear energy, and Angel lets Vivienne go.

And then she's falling.

Without Yumi, Vivienne can't track her altitude, but she's accustomed to free fall. She used to skydive in her wild gothpunk days, and she's done stuff way stupider than throwing herself out of a plane at ten thousand feet. She should be freefalling for about a minute, and then she'd be gliding down on a parachute ... if she'd come prepared with such a thing. Instead, she's just gonna hit the water at terminal velocity.

As she falls, headfirst and fingers outstretched at her sides, she sees Marcus falling with her, right-side up with his face level with hers. His face is calm, but his eyes seem a little sad.

"You sure about this, V?" he asks. "I mean, you're committed now, but—"

"I'm going to find you, Marcus," she says. "Wait for me."

He smiles distantly, then leans in as though to kiss her. Instead, he touches his forehead to hers.

She's almost done. Vivienne gazes down at the water rushing up to meet her—at her splintered and muddled image across hundreds of yards of churning sea—and wonders if she is herself or if she is the reflection. Is she looking at the stars, or has she mistaken the

44

lights in the water for the sky?

The Fearworld yawns open, the edges of the mirrors like razors, and she slides painfully inside, feeling every slice.

# CHAPTER SIX: I MISS THE MISERY

Vivienne lands hard, flat on her back, on cold, unforgiving stone.

Not the ocean. Not water. *Stone.*

She feels all the pain of crashing hard enough to crater the ground, but of course, here she can't suffer lasting injury, much less die. Azazel, after all, won't let her. Also, this is *her* world, even if she's neglected it for over half her life. That, and her body instinctively put up wards around her to cushion the fall. Still *hurts*, though—if she can imagine the pain, she can feel it.

What a perfect and terrible refuge, this Fearworld of hers. Her own personal hell.

There she lies as she waits for the pain of a shattered body to subside, all the while staring up at the sparkling, winking canopy of glass facets, barely glimpsed through the vast, misty darkness. Twenty years ago, when she first came to this place, she thought those were mirrors, but she came to realize the truth: they are distorted, fractured teeth, waiting to devour her or anyone foolish enough to enter this place. At least without a guide.

Someone moves over Vivienne, more like a silhouette against the reflecting light than a person. A shadow and a shade, but she can tell it isn't malevolent.

"Let me guess," she says, her voice a croaking murmur. "Virgil? Abandon all hope and so forth?"

"Not quite," a familiar feminine voice says. "And here I thought you never studied."

Vivienne blinks.

"Mamá?"

The shadow resolves itself into a Latina woman in her thirties. She's much younger than Vivienne can remember her mother, but it's definitely *her*. She's beautiful in a secretarial sort of way, with her hair tightly tied back and big glasses. Not at all like old Charisma Cain, and yet ...

"Am I dead?" Vivienne asks.

"No tanta suerte."

"Ha." Vivienne winces. "Wait. Is that even a real phrase? 'No tanta suerte'?"

"It's your world, mija," Charisma says. "I'm a shadow. I speak whatever language you want."

"Can you swear a bunch? I've always wanted to hear that."

Charisma smirks in a way Vivienne dimly recognizes. "Even shadows have limits."

"Damn."

She reaches up toward Charisma, but her mother's hand bounces off the wards around her own. Because of course it does. That's what the magic is for, after all, to keep out spectral interference.

"Sorry about that, Mamá," she says. "Better safe than sorry, right?"

The shade makes no reply, only regards her with distant disapproval. Now *that's* the Charisma Cain she knows. "We need to hurry," her mother says. "We're not alone here."

"How do you know?" Vivienne asks. "How long have you been here?"

"Long enough. There was one other, besides me. Now there are two."

"So far, so good."

Vivienne manages to push herself to a sitting position. Her body feels intact, but she can't say the same for the Fearworld itself. She landed on a floating island in the darkness, and the world around her is composed of dozens of these islands, like someone shattered a small town into a hundred pieces. Connecting the islands throughout the vast, misty world are rocky, treacherous bridges without handrails. Because apparently, her inner personal hell does not have OSHA.

She'll keep the protective fear magic up, just in case.

Vivienne expected the island she landed on to look like her bedroom or her childhood home—that seems like a reasonable starting place—but instead it looks like one of the on-call rooms at the Supergroup Tower back in Seattle, twenty years ago. Complete with the too-firm mattresses, utilitarian curtains, vinyl flooring, and the depressingly spare décor. Tony probably designed these, or maybe Gabriel, back before his accident. These rooms haven't even *existed* in nearly twenty years—not since the Space Needle was repurposed after the fall of Supergroup to a pretty great rotating view spot for the city and an aggressively mediocre restaurant.

"Why the fuck would I—oh, I get it. *Right.*"

The last time she was here, Vivienne thinks, she came with Tony, and they had lots and lots of sex on this very island. Of course her emotional vibe would default to this spot: as far as the Fearworld knew, it was the last place she'd been happy ... twenty years ago. Ugh, what an indictment.

"Is it?" the shade of Charisma asks.

"Is it what?" Vivienne asks.

"The last place you were happy."

"Fuck off."

The shade starts to do exactly that, fading into the gloom before Vivienne relents.

"No, wait. Sorry, Mamá. I'm just ... this is very *not easy* for me."

"Of course, mija." The shade grows more vivid again. "I want to help you."

Her voice isn't Charisma's voice—not the way it has been for decades—but it's so nostalgic, Vivienne can't help but trust her. "Are you her? *Really* her, I mean? Or are you just in my head?"

The shade moves as though to touch her, then thinks better of it and lowers her hand. After what happened last time, that makes sense. "Does it really matter?" she asks.

"Maybe?" Vivienne sighs. "So you're my guide, right? How helpful are you going to be?"

"I can tell you only what I remember, and I will only remember when it matters, and it will only matter when you face it, and only if you face it, will you understand."

"So cryptic bullshit all the way down, got it."

Vivienne cracks her knuckles, neck, and shoulders. Can't plumb the depths of your childhood trauma without your stretches. She summons the Pentagonal Hex and straps it on tight. The claws are still stained slightly with blood. Hers.

"Welp. Let's get started."

~

Having gotten her bearings in the Fearworld, Vivienne's finally ready. Only one obvious path forward: a rocky bridge that leads to something that looks like a bedroom in an Ikea showroom, albeit in the Scandinavian death metal section.

"That looks like my room," she says, stepping onto the bridge. "Sorry Mamá, I'm about to retraumatize you with my rebellious phase."

The bridge cracks and crumbles as soon as she puts her weight on it. Vivienne doesn't have time to grab onto anything before she's falling, falling, and finally she crashes hard on her right shoulder, which hurts like a bitch but starts to ease even before she pushes herself to a sitting position.

"Ow," she says. "Oh, what's *this* bullshit?"

This platform resembles a hospital room in the wake of some kind of surgery, complete with a dozen bloodied blankets and sponges, and a gurney whose bottom half is covered in blood. The mirrors all around the room are splintered into demonic grins.

"Is this supposed to mean something to me?" Vivienne asks.

Charisma floats down beside her, hair buoyant as the rest of her. "Do you recognize this place?"

"Should I?" Vivienne stays out of hospitals as much as possible—bad associations—but she thinks back to the last time she was in a room like this and draws a blank. "Looks like a surgery?"

"Where are the scalpels, then?"

Apparently, Charisma can touch physical objects here in the Fearworld, because she picks up a pair of bloodied forceps. Also on the side table are a pair of bloodied surgical scissors and a speculum.

"Do I look like a doctor?" Vivienne asks.

"These are delivery tools." Charisma frowns. "For childbirth."

For a second, Vivienne sees a screaming woman strapped to that gurney, heaving and fighting and cursing up a storm. She can't see her properly, because Tony is in the way. Tony, who is holding her hand and whispering soothing things to her. Then the image is gone.

"How do you—oh, right, you've done it before. Twice." Vivienne bites her lip. "Unless I have another sibling I don't know about? No?" She rubs her aching shoulder. "That's a relief."

The shade just stares at her levelly with no sign of mirth. Maybe the dead lack any sense of humor. "Do you remember Angelica's birth?" she asks at length.

"You mean when my bitch queen of a sister spawned my ex's baby?" Vivienne asked. "Can't say as I was in the room, no. Athena wouldn't have invited me, and I wouldn't have accepted."

"Are you certain you weren't there?"

"Pretty fucking certain." Vivienne has absolutely no memory of that night, which came about a year before the forcible dissolution of Supergroup. Probably a whiskey blackout. She remembers almost nothing about that year, actually. Or the year after. Must have been a lot of drinking.

"Because you remember you weren't, or because you don't remember if you were?"

"What is this?" Vivienne asks. "What are you trying to get me to say? That I hated my sister? Yeah, that's pretty obvious. That I envied her? For being everyone's favorite—including yours? For stealing the love of my life? For ... everything?" She bites her lip hard enough to draw blood—if the Fearworld allowed it, anyway. "Fine. I admit it. Are you happy?"

"I want you to face this moment," the shade says. "So I can tell you what you've forgotten."

"What does that mean? Athena's dead. Can't very well hash it out with her, with fists or words."

"Are you certain?"

"Is this about my abortion, Mamá?" Vivienne asks. "Because that's the closest I've come to ever needing any of this shit. About six weeks."

Charisma stares at her, eyes distant and sad.

"This is getting real annoying," Vivienne says. "Yeah, I heard her voice come out of that possessed ICE agent, and Angel said—" She pauses. "Athena isn't dead, is she?"

"Is that a question?"

Vivienne isn't sure why it took months to admit that. Well, that's a lie—she does know. It's because she spent months running from it. Refusing to think about it. Torturing herself. Drinking herself unconscious. Drugging herself out of her mind. But here, in this place, she has to face it.

Her sister is alive.

Sort of.

"How?" Vivienne asks, her voice much softer and gentler than before. "I saw her die. So did Tony. We buried her in Calvary, just like you wanted. Because you're—*were* Catholic, and so was she."

"Carmen."

Vivienne hasn't thought about Athena's real name—her *human* name, her sister would say—for decades. Carmen changed her name to Athena when she emancipated herself at seventeen, and she never looked back. Just left her hated younger sister and her increasingly dementia-ridden mother in that rotting house in Maple Leaf, while she went on to do bigger things and better people. Slept her way through Supergroup, rose to second-in-command, fucked Tony, and ...

"So she's alive," Vivienne says. "Or at least she's still active."

Charisma nods.

"I didn't need a bloody hospital room to remind me of that."

The island trembles, and Vivienne feels anger rising all around her, as though the stone itself has grown furious. The bloody gurney bends in on itself, twisting and shrieking with shearing metal, the mirrors explode into dust, and the forceps and other tools bounce and jump before flying at her like shrapnel. She conjures a fearshield on reflex and drops low behind it. The shade of her mother just floats there impassively, untouched.

A rumble goes through the island, and Vivienne sees the stone start to crack and split.

"Dammit, not again."

She turns and runs for the nearest rock bridge through the darkness, as the hospital room tears itself apart behind her. The island breaks in half, and she thinks there's something like a face starting to emerge from the core, with sick, wet sounds and a single, lingering wail. Finally, the island explodes, showering the dark emptiness with stones. Dimly, she can hear cracking glass where the rubble hits the bottom of the Fearworld. So at least she won't fall forever if she misses a step.

That's not reassuring. Especially when she hears the crunch of gnashing teeth.

~

Vivienne wasn't even looking where she ran, but now that she has arrived, she wishes she had.

This island looks like Supergroup headquarters or, more specifically, the control room where they would meet and discuss how else they could support the state during its accelerating descent into naked fascism. Or at least, that's the first thing Vivienne thinks of, because it's appointed almost exactly how it looked during the WTO riots in 1999 and for the next two years before the attack, complete with banks of anachronistic computers, swivel chairs, and ...

Thinking about the attack makes the chamber change. The walls crack and crumble, furniture overturns and breaks, and the screens of the computers splinter. The elevator up to the council chamber stands open, but the tower above it is sheared off just above the control room. She also sees bodies appear, just out of the corner of her eye, but when she looks, they're like something halfway between crash test dummies and voodoo dolls, not people. Straw protrudes from torn-off limbs rather than bone, their eyes are buttons crudely sewn on or hanging by a thread, and ... is that motor oil instead of blood? Sure smells like it. And it's not fresh oil, either.

Real nice of the Fearworld to censor itself for her. Or maybe that's Charisma's doing?

Vivienne doesn't remember the early 2000s all that well— almost nothing from late 1999 to when she was on the road, seeing Manny for the first time in 2002[5]—but she remembers the attack. Or at least, certain details, like who died and in what horrific

---

[5] See the forthcoming *The Mother of Scorpions*, co-authored with the creator of Cobalt City, Nathan Crowder, also from DefCon One Publishing! ~ Shameless Plugger Vogel

circumstances. The crumpled dummies roughly correspond to her colleagues, including the burn stain where Justice was disintegrated, the outlined multiple arms of that one four-armed guy, and ... okay, maybe her memory is blurry after all.

She finds a little button in a pool of oil and realizes it's supposed to be an eye. *Tony's* eye.

The staticky computer screens look more like teeth than broken glass. Grinning at her.

"Weird," Vivienne says. "I see a lot of Azazel, but I haven't *heard* him and his stupid demon voice. Is that your doing?"

"Maybe." Charisma appears beside her. "You're focused on me. I appreciate that."

"You're welcome. Anyway." Vivienne points at the straw puppet nailed to the wall. The dummy is dressed in Athena's superhero outfit, down to the silly little tiara that the comics depict her using as a projectile weapon. As though she ever needed that. She's attached to the wall with a dozen spears, including one through her *mouth*. "That looks definitive. But there's something else."

Now that she knows the truth, she can *look*—really look. The puppet is leaving an oily blood trail down the wall, but there's something different about it than the others. They all have button eyes, but the Athena dummy has *real* human eyes. They're wet and vital, and Vivienne realizes they're alive when they look at her. Terrified. Pleading. A gurgling sound comes from her nailed mouth.

She sees herself in those eyes. Athena is a mirror and a foil, Vivienne realizes.

"I—" Snark dies in Vivienne's throat, and she can only stare at her sister's eyes. "What do I do?"

"What do you *want* to do?" Charisma asks.

With a deep breath, Vivienne really digs. It's not easy, but she can do it.

She closes her hands around the spear through the Athena effigy's mouth, tenses, and pulls. There's no movement at first, but as her back muscles ripple with force, the spear starts to slip out with a sickly sucking sound that no straw-filled dummy would produce. It's really in there, and she pulls a full three feet of spear out before it comes free with a start.

The dummy's mouth moves, pulling itself back together with an effort. Then it speaks, in her sister's voice. "V," it says. "You came. I didn't think you would. I'm so sorry—"

"Ugh, no." Vivienne thrusts the spear back into the dummy's mouth, silencing it. She turns to Charisma, who looks a bit shocked.

"So what do I have to do, exorcise her? Finally prove I'm the superior daughter?"

The shade says nothing, but she looks distantly sad. She points, then starts gliding upward toward the next platform, accessible by a treacherous set of floating stones.

"Hey!" Vivienne hurries after her, mantling the steps. She wishes she could fly, too, but she spent most of her fear energy paralyzing Angel. "Mamá. *Mamá*, what are you trying to tell me?"

# CHAPTER SEVEN: INSIDE THE FIRE

No crumbling bridge this time, but it's more like stepping stones than stairs, making it an annoying mantling obstacle more than anything. On two occasions, Vivienne has to scramble and pull herself up. She finally has to jump and narrowly catches the edge of the platform, then her arms and lats engage full force to let her squirm up. Not the most dignified, but at least no one's here to see it.

"When were you last here?" Charisma asks.

"I think twenty, twenty-five years ago, when I threw a Nazi sorcerer in here, then fucked off?"[6] Vivienne says. "I don't remember anything like this."

This floating island resembles a school gymnasium, complete with half a basketball court, which doesn't make any sense at all. Vivienne was never much of an athlete as a kid, and she dropped out of high school. The place looks old, abandoned, and run down, and she can vaguely make out a mural on the wall of a frizzy-haired scientist. She thinks at first that he looks like her old nemesis $E=MC^2$, but then she realizes this dude's the real deal: Albert Einstein himself. The strangest part is the similarly old, green, threadbare couch someone placed at the side of the court, where the bleachers should be.

"This is weird, even for me," Vivienne says. "Did I create this island? Or the hospital room? Or?"

---

[6] That would be the pretentiously named Satanic! See *The Downward Spiral*.

"Who else?" Charisma asks, materializing at her side. "You don't recognize this place? Einstein Elementary, in Chicago? Closed in the fall of 1999."

"Should I? I went to school in Seattle, and it was that shitty Catholic private school you insisted I go to. In 1999, I was with Supergroup, getting ready for the WTO riots[7] ... The only time I've been to Chicago is the Agents of Awesome ... wait—" She thinks back, scrounging up all the memories she can. There's something familiar about this place—something nostalgic. "Wren. I saw Wren—"

For a second—an agonizing second—Vivienne sees herself sitting on that couch, holding something on her lap, while Wren flips and dances and does acrobatics. Not strictly for her amusement, but there is that. But also ...

"Wren Fulton-Gray," Charisma says. "Yes. You loved them."

"Well, yeah," Vivienne says. "And I fucked it up, just like I fuck everything up." She kicks a flat basketball off the court, and it goes sailing into the gloom. "What are we even doing here? We're supposed to be looking for Marcus. Why do you keep distracting me?"

Charisma gives Vivienne a patient, sympathetic look. "I am so sorry."

"Wait." Vivienne narrows her eyes. "Why are you different? Did dying, um, fix you? Cure the dementia, I mean? Is that why—?"

"Death freed me," Charisma says. "My memories are coming back. The ones that were stolen."

"The ones that were ... oh shit." Vivienne blinks rapidly. "What do you mean? Do you mean—?"

"Carmen's power," Charisma says. "What was it?"

"Athena?" Vivienne scoffs. "That's easy. Superhuman strength. Durability. Stamina. Speed. Flight. Your standard package. Also energy manipulation, dexterity, magic—"

"Empathic projection?"

"That's my power, Mamá. Maybe some of the dementia is still there?"

---

[7] See *Justice in Seattle*! ~ March for our Rights Vogel

"So she had every member of Supergroup's powers," Charisma says. "All but yours."

"So?"

"Isn't that odd?"

"I guess," Vivienne says. "Who knows with ... capes ... You know, now that I think about it—"

Abruptly, the flattened basketball comes flying back at her as though hurled by someone with super strength. Vivienne narrowly dodges, but the basketball smashes into the court with enough force to shatter the floating island beneath her feet. Vivienne tumbles down among falling chunks of rock.

This time, however, there's no lower platform to land on. Instead, she sees the dark void spiraling out below and around her, bordered on all sides by Azazel's grinning teeth. She's falling slower than in the real world, but there's nowhere to land except in the demon's jaws.

As she falls, Vivienne shuts her eyes, the better to think this through. The things she's seen, her mother ... are these all distractions? They must be. Azazel doesn't want her to rescue Marcus, so of course he'll run her through a labyrinth of bullshit. Play her own imagination against herself. Unless ...

The defensive magic Vivienne has put in place. She did it instinctually, when she first arrived, and it stopped Charisma from touching her. What if—?

With her will, Vivienne remolds the protective magic, and it manifests instead as a glowing purple wing sprouting from her shoulder. A bird with one wing shouldn't be able to fly, but the wing is just cosmetic, really. Vivienne arrests her fall, letting the remains of the demolished platform tumble into the darkness. It cracks a few more of the mirror teeth, which flicker and sputter like static.

Vivienne flies to the nearest platform, which looks a little like the Devil's Due, complete with booths, tables, and the music-themed décor of the place. She pulls up a stool at the bar, half-expecting Andre to be there to take her order. Instead, she sees the cracked but intact mirror that extends the width of the room. She turns away, so as not to look at Azazel's teeth.

"What's wrong?" her mother asks.

Charisma walks slowly around the pool table, inspecting each of the striped- and solid-colored balls in turn before settling on the black eight ball. Only that isn't the number eight on the ball, but four letters stacked atop each other, all of them V. She definitely created this platform, even if she has no memory of doing so. But how is that possible?

"Think about it," Charisma says.

The little differences nag at her. She knows every inch of the Devil's Due. She practically lives there. And she wouldn't have shaped its reflection with these kinds of errors. It's kind of an idealized draft of what the bar would eventually be—like a prototype, maybe? Plus, the place didn't even exist last time she was here. Did Azazel make this platform? He must have. But why?

"So," she says. "My sister is alive ... or more accurately, the thing *pretending* to be her. Right?"

Charisma hovers over next to Vivienne. "Why do you say that?"

"Athena—Carmen's spirit was still trapped in that body," Vivienne says. "But that's not all that was in her, right? And—" She bites her lip. "It didn't just appear in *her*, did it?"

Charisma nods gravely. "It was in me, too. It passed to her."

"It?" Vivienne narrows her eyes. "What?"

The shade hesitates, then pronounces a name with great gravity. "Ishtar."

For a second, Vivienne is sure she misheard. "Ishtar. The goddess of love? Seriously?"

Charisma gives her a sour look. "Ishtar, Inanna, Astarte, Aphrodite, Isis ... she is many goddesses, but all are she. She is goddess of love and of fertility—of war and of justice."

"Justice," Vivienne says. "You're kidding me."

"More like retribution," Charisma says. "When she called upon An for the power to destroy Mount Ebih, or when she turned the Earth's water to blood to punish a man who assaulted her. A vicious goddess of endless wrath and limitless vengeance ... what? What's that look, mija?"

"Boy, did she pick the wrong sister to possess," Vivienne says.

"Perhaps."

A goddess. Vivienne is up against a goddess? She's faced gods before, it's true, but rarely when they're directly opposing her. Or else she finds other, more pleasant ways to deal with them.

"It's a little strange to hear a devout Catholic say all this," Vivienne says. "Don't you, y'know, believe in Jesus and all that stuff?"

"There are many gods, as you well know," Charisma says. "Including Loki, yes."

"Hey," Vivienne says. "Don't you judge me. Loki's hot."

"No argument."

"Hold on. How did you know I was thinking about Loki? I never told you about any of that." Vivienne considers. "How come you keep reading my mind? Is that a ghost thing?"

"Perhaps," Charisma says. "But it's also a *me* thing. I was a psychic, you know."

At first, Vivienne thinks her mother is making a joke, but her face is dead serious. "You ... what? What do you mean? You never had any powers. I'd remember."

"That's just it," Charisma says. "Before you were born—before your sister—I was CIA. Part of the powered unit. I wasn't a powerful mentalist, but powerful enough. Maybe that was Ishtar inside me. But as soon as your sister was born, the goddess had no more use for me."

"And your powers went away?"

Charisma shakes her head. "Not right away. But by the time you were born, she had erased most of them. I was ... a threat to her. Just as you were, but your mind was stronger. Stubborn."

"Seems legit." Stubbornness has always been one of the traits in which Vivienne takes pride. "Wait, are you saying she ... erased your powers? Or—" She realizes. "*Stole* them."

Charisma nods, relieved like she finally got something across. "That was Carmen's power. She takes the powers of others. My mind, Justice's strength, energy manipulation ... All but yours."

"What makes me so special? That I'm stubborn?" But she already knows the answer. "Azazel."

"And?" Charisma asks.

It feels like her mind is close to connecting all these dots. Carmen, the actual goddess Ishtar, Azazel, her mother, and even this strange reflection of the ... bar ...

"I created this," Vivienne says. "And the other scenes. But why? When?" She looks at her hands. "Why can't I remember?"

Charisma waits. If anything, the shade seems anxious. She's been waiting for this.

"Fuck," Vivienne says. "Athena erased my memory. Like you. Like—*fuck*, how many people has she fucked over?"

Charisma seems like she wants to say something, then her eyes widen. "We're out of time. He's coming."

"He who?"

Honestly, she should know not to ask that kind of thing by now.

She feels it first in her molars, which twinge and ache as though she hasn't brushed in years. The pain spreads forward from there, until all her teeth are on edge. Shit.

Then the sound. It's so high-pitched she feels it more than hears it, crackling in her bones and making her dizzy. But it comes down until she can finally pick it up with her ears.

*Laughter.*

The fake Devil's Due bursts into flames, and Vivienne instinctively grabs at Charisma to shield her from the explosion. Her protection is gone, so she can physically touch the shade, which feels a bit like a gelatin mold set to chill in the fridge and then forgotten for at least a week. Her arms meet resistance at first, then push through, and she hits the deck hard. She coughs, spraying dust and smoke.

A figure emerges from the back door: a vaguely human-shaped form wrapped in spiked and distorted plate armor. She thinks *vaguely*, because the creature's upper body is at least twice the size of its lower body, swelling upward in a triangle to shoulders wider than its legs are long. It's like a caricature of a bodybuilder, painted by someone who knows what the human form looks like and prefers comic books by nineties edgelords. The similarly melted armor is vicious and wicked and not at all practical for anything other than holding up a ceiling. It looks like a crude Ionic column, is what she means, or is that Doric? Who knows. Partly melted by intense heat, seven jagged spines thrust up from the helmet like the tines of a crown. It looks like something out of Lord of the Rings, and it would almost be funny if she didn't also recognize who this must be, and that makes it so much fucking *worse*.

The hellfire-melted knight raises his—its?—right hand, which has its own clawed glove like hers, except this one is fused to its arm. "Little Vivienne Cain. Oh, I've been waiting so *long*."

"Hey Heilfire or Satanic or whatever you're calling yourself these days," she says. "Long time."

"Hellknight Randall, chosen of Azazel," he says in his slavering voice. He flexes his massive arms, which are as big around as her waist, she thinks. "Randy's fine, though."

"That's right, you did have a real name, didn't you? Anyway." Vivienne channels her fear energy into a fearsword. Best she can manage at the moment is more like a dagger, but it'll have to do. "I hope you don't take the whole being buried under a 7-Eleven personally. I heard that's what they built on your mom's house, after we drowned you in concrete."

"The Many-Mouthed Devourer protects his own," the warlock says. "I was never in any danger."

"Oh bullshit," Vivienne says. "He whisked you away to the Fearworld, and you've been trapped here for what, over twenty years? All because you weren't me? Wow, what a boss."

"Over twenty years of training, of preparation, of honing my skills and magic until I can defeat you."

"You really need a hobby, or maybe to get laid?" Vivienne shrugs. "That's the thing with Nazis, right? 'While you were drinking and having orgasms, I studied race science' or something?"

"Jesus *Christ*." He lifts his two-handed sword, which bursts into scarlet and black flame. "You are every *bit* the mouthy bitch you were last time."

That's a lot of power. She can feel the heat from this distance.

"You know," she says. "When I was a kid, that might have hurt my feelings. But when it comes to pathetic little pissbabies like you, it's like Angel always says."

"And what's that?"

She points the fearsword toward him. "I don't care."

The shard of fear energy melts away into a blast of purple force. It won't pierce all that armor, but it doesn't really have to. Instead, it just has to hit him, and it practically can't miss. His distorted torso is the size of a refrigerator, and unfortunately for him, his legs aren't as strong. The power smacks him center-mass, right in the solar plexus, and knocks him tumbling back. He staggers, starts to cry out, then falls off the platform entirely.

"Shouldn't have skipped leg day for twenty years," Vivienne says.

Charisma sighs.

"Gah!" The smoke parts, and the hellknight is back on the platform, within easy reach, and he grasps her by the neck with his good hand. "Fucking bitch! Do you have *any* idea how much power I poured into that sword? Now I'll have to go find it!"

"Boo ho-urhk!" His fingers close around her windpipe, and she clutches his hand with her claw.

"No! No more of your lip, little girl!" He raises his claws to her face. "No more from you *ever*!"

He lost his helmet in the fall too, and his face is just horrific. He's invested in a little gender-affirming surgery to try to make himself look tough, but it has *not* worked. Maybe he did it on himself with the gauntlet's claws? Regardless, twenty years of no skincare, shaving with murder claws and only demon-haunted broken mirrors, and absolutely no acne care, has ravaged his skin, and his nose is barely there. Did she snip it off with her claw at some point? She doesn't know. Honestly, though, he'd probably have looked like that even if he'd spent twenty years in the *real* world. Shame about the receding hairline, though. She knows plenty of guys who struggle with that.

"Hurr—" Vivienne gestures with her free hand, pointing over his shoulder.

"Oh, like I'll fall for thaaaaaaaaaaaa—"

The word stretches as Charisma's spectral fingers emerge from his forehead. His body goes rigid and starts twitching as though he's dreaming. Which Vivienne hopes he is. Dreaming of being twerked to death by body-positive women of color, preferably. Heilfire's worst nightmare.

Slowly, the Nazi warlock sinks to the ground, armor clanking and groaning, and Charisma draws her hand once more out of his head. "That man really needs help," she says.

"Thanks Mamá," Vivienne says, her voice raspy from being choked. "Goddammit. I really gotta start solving my problems permanently, not just locking them away."

"¿Permanente, como—?"

"Murder, Mamá," Vivienne says. "*Obviously.*"

The ghost of her very Catholic mother frowns in disapproval.

"Oh, don't give me that. I'm guilty enough."

"I notice you're not killing him now, though."

"Oh, you noticed that." Vivienne kneels beside Heilfire or the Great White Cope or whatever he calls himself. It would be easy to kill him, but she thinks she probably could have defeated him one-on-one, too. He's more sad than scary. "I think Azazel lured me here intentionally, trying to get me to kill this asshole, and I try not to do what the devil wants me to."

"Since when—?"

"Mamá!" Vivienne rubs her sore throat. "This ... this was a trap, wasn't it?"

Charisma nods sadly. "Creo que sí."

"You said you could sense only one person until I got here, then two. And this asshole, no matter how pathetic, counts as a person." She sighs. "Marcus isn't even here, is he?"

She shakes her head. "Lo siento, mija. I didn't know."

"Because—" Vivienne realizes. "He never left."

Again, Charisma nods.

"Okay, so we're clear," Vivienne says. "I never want to come back to this godsforsaken hellhole. Way too My Chemical Romance. Cringe." She looks to Charisma. "You can get us out of here, right?"

"Absolutely," Charisma says. "Assuming my granddaughter catches you."

"Yeah," Vivienne says. "Wait, *what?*"

# CHAPTER EIGHT: CALL ME WHEN YOU'RE SOBER

---

"Angel! Angel!" Yumi is shouting into her earpiece. "Angel, wake up!"

Angel shakes away the paralyzing terror her aunt put in her head. God*damn* that woman, but she has bigger problems. Angel is falling, tumbling end over end toward the ocean far below, but that isn't the issue. The real issue is her arms are empty. She dropped Vivienne somewhere and ...

"Talk to me!" Yumi says. "Your vitals—"

"I'm fine."

Angel grits her teeth, rights herself, and looks in all directions. Speed, strength, and durability, those are all in her power set, but nothing extrasensory or perceptive. She has slightly better than twenty/twenty vision, but that isn't quite sufficient when you're up in the clouds.

"Angel, what happened?" Yumi asks. "Where's V? Did you *drop* her?"

"Yeah, but only because she *made* me."

"*What?*"

"Just a second!"

Fortunately, hanging onto her dad's tech means she's got the enhanced helmet and, specifically, the targeting computer. Angel taps the side of the helmet—probably harder than necessary—and a radar overlay springs to life against the visor. She scans it for any sign of Vivienne if it's set to her life-readings or, barring that, an unidentified falling object that might be Vivienne. She finds neither.

"I don't see her," Angel says.

"What do you mean? Did she already splash down?"

"I mean, maybe? She hit me with a lot, but I don't think I was out for a full minute. Hang on."

Angel fires herself back the way she came, desperately scouring the sky for any sign of Vivienne. She doesn't see a big splash or waves, so it seems unlikely her aunt crashed into the ocean already. So there must be a chance. But the computer should be picking her up ...

Abruptly, there she is, tumbling limply through the air, about two thousand feet up, two miles away. Vivienne isn't falling all that fast, as though she just appeared and hasn't been picking up momentum from falling the previous eight thousand feet. But she starts falling from there and accelerates swiftly toward the water. Also, she isn't moving, as though she's unconscious or dead.

"Shit!" Without hesitation, Angel fires herself on an intercept course with her aunt.

Angel has been doing this for a few years, and she's learned the hard way that catching a falling human body at high velocity is a tricky thing. Too fast, and the shock will shatter bone—too slow, and she misses entirely. She only hopes she'll have the chance.

"I see her!" Yumi says, helpfully. "Can you catch her?"

Angel doesn't reply. She doesn't have time.

Wind whistling, Angel covers one mile in the ten or so seconds it takes her aunt to fall a thousand feet. She's up to four hundred miles per hour but pushes herself faster as Vivienne picks up speed. Anyone watching would see a trail of fire across the sky, like a shooting star, which fades from violent red to something more like pink. Like the horizon as the sun rises.

Angel covers the second mile, and Vivienne's two hundred feet up. Angel dives down after her, trying to equalize their speed. She wraps her arms around her aunt, who's freezing cold, and slows herself, cradling her. They're going to hit the water. They're going to ...

The ocean trembles as Angel stops just short of the water's surface, then bursts apart in all directions as the force of her flight catches up. It's like an airplane in a dead dive toward the water, only to just not crash at the last instant. All that air still has to go somewhere, and where it goes is dozens of feet down into the ocean, sending up walls of water just as high that flow away from them. If they were closer to the coast, it might cause a small tsunami.

Yumi's voice crackles in her ear. "A! *A*! Talk to me!"

Vivienne's eyelids flutter. "Angel," she mouths, her lips dry and cracked.

Floating there, amidst the spray and mist and churning waves, Angel lets out a sigh. "I've got her, Y. Mission complete."

"Thank God." Yumi sounds like she's been throwing things. "What happened?"

"Oh, just V being V." Angel glares down at her aunt, who has passed out again, and grimaces. "I should really make you swim back."

Vivienne doesn't respond, of course. She looks sweet and innocent when she's asleep, more like a teen girl excited to go to the prom than a middle-aged hot mess. Angel wonders what Vivienne is dreaming of, and whether it will compensate for how loudly she plans to shout at her aunt.

Still, she's relieved, not just because three years ago, she couldn't have pulled off something like that. Angry as she is at her aunt, Angel still doesn't want her dead. And not *just* because if she's dead, Angel can't thoroughly chew her out. But that's a big part of it.

She makes sure she has a good grip on Vivienne.

~

Back on the dock, as they float toward the 2K Group control van they borrowed for this operation, Angel can tell Yumi is also not happy. The back of the van is what she would call "ADHD tantrum trashed," which is to say each and every thing has been touched and tossed elsewhere, down to an upside-down keyboard on the roof and a headset hanging off the trailer hitch. Pacing in front of the open van, Yumi herself looks about ready to explode.

When she sees them approaching, Yumi freezes in an attack pose and puts her hand out to the side. Crimson smoke flows around her hand, and Muramasa appears, cutting a brutal path through the air, like a red fan blade captured in slow motion. It leaves an energy trail not unlike Angel's own: an afterimage burned into the retina, though it fades much faster than the trail Angel's flight produces. The emotional content, though—is she really that angry? She's been pretty red recently. It stops Angel short.

The jolt of Angel's touchdown wakes Vivienne up. "Oh," she says. Then she sees Yumi. "*Oh.*"

"What did I say?" Yumi demands. "You promised you wouldn't hurt her! You *promised* me!"

"Yeah, well—" Vivienne doesn't seem in any condition to fight. She barely manages to raise her hands to ward off the furious ninja girl. "I'm sorry?"

"You're *sorry?*" Yumi's eyes burn with fiery energy.

"Stop." Angel steps between them, and Yumi pulls up short of attacking her. The two share a direct look, and Yumi finally turns away, sheathing her sword.

"So Muramasa *can* be sheathed without drawing blood," Vivienne says. "Good to know—"

"And you!" Angel rounds on Vivienne, her eyes stinging with tears. "What the *fuck* was that?"

"Hey, the only one in any danger was me," Vivienne says. "And I knew you'd catch me. Or—"

"Or what?" It's all Angel can do not to put her hands on Vivienne's collar and shake her, but that would probably kill her aunt. She puts her hands on her hips instead. "You didn't think that would hurt me? Watching you almost kill yourself?"

"Right?" Yumi shouts from behind her. "I'm an emotional idiot, and *I* know that!"

Vivienne winces. "Angel, I—"

"You know what?" Angel shrugs. "Forget it. We can talk about it later." Her eyes gleam. "Well? Did you succeed?"

Vivienne sighs. "Kind of."

At that moment, a middle-aged woman materializes from the air beside her. She's a psychic spirit, without a physical body, but enough use of her powers, and she can take a visible form. She looks somewhere around forty, her raven hair only just laced through with silver, and her dark eyes full of compassion and wisdom. And though Angel has only met her once, she *knows* her. Her eyes are clearer than ever before, because dying broke decades of gaslighting and mind warping.

70

"Is that a ghost?" Yumi starts to draw Muramasa again, but Angel raises a hand.

"Abuela?" Angel asks.

"Nieta mia." Charisma Cain hugs Angel. When they touch, her pink energy aura ripples, and she feels her grandmother's arms. They're warm, even if Charisma has no physical body.

"Fuck *me*," Vivienne says. "Add 'ghost touch' to her power set."

"V!" Yumi says. "Read the room. Dock. Whatever."

"I'm ... I'm sorry, abuela." Angel draws away from Charisma. "We only met the once, but I should have called, or visited, or something. I even missed your funeral."

"Twice," Charisma says. "It's all right, nieta—both my daughters did, too."

"Hey," Vivienne says, but Yumi's sharp look shuts her up.

The hug lingers, and Angel cries fresh tears, these happier. Finally, Charisma pulls away and touches her forehead to Angel's. Again, the energy aura flares, and Angel can feel her grandmother.

Despite her jet-black heart, raging hangover, and being basically dead just a few minutes ago, Vivienne seems touched.

"Wait," Angel says. "What do you mean *twice*? When was the second time?"

"The first time, when you were born," Charisma says, then turns to Vivienne. "Don't you remember? It was a very memorable day for both of us."

Vivienne frowns. "Not really. I was probably drunk—you know what? This isn't about me."

Angel turns on Vivienne. "Okay, it's cool to see my recently dead grandmother and all—"

"A," Vivienne says with a shocked expression. "That's rude."

Charisma holds up a hand and gives Vivienne a patient look.

"But did you find Marcus?" Angel asks. "You know, the whole reason you did this stupid thing in the first place?"

"That's what I was trying to tell you," Vivienne says. "No, I didn't find him, because he isn't there. It was a trap, and he was never there to begin with."

"Okay, so where is he?" Angel asks. "Stop being cryptic and just spit it out, V!"

Charisma fills it in. "He never left."

71

Then she fades away into the humid air—message delivered, purpose fulfilled.

"You're telling me—" Angel's lip trembles. "You're telling me Marcus is *alive*."

"Right." Vivienne swallows dryly. "So where the *fuck* is he?"

~

"Excuse me," the young man says, hefting the two bags of garbage. "Ladies?"

The development director and the executive director, who were engaged in the kind of spontaneous planning session meeting that breaks out in the halls of nonprofits all the time, blink at him and smile. "Absolutely, Malcolm," says the director. "We're blocking the exit."

"We should probably take this to your office, Linda," says the development director, adjusting her hijab self-consciously. "Thanks again, Mal, for all your help today. Couldn't do it without you."

"Of course, Marwa. Linda." Malcolm would put his hands together in thanks, but since he's carrying two bags of trash, a bow will have to suffice. His rainbow skullcap makes for a particular bright spot at the shelter. "Those guys out front are gone, but be careful on your way home, okay?"

Marwa nods rapidly. Malcolm can tell she desperately wants to ask him to walk her home, but not because she feels unsafe. He's not sure how he knows that, but over the last few months, he's been getting these feelings, and they're never wrong. He assumes it's just a new thing, and that's just fine.

Before Marwa can speak up, though, Linda takes the lead. "Always," the executive director says. "With Prather pulling nonprofit grants, though, we've got a lot of work. It might be an all-nighter."

"I hear that," Malcolm says. "See you tomorrow, then?"

"You bet." Linda shepherds Marwa into her office, despite Marwa stealing a lingering glance at Malcolm. He grins and shakes his head. Too bad she's not his type.

Malcolm heads out through the emergency exit into the alley, with no alarm sounding. It hasn't worked since before he started working here. The House of Muhammad, Peace Be Upon Him, or, as it's called on the street, "the Muslim Peace House," operates at incredibly thin margins, just barely able to keep the doors open and the community served. Especially with the opiate epidemic, it's been tough.

For Malcolm, it's a minimum wage job—his favorite of his three—but that's Prather's economy for you. Oh sure, the Republicans keep *saying* they give the tiniest shit about jobs and standard of living, but they just mean for themselves. Meanwhile, they keep instituting policies to make life worse for everyone who isn't worth a million or more, and those idiots keep voting for them. He knows it's not about the money, though. It's not about the Constitution. It's not about democracy.

It's about the other thing.

The temptation to just ... make different choices is always there. But at this point, it's the principle. Stealing, dealing, or whatever would just be admitting defeat, and Malcolm Ali has always been stubborn. That, and he still remembers one of his father's lessons: from each according to their ability, to each according to their need. You get what you earn, and you help those who need it.

Still, the option's there. Things haven't gotten that bad yet, but never say never.

Just after he lets the dumpster lid fall closed, Malcolm thinks he sees something in the boarded-over window at the back of the shelter. It reflects the fire escape behind him, across the alley, and perched on the landing is ... is that a bird or a *person*?

He turns, but there's no one there. Just seeing shadows.

"Hey!"

There they are, the two Prat Hats from earlier today. Solidly built white guys, skipped a few leg days in favor of happy hours, exactly what you'd expect. One of them has a baseball bat and a red Prather hat with the yellow text, of course: "America First, America Only."

"What's the matter, boy? Didn't get the memo?" The bearded Prat Hat points to the Prather poster. "This ain't your city anymore. Ain't no more sanctuary cities, order of the Commander in Chief."

"Hey, give 'im a break, Chad," says the one with the baseball bat. "Muhammad here probably can't read American. Let's make it

73

clear." He pokes the baseball bat toward Malcolm's chest. "Get the fuck out, DEI. You ain't replacing us. Tainting our blood—"

"Yo, man." Malcolm slaps the bat aside with unexpected strength, making the Prat Hat stumble. "I ain't fucking any white women, let alone your Nazi barbies. I'm gay."

The Prat Hats exchange a distinctly "that's worse" sort of look, then the one with the bat takes a swing at Malcolm. He starts to say a word that starts with "F" but doesn't get the chance. Malcolm casually raises one arm to block the blow, and the bat shatters into a thousand pieces as though the Prat Hat in question hit a foul ball so bad he took out his coach and the guy on deck.

The other one pulls a gun, but the bullets just bounce off Malcolm, though they do leave little holes in his shirt. The increasingly alarmed bigot's eyes get wider as he empties the magazine, until the pistol clicks over and over again. Malcolm frowns down at the wide spread, even at this short range.

"I wasn't finished, you Nazi fuck," Malcolm says, static dancing around him. "I ain't your 'boy' or 'DEI' or any of that. The name's Malcolm Muhammad Ali, and it's *Reparation* time, bitches."

He cracks his knuckles, his fists starting to hum with kinetic energy.

"Time to get it."

# CHAPTER NINE: REBEL WITHOUT A PAUSE

"And he defeated both of them quite thoroughly," Antonio DeSantes says into the phone. "I wouldn't say efficiently—he evinces no sign of formal fight training beyond street boxing—but—"

"And why," says the voice on the other end, "are you telling *me* this? What have I done that gives you the impression I know or care about fisticuffs? Please let me know so I can avoid it in future. I'll have Arsho put it in my calendar. Perhaps a class—"

Tony holds the phone away—he muted it as soon as she started her rant—and sighs. Ruby Killingsworth will never like him, he's quite sure, but he's doing his best to avoid giving her an in for snark and spite. She is, however, a master at both, so he isn't always successful. In fact, he misses a *lot*.

The room where he's squatting isn't much—a mattress, a table, a single creaky chair—but it has an easily guarded entrance, a fire escape inaccessible from the street without an enhanced suit or powers, and an excellent sightline on his target. Tony doesn't mind the barebones work—quite enjoys it, in fact. Since he left Valhalla behind with the bulk of his resources, he's kept a low profile and avoided hotels, customs, that sort of thing, especially this close to the festering anti-democratic think-tanks in Silicon Valley. He could be one of those tech bros if he wanted to—if he sold out all his principles and bowed at the altar of ghouls like Thiel, Musk, and the rest. Instead, here he is, living the life of a vigilante without a steady source of income. What's next, boosting cars?

It's like the old days, but he refuses to succumb to nostalgia. The worst thing you can do is relive the glory days. Whether it makes you maudlin or overconfident, that's a recipe for disaster.[8]

As Ruby goes into some defamatory insinuations about his sex life, Tony leans over to the window to check out the Muslim Peace House. The nonprofit shelter and cultural center has been the subject of a number of hit-and-run attacks by Prat Hats—no organized protest, because the last thing supporters of Lyle Prather are is *organized*. But there's increasing right-wing chatter about some kind of "big hit" on the place, and Tony has staked out the shelter for several days now. It wasn't until the day before that he saw their protector in person, but now that he has, they can't just wait. Who knows what weaponry the Prats will bring against the center, now that Malcolm Ali—or "Reparation," as he calls himself, what a great name—has put two of them in traction for at least six months?

He checks, but Ruby's still going strong. Ordinarily, he'd wait until she was finished or at least winding down before he spoke again, but today's special, and they only have so much time to indulge in their unique form of banter. This is an opportunity they can't afford to miss.

"And another thing—" she's saying when he cuts her off.

"The subject," he says, "has shown up on local Prather bulletin boards and the dark web."

Ruby does him the favor of suppressing her annoyance at being so rudely interrupted. She must have been nearly done. "And that means, what exactly? He has an OnlyCapes page?"

"It means," Tony says, "that they're planning an assault on the center where he works. They've studied him, and they think they can take him."

Ruby pauses. "Can they?" she asks at length.

*Nice of you to care*, Tony thinks but doesn't say.

---

[8] Tony's too polite to say or think it aloud, but he means his clash with Jaccob "Stardust" Stevens in *Eye for an Eye*, where Stardust got a little too excited and made what Tony would deem "rookie mistakes." And that was before his life fell apart. Poor Jaccob! ~ Commiserating Vogel

"Unknown," he says. "I've only been able to measure his power level from observation."

"Can he defeat you?"

"That's uncalled for."

"Well, you called me—and with nothing to offer, I might add. That's what you get."

Tony figures he deserved that. "By all means, abuse me more, Lady Disdain."

"You get off on this, don't you?"

"No."

"Liar. I'm hanging up now."

"A question," Tony says. "How's the ritual to separate them coming?"

"I'm working on it, Tony. You can't just rush sorcery. It's not as clumsy or random as *tech*."

"I don't suppose you have an ETA?"

"How about *eat me*?"

"Nice."

"I'm glad you appreciated it. I got that one from—"

She trails off, but they both know what she was about to say, and the rant it was about to trigger. Ruby has not spared Tony her opinions about Vivienne, her frequent lapses in judgment, her neglect of her health, her absolutely wasted potential, and her many, many, *many* character flaws. It's obvious to Tony that Ruby wants him to know how much she hates and is entirely over Vivienne, and it is equally obvious that neither is the case. But of course he can't point that out. If he even lets on that he knows, Ruby will be so angry, it'll make the destruction of Valhalla look like an awkward middle school Valentine's Day sock hop. So they dance this careful dance, each pretending not to know, and not to feel. Just to focus on the job at hand.

They have way more in common than either of them can say, though at least Tony can admit it to himself. Maybe Ruby can too, but Tony expects he'll never again get close enough to know.

"Movement." Tony peers through the scope. Sure enough, there's Malcolm heading out for the night, a little earlier than usual.

"Maybe he has a hot date," Ruby says.

"Don't do that."

"Do what?"

"Read my mind. I know you're showing off."

"Why, what*ever* are you talking about, Mr. DeSantes," Ruby says, which isn't a question. "Why, you *must* have said that aloud. *Surely* I couldn't be in your head at *this* distance."

"Laying it on thick today, I see."

Tony *knows* she can, in fact, thanks to her curse binding his heart. He's sure Ruby didn't intend to connect them in this way, but she's not shy about flexing on him from time to time. He also knows she only hears surface-level thoughts, as he's tested her a few times to confirm. Those thoughts and feelings that Antonio "The Raven" DeSantes holds deep inside are things about which Ruby Killingsworth physically could *not* pass up the chance to snark.

"Well, are you going after him or what?" Ruby asks. "Make it quick. I have a conference call in five minutes with the president—"

"Send him my love," Tony says with a completely straight face as he holds out his arms for the automated activation process to enclose his torso, arms, and legs in black armor.

"Darling, if I were the punching type, you know I'd be first in line."

"Heh." His cape wraps around his shoulders and unfolds in a glittering cascade of blades. He flexes his hands and arms to ensure a tight seal.

"Was that a laugh just now?"

"No." His helmet closes over his face, leaving just one burning red eye visible.

"I'm hanging up now. Don't get killed. Or, better yet, *do.* I'd consider it a great personal favor."

The phone clicks.

The Raven goes out the window and to work.

~

Fog rolls off the bay to blanket San Francisco, making the streets seem cramped and tightly enclosed, like a maze for rats. Winter has clung on hard and won't let go. The wet chill gets into the bones and lingers. Not many residents would be caught dead out after dark, except in organized gangs or marches, out to fight seemingly every night.

Tensions are high. The city is a battleground for an increasingly desperate President slash Would-Be-King Prather heading into a re-election fight and the local progressive populace, which has been at war with the fascist regime since the beginning. ICE has increased its presence in the city, especially over the last years, emboldened by roving bands of Prat Hats armed with pepper spray and telescoping batons. The constant presence of these dudes in sweat-yellowed shirts erodes the patience and morale of liberals, who would prefer to hide in their overpriced lofts and studio apartments and hope it all blows over. It falls, as it always does, to just a handful of people out on the streets, making a difference.

Like this Malcolm Ali.

*Maybe.*

And that's a big maybe. Who knows what this man really wants? What his goal is? He beat a couple of white supremacists into the hospital, but who hasn't, really? That isn't proof that he's on the side of the angels. Just that he takes no shit. The Raven respects it, but he's wary, too.

As he leaps from rooftop to rooftop, using the booster jets as little as he needs to, The Raven thinks back to his Black Bloc days. The '99 WTO riots in Seattle. May Day marches. Cyclical marches against the wars in the Middle East. Until the unexpected gubernatorial election of 2008, he hit basically every march he could and financed those he couldn't. Even as the governor of the great state of Colorado, he was still an outspoken advocate of protests, marches, and fighting with the cops as needed. He was well used to wearing the mask. It kept him anonymous. The Raven could be anywhere, poised to crack a few white supremacist skulls and defend others' right to protest.

When he lands atop the far building, his creaking joints stage a protest of their own.

He's getting too old for this.

Maybe they're right, his joints. Maybe he should have stayed in that chair and made a difference with his pen, not his fists.

Other than occasional weekends in Black Bloc, he's spent the last twelve and especially the last four years as basically a bureaucrat, sitting in that chair in the state house or in his own high-rise base of operation. It took him until his second term to understand that he could do more at a desk rather than on a rooftop or the pavement. Under his leadership, Colorado became practically an autonomous nation-state, refusing to bow to the will of the growing fascist powerbase in Congress, and it was well positioned to defy Lyle Prather and his ilk when they stole the election of 2016. Tony "The Raven" DeSantes has always been the first one to paint a target on his back, and Prather has taken shot after shot at him, until finally, he mostly succeeded.

Now, off the grid and underground, with just himself to rely on, The Raven wonders if he was a little too hasty seizing the opportunity afforded by Prather's blatant attack on his powerbase. Disappearing after the attack on his tower has left Colorado in political chaos, though at least his lieutenant governor stepped up. Apparently, momentum is building in Colorado and around the country, with the people expressing disgust and loathing toward Prather for trying to assassinate an elected official. Colorado will definitely go blue this year, and probably a few other purple states as well.

Meanwhile, Tony DeSantes is missing, presumed dead, but The Raven is haunting the streets.

Interesting how life circles back around.

The fog ruins his night vision—too many particles in the air—but his eye is adapted well enough to the gloom to make out the bright rainbow pattern of his mark's skullcap, just visible over a dumpster behind an old brick apartment complex. The Raven slows his roll and waits a minute, then springs down to the street level, booster jets cushioning his fall enough that he hardly feels it in his legs. Old joints.

"Malcolm Ali," he says, his voice rough through the modulator. "I'm—"

Before he can say another word, an electric whine rips through The Raven's helmet, and his suit abruptly glitches out, firing razor feathers in several directions before going dark entirely. Shocked, The Raven staggers back and activates his reboot cycle with a trembling finger, but that'll take at least a minute. He was EMP-shielded, but apparently not enough. Should have built in backups. Careless.

"You the one's been watching me, huh?"

Malcolm steps out of the shadow of a dumpster, energy crackling around him in a blue corona. He has unzipped his jacket, under which he wears a white tank-top that contrasts sharply with his dark skin. As The Raven struggles to get up, he bends down and retrieves his rainbow skullcap, which he places over his meticulous cornrows and adjusts carefully.

"You Prats never learn, do you?" Malcolm pounds his fists together, sending out crackling blue electricity. "You gon' send a cape after me, at least send one with powers. The disrespect, for real."

Twenty percent restored. De-escalate. Buy time. "There's been a misunderstanding," The Raven says, shivering with leftover electricity. "I'm not here to fight."

"Yeah?" Malcolm raises his arm, which has three Raven feathers sticking out of it. He plucks one out, and there's no blood. "Funny way of showing it."

He's the one who shorted out the suit. Embarrassing. "Reflex."

"Bitch, shut the fuck up." Malcolm strips off his damaged jacket, revealing bare arms tightly corded with muscle and sinew. No feather wounds. "It's Reparation time."

As Reparation throws the first punch, it occurs to The Raven—in that sardonic, darkly ironic way of his—that this is what being a leftist is like on a daily basis. Punching Nazis, sure, but also punching each other just as hard. Especially when we don't see eye to eye.

The Raven slips the jab, but it still wings his helmet with enough force to disrupt his balance. The resulting cross smashes straight into his guard, making The Raven's right forearm go numb to the elbow. He's hideously strong—as strong as any enhanced fighter The Raven has ever faced. And his suit is only at thirty percent. He has to stay in the fight until it recharges, and he can't give ground, because Reparation will just shock him again. And talking it out isn't working. Also, he picked a helluva year to give up using guns.

He's *definitely* too old for this.

Still, even recently electrocuted, The Raven isn't one of the best hand-to-hand fighters in the world for nothing. He tests Reparation's range and technique, giving a step here and there, but never allowing enough distance for the vigilante to bring his energy powers to bear. It didn't seem like a targeted blast, more like lashing out and hoping for the best, but The Raven can't take that risk. Not with his suit at fifty percent. Another blast could *kill* him.

After thirty seconds of boxing, one thing becomes very clear to The Raven: Reparation is new at this. The younger man is a straight-forward boxer, evincing the kind of training you'd get at a YMCA or a local gym. He's totally untrained in the dirty tricks The Raven picked up on the street and has refined over thirty years in the game. He keeps falling for feints, opening himself up for a body shot here, a tag to the face there. Now, if it weren't like punching solid rock, that would get him somewhere.

Sixty percent. Come on. Andale, *andale.*

As he ducks a hook that shatters a fistful of brick out of the corner of a nearby building, The Raven wonders if he should be running. He doesn't feel fear anymore—not since he burned out his amygdala and its associated fear-processing response. He had that done so he could take down Lady Vengeance if he needed to—rendering him immune to her powers—but he can't deny it's made him reckless.

Seventy percent.

Reparation finally turtles up, going on the defensive to catch his breath, and The Raven presses the attack. He activates his spring-loaded titanium claws, which spring out of his bracers. The diamond edges cut a little into Reparation's arm, but The Raven realizes it's just the skin indenting, not being cut. The man really is indestructible, isn't he? Not only that, but he casually backhands The Raven across the face, snapping the claws off at the bracer and tagging his faceplate. His eye-port cracks and he staggers back against the wall as warnings flash inside his helmet and across the staticky heads-up display.

"Yo, man, I see you tryin', but you got nothin'."

Eighty percent will have to do.

Driving forward, The Raven channels all his recharged power into one lethal kinetic strike, punching both fists into Reparation's midsection. He built this upgrade into the current suit to help him deal with enhanced pugilists, letting him hit like a freight train at full speed, and he once tore open the side of a *tank* with it. That kind of hit would shatter every bone in the body of a normal human, which, of course, Reparation is not. Hopefully, it will at least buy The Raven some time.

It *does* knock Reparation back several feet. As tough and strong as he is, he just doesn't have the *mass* to stand unscathed by the hit. He slides backward, arms crossed, feet scraping the pavement, which cracks under the force, and finally into the brick wall behind him. He caves in a crater that's at least a few inches deep. Meanwhile, The Raven's suit is down to fifty percent again, and he stands there panting. Maybe he really *should* run—come up with a better strategy ...

Then Reparation does something The Raven has only seen Marcus Orestes do on occasion, and before him, only Justice with any regularity.

"Enough!" he roars.

Then he propels himself like pure energy, darting through the space between them like lightning, and impacts The Raven with a thunderous boom that rattles his bones and steals his breath. Reparation grasps The Raven by the throat and holds him up against the wall, feet kicking several inches from the ground. Before The Raven can fight back, Reparation slams his charged free fist into his side, denting his armor, blowing away his breath again, and making his ribs quake.

"Enough," Reparation says, his voice softer but no less dangerous or violent. "Where's the dude that sent you?" He punches again, shocking The Raven with jangling nerves. "I gotta pay him a visit next."

"Wait—" The Raven says.

"You from ICE? Paramilitary? Mercenary?"

Reparation punctuates each question with another hit, and each one breaks off pieces of The Raven suit. Even worse is the energy in each punch. It's a little like a cattle prod or a stun gun, but it isn't just electricity. It's like he's disrupting the energy flowing through The Raven's body, eroding his life force itself. He hasn't been hit like that since ... he can't even remember.

"What?" Reparation glares, sweat running down his face. "Nothing to say?"

The Raven manages to croak out broken words. "I'm ... The Raven—"

"Yo, is that supposed to mean something to me?" Reparation smirks. "Caw caw, motherfucker."

Young people these days, though Reparation is probably about thirty. Not a kid by any means. The Raven has definitely lost some of his edge with the youths.

"Not ... Prather," The Raven says. "Here ... to help you—"

"Help *me*?" Malcolm considers him for a second. "Nah. You ain't."

Then he slams his fist so hard into The Raven's helmet it shears steel and shatters his eye-port. The pressure pushes his prosthetic out, and it bounces into the street. The suit's systems go entirely dark, and he collapses to the ground, wheezing and coughing.

"Eh, yo, you Mexican or something?" Reparation asks. "Why you siding with white supremacists, brother?"

"I ... told you—" The Raven says. "I'm not ... with Prather—"

"Maybe, but you still stepped to me, and I can't just let that slide." Reparation bends at The Raven's side. "Don't take it so hard, old man. You ain't a Nazi, so you get to live. But if you ain't helping, get out of the way."

Reparation leaves The Raven lying there, struggling to breathe, and heads down the alley. He's limping faintly, but that's really the only consolation he has to offer.

"Fuck," The Raven says, his voice raw and broken.

His right arm doesn't obey his commands, and his left arm feels like it weighs as much as his whole body. He raises it with significant effort and hits the emergency release on the side of his helmet. It clicks but doesn't come open until he hits it a couple times, making his ears ring. Half the faceplate falls off, while the other half grinds open. That sound makes it very clear it won't close again. Also, his communications system is profoundly shot.

Wincing at the effort of reaching down again, The Raven hits a button on his utility belt, unlocking his cell phone. It falls from his numb fingers onto the ground, and he leans down so that he can dial with his broken nose. With his last bit of strength, he hits redial and turns on speaker.

"Don't you know you're not supposed to call back until at least three days later?" Ruby asks, her voice echoing around the alley. "Honestly, this is just common sense ... Am I on speakerphone?"

"Ru ... by—" The Raven gasps as his vision narrows. "Call ... V—"

"What? Oh *no*, no no no, I'm not calling that woman. And that's *your fault*, let me remind you. If you'd just kept your admittedly excellent dick in your bird-themed tighty-whities—"

"Ru ... by—"

"DeSantes? Do you hear me? I hope you're dying because one, that's my fondest wish, and two, you're being very rude right now. Do you hear me? *Rude.*"

The Raven can't speak through his swollen throat and mouth. Everything goes dark.

"Ugh, goddammit, why do I have to do *everything*—"

The phone clicks. The Raven passes out.

~

Or at least he *should* have.

Tony was going to lose consciousness and possibly bleed out internally right there in the filthy alley. His suit has sustained so much damage the alarms have shut down, plus the backup alarms and the backups to the backups. His body feels cold and growing colder, with numbness spreading inward from his extremities as his heart desperately tries to salvage what it can of his internal organs. He's been near to dying before, and he recognizes the signs. Consciousness should have left by now. And yet somehow ...

"Somehow, you're still alive. How very unexpected."

Tony realizes he can move almost normally, as though he's mostly recovered from his wounds. He doesn't push it, though, and just leans against the building. "Are you here to gloat? *Ishtar?*"

"Remarkable." The statuesque Black-Latina woman stares down at him imperiously. "To think, you, who are just a man with no powers or magic of your own, continue to defy me."

"No, there's another reason," Tony says. "You want the boy, too."

The goddess shrugs. "I have no need to deny it. That boy is infused with the spirit of my husband and my great rival, whom I have loved and fought for eons."

"Dumuzid? The God of Milk and Shepherds?"

"Again." The goddess sounds intrigued. "I thought you only cared for Odin and his ilk. Those drunken oafs."

"I read." Tony bites his lip. The pain is returning. Whatever magic she worked upon him, she's pulling back. "The spirit of justice is in that boy. How is a god of fertility associated with justice?"

"You ask after the source of our conflict. It is beyond your mortal understanding—"

"Because humans need justice to grow and flourish."

"Apparently not," she says, raising her hand, fingers splayed. "You're wiser than I took you for."

"A compliment." Tony coughs, especially when she starts closing her fist. His heart trembles, as though it's inside her closing hand. "How ... how unlike you."

She smiles. "Goodbye, chosen of Odin. We shall not meet again."

The goddess starts to close her hand, then sneers as though she just tasted something very sour. She fades into the mist and disappears as a hulking shape appears over Tony. The last thing he sees is a rainbow bowl floating down toward his face ...

# CHAPTER TEN: ANTI-HERO

Speeding along at four hundred and fifty knots at thirty thousand feet isn't typically the context in which one expects a dark emo ballad to start playing. Specifically, it's a depressing heartache sort of song—a lament of one's long-lost love who has moved far away, loves someone else, died, or perhaps just got sick of the singer's nonsense. Seeing as it's Vivienne's phone, any or all of that could be the case.

Vivienne is, however, deeply asleep in her seat on the third Kujikawa family Cessna Citation after her most recent near-death experience, so she makes no move to answer the phone. It's a new one, to replace the one she broke, but all her contacts and ringtones were saved to the cloud, so ...

"I'll get it." Yumi bounces up from her comfy leather chair, only to hesitate when it comes to actually touching the sleeping woman. Her hands open and close nervously. "Um—"

Angel looks up from the latest issue of *Glamour*. "Aren't there supposed to be no signals on a plane? Messes with the radar or something?"

"I dunno, I'm not a tech hero." Yumi winces. "Excuse me!"

Increasingly flustered, Yumi reaches into Vivienne's jacket and checks each of the pockets for the source of the crooning heartbreak. Motorcycle keys, her apartment key, a keycard, wallet, thirty-seven cents worth of coins, pocketknife, a condom, a mostly empty hand sanitizer ... but no phone.

"Why doesn't she just carry a purse?" Yumi asks, growing positively manic.

Angel rolls her eyes, leans over, and reaches into her aunt's neckline. "She keeps it in her bra."

Easily enough, Angel retrieves the phone and tosses it to Yumi, who fumbles it despite her superpower literally being heightened dexterity. Vivienne didn't make a sound, though her expression is troubled. By contrast, Yumi's face is so bright red, it's a miracle she's still conscious.

"Amy Lee," Yumi says, reading the caller ID. Her eyes widen. "You don't think it's *the* Amy Lee?"

"Who?" Angel takes the phone back and, sure enough, that's the name it shows.

"OMG." Yumi shakes her head. "It's like you never had a goth nu-metal phase."

"Nu-metal?" Angel's about to answer the phone, but Yumi touches her wrist.

"Wait," Yumi says. "How do we answer? Like, is this a professional contact or a civvie?"

"Civvie?"

"You know, a normie. Not a cape. Does V have a secret identity? Apparently some people do."

"I don't think so?" Angel sighs. "Maybe we let it go to voicemail."

"We can't do that!" Yumi looks shocked. "What if it's *the* Amy Lee?"

Angel answers the phone, though what she was going to say goes immediately out of her head. "Um." She looks up at Yumi, totally blank.

Yumi seizes the phone and activates the speaker. "Um, V's phone?"

Angel nods. That makes sense. That could be either her name or her codename.

"Who is this?" asks a woman's voice, suspicious. "If this is a prank, V, I swear I will *end* you."

"Um, no, she's, uh, asleep?" Yumi says.

"Ugh. Typical." The voice on the other end utters a deep, long-suffering sigh. "This isn't about you, dear, but take some advice. That woman will ruin your life, and you should get out now. Before she wakes up. Take whatever's in her wallet, but it's probably not much. Count yourself fortunate." She murmurs something unintelligible. "Probably for the best. Sounds so *young*, too—"

"Um, no, uh, this is a friend. We're just friends, and I'm here with V's niece and—"

Angel gives an exasperated shrug. She wants no part of this.

"I see." The caller pauses for a second, considering. "This is Ruby Killingsworth. I assume you know who I am."

"Um?" Yumi says. "I don't—"

Angel leaps up and takes back the phone. "Ruby Killingsworth, CEO of Goblin Media?"

"The one and only."

"Oh!" Yumi says, going red. "Her g—" She mutes the phone. "V's girlfriend!"

"I think they broke up?" Angel shrugs. "But she's huge in the music industry."

"Hello?" Ruby says. "Are you there?"

Yumi unmutes the phone. "Hi! Nice to meet you, Ms. Killingsworth. I'm Yumi Kujikawa. And, um, I'm here with Angel. Angel DeSantes—"

"Miss," Ruby says by way of correction. "Kujikawa ... as in Akira Kujikawa, of the 2K Group? Your father, I assume?"

"Uh, yes."

"Adorable," Ruby says. "Our V certainly *does* have a type."

"Should we wake her up?" Yumi is blushing. "I mean, if you want to talk to her—"

"No," Ruby says, the word sudden and forceful, hot with anger. She cools a little. "No. This is better. Can you take a message, or should I call back and leave a voicemail? My time is valuable."

"Um. Yes!" Yumi shoves the phone into Angel's hands. "Let me just ... hang on."

Angel stares down at the phone, which incorrectly identifies *Ruby Killingsworth* of all people. In a way, she actually wishes it were indeed *the* Amy Lee.

"Hello?" Ruby asks, her smooth voice tinged with irritation. "Honestly—"

"Hello," Angel says, because she doesn't know what else to say.

"Ah. You must be Angel DeSantes." Ruby's voice is very level, allowing not a hint of emotion. "I'm told your set in Pensacola was decent. That town has a special place in my heart."

"Oh." Somehow, Angel thinks she should be overjoyed, but at the moment, she just feels numb.

"So I'm told. I haven't listened to your music myself, you understand. But I am intrigued."

"Okay."

"Your friend is ... a lot."

"She really is."

"Here!" Yumi hurries back over with a notepad of 2K stationary and a lipstick. It is apparently the best she could do. "Hi, Ms. Killingsworth! It's Yumi again. What's the message?"

If Angel could feel a migraine through the phone, she would be feeling it. She sympathizes.

"The boy—Marcus Orestes, is it? Anyway, Tony thinks he's in San Francisco."

"What?" Yumi asks.

Angel just stares at the phone.

"He said V would know what that meant," Ruby says. "Go to San Francisco. Look for a Malcolm Ali. At the Muslim Peace House." Then, as an afterthought: "Oh, and he beat Tony unconscious. Possibly dead."

"Wait, you mean—?" Angel starts to ask, but the phone beeps. Ruby hung up.

"A," Yumi says, eyes wide. "Tony as in your *dad*, Tony?"

Angel squeezes her hands into fists, and it's only Yumi's heightened reflexes that let her snatch the phone away before she can break it. "Change course. Fly to San Francisco."

Yumi frowns. "We can't just—"

"Change course, or I will open that door and fly there myself."

It seems like Yumi might object, but instead she smiles wildly. "I'll tell the pilot."

As Yumi heads up to the cockpit, Angel stands there, staring at the phone on the table, hardly daring to think. Her father being in danger—well, he's The Raven, he's going to be fine—but Marcus? Alive? In San Francisco? Literally just a couple hours away? It feels so real. So possible. And yet ...

Aunt V has already given them hope, and Angel's spent so many nights crying herself to sleep because of *hope*. Only in the last few weeks has she finally stopped crying, and she can almost sleep through the night. Almost.

She's afraid, she realizes. Not of some unhinged super maniac in San Francisco that attacked her father. She's afraid that they'll get there, and they'll be wrong. V. Her father. Ruby. Herself.

She clenches her hands into fists.

"Let's go," she says under her breath.

~

"What was that?" Yumi asks. "I must not have heard you correctly."

"We're under specific instructions to return to Seattle," says the pilot, whose flashy red cravat, slacks, and vintage cognac leather blazer aren't anything like a uniform. "Orders straight from the top. I'm sure you understand."

Yuriko scowls but says nothing. "I should do a drink service."

"Arigato, Yuriko," Yumi says, and stares at the recalcitrant pilot until the hatch closes.

It just *had* to be Desmond Stein. He's young—about Yumi's age—but those eyes have seen a lot more danger and death than she has. Apparently in addition to his History major at the University of Cobalt City, he's also an aviation enthusiast. Probably not officially licensed to fly a commercial airplane, but whomst at the Factory lets a little thing like safety regulations get in their way? Probably her father attached him to this job to annoy her—or maybe Desmond volunteered so as to annoy her. *Regardless.*

Being trained by an international assassin syndicate, he's also a brutally efficient killer, obviously. He even has a suit with poison spines and a harpoon launcher. He doesn't use his codename much, after Yumi giggled and said "no, really" when he told her about it. Clearly, he doesn't care about her opinion *at all*. What a brat.

Yumi slumps down into the copilot's chair. "Okay Desmond. What do you want."

"What do I want, huh?" With a sly, sidelong look, Desmond puts a hand on her thigh. "The hatch locks automatically, you know."

"Stop that," Yumi says.

"Stop what." His fingers tease along the inside seam of her jeans.

"The seduction thing. We both know your heart isn't in it, *Lionfish*."

"Hmf." He recoils from her as if from a hot stove and goes back to the controls. "I'm offended."

"Professionally?"

"Obviously." He nods back over his shoulder. "You have your hands full anyway."

"A-Girl?" Yumi laughs. "We're just friends. She's straight."

"Oh, don't make me ask questions about you bringing a notorious property damage expert onto a plane—one who is having a well-publicized psychotic breakdown."

"She's not—look, it's complicated."

"I'm sure it is." He sneers in that cruel way of his. "But I meant Lady Vengeance."

"What?" Yumi's cheeks feel warm. "I don't know what you mean."

"Stick to fighting—you're a *terrible* liar."

Yumi rolls her eyes. "Look, are we flying to San Francisco or what?"

"And face the wrath of Akira Kujikawa?"

"I know how to handle my father."

"Hmf. *Right*."

"Desmond." This time she lays her hand on his arm. "You do this, and I'll owe you a favor."

"Two favors. One from you." He looks into her eyes, then looks back at the hatch. "And I want a favor from A-Girl."

Yumi frowns. "I can't guarantee she'll do whatever you want her to. She's not like us. She's a hero, you know?"

"Settle down, Stabbity." He produces a CD case. "Get me her autograph."

"You—wait, what?"

"What, an assassin can't be a fan?"

Yumi doesn't manage to keep from smiling wryly. "Is that the favor from me or from her?"

"I guess it could be either. Which would you prefer?"

"Why are you always like this?" Yumi groans. "Fine, that's *her* favor. I'm sure you're not going to defy the American Vice President of the Factory for some stupid autograph."

"Are you kidding? Do you know how much a signed, limited-run, A-Girl EP goes for on eBay?"

Once she has confirmed that the Cessna has changed course—she literally watches Desmond do it, the sneaky bastard—Yumi heads back into the passenger cabin to check on Angel. Having discovered she can use her phone on the plane, her friend, the pop star, is rapidly texting with a look of concentration that tells Yumi not to bother her. Which is fine.

Also, there *is* the little matter of the ghost woman floating just behind Vivienne's chair. If Angel or even Vivienne can see the ghost after that encounter at the docks in Florida, they've shown no sign, but that's unsurprising. Yumi has a history of seeing ghosts that just won't go away, and she's not keen on collecting another spectral follower. While the ghost lady doesn't seem hostile, she also doesn't seem to have noticed that Yumi can see her yet, and Yumi's spent enough time around ghosts to know to avoid their attention. She did, after all, live in a ghost dorm for a while, while dating a dude who's at least a quarter dead,[9] so ... The ghost seems familiar, and Yumi wants to figure out who she is before trying to make contact, and she can't very well ask V about it while the ghost is there.

Acting as though she sees nothing, Yumi heads into the onboard bathroom and locks the door, flicking the display to "occupied." The 2K Group has spared no expense on even this, the third and least lux of its private jets, and the bathroom here is bigger and nicer than the bathroom in her apartment. Impeccably clean, orderly, and positively reeking of floral air freshener.

Yumi sits on the toilet, but not to pee. Instead, she pulls out her phone, takes a deep breath, and dials. Her call is answered on the second ring. "Hey."

"Hi," Lisa says. "Where are you? Weren't you supposed to be back *yesterday?*"

---

[9] Yumi means Mark "Ghost House" Obayashi, a character in several Cobalt City works, including *Cobalt City: Resistance* and a cameo role in *We are the Champions*. As for the "at least a quarter dead" part, well, his grandfather is a ghost. That might have something to do with Yumi seeing ghosts! ~ Spooky Vogel

"Yeah, sorry," Yumi says. "It just got, you know, more complicated."

"Family stuff, right." Lisa sighs deeply. "I can't keep covering for you, Y. You've got to show up for your classes at *some* point. There's that gender studies midterm coming up soon. Have you even studied? Also, Hank was asking questions at the café—"

"Oh yeah? I'll call him." Yumi winces. Since making the deal with her father to gain access to her trust fund again, Yumi has kind of ghosted Hank at her part-time job at the Cup o' Chino on campus. It wouldn't be such a big deal, but Lisa's been visiting her there the last few weeks, and she can't keep pretending to work the night shift because Mark works the night shift, and it's only a matter of time before someone talks to someone else. Juggling being not only a superhero and a college student but also a secret heiress (again) and part of an international assassin network is getting harder and harder. She hasn't told her girlfriend about the latter half of that, and so far, Lisa hasn't asked where the rent money comes from, but ...

*Just tell her,* Yumi thinks. *How mad can she be?*

Considering Danielle Swain and Desmond Stein have both tried to kill Yumi on multiple occasions, and she has a will-they-won't-they thing with Danielle, and now they're both her colleagues, which Yumi has been keeping from Lisa for months now? Pretty mad.

"You there, daarin?" Lisa asks, which is mostly an in-joke between the two of them. They've spent entirely too many hours watching anime together, including one overwrought sci-fi romance that made heavy use of the Japanese adopted word "darling." English isn't the only language that stalks other languages into alleys, clocks them with a heavy dictionary, then goes through their pockets for loose grammar. Never mind that it makes them sound like an old married couple.

Yumi smiles. "I'm here, hanii."

Lisa laughs, and it feels okay, at least for now. She'll have to tell Lisa eventually, but she can put it off for a little longer. At least until she gets back.

"When *are* you getting back?" Lisa asks, almost like she read Yumi's mind. It's not the first time she's seemed to know exactly what Yumi's thinking.

"Not sure," Yumi says. "A couple days. My dad's being ... my dad. You know."

"I don't actually, as I haven't met him," Lisa says to clarify. "Or any of your family. Do they ... They do *know* about me, right?"

"What?" Yumi taps the phone against her forehead. Dang it. "Of course they do."

"*Daarin.*"

"Well, we've been estranged for a while, and I'm getting things sorted. It's complicated."

"They do know about, y'know ... you dating a girl?"

"Yes." No. "And they'll love you. Don't worry. Maybe we can do a Christmas thing?"

"Sure. That's only like nine months away."

"Where's this coming from?" Yumi asks. "Why so eager to meet my family? I told you, they're a bunch of stuffy rich people who wanted too much control over my life. And they're very ... traditional."

"Traditional, like—?" Lisa asks.

Traditional like samurai. Traditional like training a small army of assassins with swords and shuriken. Traditional like the Yakuza. "Traditional like black tie and fancy cocktails. But the dress has got to be just right. Let's go shopping when I get back."

"You know I love you in a tux."

"You know I love you in general."

"Are you trying to get *me* to wear the tux?" Lisa asks. "Because I'm not sure I can pull that off."

"Because of your butt?"

"Hey, what's wrong with my butt?"

"Absolutely nothing. It's perfect."

"Okay, well—" Lisa sighs. "I miss you. It's cold without you here."

"I know. And I'm ... I'm almost done. I'll be back soon. I promise."

"Love you."

"Love you too—" Yumi starts to say, but the call cuts off.

She sighs and presses the phone to her forehead again. She should be heading back to Cobalt City right now, straight into the shower, and then into bed with her girlfriend. But V and Angel need her help, and if there's a chance to get Marcus back ... she's got to be part of it.

She just hopes that isn't an excuse.

There's a folded square of paper in the pocket of her skinny jeans, and she pulls it out to review one last time. Vivienne passed her this note before falling asleep, avoiding Angel's notice. The folded yellow sticky note has a crossed through circle with the letter "A" in the middle, as if the implication to keep it a secret from her best friend wasn't already clear. Yumi unfolds it and reads.

It doesn't seem possible, but stranger things have happened.

She deposits the note in the onboard toilet and flushes. She's not going to forget.

# CHAPTER ELEVEN: SWEET BUT PSYCHO

When the three women walk through the doors of The House of Muhammad, Peace Be Upon Him, colloquially known as "the Muslim Peace House" to locals, they cause a bit of a stir.

As its name suggests, the Muslim Peace House in Bernal Heights is one of many such organizations that service San Francisco's large and growing Muslim community. It combines the features of a homeless shelter, community center, and free or subsidized clinic. Some 250,000 Muslims live in the Bay Area, which is only about three or four percent of the population, but that—and the city's sanctuary city status—still make San Francisco a target for Prather's reign of culture war terror.

It's not like Prather was the start of Islamophobia in America, but it's definitely become worse lately. Domestic terrorist attacks on the Peace House, both new and old, have left noticeable scars: broken and cracked pavement, spray-painted slogans from white supremacists, Nazis, and Prather blather, which is to say, it's hard to differentiate. Many of the windows, locks, and signs have had to be replaced multiple times over the last four years. Most gutting of all are the names etched on gold plates, identifying victims of Islamophobic violence.

It's probably how the three are dressed, honestly. The one who stands out the least is Vivienne in her black jeans, black leather jacket, and a shirt that says "I lost everything in Vegas except this shirt." Yumi has gone with red leather hotpants and a fur-lined black jacket over a white tank top that probably cost four digits. Angel herself has even more unusual attire: high black boots, black fishnets on top and bottom, black short shorts, and a kind of crop-top sweater that covers her upper arms and her upper torso, leaving her midriff bare. Her agent once described it as a "mantle," but honestly, Angel just thought it looked cool. A bit hard to move in, but still cool. By contrast, everyone here is dressed conservatively at best.

The Peace House doesn't exclusively serve a Muslim clientele, and all are welcome under the peace of Allah, but realities are what they are. As such, when Vivienne, Angel, and Yumi come in—only the first of whom is even plausibly of Middle Eastern heritage—they naturally draw some suspicion, as much for their unusual clothes as for being total strangers. A number of eyes glower at the three from the narrow span of niqabs, and several women wearing colorful hijabs frown at them as well. There's even one woman wearing a burqa, making it hard to tell where she's looking.

"Maybe they're fans?" That's Yumi, always trying to put a cheery spin on things.

"Relax. They're just a little anxious." Facing the nearest woman, Vivienne bows her head slightly and puts her hands together. "Salam alaikum."

The woman nods, fingers easing on the tail of her hijab. "Wa alaikum assalam."

"I didn't know you spoke, um, Arabic?" Yumi asks.

"Sort of," Vivienne says. "That's a pretty standard greeting. It means 'peace be upon you.'"

Vivienne repeats the greeting to each of the waiting patrons they encounter, most of whom bow their heads in reply and murmur in kind, or they say "inshallah." Angel has at least heard that word, which she thinks means something like "God willing" or "hopefully." She notices a few glances turned from suspicion to curiosity focusing on her, and she tries out "inshallah" on one young woman in a red hijab. The woman blinks and smiles at her, which Angel chooses to take as a good sign.

All the patrons in the waiting room are women, as is the perky young woman behind the counter in the purple and red patterned headscarf that really flatters her deep brown complexion. Angel knows there are Black women who are Muslim, but she doesn't think she's ever met one in person. She's wearing normal street clothes, like about half the patrons, and if not for the headscarf, you'd never know she was Muslim.

"Good morning," the woman says, correctly guessing that neither Arabic nor Urdu is Vivienne's first language. "How can I help you, Miss—?"

"Cain," Vivienne says. "We're actually looking for someone—" She glances at the woman's nametag. "Marwa."

"That's a lovely name," Yumi says, attempting to be helpful.

Vivienne gives Yumi a sidelong look. "Malcolm Ali. Know him?"

The name makes Marwa's helpfulness evaporate, and her eyes narrow slightly.

As they negotiate, Angel becomes aware of a little girl probably around four standing at her side, reaching up to about mid-thigh. Unlike the others in the waiting room, the child wears no scarf over her messy black curls and is just dressed in normal clothes, including a slightly faded pink t-shirt with ... is that *her* on the shirt?

Sure enough, that's A-Girl in her white costume with pink piping and a pink energy trail. In one hand, the little girl clutches not only a first-run A-Girl doll, its blonde hair a little threadbare and stained from age, but also one of the limited-run Marcus "Kid Justice" Orestes run that neither turned out particularly well nor sold many. Still, seeing the dolls pulls Angel into a whirlpool of existential uneasiness, buffeted by waves of nostalgia, and ...

The little girl is staring up at her, wide-eyed, her little mouth forming a question in a language Angel doesn't speak. Instead of replying with words, Angel gives her a wink and presses her finger to her lips. The little girl mimics the gesture, then smiles and holds up the Orestes doll in offering.

"For me?" she asks.

The girl nods very solemnly.

"No, that's okay," Angel says. "I don't—"

"Aaliyah!" a woman says sharply. "Ab yahan aao!"

The girl shoves the doll into Angel's hand, then hurries back to her mother. The woman gives Angel an apologetic look, then chides her daughter gently but firmly. Angel is left staring down at the doll in her hand, with its dark skin and goofy smile. Her fingers tremble.

"Angel?" Yumi asks. "Are you okay?"

"What? Oh. Yeah." She tucks the doll in her purse, as much to hide it from herself as from Yumi. She also sees that apparently there's a voicemail on her phone, but she doesn't remember it ringing. Who uses a phone as a phone, let alone leaves voicemails anymore? She doesn't recognize the number.

"Sutter?" she says under her voice. "Who do I know named 'Sutter'?"

She opens the voicemail and listens, warmth and color draining from her face. And even so, a fire ignites in her stomach, fueled by long-simmering rage she's kept stuffed down for too long.

"A?" Yumi asks. "What is it?"

"We need to go," Angel says. "Right now."

"Malcolm Ali," Marwa is saying, "is a good man. A gentle giant who would never hurt a fly. He's a firm believer in the Quran, after all. 'Whoever kills an innocent'—"

"'It shall be as if he killed the whole of humanity,' yeah. Unless it's to punish evil."

*To punish evil.* Angel listens to the voicemail again and makes note of the address. Her whole body is tense. Ready to do some punishing of its own.

"I'm sorry, ma'am," Marwa says, politely but firmly. "But unless you have identification as a law enforcement officer and a proper search warrant in compliance with federal law, I simply cannot help you. It is a privacy issue. I appreciate your understanding."

She points to something framed just to the side of the desk, which is the Fourth Amendment of the U.S. Constitution. That they've had it framed in plastic suggests they've had plenty of cause to refer people to it during the Prather administration especially.

"It's not like that," Vivienne says. "We just want to find—"

Marwa taps the sign.

"Aunt V," Angel says, holding up her phone. "Let's go."

Vivienne looks at her, clearly annoyed, but whatever she sees in Angel's expression, it makes her hesitation evaporate. "Okay."

"Excuse me, is there a problem here?" The newcomer behind the desk is a white woman, probably around fifty, dressed in colorful robes and a white headscarf in the fashion Angel associates with Muslims generally. Not a single hair escapes her hijab, but Angel guesses she's blonde. "I'm Linda Logan, Executive Director of The House of Muhammad, Peace Be Upon Him. Can I help you?"

"No. Thanks anyway." Vivienne glances at Angel. "We were just leaving."

"Wada'an," Linda says, sharply.

"Assalamu alaykum," Marwa says, which sounds a little more polite.

~

California Pacific Medical Center Emergency, Mission Bernal Campus and Orthopedic Institute, is a brand-new hospital, fresh and highly modern, with some one hundred and twenty beds and the sort of green and seismic updates you'd expect in one of the most liberal areas in the United States that just so happens to stand entirely too close to the San Andreas Fault. Angel, who has had some experience knocking down buildings, suspects that if hospitals in Seattle were upgraded like this, they might weather the Big One, whenever it comes.

She also realizes she's trying to distract herself during the town car ride, and when they get stuck behind an ambulance heading for the ER, it's all she can do not to fire herself out the window. But Yumi puts her hand on Angel's, and that keeps her anger in check. She can hold it together ... at least until she's got an enemy to attack. And it's only a matter of time until her targeting solution is set.

The nurse in charge—a short-haired, solid, and no-nonsense white woman of about fifty, whose nametag says "Melinda"— appears to be something of a capes fan, as she recognizes Angel and Vivienne immediately, despite their street clothes. Since they ask to see "Tony DeSantes," it's a pretty dead give-away, though it seems Melinda has kept his identity under wraps, and she was the one who called Angel's phone. They follow her past a broken safety glass wall, which is cordoned off with orange cones and hazard tape. Looks like a recent workplace accident.

"I never thought I'd meet an actual superhero, much less *you!*" Melinda says, increasingly excited, despite the clear suffering and sickness around her. "Wait until my niece hears about this. She's a total fangirl. That's still a relevant term, right?"

"Um." Vivienne looks at Yumi, who shrugs. "Sure?"

Nurse Melinda titters in pleasure, and launches into stories about CapeCon the past fall, where she and her niece cosplayed Lady Vengeance and A-Girl, in fact, though they both wore the white costumes. Despite Aunt V's apparent amnesia regarding ever wearing white, Melinda explains that Vivienne *did* wear a white costume, once upon a time, for a short-lived and ill-conceived rebrand.

"No one expected Lady Vengeance, bad girl of Supergroup, to wear *white*, even at a wedding." Melinda laughs. "I saw this one Lady V cosplay in a purple wedding dress, bloody claw and everything."

"Seems legit," Vivienne says. "Though I've never been married, thank Lilith."

"Anyway, we didn't make it to SuperCon this year, just a couple weeks ago? I had to work, and she's in this cosmetology internship—"

Angel can barely follow the conversation and barely wants to anyway. All she wants is to see her dad, if he's even really here. The message—which Melinda had left, in hushed tones, because she recognized their names—had claimed as much, but she won't really believe it until she sees it.

As she goes on about the finer points of outfit construction, the nurse leads them into the ICU, which has fewer rooms and fewer people than the ER or trauma. There's a San Francisco police officer: a sweaty white guy with a graying moustache guarding one of the rooms, but his bulky ass is no match for Angel "I can bench-press a jetliner" DeSantes. He does step to her, hand raised, and she's about to shove him through the ceiling when the nurse intercedes.

"They're family." Nurse Melinda indicates Angel. "This is the patient's daughter."

The SFPD cop eyes them quizzically—especially Yumi, being obviously Japanese.

"Adopted!" Yumi says brightly.

"And he's my ex," Vivienne says. "Amicable. We still sleep with each other sometimes, though. You know how it is."

The officer quirks an eyebrow, but he's clearly had a long day and wants none of this nonsense. "You identified the Juan Diaz, then?" he asks Nurse Melinda.

102

"Juan D——? Oh, I get it," Yumi says. "Instead of 'John Doe.' Racist microaggression, of course."

The officer bristles and turns pink around the neck. "Now listen here, miss——"

"No, actually." Vivienne's eyes have gone black, and fear energy swirls around her. "You listen to *me*, little piggy."

Angel pushes past the transfixed officer, not bothering to watch what fear fuckery her aunt is going to pull, and hurries to her father's side. Sure enough, there lies Antonio DeSantes, hooked up to a heart monitor, oxygen machine, and at least two IV drips. One of his arms is in a cast, his nose is broken, and he clearly has a fractured orbital over his empty eye socket. The prosthetic was either lost or destroyed during the attack. Much of his body is heavily bandaged, and those parts that show are blackened or yellowed with developing bruises. Someone beat him within an inch of his life, and seeing his injuries fills Angel with a rising fury that pounds in her ears.

Someone approaches the bed, and Angel rounds on her with a glare.

Nurse Melinda holds up her gloved hands innocuously. "I need to check his vitals."

Angel allows it. Her legs suddenly wobbly, she sits beside her father's bed and tentatively touches his hand. She tries really hard to do so as softly as possible, hardly daring in case her strength asserts itself. "Is ... is he——?"

"He may look rough, but believe it or not, his condition is stable," Nurse Melinda says, as she inflates the cuff to check Tony's blood pressure. She counts mentally, then lets it deflate. "Blood pressure slightly elevated. He's probably in pain." She puts her stethoscope on his bare chest.

"Oh, jeez." Yumi hugs Angel, which she accepts without moving. "A, I'm so sorry."

Angel is having a hard time thinking about anything at the moment. She almost wishes Aunt V was done with the cop. She's pretty good at keeping cool under stress. But no, her aunt is still out there "negotiating." Which is to say, she's probably loading him up with a phobia of strong women and probably also something innocuous like puppies or diapers or something.

Angel swallows through her very parched throat. "Is he ... will he—?"

"Will he be all right?" Yumi asks, filling in for her.

"He should be," Nurse Melinda says. "Broken arm, rib fracture, signs of a mild concussion—from the strike that broke his orbital—but he came through surgery just fine." She looks back toward the entrance to the room, then says, confidentially, "His armor saved him. It was trashed."

"Did its job then," Yumi says. "You done checking his vitals?"

"Yes," Nurse Melinda says. "I was thinking about waking him, but he's resting. Maybe we—"

"Should give them a moment?" Yumi suggests.

"Oh. Of course." Nurse Melinda looks at Angel sympathetically, then nods. "If he wakes up in pain, you push that call button. I'll just be right out there."

"Right."

Yumi squeezes Angel's shoulder and follows Nurse Melinda out. The cop is gone—probably wandered off to lock himself in a toilet stall or something—and Aunt V stands there outside the ICU room, leaning against the wall. She looks away when Angel tries to catch her eye, and it's obvious she's not emotionally steady either, but she's giving Angel some space. That's something, at least.

"Dad," Angel says. "I'm sorry. I should have been here. But I've been ignoring your calls, and so has Aunt V. We'll get the asshole that did this to you. We will."

Tony's machines beep, but he himself doesn't stir.

"Okay," Angel says. "But seriously, what the *fuck*, Dad?" She rolls her eyes. "Sure I was being a brat and V was being ... V. But you still could have made a little effort, you know! Instead, you run down here on your own and get hurt and ... gah, eres tan *estúpido*, papá!"

His hand squeezes hers, just a little.

"Angel," Tony murmurs, his voice thin.

"Dad?" Angel takes his hand in both of hers, careful not to squeeze past human limits. The last thing her broken father needs is a fractured hand. "Dad! Can you hear me?"

"N ... Not so loud, mija. We're in a hospital."

Angel groans. "Now's not the time for jokes, Dad."

"The Raven ... doesn't tell jokes—"

Angel wants to shout at him, but the words catch in her throat. Instead, she just squeezes his hand. A little too hard, as he winces. "Are you in pain? The nurse said to use the call button."

"No," her father says. "Not yet. She'll give me morphine, and I need to concentrate. Tell you—"

He doubles over in pain, and Angel's chest seizes hard in sympathy. She doesn't hesitate to push the button.

"He's awake?" Yumi reappears alongside Nurse Melinda.

"He's in pain," Angel says, feeling stupid. "Help him."

"Wait—" Tony says. "I need to ... need—"

"You need to *rest*, Mr. DeSantes," Nurse Melinda says. "I'm going to give you your meds."

"I with ... withhold consent," Tony says.

"You heard him," Aunt V says from the doorway, her voice dark. "He doesn't consent. You give him those meds, that's assault."

Angel glares at her, and red energy starts to burn around her hands.

"A," Yumi says. "A, calm down—"

Nurse Melinda hesitates and looks pleadingly at Angel. "Can you talk to them?"

Tony sweats and gnashes his teeth as he tries to speak. "Peace House ... Malcolm—"

"Malcolm Ali, we know," Aunt V says, avoiding Angel's glower. "Ruby called us. Told us where you were and who you were following. We checked the Peace House, no luck."

"I really have to give him his meds," Nurse Melinda says. "His blood pressure's elevated. He could go into arrest—"

"Do you have any other leads, Mr. DeSantes?" Yumi asks, earning a glare from Angel. She returns a helpless shrug.

"He's ... strong," Tony says. "Reparation ... he calls himself ... Strong as ... Justice—"

"That's encouraging," Vivienne says.

"But *how* though?" Yumi asks, but Tony isn't finished. "He has Justice's power? How?"

"Skull—" Tony says. "Rainbow—"

Then his eye rolls up in his head, and he starts to shiver.

"Dad? Dad!" Angel looks at the nurse. "Give him the meds! Do it!"

Nurse Melinda doesn't need to be told twice. She pumps morphine into Tony's IV, and the shaking subsides almost immediately. Tony relaxes, and his eye rolls around to focus distantly on Angel. He raises his hand to touch her face, smiles, and goes right to sleep.

"There," Nurse Melinda says, relieved. "He'll probably sleep for the next few hours, so maybe I can show you to the waiting room?"

She's playing it cool, but she's got her hand over the call button for security. Anyone can see Angel's upset, what with the fiery energy aura shrouding her.

"Yeah. Sure." Angel kisses Tony on his unbandaged cheek. "Let's go."

~

Nurse Melinda shows them out to the waiting room, looking positively relieved when they take their argument with them. No doubt she's encountered more than a few situations like this, and prioritizing her patient seems like the right call. Especially since Angel and Vivienne seem just about ready to blow. When the nurse excuses herself to check on other patients, Yumi feels her departure like a severed limb. Now she's the one who has to defuse the two, and resolving conflicts peacefully is not among her power set. Quite the opposite, in fact.

"The fuck," Angel says, "was *that*."

"A, don't—" Yumi says, but Angel silences her with a glare.

"The fuck was *that*, Aunt V?" she asks. "You nearly killed him!"

"Don't be dramatic." Vivienne, who's been knuckling her forehead in thought, waves dismissively. "Tony DeSantes can handle a little pain. He needed to tell us something, and he did."

"Did he?" Angel takes a menacing step toward Vivienne, who stands her ground. "And what was *that*, exactly?"

"I'll let you know when I figure it out."

"You—you don't even *know*?" Angel has turned bright red, both in the face and in her aura. By contrast, Vivienne looks unbothered, as though she hasn't even *noticed*. Which Yumi knows is bullshit, since Vivienne is an empath and can *literally* feel other people's emotions. But there she is, nonchalantly tapping away on

106

her phone—one Yumi bought her, and she hasn't even thanked her for, by the way—as though she's just shopping online or on a dating app or something. Meanwhile, the ghostly woman who's been following them—never more than ten feet from the anchor of Vivienne—is looking between aunt and niece with increasing despair.

Yumi clearly has to do something.

They're in a disused corner of the waiting room far from other patients, but even so, the argument has drawn a few wary glances. It's only a matter of time before they call security, and Yumi will have to deal with a few SFPD officers so they don't get suplexed into the basement or lose all bladder control for the rest of their lives. Man, the three of them are packing a lot of power, and Yumi realizes *she's* the weakest link here.

Better start with her best friend.

"A—" Yumi puts on her best Dulcamara[10] impression in the hopes that it will be calming. "Emotions are tense, but remember, your dad's okay. He's being well cared for. Nurse Melinda seems to love capes, and she didn't out him even to the cops. He's in good hands."

"I guess," Angel says, a touch of sulk in her tone. "But *she* put him in danger for no reason. And she doesn't even care. What kind of psycho are we working with here?"

"Oh sure." Vivienne doesn't look up. "Call me a psycho. Like I've never heard *that* before."

"V," Yumi says. "Don't you think you were being a little insensitive? With Mr. DeSantes?"

"Eh," Vivienne says. "Suffice it to say, Tony likes pain. Unless you want more details."

"I ... just ... um—"

---

[10] Yumi's colleague and former teammate on the teen superhero team Justice or Something, Friday "Dulcamara" Jones (first appearance, "Dead Souls" in the *Cobalt City: Dragonstorm* anthology), plant manipulation, avatar of Freya, typically the adult in the room. Also, one of my signature characters! ~ Nonbiased Vogel

"Didn't think so." Vivienne purses her lips. "Rainbow skull ... Dia de los Muertos? Nah, that's six months away. Luchador mask? Hmm—"

Yumi tries a few sentences, but they all dissolve. Possibly boiled straight out of her mouth by Angel's growing rage. Yumi doesn't have to be an empath to feel her anger—like a blazing fire, about to set the hospital alight.

"You—" Angel is staring at Vivienne as though she could set her on fire with a look. "You just—ugh, God!"

Angel thrusts her hand into her purse with enough force, Yumi's surprised she doesn't punch right through. She's probably going for her phone, but instead she gets a confused look on her face and pulls something else out instead. It's a brown-skinned action figure that looks a lot like Marcus, and the sudden juxtaposition is jarring. Has Angel taken up sympathetic magic while Yumi wasn't looking? But no, that doesn't look like a voodoo doll or an effigy.

"That," says a familiar voice, and Yumi realizes the ghost woman has spoken. She's pointing at the action figure like it is an object of great import. As though it draws her with a gravity all its own, she drifts toward the toy in Angel's hand, her feet sliding right through the floor. The ghost doesn't touch it, of course, but she seems to think it's important.

"That." Yumi ignores the ghost's gaze and indicates the toy. "Where'd you get that?"

"Some kid gave it to me," Angel says. "I'm a little old for dolls."

"Excuse you, that's an *action figure*," Yumi says. "I thought they stopped making these when—"

She trails off, because Angel's eyes have suddenly gone watery. Even though she's about to cry, Angel looks confused, and it isn't until Yumi hugs her that the waterworks start.

"Stupid," Angel says between sobs. "My dad's in the ICU, and I'm crying over some stupid *doll*."

"Action figure." Yumi clutches Angel tighter. "Don't worry. We'll find him."

"Maybe," Vivienne says.

Angel bristles. "*Maybe?*"

"Hey, that's not helpful, V," Yumi says. "Try to stay positive."

"Stay positive?" Vivienne sneers. "The one lead we had was this Malcolm Ali guy at the Muslim Peace House, which was a bust. Tony has given us one more lead—the words 'rainbow' and 'skull.' Now unless you're a super genius or something—"

"If only one of us knew a sorceress," Angel says.

"Oh, no no no, that is not an option," Vivienne says. "She barely talked to you. She won't talk to me, let alone do me a favor."

"But she was working with my dad," Angel says. "And she hates him, right? Because you keep *fucking* him—"

"Whoa whoa whoa, hey." In a last-ditch effort, Yumi steps between the two, the Orestes action figure raised like a talisman against their rising antagonism. "This is a hospital. Stay cool."

The standoff outlasts Yumi's attempt to defuse it, as both women stare daggers at one another. The friendly spirit looks between them, deeply saddened. Yumi makes a concerted effort not to meet her gaze.

Honestly, she's getting tired of this. The adult-in-the-room role does not fit Yumi at all. She's much more accustomed to being the one mediated, not the one doing the mediating. Also, she's just bad at it. She can't keep trying to keep these two women in check when they clearly want to have it out. And based on the energy swirling around Vivienne's hands and the red power aura starting to hum around Angel, it looks like that's exactly what's going to go down.

What should she do? Try to move them somewhere away from a whole bunch of sick and injured people? The parking lot is relatively safe, but it's packed with cars, at least some of which are occupied. She saw a park on the way here that looked pretty nice ... Though even Prather's incompetent press secretary would have a field day with a major superhero brawl in San Francisco.

"That looks like him," Nurse Melinda says abruptly.

The three women look to her, their power easing slightly. The nurse may be a cape fangirl (and possibly a cape chaser), but she's all business now. Probably one of the patients complained about them, and they sent Nurse Melinda over to deal with the situation. Probably a good call, as she has clearly activated her conflict resolution and de-escalation techniques. Interrupt the dance with a random observation. Not a bad technique, honestly. Practically a superpower itself.

"What looks like who?" Angel asks.

"Looks like *whom*," Vivienne says.

Angel narrows her eyes. "I swear to God, Aunt V—"

"That doll." Nurse Melinda carries right on. "Looks like the man who dropped him off ... Mid-thirties. Big. Muscular. Muhammad was the name he left. Nation of Islam, you know?"

Angel looks confused, and Yumi can't say she gets the reference either.

"Black Muslim," Vivienne says. "Sounds like our guy. He do this?"

The nurse shrugs. "He left before the police could figure that out. Shoved one of them hard enough to put him through that glass wall in the ER. He's wanted for questioning."

"So it sounds like he sure could have done this." Angel curls her hands into fists.

"Did he have a ... like a costume? With a skull?" Vivienne asks. "Maybe rainbow colored?"

"What? No." Melinda frowns, then brightens. "Oh, but he was wearing a rainbow skullcap."

"That ... makes more sense," Vivienne says. "Like a colorful, Middle Eastern pattern?"

"Like a Pride flag. It was a little odd, but I got the sense he was, y'know—"

"Gay?" Yumi asks.

Nurse Melinda nods solemnly. "What a nice young man. He seemed determined. But also sad."

"Do you know where he went?" Vivienne asks.

"No ... but he did leave some contact info. Hospital policy." Nurse Melinda frowns. "I can't just give that out, though—"

"This is a matter of life and death," Yumi says. "Maybe a donation to—?"

"I could enspell her," Vivienne says. "A little fear magic would—"

"Please."

All gazes turn to Angel. Even that of the ghost lady, who—especially in that moment—bears a striking resemblance to both Vivienne and Angel. And Yumi realizes, with a start, that that's Charisma Cain. She's only met the woman once, and the ghost is a lot younger, but it's definitely her.

"Please," Angel says. "It's for ... the man I love."

Charisma nods in approval.

For once, Vivienne doesn't have anything to say, snarky or otherwise.

Nurse Melinda's eyes are wet. "Yes. Okay. I'll see what I can do. Just ... Can I have your autograph, A-Girl?"

"Why does everyone want her autograph?" Yumi asks.

"Huh?" Vivienne eyes her.

"Um—never mind!"

# CHAPTER TWELVE: WHAT DO YOU WANT FROM ME

---

The lights of the club strobe, gleaming from sweat-slick skin and leather in the sea of dancers, drinkers, and revelers of all stripe, but mostly men. It is, after all, a leather bar, and such a buffet of bodies is a nightly display. Five years ago, he would have been out there at one of those tables, ordering bottle after bottle, pouring champagne over taut bodies and kissing eager mouths. He would be indulging in whatever vice and depravity he could afford, and leave planning his next payday for the morning after. Killing his liver and loving every minute of it.

Nursing his drink at the bar, Malcolm Ali thinks he left this scene behind along with his name. But everyone has a past, and sometimes memory becomes action, and past becomes present. Man was created weak, after all, and despite his strength, Malcolm is a man like any other. Those weaknesses can be overcome, however, because Allah does not place a burden on anyone greater than one can bear. Thus he drinks a club soda with lime, not one of the many colorful cocktails on display.

This is a test that he puts to himself. When his sobriety feels lowest. Vulnerable.

"You doin' good, boss?" Carlos asks from behind the bar. His favorite bartender, Carlos. An old friend, who never judges him, and prepares his club sodas with lime as carefully as any high-priced cocktail.

"Good. Thanks."

Malcolm doesn't have to be alone. Not practically, anyway. Three men and even one woman have approached him thus far tonight, and he's made basic conversation but found no spark. He isn't even getting the usual self-flagellation out of exposing himself to temptation that he usually does. He just feels more guilty for using these poor, well-meaning men for his own selfish ends. The woman he doesn't feel sorry for—who goes out with their girlfriends to a gay bar and tries to pick up a guy?

That's not it, though. The fight with The Raven weighs on him. The core of his melancholy.

A lot has happened in the last six months or so. This power that projects energy ... This is a new thing. And he doesn't know his limits or really how to control it. But that's no excuse. He should have practiced with it. Known what to do and what he couldn't. He should've controlled himself. Reined in his temper. Asked questions before he started swinging. That's always been his problem: impatience.

Malcolm is stewing when a lithe form slides up to the bar beside him. *Contestant number five*, he thinks and almost says under his breath. He stops short, however, when he looks up into the mirror behind the bar and sees the smoky eyes and easy, wan smile. The voice is smooth as silk, and makes Malcolm feel drunk even if he hasn't had an intoxicant in five years.

"Now what is a man like *you* doing here?" the newcomer says.

They're highly attractive, it's true: vaguely Middle Eastern, dark-skinned with buzzed and dyed silver hair, golden hazel eyes, full lips, and a wiry, slim, androgynous form Malcolm finds very intriguing. Malcolm has known plenty of femme sorts of guys, mostly from before his conversion but a few from after. If he has a type, it's this person right here. Is this a prank? An opp? Is he being punked?

"Buy you a drink?" the handsome stranger asks. "You look thirsty."

"I'm—" Malcolm looks at his club soda and lime, and sure enough, it's empty. "Sure. Club soda." At the stranger's raised eyebrow, he shrugs. "I don't drink."

"Is that so? I was wondering about the Taqiyah."

"It's real," Malcolm says. "So's the flag."

"I should hope so." They order another for Malcolm and a Manhattan for themself.

"Thanks," Malcolm says. "Mister—?"

114

"Mx., actually. And it's Inanna," they say, as though that's not the strangest name Malcolm has ever heard. That a Persian name? Sounds like a woman's name, but who can say. Considering how this Inanna looks—like a genie straight from a bottle, or a hip-hop star from an Arabian Nights-themed video—makes it make sense.

"Malcolm," he says. "Malcolm Ali."

"Like the fighter," Inanna says.

"You're thinking of Muhammad Ali," Malcolm says.

"I was thinking of Malcolm X."

It's the right thing to say, and it makes Malcolm ease up. San Francisco is full of eccentric twink types, and maybe Malcolm can relax. Maybe he can let this distract him.

Inanna lays a hand on Malcolm's arm. "Is something troubling you, Mal?"

Maybe not, then. But somehow, he doesn't mind. In fact, he finds himself lost in those dark eyes, and his lips move without his control.

"There was ... this dude," Malcolm says. "I ... I think I misjudged him."

"Dude you were dating?"

"Not exactly," Malcolm says. "Fool rolled up on me, and I ... it didn't go well."

"Are you okay?" Inanna's hand trails up Malcolm's arm, over the collar of his jacket, and their cool fingers play along the back of his neck. "He didn't hurt you, did he?"

"Nah, baby." Malcolm sighs. "Ya boy's unbreakable."

"I'll bet he is."

They engage in some small talk, about nothing important, and it all slips Malcolm's mind. Hard to say what it is, but something about this Inanna makes Malcolm feel so very, very relaxed. It's not their looks—really attractive people tend to make Malcolm a little wary, actually—but more their vibe. It feels like Malcolm is the only thing that matters in the world, and Inanna has focused their full attention on him to the exclusion of all others. Are there other people in the world, or just the two of them?

And as the world around them fades, Inanna grows brighter and more distinct. They're into Malcolm—*very* into him—and nothing else seems important. The gleam of those white-white teeth, the feel of their cool skin, the twinkle in their bright eyes ...

Malcolm forgets what they were talking about, forgets where they are, forgets everything outside this very moment. His memories fade, as though pushed into a deep, shadowy pit from which there's no ...

Then, abruptly, through no will or intention of his own, a bolt of blue lightning jolts out of Malcolm's neck and into Inanna's hand. The shock runs through their lithe body, making them sit up straight and recoil as though from a live wire. Malcolm is shocked too, having no idea how his energy projection would activate all on its own like that. It's a new thing, but it shouldn't be that chaotic.

"Whoa, I didn't mean—"

The words die on his lips as he sees Inanna—or at least what has become of them.

Most people never see a human being die. Over the centuries, the bulk of humans have grown so detached from death that most will *never* see anyone die in person, let alone every day. Not so Malcolm Muhammad Ali, once Malcolm Adonis Richter, who has seen his share of death. Watched his own brother gunned down in front of him when he was twelve. Held his sister's dead body while her newborn wailed in the other room after a no-knock raid. Been in drive-by shootings and gang firefights and survived revenge killings and all of it.

This ... This is like nothing he has ever seen.

Before his eyes, Inanna *unravels*. Their flesh peels away from their bones and flakes away into ash, leaving an age-browned skeleton with just a few scraps of withered flesh clinging to it. Inanna's hair grows longer and brittle, like straw hanging from their withered scalp, and their perfect lips chap, pull apart, and reveal bare teeth instead. Their stylish silks turn into stained wrappings, like a mummy out of a Hammer horror movie. Only their golden eyes remain, but the twinkle of life becomes something far worse. A dark, dreadful malice, the likes of which Malcolm has only seen in nightmares.

"The fuck." Malcolm starts to stand, but one bony hand snakes out and grasps his arm to stop him in place. The fingers are strong as a vice and cold as ice.

"Fine," the thing that used to be Inanna says in a voice like grinding bones. "The hard way it is."

116

Only then does Malcolm realize every gaze in the club is turned toward him, and all of their eyes burn like the golden desert sun. He sees the brief outline of a beautiful form next to each of them, and some part of him realizes they must have pulled the same trick on everyone else. Not that he has any idea how he knows that—up until thirty seconds ago, he had no idea magic was real, let alone could do something like this.

Which is when everyone in the club attacks him all at once.

~

The fighting in the Tomcats' Alley gay club has started to heat up when the town car drops the three women off outside. No cops, of course, because even in liberal bastion San Francisco, cops are cops, and the LGBTQ community gets unofficially shafted. Though there *are* sirens. Angel prefers it this way, honestly. No talking. Just punching.

"Welp." Vivienne reaches between dimensions and pulls out her weird Satanic claw glove. "Looks like we came to the right place. You got your comms in?"

Yumi nods. Angel touches her ear to make sure the earpiece is there.

Ironically, the three actually *are* dressed for clubbing, more or less. But now—hearing those shouts of anger and pain and the crash of breaking furniture inside—Angel feels a little under-dressed.

"Ooh!" Yumi says. "Can you magic us into our suits, V? I haven't got the hang of it—hey, wait!"

Red energy flaring, Angel strides forward without even thinking about it and kicks the doors open. One snaps off its hinges and skitters across the floor to imbed itself in the bar, tripping up several of the combatants on the way. "Hey!" she shouts. "Stop right now."

The vacant, gold-eyed stares that greet her, however, show no recognition of her feat of strength, nor her authority. In fact, a good dozen leather-clad dudes split off from where they're attacking a single guy in a rainbow skullcap to rush her instead. Red light flashes across Angel's vision.

A-Girl time, then.

"Take it easy!" Lady Vengeance says. "They're being controlled, but they're just civilians."

That's almost disappointing, but whatever. A-Girl plucks the first one out of the air and tosses him bodily into several others, bowling them all over in a heap. Half a dozen other enchanted patrons lay hands on her, though, scrambling all over each other to get at her. They move like zombies—the *fast* kind, groping and gouging and tearing with immaculately manicured nails. Her thousand-dollar outfit is definitely ruined. And much as she wants to cut loose, A-Girl knows these aren't the bad guys. She peels them off, one at a time, but there are always more to take their places.

"Hey!" A-Girl says. "Hey! Unwanted touch!"

Muramasa has more luck as she darts in, lashing this way and that with her scabbarded sword to trip up, overbalance, and otherwise thwart the attackers. Half of the patrons look big or otherwise trained to handle themselves in a fight, but whatever's controlling them seems to have bypassed complex motor functions and training. They hurl themselves at her, and she dances, weaves, and leaps her way around them like the gymnast she is. Ironically, it's actually a few of the smaller guys who give her the most trouble, and she yelps as one of them gets in a solid punch.

"Ow!" Clutching herself, Muramasa sweeps that guy's legs out from under him, seems to blur with speed, and push-kicks him back into the bar. She lands with a wince. "He hit me right in the boob!"

Lady Vengeance growls in frustration, and they've fought together often enough for A-Girl to realize she's pulling power for one of her jury-rigged spells. Some of the enchanted patrons are heading for her, and A-Girl makes sure to toss her own attackers at them to try and trip them up. It mostly works, though her aunt has to take down one or two with fear blasts, overwriting whatever voodoo is controlling them with her own horrific power. A-Girl's not sure which is worse.

But for some reason, Lady Vengeance is just not getting *on* with it. Instead, she's fixated on something A-Girl can't see beyond the wall of bodies. It takes all of A-Girl's attention to hold them at bay without hurting them. Some of the zombies have even started biting. *Ugh.*

"V!" Muramasa says over the comm, sounding like she's in trouble. "V, what are you doing?"

Good fucking question. Maybe she's clashing with the guy they came to find? Is he behind this? Angel wasn't expecting a psychic or a mesmerist, or maybe this is sorcery? Ugh, she *hates* magic. And yes, she's aware of the irony, seeing as her powers are technically magic based.

A big bear of a man slams into the twelve guys trying to wrestle her down, and A-Girl slips in spilled beer, bringing the whole pile of dudes down to the ground with her. They can't hurt her, obviously, but the groping and squeezing and clawing is too much, it's just too *much*, and ...

A-Girl sees a leering face with a prehensile tongue drooling acidic slime on one of the zombies.

"Get *off!*" she screams, and shoves with just a fraction of her strength, sending enchanted patrons flying and scrambling. Several of them smash into the ceiling, then drop to the floor, where they lie groaning in pain. She sits up and realizes she's surrounded by injured men. The fiery red energy of her rage dances among them, like they're logs tossed onto a fire. In the strobing rainbow lights, their faces look lost and confused, but their eyes still glow with a cruel, metallic yellow light.

Then they just get back up and stalk toward A-Girl, moaning as the golden magic propels their bodies forward. They aren't undead. They're very much alive, just in the grip of a fouler magic. Honestly, A-Girl would have preferred shambling corpses. At least those, she can splatter without compunction.

"Dammit. Oh, come on!" Muramasa cries out in annoyance and pain. "A! A, hold on!"

Fast as Muramasa is, there are too many of them, and she can't draw her sword lest she drain some poor happy-hour dude's soul. It's not the zombies' fault some asshole enchanted them.

A-Girl picks up a pool cue and swings it around herself to ward off the attackers. She certainly doesn't need a weapon, but she's much less likely to hurt someone this way than with her bare fist. Someone is going to get hurt—probably a bunch of someones already have—and she's running out of ideas. And that rage, like crimson fire churning in the pit of her stomach, is rising. Every punch, every kick, every gouge—they don't hurt her, but they fuel the fire.

Sure enough, the pool cue snaps off on the side of one bespectacled nerdy guy, knocking his glasses away. Blood starts to trickle from his brow, into his glowing golden eyes, but he just keeps coming. Angel throws down the shattered pool cue and crosses her arms defensively. All down her arms, barely covered in torn fishnet sleeves, her fiery red power spills out like foam from a pot left to boil. She's about to blow, whether she likes it or not.

"Dammit, Aunt V," Angel grumbles under her breath. "If you're gonna do something—"

"Oh, fuuuck *off!*" Lady Vengeance cries behind her.

A wave of purple fear energy floods the bar, sweeping over the fifty or so patrons. Instantly, they stop attacking and either stand there dazed for a second, or else lean wearily against pillars or walls. The eerie golden glow is gone from their eyes, and they look tired and confused. All attention goes to Lady Vengeance, though, whose eyes have turned utterly black in the depth of her powers.

"Get out," she says, her voice like thunder. "*Now.*"

Not a single complaint is raised, as though they really could have. In the grip of purple terror, the patrons beat a hasty if orderly retreat, giving Lady Vengeance the widest berth they can manage. Through it all, she keeps staring straight ahead, claw poised and pointed with deadly purpose.

What is she looking at?

"What's the matter, Angel?" asks a voice. "Fallen into my trap, have you?"

That voice. She *knows* that voice.

Slowly, A-Girl turns, and sees something out of a horror movie. The creature—don't call it a person, because it hasn't been a person in a *while*—standing atop the bar is the source of the voice, and of the dark power controlling all these patrons. It, no, *she* looks more like a walking corpse than a person, with yellowed bones poking through yellowed bandages wrapped tightly over withered brown flesh. But how can that be? She was just a hallucination. Wasn't she?

"Come." Athena's corpse mouth, which is mostly teeth, curls into a cruel smile. "*Daughter.*"

A-Girl has no choice. She tenses her legs under her, ready to spring, but concussive force smashes into her from the side, sending her crashing into the leftmost wall. That wasn't some enchanted leather daddy or bear hopped up on evil magic. Purple flames dissolve around her.

"V?" she asks, shocked and betrayed.

"Muramasa!" Lady Vengeance says over the comm. "Yellow sticky!"

Yellow sticky? What does that mean—?

A lithe figure hurls itself from the shadows, moving so fast the air blurs around her. A-Girl recognizes Muramasa's powers at full blast, allowing her to move faster than any normal person and even most capes with enhanced speed. The sword for which she's named sings free of its scabbard and flashes a blood crimson arc through the strobing light ...

And hits nothing. The mummy that was Athena fades away as though it were just an illusion.

"Not yet, sister," Athena says, her voice echoing around the destroyed bar. "Not yet."

~

The three of them stand there panting. It's not every day you fight off an entire horde of divinely enchanted people, after all, and of the three, Lady Vengeance herself is the closest to crowd control. At least the building hasn't collapsed, so that's something.

Not that it reassures Lady Vengeance, whose heart pounds a hundred miles an hour as she stares at the spot where her undead sister stood before she dissolved into floating golden mist. She believed, sure, but something about *seeing* it ... About bearing witness to the horror.

Her mother was right. Athena *is* alive. Or, well, not *alive*, but still on her bullshit.

A low growl draws her attention. "Aunt *V*."

Shit.

Standing there, trendy outfit reduced to ripped fishnets and scraps of cashmere, eyes and hands and whole body shrouded in blood-red flames, A-Girl is the *picture* of rage. If Lady Vengeance thought she was pissed at her concert, this is like a supernova where A-Girl makes little to no effort to hide it. She's a volcano in the process of erupting, and only a shred of willpower holds it all together.

Lady Vengeance knows all this because she can feel the anger pouring out of the young woman, but also because Charisma Cain is floating right beside her, vainly holding her back.

"Aunt V," she says, shoulders heaving. "You knew. You *knew*."

"I didn't ... *know*, know." Lady Vengeance blows out a sigh. "But yeah. I suspected."

"And you." A-Girl turns on Muramasa, who is trying to remain unobtrusive near the bar. "You knew too? She told you? You had a codeword and everything!"

"It was ... a contingency," Muramasa says. "I didn't think it was really possible."

A-Girl turns her rage back on Lady Vengeance, where it probably should be. She's about to propel herself forward, and Lady Vengeance pulls what little fear energy she has left after that big crowd control burst. Not enough to conjure a shield that will deflect a straight-up A-Girl charge, especially not considering how much more powerful she seems to be these days, but maybe bodily enhancement ...

"V, look out!" Muramasa shouts.

A door comes flying at her, and Lady Vengeance just barely has enough power to strengthen her body so it doesn't crush her. The door goes skittering into the street.

A muscular Black man, his clothes shredded and his Pride flag skull cap slightly askew, climbs out of the wreckage of the back of the bar. Though he's clearly been fighting, he doesn't seem injured other than a few bruises here and there. Blue energy crackles around him, and Lady Vengeance recognizes Justice's energy signature. But this man isn't Marcus Orestes.

"Malcolm Ali?" Lady Vengeance asks. "*Reparation*, right?"

"Yo, who the fuck are you?" he asks, eyes narrowed. He adjusts his Taqiyah and cracks his knuckles. "You come literally *bash* a gay bar, and now you wanna talk? Nah."

"We didn't—oh." Muramasa winces. "Oh shit, he's right, we *did* do that."

"There were extenuating circumstances," Lady Vengeance says. "Listen—"

But it's too late. Reparation lunges at her, lightning crackling around him as he propels himself like a bullet. Muramasa blurs and leaps for them, but she used up too much power just a second ago and can't get there in time. Lady Vengeance hopes she has enough fear energy left to block Reparation's charging attack, but somehow, she doubts it.

A blur of crimson intersects with Reparation's charge and shoves him out of the way. Dust bursts and a column splinters, revealing A-Girl holding Reparation's fists in her hands, his strength struggling against hers.

"No one gets to fuck up my aunt," A-Girl says. "No one but *me.*"

Abruptly, she fires herself up into the air, dragging Reparation with her. They smash through the ceiling and at least two more floors, then up through the roof and into the overcast San Francisco sky.

Lady Vengeance looks over at Muramasa, at the thin trail of blood dripping down her face.

"Well, shit," she says.

# CHAPTER THIRTEEN: REAWAKER

Wood and concrete exploding and rebar twisting all around them, A-Girl carries Reparation up and up through the floors of the building, through the roof, and out into the twilight. They might have kept flying into the sky, but he lands a glancing elbow to her face that knocks her head to the side and throws off her whole trajectory. He pushes himself clear and crashes down onto the rooftop while she tumbles through the air, struggling to control her careening flight.

"A," Lady Vengeance says over the comm. "A. You alive?"

"Yeah, yeah." A-Girl rubs her jaw. "Ow."

Damn, that was a good hit. He's nearly as strong as she is. It's like fighting Injustice—the insane clone of Marcus's father—only this Reparation guy knows his stuff. His elbow had skill and precision behind it, and if he had the leverage of his feet beneath him, that blow might have stunned her.

When A-Girl rights herself, she doesn't see him. Flashing reds and blues are coming toward them, and she hears sirens growing louder as the police respond. But no Reparation anywhere in sight …

Then he comes flying at her, crackling with blue lightning, fists raised over his head. She manages to raise her arms to block, but his strike still sends a shock through every shuddering bone in her body, and the force sends her crashing back through the hole they made in the building. He rides A-Girl back down, continuing to punch at her face while lightning crackles around and through them both. It's a ground-and-pound with extra steps, and fortunately, A-Girl has trained enough to react appropriately, defending her face and head from his too-strong strikes.

"Incoming," she manages to say into the comm.

"Roger!" Muramasa says. "We'll be ready."

At least she's optimistic.

It's more than his strength, too. A-Girl can feel her energy flowing out of her and into Reparation, or maybe his energy is just disrupting it. Regardless, her red energy aura shrinks, like the fire on a camp stove running low on propane. She feels herself growing weaker with every strike, too. Each of his punches feels a little stronger than the last one and pushes her down a little harder. This power feels like Marcus's, but where he always empowered her, Reparation *weakens* her.

They smash through the ground floor, putting a crater deep into the foundation. Before she can get her bearings, Reparation springs off her to attack one of the others. There she lies, looking at her spilled purse, and specifically at the Kid Justice doll—action figure—which honestly looks more like *Reparation* than Marcus. How much time does he spend at the gym?

"A! A! Are you all right?" Muramasa asks, panting.

"I'm fine," A-Girl says.

Lady Vengeance's voice sounds equally strained. "Then get up ... ugh ... and help us."

"Whatever." A-Girl flails, rolls over, and pushes herself up to peer through the swirling dust. Even with her short hair, she has to brush it out of her eyes.

It's not good.

Reparation is hammering on Lady Vengeance's fearshield whilst ignoring Muramasa's attacks. Her fiery sword carves through his clothes but bounces right off his skin, no matter the curses placed upon it. Worse, her blade keeps pulling arcs of blue electricity out of him and into her, making her shiver, tremble, and pant. For the first time A-Girl has known her, Muramasa looks tired. Her arm looks leaden and slow, and that means she's on her last legs and about to collapse. Lady Vengeance looks only marginally better: she's down on her knees, teeth gritted, cracks spreading through her fearshield.

"Any day now," Lady Vengeance says.

A-Girl doesn't know what to do, so she does what she always does: hurls herself at the problem.

She smashes into Reparation, knocking him staggering away from Lady Vengeance and Muramasa. She must have caught him by surprise the first time, because he grinds his heels through the floorboards and not only arrests her tackle but shoves her right back, into and through the far wall near the entrance. He misses the door by about six feet, which was probably intentional. A-Girl bursts through wood, drywall, wood, and brick before she bounces across the sidewalk and into the street. She smashes into a police car with so much force it bounces up on its side, and she comes back to her senses in a crater on top of the sideways car. Damn.

A-Girl's comm crackles with static, though that might just be her hearing. She's pretty sure she collided with the car headfirst.

The police look at her with more concern than upset. "A-Girl? Is that you?" a female cop asks. Her nametag says "Gomez."

"Yeah," she says, her voice a little hoarse. "We got this."

"You sure?" Officer Gomez asks, gesturing at the dozens of cops with assault rifles and a couple cape-response vehicles emblazoned with Prather's branding. Because of course. "We have drainers—"

A memory flashes in A-Girl's mind: cops bursting into her apartment, armed to the teeth, using drainers on her. Pissed as she is at this Reparation guy, she wouldn't wish that on anyone. Also, he has enough power to take on all three of them, and he barely seems to be controlling it. What would happen if the cops went in, all guns blazing, and he retaliated? Escalation is *not* a good move.

"Just keep any civilians out of the area," A-Girl says, as she hops down from the upset cruiser. "And whatever you do, don't go in. You come in that building, and people are getting hurt."

"That a threat?" another cop asks—this one a burly asshole with a Prather patch on his vest. His nametag is covered in electrical tape because, again, of course. She's pretty sure that's unconstitutional, but since when has a single Prat Hat cared about some dusty old document establishing the rule of law?

Just a couple days ago, Angel "I don't care" DeSantes would have cursed him out or, better yet, tossed him into the destroyed bar to see firsthand how little she thought of his fascist bravado. But somehow, not only did Reparation sap her energy, he took some of her rage too. Huh.

Instead, she just ignores the Prat Hat cop, which makes him fume and sputter.

"You going back in?" Officer Gomez asks. "Can I get your autograph after? I mean, for my kid."

Because of course. "Sure, lady."

But first.

A-Girl turns to Gomez and jerks a thumb back at the cruiser on its side. "Whose car is this?"

"His." She points at the Prat Hat. "Looks totaled."

A-Girl nods and puts a foot up against the cruiser's undercarriage, like a runner bracing for the starter gun. Fashy cop gives A-Girl an angry look. "What are you doing, you pink bi—"

He cuts off mid-insult as A-Girl gives him a murderous glare, almost as though she had put her fist in his gut. His face goes bright red. "Hey wait. Don't—"

She fires herself back into the bar, shoving his cruiser entirely over onto its roof. Glass shatters, the siren whines, and the Prat Hat squeals in impotent rage.

~

The battle inside the bar hasn't developed in any positive direction.

Muramasa dances around Reparation, mostly evading his punches, which take chunks out of walls, columns, and the bar with every swing. Just about every bottle behind the bar has fallen and smashed, and it's a testament to how pressed Lady Vengeance is that she doesn't seem to notice. Instead, she keeps sending fear blasts at Reparation, but they seem to do little to nothing.

"A," she says, her voice crackling in the comm. "Get in there."

"Don't tell me what to do!"

A-Girl hurls herself at Reparation, but he slips her charge at the last second, and she smashes into the opposite wall with enough force to cave it in. She doesn't go flying through, though, and kicks off like an Olympic swimmer and sweeps his legs with her whole body. Not a moment too soon, either, because Muramasa narrowly eludes a hook that would have smashed her head in, based on the damage it does to a massive pink thermos perched on the bar.

128

Water sprays over them, lighting up with blue energy from Reparation's fury.

"Stay down!" A-Girl yells in his face as she wrestles him down.

It's like trying to restrain a snake, though, as he keeps squirming and thrashing, and energy keeps stabbing into her like electricity. He finally catches her with a punch to the jaw, dazing her for a second as she floats up into the air. He bounces to his feet and punches again, but though she's out of practice, she didn't spend two years in self-defense under Eiko "Silver Sakura" Kujikawa for nothing. She slips the punch, catches his arm, stomps the inside of his foot, and slams him back and partly into the wall, where she can at least sort of hold him. He's about to squirm away, but a blast of purple fear energy splashes into him under her arm, easing his assault just briefly, and A-Girl tightens her hold on his arms.

They lock together, pushing against each other with as much force as either can muster. They're remarkably evenly matched, except for the energy crackling out of him and into her red aura, making her limbs break out into pins-and-needles numbness. It isn't long before A-Girl is sucking hard for breath and exerting what strength she has left just to keep him in place.

She manages to speak between chattering teeth. "Do ... something ... V—"

And Lady Vengeance does *do* something, though it's not anything A-Girl would have expected.

She kneels, presses her forehead to the floor, and starts speaking in a language A-Girl doesn't know. Is she ... *praying*? The fuck?

In that moment, A-Girl is sure that—whether it's a part of Reparation's powers, Aunt V's, or just ... *everything*—she has gone completely insane. This is the moment when the world stops making sense. This is a psychotic break. Maybe she should have taken her agent's advice to see a therapist.

Even crazier, though, her opponent's force ebbs, and he finally lets go of her entirely. She falls back and puts up her dukes, but he shows no sign of attacking her again. Instead, he looks at her aunt with a bemused, curious look. Then he nods, turns in the direction she's facing, and assumes much the same posture. He presses his forehead to the floor, despite the debris.

The battle is over ... apparently?

"What's happening?" Angel asks. "Am I dead? Yumi?"

"It's ... Salah," Yumi says, leaning heavily on her scabbarded sword. "Muslim prayer time."

"Okay?" That only sort of answers Angel's question, but Yumi looks relieved, so fine.

They watch them pray together for several minutes, not sure how to break the silence or even whether they should. Out of the corner of her eye, Angel sees a couple SFPD officers approaching, assault rifles drawn, but she waves them off. Maybe they recognize her, or maybe they're just accustomed to superhero battles, because they nod and back off. They keep a perimeter but don't try to intercede. Good.

Finally, prayer time is finished, and Vivienne and Malcolm— that's his name, right?—stand up, surprisingly peaceful. "Thank you, sister," he says. "No offense, but you don't look Muslim."

"Half. And not the good half." Vivienne pops the comm out of her ear and puts the claw back in her dimensional pocket in a show of good faith. "Let's talk first, fight second."

"I assumed we was gonna start up again. Also." He puts up his fists, ready for round two. "I'm just supposed to ignore you attacking a bar full of people minding their own business?"

"Who were controlled by an evil goddess, yeah," Vivienne says. "Which I think you know."

He opens his mouth as though to argue, then nods and relaxes instead. "Who are you people?"

"That's A-Girl," Vivienne says. "And Muramasa. And I'm Lady Vengeance."

"Never heard of you."

"He's never heard of *A-Girl*?" Yumi murmurs, sounding almost personally affronted.

"But you know The Raven," Vivienne says. "You kicked his ass. Very thoroughly."

"Yeah." That catches his attention, and he looks a little saddened. "You with him?"

"Occasionally."

"Gross," Angel says on the comm, making Yumi giggle.

Vivienne continues unabated. "We don't want to fight. We got business. Can we talk?"

"Hmm." Malcolm narrows his eyes. "Those cops with you?"

130

"Fuck no," Vivienne says. "You wanna fight them, I'll join you. Could use the exercise. *After.*"

Malcolm smiles halfway. "A'ight. You got exactly three hundred seconds."

"Do we have to do this here?" Yumi asks. "I can get us the executive suite at—"

"Two-hundred an' ninety seconds," Malcolm says.

"Fine," Yumi says. "I'll ... keep watch."

"Me too," Angel says, but Yumi holds up a hand to stop her.

Silently, Yumi heads off, and Angel sighs, crosses her arms, and waits.

"Okay," Vivienne says. "The *short* version."

~

The explanation—about superheroes, gods and goddesses, transferred powers, trapped spirits, and a trip to a hell dimension— takes just under five minutes, because that's the requirement. Though honestly, no one seems to be keeping time.

Apparently, Malcolm isn't a big capes fan and knows very little about superheroes. He's barely aware of Supergroup or heard of most of its members, but he knows The Raven, and he definitely knows Justice. Honestly, the look on his face suggests he views Justice as some kind of aspirational hero. The mention of him alone might be enough to capture Malcolm's attention, however impossible Vivienne's story becomes. He listens respectfully, not believing a word of it.

Not that you can blame him. If Angel hadn't witnessed half of it, she wouldn't believe it either.

Her comm crackles again, and she wonders if she's picked up another signal or something. The voice is faint and broken up and speaking in code. Maybe it's tapped into the cops' radios?

The cops haven't attacked so far, and Angel has no idea what she said to them to get them to hold off raiding. At least the civilians are all out, and the owner of the bar actually has a lot of good things to say about Lady Vengeance, who he is confident has this in hand. Yumi got them all drinks halfway through, and Vivienne was so engrossed she didn't even touch her bourbon or chide Yumi for drinking underage. Malcolm doesn't drink either.

When Vivienne finally finishes the explanation and throws back her bourbon to soothe her parched voice, Malcolm nods thoughtfully. "A'ight."

"What?" Angel blinks. "You heard all that crazy and you're just, what, going with it?"

"Uh-huh," he says. "Some strange shit's been happening to me, 'bout six months back. I've always been strong, but the lightning? The ... seeing and knowing stuff? That's new. Like something blessed me with a bunch of new powers. And I don't mind 'em—they're helpful and all—but you need this dude back, that's fine by me. Also."

"Also?" Vivienne asks.

Malcolm bends down to pick something up: the highly detailed and articulated doll of Marcus, which he scrutinizes in detail. "Who's this supposed to be? Justice?"

"His son," Vivienne says. "Marcus Orestes. The spirit trapped inside you."

"My boyfriend," Angel says.

"You carry a doll of your boyfriend around?"

"Action figure!" Yumi says.

"Yeah." He extends the action figure toward Angel. "Let's make it right."

"Great!" Yumi says. "Let's call Ruby and—"

"Hey, yo, slow your roll, girl," Malcolm says. "I didn't say I'd do it for *free*."

Anger roils in Angel's belly, but she tries to keep a lid on it. To come this far—this close—and then more hoops to jump through.

"What do you want?" Vivienne asks.

"Something it sounds like you'd do anyway, when you hear it," Malcolm says. "I do you this favor, you hit me back. Bet?"

"Yes," Yumi says.

"Depends on the favor—" Angel glares at her, and Vivienne sighs. "Fine. Agreed."

A voice crackles over the comm—one that isn't Yumi's or any cop's. One Angel recognizes immediately. "Can't take that risk, mija," Tony DeSantes's pained voice says. Then: "Do it."

"I'm coming from a reception," a new, feminine voice replies. "This is hardly the time—"

"Do it," Tony says.

The woman sighs. "*Fine.*"

Angel knows that voice. Is that—?

The air near Malcolm crackles, reality warping and unraveling like a stretched film reel left too long under the projector. The light interrupts the ongoing negotiation between Vivienne and Malcolm, both of whom look up, startled. It starts to burn through, and abruptly a woman is standing there, her immaculate fire-red hair floating around her untouchably made-up face.

"Ruby?" Vivienne says, her voice strangled with sudden emotion.

Ruby Killingsworth is dressed neither for clubbing nor superheroing, and while Angel might not know magic, she knows *fashion*. The long-sleeved, black, beaded-lace, cocktail dress with plunging nude illusion neckline says it was an awards ceremony with high-shelf cocktails, and the simple diamond earrings say extreme wealth without ostentation. Also, those black patent Christian Louboutin So Kate pumps are at least eight hundred dollars, if not more. Is looking on-point the woman's superpower?

Actually, that would be the *magic*.

Ruby Killingsworth doesn't hesitate. A circle of runes made of white light swirling around her hand, she steps toward Malcolm, smiles up at him, and lays her hand gently but firmly on his chest.

The impact of her spell isn't nearly so gentle, though. Malcolm recoils as though A-Girl hit him at full force at the end of a Mach One charge. And something flows out of him, as though projected from the force of her touch: a crackling storm of blue energy that pulsates and stretches as though breathing. Malcolm collapses to the floor, coughing and wheezing, as the energy cloud resolves first into a vaguely humanoid form, then into ...

Angel's heart skips. "*Marcus.*"

She rushes to him, feet not even touching the ground, and catches him in her arms before he can fall. He feels warm and solid and like *him*. He's very naked, but that doesn't matter. Nothing else matters but him and holding him tight. Maybe she's gone insane, but maybe—just maybe—this is real.

"Hey," Marcus says, his voice thin. He touches her forehead. "You cut your hair."

"You like it?" Angel asks. "I could grow it back out. Gimme twenty-four hours."

"Nah, keep it. It's awesome."

Angel's gaze goes blurry, and she hugs Marcus tighter, like he might disappear if she lets go. She buries her face in his chest—in the smell of him. Like all these months were just a bad dream, and she's finally waking up.

"Ruby," Vivienne says in a broken voice, drawing Angel's attention.

The vision in black with the swirling red hair—does she use magic to do that? That's amazing—gives Vivienne a look. It's imperious, superior, and probably meant to seem entirely heartless but totally fails. Angel isn't sure how she can tell, but she can.

"Can you hear me, Mr. DeSantes?" Ruby asks in a very business-like manner over the comm. "I've fulfilled my part of the bargain, so it's time for you to do yours. *Lose my number.*"

She steps back through the rift she carved in the mortal coil and vanishes. Reality reknits itself, and then the portal disappears as though it were never there at all.

Vivienne drops her hands to her sides with a drained sigh, then looks up in shock. "Oh, shit."

Out of the smoke of the magic, Malcolm surges toward her aunt, barely fazed by magic that would have put an ordinary man in a coma. She conjures a fearshield by instinct, but he runs right past her toward ... Shit, the Prat Hat cop is coming in, complete with an assault rifle trained on them. Bullets start raining forth, and they slam into Malcolm's chest. Angel startles, but the hits don't even slow Malcolm. Instead, the bullets bounce right off, smashing into the floor, walls, ceiling, and then into the officer's leg, putting him on his back with a cry of pain.

Unhindered, Malcolm steps up to him, and the cop starts blubbering and shielding his face with his arms. Vivienne and Yumi both tense to move, but Malcolm just grabs the cop's assault rifle and tears it away from him. He looks annoyed more than anything.

"Hey!" the other cops coming in shout. "Hands up! Drop the weapon!"

Which is when a wave of purple fear energy hits them, their eyes widen, and they beat a hasty retreat. Vivienne leans heavily on a table, all but exhausted. Malcolm looks over to her, nods, and bends the assault rifle into a pretzel before discarding it on the floor. He sits down, equally tired. He stares at Marcus, his expression one of intrigue.

"Fucking pigs," Vivienne says. "I guess all that strength wasn't just—"

"Marcus, OMG!" Yumi bounds over to him, albeit a little slower than usual. She must be exhausted, too. "It's real! It's true! All of it!"

She hugs Marcus and Angel both, and Angel is so ecstatically happy she doesn't even mind that her best friend is hugging her naked boyfriend. Oh, and they used to date. But who cares?

"Not so tight. I was mostly dead a minute ago." Marcus grunts. "And where are my pants?"

"You don't need pants," Angel says, quite reasonably.

"Pretty sure I need pants."

"Agree to disagree."

"Seconded," Yumi says. "Um, I mean—"

"Okay, pants," Angel says. "Yumi. Find him some pants."

"But—"

"*Yumi.*"

She heads off, leaving Angel, Vivienne, the returned Marcus, and Malcolm alone in the room. Vivienne is staring at the spot where Ruby briefly stood, then she looks up at Marcus and smiles weakly.

"Hey kid," she says, politely looking away to preserve his modesty. "You good?"

"I think so. When I—" He shakes his head. "When I was disintegrated, it was like I was dreaming, and then I went into Malcolm. We're not related or anything, it's just—" He shakes his head again. "He's a good dude. We gotta help him."

"We what?" Angel asks, holding Marcus at arm's length. "We just got you back—"

"He has a mission, and he needs a team," Marcus says. "Especially since you ... exorcised me? I was going to support him with my powers anyway, and I'm still going to."

Vivienne groans. "Fuck."

"Good," Malcolm says. "Thought I was gonna have to kick all your asses."

"Lovely," Vivienne says.

"We gotta help," Marcus says. "It's the—"

"The right thing to do?" Angel asks.

Marcus nods grimly. "It's the right thing to do."

"How did I know you were going to say that?" Vivienne winces and shields her eyes. "How we doing on those pants, Yumi?"

# CHAPTER FOURTEEN: BAD AT LOVE

"So to sum up," Vivienne says, swirling her bourbon. "You want us to help you infiltrate and destroy Prather's ICE facility in the Bay Area. Liberate the detainees, chase off the staff, delete all their files, break their equipment, and basically destroy their facility. Right?"

"That's it," Malcolm says, cracking his knuckles. "I told you you'd like it."

Vivienne takes a sip, considering. "And this facility is located not in San Fran proper, but on—"

"Alcatraz Island," Orestes says from where he leans against the balcony railing.

"Because of course it is," Angel says, leaning next to him.

"Hell," Vivienne says. "We'd have done this for *free*."

"I like you people," Malcolm says. "Miss K, we got more of that lemonade?"

"I'll have room service bring it up. Anything else? More drinks? I could get more drinks." Of all of them, Yumi is the only one who looks a little troubled. "And it's just Yumi, Mr. Ali."

"Malcolm's fine."

They took Yumi and her black AmEx up on the penthouse suite at the historic Fairmont San Francisco, with stunning views of the city, the bay, and the famous Golden Gate Bridge. Which Orestes has always wondered about, since it's *red*, not gold. But that's not the point. He can see Alcatraz from here, the recently upgraded facilities blinking with ominous yellow light. That's their target. Who would have thought his first time there would be in a superhero costume, rather than as a tourist?

Everyone seems to be in a restful, jovial mood, with two clear exceptions. Yumi is doing that thing where she's constantly moving, soliciting everyone's drink orders, and basically trying everything to avoid an uncomfortable thing she has to say. Angel also seems distant, but that's a different thing. She stands next to him at the railing, clutching his hand as though he might disappear at any second if she lets go, and her grip only gets stronger as the conversation goes on. He can tell she needs to say something to him. At this point, it's a race to see which of them cracks first.

And with his Godsight, he knows who it will be.

His time inside Malcolm Ali has changed him, he realizes. Empowering him in some ways, weakening him in others, and generally shaping him into something ... not quite himself. He's not entirely sure of the scope of these changes, but he knows his Godsight is more powerful than before, and he usually knows what will happen before it does. For instance ...

When the room doorbell sounds and Yumi jumps nearly a foot in the air and tosses the ice bucket over the railing in surprise, that answers that question. Orestes sighs inwardly.

"I can't go!" Yumi says to the group, who all stare at her wordlessly. When no one speaks for half a second, she launches into a stream of words to explain. "I'm happy to bankroll you all this far, but I really can't be involved in direct action against the United States government even if it is ruled by a fascist who's hired a bunch of supervillains to do all his dirty work—"

"Because of your father," Vivienne says.

"You—you know about that, huh?" Yumi asks.

"That you got the hookup? Girl." Malcolm gestures around the balcony. "You're rollin' in it."

It's ironic, that Yumi's got all this money, but Orestes is still walking around in worn skinny jeans, a t-shirt that says "I heart SF," and a pink jacket someone left at the bar. But then, they grabbed what was available, and it hasn't occurred to Orestes to ask for new clothes.

Orestes goes to the door to let in the room service cart, but there's no one there. Just the cart and an empty, discarded bellhop uniform. He didn't expect anyone, of course, and he takes the cart of drinks inside, then closes the door. When he gets back to the balcony, the conversation concerns the political implications of Yumi continuing to bankroll their little freedom fighter operation.

"I don't know what deal you've made with Akira," Vivienne says. "But if you get spotted attacking a Prather installation, that could be a whole thing. Especially with the 2K Group's public support of the administration."

Yumi, who was queuing up for another string of run-on sentences, stops short and hangs her head. "Much as I love punching Nazis, I've already defied my father's instructions a couple times. I should really be back in Seattle tonight, and if I miss family dinner tomorrow—"

"It's fine," Vivienne says.

"It—it is?" Yumi's eyes have gone wide. "But I don't want to just leave you hanging or anything. I'm just—I'm worried I'll be a liability if my father starts sending Factory assassins after me."

"Assuming he doesn't already have a tracker planted in your skull or something," Vivienne says.

"Tsch," Angel puts in. "We're talking about *her* dad, not mine."

"Tony DeSantes, right?" Malcolm asks, clearly doing some relationship mapping in his head.

"Fuck, don't say his name out loud. He's probably listening right now. But you're right." Vivienne sips her bourbon. "Akira Kujikawa would use a tracing spell I couldn't break even if I could find it."

"We could always call Ms. Killingsworth again?" Orestes suggests.

Orestes winces as everyone gives him a sharp look, including Malcolm. After all, she did punch Orestes out of Malcolm when they first met. He probably doesn't have good feelings about her.

"Pass." Vivienne shrugs. "It's cool, Y. I mean, you've already wasted a *lot* of corporate money on our nonsense."

"I guess that's true," Yumi says. "The caviar, for instance."

"That what this is?" Malcolm slathers a generous amount of the spread on another hunk of fresh sourdough bread from the Boudin Bakery. "Yo, this shit's pretty dope."

"It's also about five hundred bucks an ounce." Vivienne shrugs. "What? Ruby doesn't pay attention to price tags, but I do."

"I'll have room service bring up some more," Yumi says. "And besides, I'm sure everyone knows I'm carting you around the country on the jet. If anyone's following you—"

"Like Athena," Orestes says, making Angel squeeze his hand harder.

"Right," Yumi says. "They might assume you're flying back to Seattle with me."

"So we'll have the element of surprise," Vivienne says. "Good thinking, Y."

Yumi beams. "I still feel bad, though. Maybe I can set up an expense account for you? Or would that be embezzlement?"

The Godsight flares, and Orestes wraps his arm around Angel.

She stiffens, surprised, and looks up at him quizzically. "Hey. Listen, I wanted to talk with you ... alone—"

"I know," he says. "Just ... don't be upset."

"Upset?" Her face falls in confusion. "Why would I be—?"

Which is when the dark shape climbs over the rail, a few feet from where Orestes and Angel stand. It's not The Raven's best suit—that one, Malcolm destroyed with a little help from Orestes's power boost—but it's powered and supportive enough to let him climb high up on a twenty-three-story building in the dark despite practically being in a coma the previous day. That and the energy Orestes infused into him after the beating. Though the effort has still left him trembling.

"Fuck, of course," Vivienne says, and drains her bourbon.

Yumi has already summoned Muramasa into her hand, leaving an arcing trail of crimson fire in its wake, but she does a doubletake when she sees the red eye. "Mr. DeSantes?"

Of all of them, Malcolm is the one who looks the most surprised. And a little uneasy, in fact.

"I heard—" The Raven's voice rasps through the speakers, until at the press of a button, the helmet retracts from Tony's face. He still has a black eye, and his eyebrow is heavily bandaged, but he's mobile, at least. "I heard you might need a new source of funding."

"Yes!" Yumi smiles and claps her hands. "Perfect!"

Vivienne rolls her eyes.

Orestes's focus goes to Angel, however, who stares at her father with shock and disdain. He can feel her bubbling emotions and knows the exact moment they boil over.

140

Without a word, Angel marches away from the railing and into the master bedroom. The door slams, hard enough to shake the penthouse but not to shatter into a million pieces. Good construction here at the Fairmont.

Everyone looks awkward and not a little ashamed. Tony, in particular.

"I'll go talk to her." Orestes pushes away from the railing and heads back inside.

He already knows what to expect. The Godsight is, after all, never wrong.

~

"Heh, straight people, amirite?" Yumi smiles at Malcolm as though he'll get the joke.

Not only does no one laugh, but no one seems to have noticed her attempt at humor.

"Well, that's just great," Vivienne says, when it's just the adults (plus Yumi) on the balcony. She stands and crosses her arms as she stares daggers at Tony. "You couldn't have stayed in that hospital for even one more day? Just until we were gone?"

"I thought—" Tony coughs. "I thought I could be helpful. I called Miss Killingsworth, didn't I?"

"Yes, and that was very helpful," Yumi says. "Though ... Mr. DeSantes, you could have told us."

"I know, and I ... I'm sorry," Tony says. "Miss Killingsworth and I have been working together for months, and that was our best and only chance to see it done. Still. I want to apologize. To all of you. Especially—" He glances into the suite. "Especially to her."

Vivienne really should rebuke him, yell at him, maybe shove him off the balcony while she's at it. If his suit let him climb up here, surely it'll help him land safely. But just then ...

Ugh. *Idiot.*

She takes a step toward Tony, who looks at her warily. Not that he's afraid of her—he's made it very clear that he doesn't feel fear anymore, and she's unable to absorb any from him—but he's concerned. Concerned about how she will react, what she will do, and the impact it will have on Angel. And that—*that* is why she can't yell at him.

It's clear he's done all this for his daughter. He's worked with Ruby—a woman who hates and almost killed him, *multiple* times—for months. He kept up the search even after the Valentine's Day attack, and he left his powerbase behind in Colorado to pursue it. He fought a terribly overpowered Malcolm, and then he fought his way out of a hospital bed to tap their comms, monitor their own fight, and bring in Ruby—the woman who wants to murder him—to get it done. All for Angel.

Vivienne puts her arms around him. "Thank you. You're an idiot, but you did good."

He relaxes a little and nods, and for a moment, Vivienne wants to kiss him, but she restrains the urge. It wouldn't do to reward this behavior. That's been a problem before.

"You could have used the door, you know," she says.

"I did. But no one answered, so I came around the outside." He smiles crookedly. "You don't honestly think I climbed all the way up here. I just—" He coughs. "I just got out of the hospital."

"Knowing your crazy? Yeah. There was a good chance."

Tony slips gently past her and regards Malcolm. "I want to apologize to you, as well. I should have de-escalated and explained the situation. I handled our meeting poorly, and the fault was mine." He extends his black-gloved hand, which Malcolm inspects dubiously.

Finally, Malcolm takes it. "Enough blame to go around. We're even."

"Even."

Yumi, who's been watching the whole interaction unfold, breathes a sigh of relief. "Can I get you a drink, Mr. DeSantes, sir? Tequila, right?"

He waves away the offer of hard liquor. "I'll take a beer if there's beer."

Yumi scurries off to make it so.

"Gotta wash down some more pain meds?" Vivienne asks.

Tony shrugs. "I'm feeling better than you'd expect. Are you a healer as well as a fighter, Mr. Ali?"

"Malcolm," he replies. "Hey, yo. How'd you know to show up right then?"

"The Norn Seeing protocol," Tony says. "Listening program on your devices, programmed to activate when—"

"When someone says your name?" Vivienne sighs. "Because of course."

Vivienne winds back to throw her phone off the balcony, but Yumi snatches it out of the air. "Do you have any idea how much this cost? Let me just uninstall the program this time!"

"*Fiiiine.*"

~

Orestes waits outside the door of the master bedroom until the moment is right. How exactly it's right, he doesn't know, but he knows it is. If he acts too early, it will ruin things, and if he acts too late, it will be worse. And so he waits until his Godsight tells him to knock.

He knocks.

"Go away," comes Angel's muffled shout.

"It's me." He pushes the unlocked door, because Angel broke the lock when she slammed it earlier. "I'm coming in."

He isn't two steps inside the door when Angel is on him, arms around his shoulder, lips pressed to his. "Finally," she says, her voice heavy. "So much talk, talk, talk, and finally I've got you all alone." She starts unfastening his belt. "Lock the door."

"Can't," Orestes replies. "You broke the lock."

"Eh, fuck it," Angel says against his neck. "If anyone's stupid enough to walk in on us—"

She is burning with energy and lust and *fuck*, is she hot. Orestes does the hardest thing he's ever had to do, and that includes dying. He pushes her gently away.

She's so surprised that it doesn't even occur to her to stop him, which she could easily do. She's stronger than fifty of him. Instead, Angel just stares at him, blinking her big contacts-blue eyes.

"We need to talk," he says.

"Talk?" Angel seems even more surprised. "You've been dead for six months, and you just want to talk?" She narrows her eyes. "Did being inside a gay man—?"

"No," Orestes says. "You are the most beautiful and wonderful thing I have ever seen, and I absolutely want to have sex with you right now, all night, and through tomorrow. Is that better?"

"A little. But then why aren't we doing that?"

She takes a step toward him, and Orestes holds up his hands. "It's not right."

"Not *right*?" Angel asks, exasperated. "Not right *how*? It's not like we broke up or anything. You died. Right when—Jesus Christ, Marcus, what the fuck?"

Orestes sympathizes. *God*, does he sympathize. His Godsight is being frustratingly nonspecific as to why he needs to deny her, but that's what he's doing. Agonizingly. "It's just, a lot's happened, and—"

"Is it about my elevated body count? Because if it is, let me reassure you, all those groupies meant nothing. Absolutely nothing. I never even learned their *names*, Marcus."

"What?" Orestes did not expect that argument. "Put a pin in that. We'll circle back to that—"

"I knew it. I fucking *knew*." Angel crosses her arms. "What was I supposed to do, wait for you? You were dead. And I was lonely and in a dark place and—"

"That's not you!" Orestes shouts, unable to hold back anymore. "It took a long time for you to feel comfortable with me, and you went and had meaningless sex with a bunch of people?"

Angel glares. "Oh, don't you *dare* slut-shame me, motherfucker. V's bad enough, but you—"

"No, that's not—"

He tries to grasp her shoulders, but she breaks out of his grasp trivially easily, pushing him back against the wall with only a fraction of her strength. The full-length mirror groans behind him, and a single crack splinters through it. His shoulder starts to ache.

"Don't *touch* me," she says. "Don't you *fucking* dare."

"I'm sorry." Orestes puts his hands carefully down to his sides. "But you've gotta see what I mean, A. You're not acting like yourself. You're ... you're not okay."

At first, he expects her to argue, but her trademark stubbornness comes out in the opposite way. "Of *course* I'm not okay!" she cries, loud enough to shake the room. "The man I loved just fucking died, my aunt had a nervous breakdown, and I'm on the verge of a psychotic break, and just when I think it's all going to be okay, you cold-fish me and—"

"Angel," Orestes says. "That isn't what this is. I'm worried about you. I think ... I think you have to worry about you, too. You haven't been taking care of yourself, and I don't want to make it worse."

"You don't think rejecting me will make it worse?"

"I think taking advantage of you will."

"You're not taking advantage of me—I invited you. I consent. See? Enthusiastic consent."

"I need to take care of you. Let me take care of you."

"No problem, it's always ladies first with you anyway."

"That's not what I mean."

"Ugh, *God!*" Angel hurls herself onto the bed with enough force to make the frame strain and groan concerningly. She puts her hands over her face. "This is so humiliating."

"Angel—"

"Look, O, two choices," she says. "Take your clothes off and get on this bed with me right now or fuck off. Easy choice."

He wants to. He wants to so badly, but he knows that if he does ... "I'm sorry, Angel."

"Ugh, just get out."

Heart sinking into his stomach, Orestes heads for the door, but he pauses, one hand on the frame. "I love you, A. That's not gonna change."

For a hopeful second, he thinks she might say it back, but instead she just sighs.

He shuts the door behind him.

~

Angel groans in unfulfilled frustration up at the ceiling. This was not how she expected this to go. Not in a million years.

The worst part of it was that he was right.

When he died, it devastated her. She barely remembers anything after that moment. Blue Steel smiling with Athena's mocking smile and disintegrating Marcus right in front of her. He disappeared, and her world went red, then black. For days after, everything was a fractured mass of images and moments, and in all of them, she felt utterly, hopelessly alone. She couldn't talk to her father, her aunt wouldn't take her calls, and she couldn't face any of her friends. No one understood her. She was alone.

Oh, she didn't *stay* alone, of course. She watched herself, like an outside observer, make all kinds of bad decisions. Drinking progressively higher proof liquor until Everclear finally made her feel drunk. Going on loud, crazy dates where she trashed clubs, made out with scumbags, and stripped mostly naked more than once in public. Writing a shit ton of even shittier music, then letting Yumi talk her into going on a national tour of all things. So many distractions to keep herself from facing the truth.

And of course, as much as she tried to destroy herself, her own stupid powers wouldn't let her. She'd paid for dozens of tattoos that never set, because her skin healed them by the next day. Piercings popped free within minutes. Booze and drugs and demeaning sex never fazed her for longer than a few minutes at a time. She couldn't even properly suffer through her misery, not in any lasting way.

And so she hurt herself the only way she knew how: breaking her heart over and over. Reliving that loss over and over. Sitting with her loneliness. Constantly scratching and licking at her emotional wounds so they would never heal. Because she didn't *deserve* to heal, and the concept of being better only made her hate herself more.

And now he's back, and he's perfect, and he's right to turn her down and—*argh*!

Angel lies there on the master bed for a long time, staring up at the ceiling, hands clenching and unclenching. Eventually, sleep claims her, but not before she has sworn to herself to take all of this out on Prather's goons tomorrow. That makes her feel a little bit better. Not as good as you've-been-dead-for-six-months makeup sex would, but she'll take what she can get.

And much as her stubbornness wants to prove Marcus wrong ...

She slips into a gentle sleep full of annoyingly sexy dreams.

# CHAPTER FIFTEEN: BURN IT TO THE GROUND

The March morning mist has settled thick over the bay, obscuring all but the tips of the Golden Gate Bridge, and even the constant honking traffic can't disrupt it. The low render distance really makes sentry duty on the walls of Alcatraz feel both impossible and unnecessary.

"Some real Silent Hill shit here." Private Stevie Miller grins his big, toothy grin, which coupled with his basically vanished hairline at age thirty only increases his vampiric vibe. "I like it."

"Bruh," Corporal Don Trumpet says. "Bruh, I was with this hottie last night, oh my God."

Miller rolls his eyes. "Sir, with all due respect, sir, do you really need to tell me about—"

"Bruh, you gotta hear this," Corporal Trumpet says, just carrying right on in a way that he would never be able to get away with without his rank. "There was this girl, right, and she was really into the Army, right? They'll let you do anything if you're in uniform. Anyway, I moved on her like—uh?"

Miller looks around as though to investigate, but his buddy has just disappeared. A second ago, he was standing right there, bragging about yet another sexual harassment, and now he's gone.

"Sir?" Miller asks. "Sir, this isn't funn—ahh!"

His word turns into a cry of alarm as A-Girl swoops through the fog, plucks him up like a kitten, and deposits him, none-too-gently, about half a mile away from the island in the middle of the bay. She drops him from just high enough for him to feel the impact without breaking any bones, but honestly, that's because the

147

goal of this operation isn't to kill anyone, even serial predators and vampy weirdos in service of the Prather administration.

"Good job, A," her father's voice crackles over the comm. "Two more on the north face."

"Yeah, whatever," A-Girl says, and zips back toward Alcatraz. She's careful not to go too fast, as a sonic boom will definitely destroy the element of surprise.

Why exactly The Raven wanted to make this a stealth mission is beyond her. After last night, the last thing she feels like is going quiet. But she supposes picking a fight with the U.S. military isn't the best of ideas, even if she really, really feels like seeing how far she can hurl a tank this morning. At least they're in the black costumes, which suit her mood.

The Raven speaks over the comm again. "A, report."

"Just about—there."

"No casualties," The Raven says.

"Yeah, yeah."

A-Girl swoops in on two more sentries, so fast she basically appears between them as they stand there confused, rocking slightly from the air displacement of her arrival. She grasps them both by the backs of their necks, knocks their heads together, and flies off with them. It takes less than a minute to drop them in the drink, though she makes sure their heads are up, out of the water.

"Unconscious men can't swim, A," The Raven says over the comm.

"Human bodies float, T," Lady Vengeance puts in.

"Maintain radio silence, V."

"Someone's gotta call you on your shit."

*She's right*, A-Girl thinks, but doesn't say. She doesn't want to give her aunt the satisfaction.

Lady Vengeance isn't done. "And since when do Nazi lives matter?"

"I told you, I—*koff koff*." The Raven takes a coughing break. "I'm trying something new."

"Sure, T."

"Stop flirting and direct me." A-Girl is already heading back toward the dock.

"We're not—" The Raven sighs. "Step two. Insertion."

Lady Vengeance snorts, but Kid Justice's voice comes over the comm. "Just be glad Y isn't here."

"You're right, she wouldn't even *hesitate*."

Reparation grunts. "Y'all are *weird*."

~

The fishing boat skims through the fog with unnatural speed and no sound of cutting waves. This is, of course, because A-Girl is carrying them from the dock toward Alcatraz.

"I still think using the boat like a *boat* would have been easier," Lady Vengeance says, as she holds a fearshield against the fog. "And way more comfy."

"Radar, V," The Raven says over the comm.

"Oh, and they won't see a flying boat?" she asks.

"The fog disrupts it." Kid Justice says. "And I can manipulate the radio signals anyway."

"So why didn't we just take a boat?" she asks again.

"Starting to regret bringing you weirdos along," Reparation mutters.

Lady Vengeance has to admit that having A-Girl carry the boat is much faster than rowing or motoring over, if nothing else. They make landfall in just a couple minutes and pile out of the boat in various postures of stealth. In his black outfit, Kid Justice—nah, that's too cumbersome, she's just going to refer to him as Orestes—gets out, crouches, and crab walks as best he can to take cover behind a nearby boulder. Reparation does similarly, though he's a little less awkward about it. As for Lady Vengeance herself, she steps out in full view, adjusting her covert black costume. Man, this thing gives her such a wedgie. A-Girl lands next to her, annoyed.

"Boys, it's fine," Lady Vengeance says. "A's handled all the sentries—"

A cry of alarm goes up from the watchtower.

"Ugh," A-Girl says. She projects herself away, making Lady Vengeance stagger from the force.

A man in military fatigues goes flying from the tower into the open water. Then A-Girl is back, leaving a little crater in the uneven concrete underfoot. She crosses her arms and refuses to meet anyone's gaze.

"Report," The Raven says. "What's happening? Contact?"

"Just a guard," Lady Vengeance says. "A took care of it."

As if on cue, an air raid siren starts blaring, and alarm lights flash throughout the complex.

"Not fast enough," The Raven says. "Prather forces mobilizing."

"Welp. Time for that distraction." Lady Vengeance nods to Reparation and A-Girl. "Ready?"

Reparation grins, his teeth shining in the diffuse light. He bashes his metal-shod gloves together. "Time to get it."

"Whatever," A-Girl says.

Lady Vengeance puts her hand on Orestes's shoulder. "Kid, you're with me."

Orestes gives A-Girl a long look, then nods. "Let's go."

~

"Yo," Reparation says, as alarms flash and whine. "You here, girl?"

A-Girl shakes her head, forcing herself to stop staring after Orestes. She doesn't much like Lady Vengeance's arm around his shoulders, but that's ridiculous. She should be furious with him, and she is, but it's not like he's going to sleep with her aunt. Right? She's got to focus.

"Stealth isn't my thing anyway," she says. "And I'm not a girl. I'm a grown woman."

"Yeah, right. How old are you? Sixteen?"

"Nineteen."

"Damn." Reparation grins. "I'm gonna fight with a teenage girl? *Shit.*"

"Listen, asshole—"

"No shade, no shade, sure you'll do your best."

A-Girl rolls her eyes. This Reparation dude seems cool and all, but the paternalism is starting to get a little annoying. Some deeply ingrained misogyny, maybe? She'll show him.

They've made their way to the recreation yard, which is surrounded by a fence and razor wire to keep out curious tourists.

A-Girl offers Reparation a hand, but he declines with a wave, then bounds over the fence, no problem. She floats over and touches down in the firing solution of Prather's ICE goons, who all shout down at her from elevated positions about this being "a restricted area" and to "get on the ground" and "hands behind your head" and things like that.

"What you waiting for, girl?" Reparation asks.

"Calm your tits," A-Girl says. "Just wait—"

There. She sees the telltale flash of green light that indicates a power drainer being set up.

"Just a second."

One instant, she's there, and the next she projects herself toward the elevated walkway, leaving a crater in the yard. She smashes into the crenellation, exploding it in all directions, seizes the drainer, and projects herself back into the yard. She lands beside Reparation with enough force to make him stagger a little bit in a very satisfying way.

Above, panicked shouts to "hold your fire!" rain down as the ICE goons try to get their bearings. A few isolated shots ring out, and Reparation holds up his arm to bat them aside like annoying mosquitos. His suit isn't bulletproof, but it's the kind of flexible atomic mesh The Raven uses to make all their outfits. It also coincidentally makes Reparation's backside look particularly nice. Not that A-Girl was looking or anything.

"Hold up, is that goofy looking thing—?" he asks, pointing at the big sci-fi rifle that is the drainer.

"Sure is." A-Girl holds up the rifle, then shatters it over one knee. Green energy fizzles out with a disconsolate series of pops.

"Damn, girl." Reparation nods. "Respect."

A-Girl shrugs and tosses the splintered halves of the million-dollar piece of machinery aside. "You sure you're ready for this?" she asks, dusting her hands clean. "Not that I care."

"Is a bulletproof Black man ready to take on a team of Nazi scum?" He nods. "You *should* care."

"You—you're right, I'm sorry. It's just ... Life sucks, you know?"

She fully expects Reparation to rebuke her for being a whiny, selfish little asshole right now, but instead he nods again. "Allah gives us no challenge we cannot overcome," he says.

"Huh." A-Girl will have to think about that one. "Why aren't they shooting is the question."

"The fash are always cowards," Reparation says. "No one wants to be the first one we target."

"Maybe." She wonders, though. Are they just that afraid of the two bruisers in the yard? Or maybe they realize A-Girl could take them all out in seconds, and not in a pretty way?

Which is when the lights start flashing around a loading bay door at the far side of the yard. Reparation braces for a new threat, while A-Girl just stands there blinking.

"Oh," she says. "That's ... not good."

~

"Turn right," The Raven's voice crackles over the comm.

"T, I'm telling you, there's no door there," Lady Vengeance says. "Just a solid wall, slightly chipped, but not like a secret door or anything. When did you say you got those schematics?"

"This map is original, cross-referenced with public records and my own exploration," he says, a little huffy. "You remember our trip to San Francisco."

"In '97?" Lady Vengeance scoffs. "Not really. Just a lot of sneaking around. The sexy kind."

"Fine," The Raven says. "Straight forward. Watch for a concealed door on your right."

Lady Vengeance rolls her eyes, then flashes Orestes a grin. "Bet you missed this, eh, kid?"

Orestes can't help but smile. Not that he's at all interested in listening to The Raven and Lady Vengeance do their usual arguing and/or flirting banter, but because it all feels comfortably familiar. He was locked away so long, he started to forget what it felt like to be his own independent person, let alone spend time with people he cares about.

The under tunnels of Alcatraz aren't nearly as awesome as Jerry Bruckheimer's filmography would lead you to think. They're mostly cramped and disused rooms full of dust and broken furniture. No mine cart or track in sight, let alone a boiler that spews flame at set intervals. Which is a shame, because with the Godsight, Orestes could definitely get through any number of time-based traps. As it is, it's mostly dark, grimy, and unpleasant.

"So," Lady Vengeance says, as they fail to find The Raven's mythical access door for another ten paces or so. She touches her earpiece, cutting off her mic. "How'd it feel, being dead?"

No question really surprises Orestes anymore—not with the Godsight operating on full blast since the Goblin Queen's spell punched him out of Malcolm Ali—but he hasn't formulated a proper response to this one. He knew it would come up, but during a mission?

"Strange. I don't think I died so much as moved. Y'know, got a new apartment?" He shrugs. "One second, I was in that hospital room, the next, I was inside Malcolm. And while I was there, I could see what he was doing, feel what he felt, understand what he wanted."

"Even, like, romantically?" Lady Vengeance asks, because of course she does. "Sexually, even?"

"Malcolm's a very fastidious man," Orestes says.

"You mean closeted."

"No—not exactly," Orestes says. "But he didn't hook up with anyone while I was inside him, if that's what you're asking. Just beat up a bunch of Prather's goons. Bro really hates Nazis."

"Who doesn't."

"The twenty percent of Americans who voted Republican in 2016?"

"Whoa. Look who got radicalized inside a modern-day Black Panther." Lady Vengeance gives him a sidelong, approving look. "It's a good look on you, kid."

Orestes almost argues, but he has to concede the point. That's not a quip he would have made before last year. His white dads raised him to look for nuance and go along to get along. But between Prather's policies, street violence, and more discrimination packed into those six months than in his whole life in Seattle, his time spent inside Malcolm has clearly changed him.

"If anything, he has some chemistry with T—with you know who."

Lady Vengeance does a double take. "You mean Tony? No shit."

"None." Orestes nods. "Are you two ... on again or off again?"

"Oh, kid, that is so complicated, I don't even know how to *begin* to answer."

"Well ... what do you *want?*" Orestes asks.

"That question doesn't even *have* an answer."

"Hold up." Orestes steps in front of Lady Vengeance, arms crossed, forcing her to stop. "I know deflection is your thing, but you know you deserve to be happy, right?"

Lady Vengeance stares at him quizzically. "What does that even mean?"

Orestes isn't sure what to say. Which is to say, he *knows* what to say, but isn't sure if he should. The path ahead seems dark and clouded regardless of how he puts it, and he doesn't want to follow the Godsight's course. Instead, he adjusts his sight and his plan.

"Only when you're willing to face things," he says.

That definitely means something to her, but she hides the flash of recognition beneath her wry half-smile. "Okay." She crosses her arms. "Enough cryptic bullshit. Do you know something?"

"A lot of things," he says. "But this is a longer conversation."

"Fine," she says. "So open the secret passage so we can get this over with. I know you know where it is, Godsight."

Orestes pushes open a door mostly hidden by cobwebs and an old tarp.

"You could have done that this whole time," Lady Vengeance says. "If we're late, that's on you."

He resists the urge to correct her.

The Raven's map was, in fact, accurate, at least in identifying the hidden utility corridor that leads up toward Cellblock B, identified by a peeling painted letter on the wall. Handprints and muddy footprints mark the floor and walls, and his Godsight tells Orestes this corridor was part of the great escape Alcatraz is famous for. Lady Vengeance is a little too determined just at the moment to bring it up, though, so he privately enjoys that bit of historical trivia.

The Alcatraz blocks are organized in two levels of cramped, outdated cells that lack the amenities of unpleasant and poorly modernized American prisons. The place was last used as a prison fifty years ago, after all, and the cells were only just getting upgraded with hot water shortly before the place closed. They're small, stained, have no privacy, and smell like rot, blanketed over with the ever-present tang of salt water.

And in those cells are people.

Not criminals, and certainly not anyone who's had anything like a trial, but just people abducted off the street or from their places of work. Hispanic, Middle Eastern, Black ... all sorts of marginalized people the Prather administration campaigned on as "undesirable" in his "restored" America. They stink of body odor and buckets of human waste that haven't been emptied in a couple days, at least. Orestes has only to look at the huddled forms with their gaunt, desperate faces and empty eyes to fully comprehend the horror of Prather's "America First" policies.

"Fuck," Lady Vengeance says, her confidence faltering with horror. "This is Auschwitz shit."

Orestes agrees, but the atrocity hits differently for him. Disgust, rage, unreasoning urge to destroy Prather and his minions, yeah, sure. But a year ago, he'd have been shocked to see such reckless and inhuman abuses. Now, though? After six months inside a bulletproof gay Black man called "Reparation"? Now all of this just seems inevitable.

Elect a Nazi, get a Holocaust.

He reaches out to stop Lady Vengeance before two guards, toting assault rifles, come into view at the far end of the cellblock, their route pointing in this direction. The blaring alarm outside the cellblock doesn't seem to have pulled them away from their patrol route, which is annoying. Orestes and Lady Vengeance take cover behind a stack of equipment crates, bodies pressed close together in the cramped space. Orestes feels the thrumming tension in her, even if he couldn't also pick up the vibe of her mounting rage. She's about to explode, and unless he finds something to point her at—and soon—she's going to go nova and give them away.

"Stay calm," The Raven says over the comm. He can see what's going on because he hacked into the security cameras to cover their infiltration. "A and M have engaged in the exercise yard."

The guards have come close enough that their voices carry. "Man, you know what's going on upstairs?" one asks.

"Probably some kinda drill," says the other.

"Yeah, probably." The guard grimaces, making his sparse moustache distort in a blob on his pasty face. "Stinks in here. Can we hose them down again?"

"Once a day. Orders are orders."

"Ugh, *fine*."

Lady Vengeance suddenly goes very cold and still. "How many?" she asks between her teeth.

"Four," the comm buzzes. "Two on the ground floor, two above—"

"How many *prisoners*?" Lady Vengeance asks.

"V," Orestes says in a warning tone.

"Manifest says two hundred," The Raven says. "Can't confirm. ICE keeps terrible records—"

That's the straw that breaks the camel's back. First Lady Vengeance switches off her comm, then she's suddenly moving from behind cover, and it's only the Godsight that allows Orestes to follow quickly enough to do anything.

The guards' eyes go wide, and their rifles come up awkwardly, but Lady Vengeance is faster. She levels one of the guards with not one, not two, but *three* blasts of crackling purple fear energy that smash into him like multiple strikes from a battering ram. The bolts of force project him backward, through the air, to crunch into the far wall with enough force to put a crater in the plaster. The other guard's rifle goes off, but Lady Vengeance has grasped the barrel in her claw and moved it to fire uselessly into the floor. The man starts to cry out, but she seizes his throat in her other hand, oil-black eyes burning, and she roars her rage into his face like a horror out of a nightmare.

Orestes realizes she pointedly didn't blast him away so she could take him out in a more personal fashion, and he can't say he disagrees. Not that he has time to comment, as the guards on the upper level alert and raise their weapons. Orestes is already tapping into the electrical flow of the devices rigged up in the cellblock, and he rides the flow onto the upper walkway. The power puts him right in the faces of two guards with assault rifles. Both weapons come up but pointed toward the detainees rather than Orestes himself. Maybe they're under orders, or maybe they're just desperate.

"Back off!" one of the guards shouts. "Back—"

Orestes taps into the kinetic potential of their weapon's magazines, and as they start firing, their guns click uselessly. "Attempted murder of unarmed civilians," he says, as he stalks forward. "That's not just a crime, it's a *war* crime."

The farther guard fiddles with his rifle, trying to clear what he assumes must be a jam, while the nearer one turns to Orestes and fumbles to draw his sidearm. "Stay back, you n—"

The slur cuts off as Orestes closes one hand, enhancing the guard's gravitational force. He collapses to the floor, crushed by a body that suddenly weighs a thousand pounds.

"Hate speech is technically protected by the First Amendment," Orestes continues, calmly laying out his case. "But I think you'll find that use of slurs is evidence of racially motivated animus, and under local law, that elevates your attempted mass murder to a hate crime. Not—" He steps close to the soldier's face but takes care not to touch him. "—that it much matters at that level of prosecution."

The second guard finally throws his useless rifle down and goes for his combat knife. "You better stay back. We're United States military, boy—you mess with us, you mess with—"

Orestes casually waves his other hand, unshackling the guard from gravity. The man's bravado trails off in a series of wails as he floats away from the floor. His sidearm slides from its holster, he fumbles it, and it goes spinning off to slap against the ceiling, pulled there by its own individual gravity.

It's actually a lot of effort to sustain three different gravitational fields, and Orestes's head starts to pound. He didn't even know he had these powers until his untimely disintegration, and he's never used them, but they feel as natural as breathing. Justice had these powers too, he understands, and he's so close to a higher level of knowledge that he can almost taste it.

"You okay?" he asks the detainees through the bars. "¿Estás bien?"

They nod. "¿Quién eres?" one of them asks, a tween girl who looks shockingly thin.

"Hijo del Justicia," he says, which he hopes makes sense.

Whether she understands, she stares up at him with wide, appreciative eyes.

A man's scream from below tells him Lady Vengeance is done with her guards. The irony of what he just said makes him wince inwardly. "You good, V?" he asks.

"Better," she says. "Can you open the cells?"

Orestes puts his hands on the bars, connecting to the rest of the cells and the locking mechanism. It's a simple matter to unlock all the cells on the block, which pop open with a buzz. The people shuffle out, exhausted, deprived, and on the verge of collapse, but mobile and alive.

Mission accomplished ... assuming they can get all these people off the island.

"O, you better get down here," Lady Vengeance says.

With a reassuring nod and an awkward pat on the head of the girl, Orestes hops over the railing and floats down by manipulating his own gravity. When his powers first manifested, he could only control electricity, and eventually fire, but now all the forces of the universe seem to be his to direct. Energy manipulation was only the beginning.

For her part, Lady Vengeance doesn't seem surprised to see Orestes flex these powers. Impressed, yes. Maybe even a little wary, sure. But surprised? If anything, the attitude he gets from her is more like "about time." One guard lies crumpled against the wall, groaning, and the one she attacked hand-to-hand hangs twitching from her claw, eyes rolled up in his head to show only the whites.

"Any trouble?" she asks.

He shakes his head. "What's the problem?"

Lady Vengeance points at a sigil—no, a *sign*—painted in yellow over a doorway marked with a D and an arrow. Is that just an optical illusion, or is the yellow symbol *moving*? It makes his mind swim and his head ache, as though his brain wants to claw its way out of his skull.

"That's—what is that?" he asks, averting his gaze before he throws up.

"Nothing good." Somehow, she's holding it together, but she's not looking directly at the symbol either. "That's a ritual mark. Whatever's going on here, it's not just a concentration camp. We're dealing with cultists, and who knows what heinous shit they've unleashed."

Horrifically, Orestes realizes the symbol is visible to all the cells in the block, and he wonders if having to stare at that thing was part of the cruel and unusual punishment ICE has subjected the detainees to. No, it doesn't even feel right to label this facility as ICE. It's something above and beyond—something cosmically evil in a way that even his enhanced Justice powers might not be up to defeating.

"What do we do?" he asks, his voice a hoarse whisper.

"We? Nothing." Lady Vengeance invokes power to fill her gauntlet. "Me? I'm going in there. You head to the yard and support the others."

"You're going alone?" Orestes asks.

He realizes his comm has been switched off this whole time, and he turns it back on to a barrage of A-Girl's sharp reports and Reparation's grunts. There's a battle going on.

"A?" Orestes asks. "A, are you—?"

"Contact in the yard. Hard targets." The Raven's voice crackles. "V, stay on mission, don't—"

Lady Vengeance pulls out her comm and stuffs it into her cleavage, as these suits have no convenient pockets. "Eldritch horrors are my specialty. But you've got to keep the cult busy. Can you do that?"

"V—"

"Can you do that?" she asks again, her glare brooking no protest.

He nods. "Be careful."

She smiles crookedly. "I'm always careful."

They both know that's bullshit, but neither spoils the illusion.

"Hey! Hey! You little Black bastard, you put me down right now!"

Orestes almost forgot about the guard whose gravity he all but suspended. The man has floated out over the railing and now stands to drop twenty feet to the cellblock floor. "You sure, bruh?"

"What? Of course I'm—" The guard's eyes widen. "Wait. Wait!"

Orestes releases him, and the guard falls with a crunch. The detainees stand around him, blank-eyed, as he lies groaning. Maybe he should do something about this, but just at the moment ...

As he heads out of the cellblock toward the exercise yard, the last thing he hears is Lady Vengeance's voice.

"Sit tight, people," she says. "And if anything happens to those guards, well, I didn't see it."

# CHAPTER SIXTEEN: ENDLESS WAR

The observation windows might as well be gray walls for all anyone can see through them. It's not that far away, but even the Golden Gate Bridge successfully hides in the damned fog. Let alone the other supposedly beautiful sights of the San Francisco Bay.

Not that Clinton Nash, Cabinet Secretary of Immigration and Customs Enforcement under Lyle Prather, Forty-Fifth President of the United States, wants to see any of that shit, but it feels particularly disrespectful that the fog set in when his private jet touched down yesterday. Oh sure, the limo driver told them it's been foggy for the last week, but that doesn't stop Nash taking it as a personal affront.

"The dreary shitty weather of this godless city, I swear to God," the man in the tight, poorly fitting business suit grumbles under his breath. "Fucking commies, probably doing this on *purpose*."

"Sir?" asks the ICE manager nervously showing him around the facility. "Mr. Secretary, sir?"

"Yeah, yeah," Nash says, already exhausted of the Alcatraz inspection. "Keep going."

Neither of them wants Nash to be here. The manager doesn't want the surprise inspection, and Nash would much rather be on the range or out hunting. But nooo, he's got to do some actual *work*.

Nash has had a tiring week.

The last few months, really, ever since that fiasco in Nevada back in the fall. A lot of heads rolled over that mess, and Nash himself almost lost his job. Prather blathered and fumed and threw a whole temper tantrum about it, especially how he'd been out of the loop and not informed. This despite the fact that Nash had filed repeat briefings to the President literally every day during Operation Fallen Angel,[11] and he'd had them reproduced in triplicate. After his work as Solace in 2008, Secretary Nash knew how to cover his ass, and it came in handy this time.

Prather wasn't happy, but then, when was he? If he'd ever been happy for one minute in his whole miserable life, he wouldn't have started a radio show about hating people or run for office as a Republican. Mr. President hates himself, and honestly, Nash is here for it. Prather deserves every instant of hate he heaps on himself, and Nash would happily add to said load if the little fool weren't his meal ticket.

Even so, Nash is looking forward to Prather's retirement from relevance. The thought of putting his fingers around that greasy little neck of his and squeezing ...

"Sir?" asks the manager, who's currently leading Nash down a damp, shitty hallway in the long disused prison. "Are you all right, sir?"

Almost raged out again. Goddammit.

"Yeah, get on with it." Nash affects a gruffness of voice that reminds him distantly of his time as Solace. Not that it would intimidate any gangbanger or pimp on the streets of Cobalt City or New York, but it has the desired effect on this officious little pussy.

"Right this way, sir," the worm of a middle manager says, clutching his clipboard.

The man isn't a warrior. Probably hasn't worked out a day in his life. Barely a scientist, either—just a bureaucrat who's good at kissing Prather's ass. Probably a homosexual, too. Everyone in this queer hellhole of a city. Nash instinctively reaches for his sidearm, but of course they disarmed him when he entered the facility. Some champions of the Second Amendment, stipulating their workplace some sort of gun-free safe space. Why does Prather even hire these liberal—?

---

[11] What a coincidence, because that's the novel that covers the events ex-supervillain Clinton Nash is thinking about: *Fallen Angel*, the previous book in this very series! ~ Editor Vogel

No, no, that's not fair. These people work for *you*, Clint. You wouldn't hire no rainbow brigade. Mindful of his heart, he pops one of his soothing pills and focuses on his breathing.

"I control myself," he murmurs to himself. "I control how I think about others."

Focusing on his breath, Nash forces the red out of his vision, practicing the biofeedback techniques his therapist taught him. He's seen a succession of commie thought police in armchairs— never wanted to go to any of that hippie-dippie, new-age crap—but finally he found a therapist out of Chicago who had managed to get some of it to stick. He never gave a shit about pronouns—not like Prather or the rest of his lackeys—but only whether someone was useful. And Dr. Fulton had taught him some good anger-management techniques. Not that he'll go back because, well, hippie-dippie, new-age crap. You can only go to so much therapy before you become a gay, after all. Or a commie.

They pass through Cellblock A, which Nash is disappointed to see doesn't actually house any detainees. The rooms seem to be mostly set aside for storage, and he wonders why the manager would bother showing him this. It would really help him if he had a gun to finger.

"Show me the Hole," he says. "I want to see where these illegals suffer most."

"Sir." The manager—whose badge says "Schmidt"—smiles awkwardly. "ICE isn't punitive. We don't punish or torture."

"Oh, of course." Nash gives the man a wink, which gets returned. "Hoses, right?"

"Definitely, there are hoses, sir."

"Good man. That's what I like to hear."

Alcatraz isn't so bad, when you get down to it. Not even remotely a modern facility, but that's what Nash likes about it. You could throw some brown-skinned scumbag in one of those cells and forget all about him, except for hosing him down with salt water pumped straight from the bay. He can practically feel the pain and suffering from decades of cruel and unusual punishment, and that provides a welcome silver lining to flying all the way to the deviant dumbfuckistan that is San Francisco ...

Which is when the alarm goes off, sounding klaxons like air raid sirens that fill the facility with an ear-splitting shriek. Lights flash, boots pound the creaking floors, and soldiers stream past on their way toward the exercise yard. All his instincts kick in, and Nash immediately goes into fight mode. He's suddenly aware of nearby cover and remembers the armory Schmidt showed him a couple rooms back. He has to practice more biofeedback to stay calm and business like.

"What's that?" Nash asks. "What's happening?"

"Intruders," Schmidt says, tapping his earpiece. "Don't worry, we're safe."

*Fuck* being safe. He wants to get in on the action.

"Get me a gun," Nash says.

"Sir?" Schmidt asks. "I'm afraid I can't let you ... wait. Really? Enhanced?"

Nash practically starts salivating. Suddenly, it's a decade ago, and he's getting ready for a fight. He's put on a few pounds since then, and his chiseled muscles have softened, but he's still a crack shot, if those assholes at the range are to be believed. "What kind of anti-cape ordnance do we have on-site?"

"Standard issue drainers and ... well." Schmidt gets an evil little grin. "I was saving this for the end of the tour, but would you like to see something really cool, sir?"

Nash is a little frustrated that Schmidt isn't giving him a gun, but something about that smile reassures him. "Operation Heavy Hitter?"

"The same."

Now it's Nash's turn to smile. This was the other reason he wasn't upset about this inspection. "Show me to command. I get to use the controls, right?"

Schmidt fairly salivates. "You can drive stick, sir?"

"What are you, gay?" Nash asks. "Of course."

~

The creature that comes out of the exercise yard gates looks at least vaguely like a person, if you expand your definition of "person" to include eldritch horrors from weird Nazi science. Part of it was human once—a withered, desiccated corpse, specifically—but there's so much metal bolted on that it's hard to see how much is organic and how much is robot. Its arms and legs are massive constructs, and a yellow light burns in the riveted metal breastplate that protects its torso. The cyborg zombie lurches forward, groaning and roaring like a dying animal.

"What is that?" A-Girl asks.

"Not what," Reparation says, his voice grim. "*Who.*"

"Huh?" Now she's even more confused.

The awkward and ungainly ten-foot-tall monstrosity moves much faster than it should, and A-Girl abruptly stumbles aside as Reparation strongarms her out of the way. The cyborg zombie smashes into him with enough force to drive him ten feet backward, leaving deep furrows in the dirt. The strike mostly staggers the zombie to a halt, but its arm has followed Reparation, telescoping out on clanking pneumatic pistons. It grinds him into the ground, despite Reparation's attempts to hold it at bay.

"Ahh!" A-Girl propels herself at the zombie cyborg's arm and smashes her fists into it with a clang. A wave of electricity rips through her, and she bounces off to sizzle on the ground, like a fly caught in a bug zapper. When she comes back to her senses, shaking her head to clear it, the robot has inched closer to Reparation. As it brings its other fist to bear, the limb opens to reveal ... is that a *flamethrower?*

She flies across and catches the flamethrower just before white-hot flame rushes out, narrowly missing Reparation's face. She holds it away, allowing fire to jet out into the yard, burning the last of the fog away. This is utterly ridiculous.

"Tyrone," Reparation says. "C'mon, Ty. Snap out of it."

For three blessed seconds, A-Girl has no idea what he means, until it dawns on her that he's addressing the body at the center of the cyborg, which she thought was a corpse but is, in fact, a living person. A skeletally thin man with deep brown skin, wisps of black and gray hair, and yellowed teeth with deeply receded gums. His eyes are yellow with jaundice and also some weird hazy glow.

"Oh, God," she says. "What the f—?"

The cyborg's defensive measure activates again, shocking her with several thousand volts of electricity, but this time A-Girl's ready for it. The voltage flows into her, and her red energy aura flares. With heightened strength, she twists the flamethrower nozzle, making the fire peter out. The arm hurls her aside, however, and she smashes into the wall of the exercise yard with enough force to jar her helmet loose and stun her, not to mention put a crater halfway through the wall.

"Ow," she says, head reeling. Then bits of the wall start exploding around her, and she puts up an arm to shield her face. "*Jesus.*"

It seems the ICE guards were holding their fire when she was close to the robot zombie, but now she's far enough away, they can take shots at her in relative safety. Those are high-powered rifle rounds, which aren't going to cause her any serious harm, but it's been a while since she's tanked concentrated gunfire, and those little stings are definitely distracting. She climbs to her feet, holding up her hand to block bullets, and looks at the overlook. A dozen shooters with high-powered rifles and ...

Abruptly, something slugs her right in the face, her head snaps violently to the side, and her vision goes halfway red as her right eye explodes.

~

"*Fuck.*" Lady Vengeance feels a sharp pain in her head and covers her right eye. It's almost like a mosquito flew right into her eye, but she blinks rapidly and there's nothing there.

Nothing but the squirming madness of the Yellow Sign carved onto the doors to Cellblock D.

She was wondering why the notoriously plentiful ghosts of Alcatraz hadn't reached out to her. She could feel the misery and suffering soaked into the place like mildew turned to black mold in the foundations. One doesn't have to be an empath to pick up on the long history of human torment, agony, depression, and just a tinge of useless hope that grips any long-operating prison, and especially the Rock. But a sickly film has covered all of it this whole time, blocking her psychic perception. The ghosts of this place are scared. They especially avoid Cellblock D, and now she sees why.

Over her long career, both in and out of the costume, Lady Vengeance has encountered any number of cosmically horrific entities, and the King in Yellow is very, very, *very* low on the list of threats she would ever want to get involved with again in any way. Her memories of that whole episode are fuzzy, though she's fairly sure they bear no resemblance to the actual events. She remembers a pallid mask sculpted from suspiciously human-like skin, which she only managed to avoid putting on because of ...

Suddenly, he's there, in a mostly human shape, leaning against the wall near the door bearing the sigil, clad in a slick black suit with dozens of white patches that she knows aren't patches. The filthy puddle in that part of the room doesn't touch his perfectly shined shoes, but it goes the other way around: his darkness seems to seep into this reality, warping the stone floor instead. Cracks extend through the stone, and the water starts bubbling as though simmering with intense heat. He has no eyes, no nostrils, no face— only teeth.

Otherwise, he looks like Tony.

"Vengeance," the avatar of the Many-Mouthed Devourer says, its voice smoky and bedrock-deep. "I come to you in your hour of need. I offer you my aid, this second time."

Lady Vengeance does consider it. For about two seconds.

"Pass," she says, and heads closer to the Yellow Sign, keeping her gaze carefully averted.

Azazel doesn't seem surprised, but he is still a bit bemused. "In your stubbornness, you would sacrifice fragments of your mind rather than fulfill our pact?"

"Why yes, I'd rather lose some braincells than give you my body or my soul."

Azazel chuckles. "Oh, Vengeance ... you say that as though you have a soul to lose."

Most people would not ignore a manifested demon god standing about ten feet away. Most sane people would start screaming, shit themselves, and/or prostrate themselves to its profane grace.

Vivienne Cain is not most people, and she hasn't considered herself sane since she was nine.

"There are powers gathering that you do not understand," Azazel says. "Much less can you resist them. Not alone. Not without me."

Wordlessly, Lady Vengeance inspects the edges of the Yellow Sign. She's seen some shit, but she still has a human mind, and it can only stretch so far. She avoids staring too long at the geometry that cannot be—at the twists and turns that seem to undulate as one watches—because she knows from experience that will only make it worse. She'll be trapped, constantly trying to understand the incomprehensible—scrabbling at the cosmic and ineffable—and in the meantime, her self will cease to exist or worse. Much like what Azazel wants from her.

"Vengeance," the demon says, his voice surprisingly gentle, like a kitten's first velvet purr.

She feels rapidly escalating pain—a scraping, tearing, gnawing sensation on her upper arm—and realizes Azazel's gnashing hand has touched her there. She jerks her arm away and staggers, but the lingering feeling of the demon's teeth remains. Ripping through skin and flesh and muscle and bone ...

And there is something so irresistible and compelling there that she can't help but focus on the feeling. Breath comes shallow, her blood courses fast, and her heart thuds at a rabbit's pace.

Abruptly, he pins her against the wall, a void of ceaseless hunger, and his mouths hover over her cheek, her lips, her neck, her breast. Lady Vengeance cringes away, her own teeth set on edge, and refuses to look upon him in his horror and magnificence. He speaks with a hundred voices: some pleading, some teasing, some screaming, some worshiping. All to her. All upon her. All *for* her.

"You need me," he says in her ear, sending shivers through her comparatively frail body. "You will call for me. And I will be there for you. When all others abandon you, *I* shall be there."

"Oh ... oh yeah?" she manages. "Prove it, then."

She feels his grin on her face.

Abruptly, a clap of thunder, the shriek of steel, and a horrific sound like the rending of fabric deafens Lady Vengeance and knocks her to the floor. Rocks and dust and bits of plaster fall all over her, and she manages to cover her head with her arms to protect it. When she looks up, ears ringing with the impact, sure enough, the doors to Cellblock D marked with the Yellow Sign aren't there anymore. Azazel reached through reality and tore the mark away, leaving mere traces of its foul malevolence to dance and writhe and crisp away like those snake fireworks that produce squamous coils of ash, only this ash is sickly yellow. She pointedly looks away from those leavings of the King in Yellow's power as she climbs haphazardly to her feet. At least the door is open: a yawning, smoke-filled portal into further horrors.

"Fuck," she says, though she can only dimly hear herself.

She heads into Cellblock D, braced for the madness that awaits.

~

A-Girl drops to the ground, gasping and crying out, covering her right eye, which is bleeding and watering in equal measure. Did someone just shoot her in the *eye*?

Her eye's still there, she confirms, but it's full of blood and seeing red. No one's ever shot her in the eye before, and she has no idea if her powers will heal it or not.

A-Girl sees the sharpshooter without a lot of searching, mostly because he's wearing a goddamn suit, rather than a tactical outfit. She almost thinks she's imagining things, but sure enough, there he is: a white guy, probably fifty-ish, with that slightly softened but still chiseled look of former military. And if she had any doubt, it goes away immediately when he grins a self-satisfied smirk at her.

That's *fucking* it.

"A ... ay on mission," her father's crackling voice says over her damaged comm. "Stay—"

A-Girl projects herself right at the sharpshooter, but he moves well for an old guy, throwing himself aside as she smashes like a railgun round into the elevated walkway. Stone and dust tumbles around her, and she sees that she has inadvertently shielded one of the ICE shooters from the collapse. Not the motherfucker who shot her. The ICE shooter blinks up at her, confused, and maybe he's about to thank her for saving his fascist life. She'll never know, because in the next second, she grabs him by his tacti-cool vest, whirls him around, and hurls him out to sea.

"A!" The Raven is shouting. "A—stay on—"

She smashes and crashes through the crumbling edifice after the sharpshooter in the business suit, who beats a tactical retreat along the walkway, shoving past ICE troopers in bulletproof vests that won't do *shit* against a human wrecking ball like A-Girl. They're just lucky they're not her target, and they get to go tumbling down into the exercise yard without every bone in their bodies shattered. That fucker in the suit, though ...

She busts through a load-bearing wall and a whole floor of the building tilts toward her. Not that she cares if this historic landmark collapses, but she isn't quite fast enough to get out of the way, and she catches the slumping building on her shoulder, forcing her to one knee as the red flames of her energy aura leak around the crumbling stone. It might not be the heaviest thing she's ever tried to lift, but it still pins her in place with sudden crushing pressure. So much power goes into just catching and holding the bulk of the thing that her energy aura dulls and gutters. A bunch of ICE agents sit or stumble nearby, braced for disaster, and she has, again, inadvertently saved them.

Her suited quarry pauses and glances out from behind a pillar. He grins.

"No," she says. "Don't you fucking *dare*—"

The rifle cracks, and a bullet slams into the side of her knee. It doesn't break the skin, but it strikes with enough force to disrupt her balance. The full force of the upper floor crushes the walkway under her, and she slides down in an avalanche of crumbling concrete, rebar, and tile. At least the cowering ICE agents go down as well, shouting and cursing in the collapse.

Her mistake, she thinks, as tons of rubble bury her in the yard, was thinking these fascist assholes give the tiniest shit about each other. And now they're all gonna be crushed under tons of rubble.

Only that isn't what happens. Instead, the rubble slows and stops, floating above A-Girl. It doesn't crush the ICE agents, either, who scramble or crawl away, mewling and cursing. She looks up, just the faintest flames flicking around her hair, and there he is, floating in a shimmering cocoon of blue energy, his eyes blazing with lightning, one hand extended down to restrain the debris.

Marcus Adonis Orestes.

"Look out—" A-Girl cries in warning, but Orestes raises a hand casually and stops the bullet to hover in the air next to him. Little sparks of lightning crackle off the spinning bullet as it slows, and it finally floats off into the air, its destructive potential entirely spent.

The shooter takes aim again, but Orestes sends the rubble he's floating with his mind toward that corner of the yard, where it smashes the supports and brings down the entire overhead walkway. The shooter vanishes in the avalanche of concrete and tile.

"Need some help?" Orestes asks, as the dust settles.

"I had it." A-Girl nods and climbs woozily to her feet. "Eventually."

"I'm sure you did." Orestes gives her a quirked smile, then floats down toward her. He touches her cheek, and she feels power sparkling inside him. Her body yearns for it—for him—and she forgets she's supposed to be angry. His other hand touches her other cheek, and he's cupping her bruised, dusty face. All her pain is gone, and it's everything.

"Hey," he says.

"Hi," she replies.

"Your eye," he says. "Are you okay?"

"No, but it'll heal."

He purses his lips. "May I?"

"Finally."

They kiss, and power explodes into and through her, as though she just touched a lightning rod. Instantly, her aura sparks and flares back to life, blazing pink instead of blood red. When she pulls away from him finally, all she wants to do is kiss him again, but there are some bad guys in need of punching first. He grins sheepishly, as if he can read her mind and feels the exact same way. No more words have to be exchanged.

Time to go to work.

# CHAPTER SEVENTEEN: THE THING THAT SHOULD NOT BE

Cellblock D is dark, but not in the mundane sense, like the lights just happen to be off. The darkness here is a palpable thing with depth and texture. A cloying mist of nothing that blocks light and warmth and life. It's like swimming in the deep end at night, but you can still breathe. For now.

This kind of darkness is familiar for Vivienne Cain. In some ways, it feels as though her whole life has been lived in the dark like this, grasping and flailing for a light switch that she'll never find. Her entire life, she has felt lost—like she shouldn't be here, but she is, and there's no path pre-blazed for her. Just a lot of fumbling and failing and falling flat on her fucking face.

How many nights has she awakened in a cold sweat, whether in a stranger's bed or her own, and desperately searched for something—anything—to ground herself? She's used everything from sex (frequently), booze (constantly), harder drugs (on occasion), and even magical intervention (never again) to try to fix herself, but nothing works. She just doesn't belong.

Maybe it started with the death of Supergroup, when she went on the run and faked her death, or maybe it was before that. Maybe Azazel should have taken her when she was eighteen. Or maybe even earlier—that she should have been the sacrifice to keep the world turning. She would have been, had not Tony DeSantes refused to let her die. That idiot.

Vivienne should have died a thousand times over, but here she is, still breathing, still fighting, when so many who should be alive aren't. Maybe she should just ...

She stops herself. This is bullshit. She has never once, in her whole miserable life, actively thought about killing herself, and that she's doing so now means something else is going on. Intrusive thoughts are nothing new, but that's going a bit far. Something is messing with her mind, and whether it's a ward or a cosmic horror is beside the point.

"You don't know who you're fucking with," she says to the black fog.

"He ... hello?" says a weak voice. "Is someone there?"

Fuck.

Vivienne bolsters her mental defenses with some of the fear energy she's carrying, and the existential angst fades to its usual dull rumble in the back of her mind. At the same time, she raises one hand and conjures a fearsword. It's more like a feardagger, honestly, but what she wants is the light, not the cutting potential. Purple radiance diffuses to the corners of the room like drops of blood in a stagnant pool. Hardly enough to light the place up, but enough she can faintly see.

It doesn't make things any better.

If she remembers the briefing correctly, Alcatraz's Cellblock D is where they kept the least desirable prisoners: the ones who fought with each other, fought with the guards, or otherwise caused too much of an uproar. Which, in early prison industrial complex speak, probably translated to requests to use the phone, complaints of food poisoning from the shitty cafeteria fare, or just looking at the guards for too long. Deeper in Cellblock D is "The Hole," the culturally ubiquitous euphemism for solitary confinement, which society would only learn fifty years later is basically the worst thing you can do to a human being. Learn it, but not care much about it, based on how prisons are run to this day. Because fuck convicts, right? They're barely human, who cares about their basic rights and needs?

Vivienne advocated long and hard for destroying the entire complex during their planning, and Tony pushed back. Not in principle, but in practicality. They didn't bring enough firepower to destroy the entire island, and the goal here is to minimize casualties, not squish or explode all the ICE agents and the detainees. Grudgingly, Vivienne had to concede the point. Killing all those hostages *would* suck.

What she sees now, however, fills her with such horror and dread that she wonders if preserving the facility, the island, or the bay itself is going to be an option.

The cellblock has been converted into the nightmare hate-child of a mad scientist's laboratory and a sacrificial ritual chamber to the Great Old Ones. She can't possibly guess at the function of the devices set up here. Best she can do is analogy, and she lands on something halfway between blood-saturated operating room where a dozen patients have died on the table, but no one has bothered to clean up, and an auto mechanic's stall slash chop-shop that fails every OSHA standard set in place, even the ones Prather hasn't stripped away. The connections among the bizarre science installations resemble tentacles more than wires, tightly wrapped in bandages soaked through with yellow-green blood and pus. The walls are twisted and warped: more flesh than concrete but not one hundred percent either way, oozing liver-blackened blood from weeping sores that look like eyes.

The chamber is, in short, a Lovecraftian horror show. Howie P was a neurotic, small-minded bigot, but he caught some glimpses. And this room would have given him an aneurysm or two.

Vivienne's immediate impulse is to channel as much fear energy as possible into breaking everything in sight, but there's a body actively on the table—in work, as it were. It takes her a second to understand that it's a person, mounted inside a bipedal mech. From the flippers and fins, she suspects this one is supposed to be aquatic, like some kind of partially human submarine. What's most striking, however, is the femme face peeking up at her from amongst the sci-fi horror.

"K ... kill ... me—" the heart of the robo-zombie says. "Please—"

This, Vivienne realizes, is the source of that plaintive whisper.

"What's your name?" Vivienne asks, touching the woman's face.

"N ... Naomi," she says. "Please—"

In Naomi's face, Vivienne sees any of a thousand young women she's met. Desperate, scared, so beaten down by the world that they don't think there's any way forward. Can't find any place where they can exist and be themselves. A woman loathed just for existing. She knows that woman. She's *been* that woman. And the

King in Yellow, his priests, Azazel, Prather, any of a horde of shitty waste-of-space men want her to be that woman again. Want all women to be that woman.

"Not today, Naomi," Vivienne says, lighting up the room with purple. "Not ever."

~

When the pink streak of energy comes flying toward him, as Reparation holds back the robo-zombie's crushing fist slowly driving him into the ground, it's the most beautiful thing he has seen in a long time. This fight has not been going well.

Tyrone Hughes and Malcolm Ali have been fighting all their lives, from that first day on the street in Fillmore, all through school, and as young men. They wore the same colors, fought the same stupid fights, scrabbled for the same prestige, and gave each other bruises and scars and good memories too. They're friends the way street kids can be friends: rivals, constantly trying to one-up each other and push the other down. Or at least that's the way it was until a few years ago, when Malcolm converted, changed his name, and got out of the life, while Tyrone stayed and just got worse.

Malcolm tried to fix things. He challenged Tyrone to have an earnest, vulnerable, man-to-man conversation. Invited Tyrone to come with him. Stopped short of confessing his feelings, but it didn't take a mind-reader to know what was up. Tyrone wasn't there for it. He blamed that nonsense on Malcolm being gay (though he didn't use such polite language) and his "weird Muslim shit." Malcolm would like to claim that he'd taken this all in stride and kept his temper, but obviously that wasn't true.

They hadn't seen each other for two years, but as soon as Malcolm heard Tyrone got picked up by ICE, he made it his mission to get him out.

It hasn't gone well.

Whatever Nazi science or magic or shit they put into this walking corpse that used to be Tyrone, it's too much for Reparation to handle alone. The thing is every bit as strong as him, if not stronger, with greater reach and punching power. The ICE agents firing their guns at him didn't hurt, but it didn't help either, as even though the bullets bounce off him to no effect, he still feels the impacts, and they distract him. If A-Girl hadn't twisted its flamethrower to uselessness, he'd be dead by now.

And speaking of—where the fuck did she go? Something happened, and she flew off and started bashing up the place. Not that he objects to destroying a symbol of the white hegemonic prison state, but he needs some damn backup here, and there she goes having some sort of emotional outburst. He should've known better than to rely on a teenage girl, despite the help she's provided.

Speaking of, as they're locked together, the abomination brings its left arm down at him like a super-heated club. The metal glows bright red from all that trapped fire, and Reparation doesn't need Godsight to tell him to steer clear. He bobs and weaves under the wild swing, and when it strikes the ground, it explodes in a shower of flame, smoke, and shrapnel. The impact knocks him to the ground, and the creature staggers too. Reparation lies there for a bit, unable to hear through the whine of the explosion, his eyes swimming and blurry in the smoke. Maybe the robo-zombie took itself out. Maybe ...

No such luck. The creature looms back up to its feet through the smoke, and Reparation knows he's fucked. Its left arm ends in a ragged mess of wires and tubes that pour noxious fumes into the air, but its grasping right hand is still there, and it closes around Reparation's throat. The pistons start to push, and his windpipe contracts.

"Tyrone," he tries to say. "Ty—"

Which is when A-Girl swoops back in, leaving a trail of pink fire behind her, and smashes into the robo-zombie with enough force to make it stagger. The pressure lets up, allowing Reparation to fall back to the ground and catch his breath. Before the robo-zombie can attack again, A-Girl flies in from the other side and wrenches its arm harmlessly toward the sky and pulls the whole monstrosity back against the building, where she pins it in place. It tries to shock her, but that only makes her pink aura flare brighter.

"Go!" she cries. "Get it!"

Blood surging through him, heart racing, Reparation climbs to a crouch and launches himself forward, fist cocked back. His rage is popping off, and he sees only red. These Nazi fucks have done enough, and it's time to end them. Put them all in the ground.

He brings down his hand and chops through the robo-zombie's exposed arm, shearing it off at the elbow. Electricity crackles and pops uselessly from the severed stump, and the monster slumps, waiting for the killing blow. Reparation grasps his hands over his head, ready to bring them down on the thing's toxic heart.

A wave of power flows out from the heart of the prison, and Reparation hears a sound like a scream from another world and another time. The cacophony of thousands of long-dead voices, some human and others very much not. A bitter malaise strikes him, filling his mind with squirming, writhing madness, and for a terrifying second, his body feels as though it will unravel into its constituent parts, skin flaking off and organs rupturing, but it disperses as soon as it touches him, leaving him shivering and panting. Forever after, he will remember only a lingering sense of brushing against something man was never meant to know.

He sees Tyrone's face, sputtering and spitting at the core of the monster they built around him. The yellow light lifts from his eyes, and he looks up with confusion. "Mal?"

Malcolm Ali stops at the last second, holding his fist cocked over Tyrone's face. "Ty?"

"Do it," Tyrone says. "Look what they done to me. Look—"

Malcolm lowers his arm and instead presses his forehead to Tyrone's. "I gotchu, brother. I gotchu."

Bloody tears squeeze out of Tyrone's jaundiced eyes, and he cries for the first time in decades.

A-Girl watches, her pink glow a stark contrast with her black costume, but it still works. Then the stone next to her head explodes from a high-velocity round.

"Oh, yeah," she says. "Be back in a minute."

"Nah." Malcolm puts a hand on her shoulder. "I got this."

~

The radio crackles with the cries and disorganized confusion of officers freaking the hell out.

"Goddammit," Clinton Nash says, as he loads a fresh magazine into his assault rifle. His leg still hurts from the fall, but he managed to stay upright and mostly hidden.

He tagged A-Girl with what should have been a kill shot. Prather may be all about trimming budgets, but Nash made sure his facilities had top-of-the-line weaponry, including these anti-cape rifles that fire hollow-point, depleted-uranium rounds that can take out an Abrams tank with a well-placed shot. Putting a bullet in her eye should have put her down for the count, but somehow, she's still up and moving. Worst of all, there's some Black punk floating there stopping his shots with his own ridiculous powers. And they take a moment to fucking *kiss* of all things?

That is the most infuriating part of what is already a shitty battle. It's the disrespect that gets him. They don't even seem to think of him as an annoyance, let alone a threat.

"Motherfucker," he says, teeth gritted.

A-Girl flies off, opting to attack the mech, and that annoys him further.

"It's not over, you pink bitch," he murmurs. "But fine, go ahead. I'll just kill your boyfriend before you get back."

He'll show them. He'll pull out the victory.

He has an opportunity. Blue Boy doesn't seem to be looking his way. Probably assumed he went unconscious in the collapse. So if he times this just right ...

He leans out of cover to assess his target. No point shooting at Blue Boy, not if his ridiculous powers will just stop the shots. But if Nash can distract him, that might give him a chance. He took down A-Girl with one hit to the eye, and if he can land a second, it might penetrate. If he can kill the pink popstar, what a coup that'll be. What ...

A wave of nausea washes over him abruptly, leaving Nash sputtering and confused. His mind is filled with a jumble of bizarre, disturbing images, mostly of dismembered human bodies and tentacles, but he shakes it away. He's seen worse. *Done* worse.

It's going to take more than some stupid mind-games to stop *Solace*.

That's right. That's who he is. The vigilante who took out a string of convicts who escaped justice. Who saw justice served. Who protected America from the foreign invasion poisoning its blood.

And he's going to do the same thing here.

The radio crackles again with an official withdrawal order, but Solace ignores it. Fuck these cowards. They're all fired, as soon as he gets back to the office. They'll be better off if they die in battle here. That way they'll be heroes, rather than traitors.

The wave seems to have had more impact on the boy with the blue lightning, who looks confused and troubled as he starts to sink toward the ground. Solace finds the unmoving body of an ICE agent—idiot got himself half-buried under rubble—and strips the two grenades from his belt. One flashbang, one fragmentation. He pops the pin on the flashbang and lets it cook. He can do this.

Even if he's the last one standing—the last one with any balls—he's going to win the day. No mercy for the enemies of America. Death is the only justice for these terrorists.

Especially the brown ones.

Solace leans back out of cover and hurls the grenade.

Blue Boy hardly seems to realize the attack is coming. The grenade explodes, and he looks up in the half-second after the flash and thunder.

No point aiming at Blue Boy, so Solace targets A-Girl. There's a lot of haze, but he can hit that weak spot ...

Blue lightning crackles, warping the air and wind, and the bullet goes wide. It shatters off the wall behind A-Girl. She and the other guy—another Black dude, Jesus, there are two of them?—look in his direction. Shit.

At least Blue Boy seems to be wavering a little. Solace pulls out the second grenade and tosses it. Even as the grenade flies, he raises the rifle to his shoulder and takes aim through the scope.

As such, he has a perfect view as the older Black dude steps up next to the guy with the blue powers, catches the grenade, and holds it against his chest. That can't possibly be what Solace just saw, can it? Who would do something so insane? But sure enough, the grenade goes off, and instead of a dismembered brown body, the guy only loses the front half of his shirt. He looks at Solace, eyes narrowing.

"Shit," Solace says, and starts firing.

Too late. The shirtless guy steps in front of blue boy and blocks the bullets with his rippling pecs and chiseled abs. Is that an eight pack? Ten? Solace shivers.

He clicks the rifle to full auto, unloading dozens of bullets into the guy as he approaches, but to no avail. He tries to flee to a better position, but his leg refuses to work. The Black guy grabs his still-firing rifle and bends the barrel nearly double.

"Fuck you!" Solace shouts. "Do you know who I—?"

A gentle tap to his stomach is still hard enough to double him over, and he collapses to the ground.

"Nah," the guy says. "No one gives a shit."

~

"Marcus!" Angel is saying, though he can barely hear her over the buzz. "Are you okay?"

Orestes nods in what he hopes is reassurance, though he's a little embarrassed the flashbang actually stunned him. It never even occurred to him to try to control light and sound. Learn something new every day, apparently. When Angel puts her arms around him, though, it all fades in her embrace.

Malcolm reappears, dragging the guy in the suit with the assault rifle.

"Is that ... Immigration Secretary Nash?" Orestes asks. "The head of ICE?"

Malcolm shrugs his impressively muscled shoulders.

"That's the son of a bitch who shot me in the eye," Angel says.

Orestes blinks. Is that what happened? Her eye is red with blood and clearly damaged, but when he overcharged her, it started healing as fast as she always does. Also, her hair is longer.

"You're not going to kill him?" Angel asks Malcolm.

Orestes looks over at Malcolm as well, suddenly tense. Tony DeSantes insisted on minimal casualties on this mission, but the head of ICE? A member of Prather's cabinet? And a former supervillain at that?

"He who kills a man," Malcolm says, "it is as though he killed the whole world."

And with that, he drops Nash unceremoniously to the dirt and goes to the wreckage of the robo-zombie, kneels, and starts reassuring his friend.

Orestes knows this isn't over yet, and he looks at Angel. She stands over Nash, her knuckles cracking. Blood still smears her face, and her body trembles all over with tension.

The radio crackles, and it sounds like Tony has caught on as well. "Angel, think about this. Don't make that man a martyr. He—"

In one fluid motion, Angel digs out her comm and crushes it between her fingers.

"Angel, don't," Orestes says. "He needs to be tried and held accountable."

"By Prather's corrupt SCOTUS?" Angel scowls. "Not likely."

"Angel—"

"Don't try to stop me, O."

"I won't," he says. "But think about this. This isn't you."

She doesn't look at him, but she bites her lip. He can see the conflict in her, even without the Godsight. And he's got to talk her down before ...

"Hey." Vivienne appears out of the shadows of the broken-open prison, carrying a limp woman in her arms. "A little help here?"

The many detainees are following her as well, wandering like animated corpses themselves out into the thin San Francisco light. The fog has mostly burned off, and it's going to be a lovely day. Orestes wants to help direct them, but he feels very strongly that if he leaves, Angel will murder Secretary Nash, and that will be a step too far. And he can't expect Vivienne to take his side.

"Shit, don't all speak at once," Vivienne says. "Thanks for saving the day, V. I'm sure that cosmic horror influence you dispelled was horrible. Why yes it was, O, thanks for asking."

"V," Orestes says, his tone tense.

Angel hasn't looked up from the unconscious Nash, who is breathing annoyingly smoothly.

"Oh." Vivienne purses her lips. "Yeah, you should kill him."

Angel and Orestes both look up at her, surprised. "Huh?" Angel asks.

"Well, I don't object to killing on principle," Vivienne says. "And I'm trying to set a good example for your father, but this guy's a real piece of shit who will go on to harm thousands more."

Angel looks at her blankly.

"Hey, they were doing some really shitty stuff in there, including turning detainees into cores for their death mechs. So if you want to crush his head like a grape, I won't say a word. Like, I won't say he's Hitler, but if you had the chance to kill, like, Göring or some other mid-level Nazi shitstain before the Holocaust started, would you? Just stomp on his head and get it over with."

"Jesus, V," Orestes says. "What—?"

"Don't worry, I won't tell your dad if you don't. And even if we did? I think he'd understand."

Angel just looks ill. She gives Nash a little kick, probably shattering his leg, then walks away.

Orestes lets out a relieved breath.

"What?" Vivienne asks. "Was that a big deal?"

*Bigger than you know*, Orestes thinks but doesn't say. "You're not going to kill him yourself? After that big speech?"

"Better." Vivienne raises a hand crackling with purple fear energy. "I'll curse him so his dick doesn't work unless he's jacking it to unicorns and cotton candy."

"Gross." Orestes shrugs. "Fair, but gross."

Malcolm appears, carrying his friend Tyrone, along with some mechanical parts that he couldn't immediately detach from him. The man is, miraculously alive, and seems to be sleeping peacefully.

"Mission accomplished," Malcolm says.

"Not to toot my own horn," Vivienne says. "But I kicked a Great Old One's ass."

"Whatever," Angel says, but she's smiling faintly. The pink glow may have something to do with it. "I need a shower."

"You do," Malcolm says.

"Ugh. *Rude.*"

"After we get these people to safety," Orestes says.

"Yeah, yeah," Vivienne says. "Thanks, *Justice.*"

Orestes can't help but grin. "Is this it? Is this the moment?"

"Which?" Angel asks.

He smirks. "The slow-mo walk."

"Hell yeah," Vivienne says.

As Alcatraz crumbles and burns behind them, they head for the boats Tony has already dispatched to pick them up, escorting a small army of illegally detained humans—huddled, teeming, yearning to be free. Full of hope for the first time in a long time.

# CHAPTER EIGHTEEN: NEW RULES

The days after Operation Alcatraz Freedom have passed in a hazy blur.

Yumi extended their stay at the Fairmont to a full week, leaving them plenty of time to decompress and lay low while the Prather administration raged. And rage it does, though not to much effect. One of the things the Con Artist in Chief swears to do is round up every single "illegal" liberated from Alcatraz, but his continued failure to do just that makes him look as weak and incompetent as he is.

The San Francisco mayor's office released a statement within hours of the assault, both expressing outrage and denying knowledge of the facility, though Vivienne side eyes that. No way ICE could just take over a national landmark in their city without some paperwork. What, did people just not notice the tours stopped going? Regardless, liberal San Francisco rallies to the cause, filing lawsuit after lawsuit to restrict ICE's activities in the city or—preferably—block them altogether. Prather's war on "sanctuary cities" seems to be grinding to a halt at the San Andreas Fault.

In the meantime, Tony has the same doubts Vivienne has about the local government, so he's taken charge of getting the detainees medical attention, shelter, and protection from subsequent ICE arrest. He is, unsurprisingly, incredibly good at this, and those detainees vanish back into their American lives as thoroughly as if they were in witness protection. It does, however, take up a lot of Tony's time, and they haven't seen much of him since the operation.

Malcolm Ali isn't around either. He pronounced the lot of them "whack," exchanged one last moment with Orestes, then headed out into the night. Vivienne suspects his friend Tyrone being in surgery had something to do with that, and Tony is keeping her updated on Tyrone's progress. Prognosis is good, though he'll have a few prosthetics and a long road to recovery. Somehow, with the warm affection coming off Malcolm despite his tough exterior, Vivienne is sure Tyrone will be okay.

Which leaves the three of them alone in the penthouse at the hotel. Or, more accurately, it leaves Vivienne alone on the balcony knocking back Old Fashioneds while Angel and Orestes make up for lost time in the master bedroom. Mostly, she takes in the view, listens to podcasts on her headphones, and drinks to shut out the love and lust pouring out of the penthouse suite.

Good for them, honestly.

They meet up for meals, Vivienne pleasantly drunk and the kids exhausted. For this, the third evening, Tony left a good recommendation for a pizzeria, and while Angel shovels back slice after slice, Vivienne gets a rare opportunity to connect with Orestes. The kid is giving her the eyeball, which means he's got something to say, and she's not gonna like it.

"What's up, O?" Vivienne asks. "If you want another slice of the veggie, act fast."

Orestes purses his lips. He starts to speak a couple times, stops, rethinks, and corrects himself. Seems he's been going over this for a while. "It's gonna be all right," he says finally.

"The pizza situation?" Vivienne looks dubiously at the four empty boxes and grabs a last piece for herself.

"I mean, in general," Orestes says. "Things will work out."

"Okay." Vivienne bites into the pizza, which is a lot juicier and messier than she expected. "Like in a 'it's cool bro' sort of way, or a 'I see dead people' kind of way?"

"When my body ... dissolved, I became pure energy, and I could only use the Godsight for a while. I floated for a long time, between the physical world and the immaterial, and I could see across time with no problem. It took a long time to figure out that's what I was doing, but once I did—"

"So you saw the future," Vivienne says. "Literally."

"And the past," Orestes says.

186

"Do I work it out with Ruby?" Vivienne asks. "I know, I know, you can't tell me, or it'll change—"

"Yes," he says.

"Oh." Vivienne blinks. "That's good—"

"But you have to call her," Orestes says. "You know, 'call me or don't,' like she said."

"Goddammit." Vivienne's face falls. "I'm not sure I like this whole omniscience thing."

"Marcus," Angel says, her voice slightly whiny. She has made a mess of herself the way only someone who has rapidly eaten four pizzas can. "I need to take a shower."

"Okay," Orestes says. "I think there are fresh towels—"

"I mean," Angel says, very pointedly. "I need to take a *shower.*"

"Okay?"

"Kid." Vivienne raises an eyebrow at him.

"Oh. *Oh.*" Orestes grins, slightly embarrassed. "Let's go do that then."

"Obviously."

The kids get back to it, and Vivienne is considering whether to try to get some sleep on the couch while blasting a British horror anthology show or maybe jump off the balcony when the doorbell for the suite rings. The sound of the shower drowns it out, so neither Angel nor Orestes is going to get it, so Vivienne forces herself dizzily to her feet and heads to the door.

Standing there, in a hoodie and jeans, is Tony DeSantes.

"You used the door this time," Vivienne says.

"I did last time, too."

"I distinctly remember you climbing over the balcony like a crazy person."

"Only because—it doesn't matter. Can we talk?"

Vivienne shrugs and pushes the door open farther, then walks away.

With a grunt, Tony follows, then immediately pulls up short at the vigorous sounds from the master bedroom. It's petty, but Vivienne is glad she didn't warn him. "Is that—?"

"It sure is."

He smiles faintly. "Glad they worked it out."

"When the love of your life abruptly comes back from the dead, it's ... complicated."

He nods.

"Heh, sorry—I don't mean to be maudlin or autobiographical," she says. "Balcony?"

"Balcony."

"Beer?"

"I'm on serious painkillers."

"That a no?"

"*Viviana.*"

"I'll grab you one anyway."

She does—a couple, in fact—and they head out to the balcony, which is more like its own small park on top of the hotel. The fog that has blanketed San Francisco the last few days finally lifted for good as of this morning, making way for sunny skies and a truly outstanding sunset. The air is a bit nippy, but that's what blankets and the propane fire are for. It'd be romantic, if it weren't so fraught.

Okay, it's a little romantic anyway.

"You look terrible," Vivienne says, which is both true and not. His face still has some bruises and a butterfly bandage over his good eye to hold his brow together, while he wears an eyepatch over the missing one. One of his arms is in a sling, and he carries his briefcase suit, of course. That said, there's a certain danger and power to him that Vivienne can't help but find way too enticing.

*No, no, you're supposed to be mad at him,* she thinks.

At least they're not snuggling under the same blanket or *other* things.

Tony looks out at the horizon—at the sun sinking behind the Golden Gate Bridge and the column of smoke still rising from the destroyed Alcatraz complex. Considering how much the man hates cops and the prison industrial complex, Vivienne suspects blowing up a national monument to both might be on his bucket list. It occurs to her then how little they know each other anymore. Faking your death and going into hiding for over a decade will do that.

Vivienne pours herself a healthy glass of bourbon. She'll drink from the bottle when she's alone, but somehow, she feels like she better behave when Tony's there. "You said you wanted to talk?"

Tony takes a sip of his beer, strong meds or no. He turns his one eye toward her. "I'm sorry."

188

"Ha." Vivienne coughs, almost burning her throat on the bourbon like a goddamned rookie and not what she is: a professional. "For what, exactly? For fucking my girlfriend and breaking us up? For trying to kill me a thousand times?"

"Seventeen times," Tony says. "And yes. That. Both of those things. Don't—don't blame Ruby. She was just trying to protect you."

"That woman only tries to protect herself," Vivienne says. "And things she considers hers."

"That's not what I saw," Tony says. "You should call her."

"Yeah, no way. I think that ship has well and truly sailed." She toasts the deepening sky. "Sorry, R&V shippers!"

Tony frowns. "Shippers?"

"It's something Yumi was telling me about. It's—not important. Suffice it to say, I don't see any way we're getting back together."

"Maybe you just need to set firm boundaries."

"What, like don't fuck my ex-boyfriend?"

"That's a good suggestion."

"Oh, fuck you, Tony."

"Promises, promises." He takes another pull of his beer. "Seriously, though. Don't let her hatred for me spoil something good between the two of you."

"Something good, huh?" Vivienne sighs, long and deep. "I don't know that I'd describe anything associated with Ruby Killingsworth as 'good' in any context."

"What about Stardust?"

"Jaccob? Ha. Sure, okay." She gestures with her bourbon. "That's *one* thing."

They talk a little, about what they've been through, and what comes next. Tony's going to stay in San Francisco for a while—work with Malcolm Ali to root out and crush the rest of ICE's operations. The offensive didn't catch whatever Cthulhu sorcerer drew that Yellow Sign, after all, and the influence of cosmic madness doesn't just go away when ignored. If anything, failure to root it out will only strengthen it. It hurts Vivienne a little, knowing that Tony is going to stay behind, but it makes sense.

There's no ignoring the elephant on the patio, though.

"You sure you don't want to come with us?" Vivienne asks. "After *her*?"

Tony frowns. He's told Vivienne all about his investigation and interactions with Athena or Ishtar or whatever she's calling herself now. Vivienne isn't convinced she's actually a goddess—that shit seems too much like her narcissist POS of a sister—but she can't deny that she's alive, undead, or at least active, and that she has some power.

"I'd tell you to wait," Tony says.

"But we both know that's bullshit," Vivienne says. "She rabbited. Back in the bar. And before that, she's fucked with us who knows how many times, but that tells me what I need to know."

"She ran," Tony says, "because she wasn't prepared for you. Don't mistake that for weakness."

"Orestes is more powerful than he's ever been," Vivienne says. "Angel is pink again."

"And you?"

Vivienne pauses, biting her lip. "I'm fine."

"If you say so."

"I do."

"Fine."

Maybe Vivienne's being unfair. Tony has been forthcoming with her, at least as far as she knows. She really should tell him what she learned about Athena in the Fearworld—or just about going to the Fearworld at all—but somehow, she hesitates. He's just going to go down a rabbit hole, trying to uncover all those memories that Athena might have stripped away from him. He'll start wondering if he made a mistake, choosing the stuck-up sister over the crazy one. Who knows? There might actually be something that recontextualizes everything. But honestly, Vivienne doesn't want to deal with all of that. It's in the past, and she doesn't want ... no. She doesn't want things to change.

"Viviana," he says finally. "I know I can't stop you—"

She pours another bourbon. "You sure as shit can't."

"But I can warn you to be careful."

"When am I not?"

"Is that a trick question?"

"Pendejo."

After, they sit there in companionable silence for a bit, just the two of them, their drinks, the flickering gas fire, and the rainbow sunset. Just then, they're old friends with a complicated history that matters not at all. It's sweet and comfortable and entirely, utterly insane.

"What?" Tony opens his second beer with just his fingernails.

"Just thinking how nuts this is," Vivienne says, going full honesty. "You and me. Sharing a quiet moment like this. Like adults who aren't both completely fucking insane."

"Speak for yourself," Tony says. "I think my guerilla crusade against right-wing authoritarianism while dressed as a fucking bird is very rational."

"And the theming from a culture you have zero percent heritage in?" Vivienne asks.

"Totally understandable."

"And doing brain surgery on yourself to remove your fear response? Specifically so you could murder the best lay of your life if she gets uppity?"

"You know, you might have a point there."

"Which part? The brain surgery or the best lay of—?"

Vivienne looks over, and Tony's right there, his face only inches from hers. She likes his unshaven gray and black stubble, and the bruises and cuts on his face. He wants to kiss her, and she wants him to kiss her, so that works out. His lips are cool and rough and as strong as ever, with just a hint of vulnerability beneath. He tastes as he always has: like a comforting meal that she enjoyed too much as a teenager and still loves to revisit from time to time. But nostalgia can only go so far and appeal for so long before she remembers all the reasons she has left it in the past.

They break apart and sit quietly. That sense of quiet, calm companionship is gone, however. There's too much between them. Just too much.

He can feel it too. "Here," he says, reaching for his briefcase. "I brought you something."

"A present? You shouldn't have. And I mean that literally."

"Not exactly."

Tony clicks open the briefcase, which Vivienne had assumed contained a Raven suit. Instead, he reveals a very expensive piece of jewelry and pushes it toward her. Vivienne doesn't need to scrutinize the negation magic to recognize its familiar feel and function.

"Ruby's bracelet," Vivienne says. "I thought I lost it."

"Threw it away, you mean?" Tony asks. "Nothing's ever really lost."

"There you go being all dramatic and sexy and everything."

"Sorry. Force of habit."

"It's still *wild* that you were working with her for months. Even after—"

He nods. "Less after Valentine's Day, but she still owed me her part of the deal. I think we're done now, though. Free and clear."

"What did you promise her?" Vivienne asks.

"Never to talk to her again."

"What, she didn't make you promise never to talk to *me* again?"

"She put not just one but *two* curses on me to make that happen, Viviana," Tony says. "I think she knows that's a losing hand."

"Heh." Vivienne toys with the bracelet. "Months you were working with her. Must've been tough, seeing how much she hates you."

Tony shrugs. "I didn't do it for you, if that's what you think. It's what *she* thinks."

"You did it for Angel."

"Yes." He looks down at the beer in his good hand. "I wasn't there for her most of her life, and when I saw how much that hurt her ... I couldn't just let that go."

"You're real shitty at letting things go."

He nods.

The silence stretches, and even with the bourbon haze dulling it, Vivienne feels something from Tony that she usually doesn't. Satisfaction. Pride, even. She won't tell him how sexy it makes him. The man's already got a big enough head. And she knows he'd misinterpret it. Or maybe he would understand what she means, and they'll start up again, and again and again, and their cycle would never end. And maybe that's for the best. She doesn't want things to change, after all.

No. She's got to be brave.

"So—" Vivienne says. "Did she ever talk about me?"

"Constantly. Especially after Valentine's Day." Tony shrugs. "You should call her."

"Ugh, why is everyone telling me to call—you know what, never mind. This isn't about her." Vivienne takes a deep breath. "It's about *us*. You and me."

Tony nods. "Say what you need to say."

"I don't ... I don't think I can do this." Vivienne extends the bracelet back toward Tony. "When it comes to my emotions, I keep running and hiding and fighting and anything but *feeling* them. I keep running back to you and hurting you, and you keep hurting me ... It seems like all we do is hurt each other. Well, that's not *all* we do, obviously, but—"

"More than we *help* each other," Tony says. "Si."

"Yeah." Vivienne hangs her head. "If we're this bad for each other, maybe—"

"Maybe we shouldn't be together." Awkwardly, Tony stands. Vivienne starts to get up to help him, but he waves her back. "I think you're right."

"I hate being right." Vivienne sighs. "But we can still have sex sometimes?"

"Viviana."

"You didn't say no." She smiles wryly. "Sorry, force of habit."

With an effort, he leans down and presses his forehead to hers. "Goodbye, Viviana."

"Goodbye, Tony."

~

Vivienne sits alone on the balcony for a long time after Tony has gone. She's not sure she'll ever see him again, and for the first time in her life, she's not sure that's such a bad thing.

Even when he was hunting her—even when his entire mission in life was to end hers, for himself or for the good of the world or whatever the fuck—she loved him. *Yearned* for him, like a missing part of her body. Almost every time she woke, for twenty years, she instinctively checked the bed beside her, expecting him to be there against all odds or rationality. When the phone rang or the bells chimed to announce a customer at the Devil's Due, she had this little moment of hope that it was him. Even if he was there to kill her, at least he would be *there*. They would be reunited, 'til death do they part.

Vivienne doesn't believe in soulmates, of course. But Tony DeSantes ...

He was the first person who ever *believed* in her. Who threw away his own life for her sake. And that's not something that Vivienne "Lady Vengeance" Cain is used to. She always came back to him, inexorably drawn to the first person she had ever loved, and the first person she thought had ever loved *her*. Because if continuing to choose her despite all the crap she pulled wasn't love, then what was? If walking through flames and giving up everything for her wasn't love, then what was?

It occurs to her, in a moment of lucidity between drams of bourbon, that Tony didn't pick her, in the end. He picked Athena. Because it was the right thing to do. Because Athena was pregnant. And as much as he loved Vivienne, he honored his commitments. He showed up. He chose his child then, and he chose her again ... albeit some time later.

What's up with that? Vivienne wonders for the first fucking time. If Tony's so devoted, why did he ignore Angel for the first sixteen years of her life? Did Athena brainwash him or something to make him forget about their *child*? What a spiteful bitch.

At least he's trying to make up for it now, and he did turn his back on all that political power and money, plus got the crap kicked out of him, all for Angel's sake. So if that's what Vivienne defines as love—and that seems reasonable just now—then let Tony's love for his daughter never be questioned.

"Here's to you, A," Vivienne says, toasting with the last of the bourbon. "Congrats on having at least one decent parent."

The kids have finally settled down, maybe even gone to sleep. Vivienne can feel the affection and joy flowing out of that room, and for once, it doesn't make her want to gag. Maybe she's grown.

It also occurs to her, in a moment of lucidity, that Ruby *did* choose her. Braved flames and trickster gods and Meal Team Six and got herself *shot*, all to save Vivienne from her own bad decisions.

Fuck, she really fucked up, didn't she?

Vivienne picks up the bracelet, and for one wild moment, she considers tossing it as far as she can off the roof. But that'd probably kill someone, and it's quite expensive. Instead ...

With all that liquid courage, Vivienne opens her phone and dials.

The line connects.

"Hey, Ruby," she says. "Yeah, it's me. Listen—"

# CHAPTER NINETEEN: CRUEL SUMMER

---

**August 2020**

The filter flaps awkwardly against the box fan lodged in the window. The airflow can only do so much for the rampant heat, especially with the thick layer of smoke holding it all against the city, but it's better than nothing. Vivienne's building has no air conditioning, like at least half the buildings in Seattle, but one hundred and five degrees inside is better than the sauna outside. The concrete sizzles hot enough to cook an egg, and there are reports that I-5 is closed because the asphalt is literally *melting*.

Lolling on the ratty couch with one kicking leg thrown over the end, Angel finally surfaces from her phone. "Ugh, I'm so *booooored*."

Orestes, who has spent most of his time coughing from the smoke, cracks another bottle of water from Vivienne's fridge. "A, you could—" He cuts off when he gets a look at Angel, with her pink bikini standing out under her sweat-translucent white tank-top. "Um."

"Um, what?" Angel asks, pulling idly at her collar.

"Stop teasing the boy, A." Vivienne pushes back her heat-frizzed hair. "This is an investigation, not a wet t-shirt contest."

"Aww." Angel pulls her shirt up over her head and discards it behind the couch. She's now down to cut-off jean shorts and her bikini top. "Better?"

"Yes," Orestes says.

Vivienne sighs and wipes off the screen of her laptop, trying hard not to drip sweat into the keyboard. "A, if you're not gonna help, maybe you can stop heating up the place?"

"I can't help it that I'm hot, Aunt V."

Honestly, any third person in the cramped apartment with all the lights off brings plenty of extra body heat, but Angel burns extra hot with that superhuman metabolism of hers. If Vivienne can piss her off enough to fuck off out of the apartment, it'll probably go down at least three degrees in here.

"If you're bored." Before sitting down to rejoin the search, Orestes takes off his glasses and wipes them free of sweat smears. "You could go clear some smoke."

"Not really." Angel pouts and looks at her nails. "It just comes back."

"Well, half the West Coast *is* on fire," Vivienne says. "Good thing that climate change thing is just a hoax, otherwise we'd *really* be in trouble."

"Um, excuse me," Angel says. "Climate change *is* real, Aunt V."

"Yeah, no shit."

Angel looks confused, and to be fair, it's hard to think in this much heat.

Orestes wakes up his own computer, which is already buzzing from the ambient temperature. "I've read so much mythology, my brain feels like overcooked oatmeal. Or that's the heat."

Vivienne nods in sympathy. This is the third day of record heat in Seattle, which has broken both previous heat records, which were set yesterday and the day before. Per the news' advice, Orestes plastered cardboard over all the windows in the apartment to keep the sun out and pretty dark inside. The streets are like a bombed-out war zone where just breathing is like smoking two packs a day.

Being unable to think or move around in the heat wave isn't the only reason the investigation has stymied. Even with access to some of Tony's reports, data, and back channels, Vivienne and Orestes have only been able to track Athena's movements so much. Tony's info shows she was involved with The Aphid, with Nemesis and Injustice, and then with the ICE bozos in Nevada, all that seems clear enough. But all of them are either dead, missing, or reduced to gibbering wrecks with no useful information, which bears the distinct hallmarks of Athena sucking out their memories and leaving them hopelessly insane. They did confront her in San Francisco, but since then, she's been annoyingly invisible.

Speculation on where she might go next isn't going anywhere: Tony's notes just go around and around.

"Fucking Tony and his fucking notes," Vivienne says. "Are these written in some sort of code? Are we a joke to him? Don't answer that."

Angel, who has gone back to scrolling her socials, doesn't seem to have heard, much less have an answer. She starts making faces and hand signs to the camera, suggesting she's either taking selfies or shooting a video, and Vivienne wouldn't put it past her to do either.

"You know what we really need." Orestes leans across to whisper, so Angel won't hear. "Tony."

Vivienne grumbles. "He's busy."

She has called or texted Tony numerous times, in point of fact, with questions, frustrations, and the occasional sext, but the reply rate has dropped, and she's pretty sure he's screening her calls or has her muted or something. Based on the news coming out of San Francisco—protest marches, justice riots, Prather practically sending an army of brownshirts there to stir up trouble and run for city government in the upcoming election—it sounds like he has his hands full. Vivienne almost envies him. She'd love to be down there in the thick of protesting, punching cops and Nazis, washing out pepper-sprayed eyes with milk, and hooking up with other agitators all night long ... No, no, *focus*.

"What about Ruby?" Orestes asks. "You two are ... back together, right?"

"Sort of. But don't let her hear you say that." She checks her messages—no update. "She's been dealing with something back in Cobalt City. Time travelers or something?[12] Not that she's mentioned it to me. Mostly I hear about it from Yumi."

"Oh is *that* what she keeps messaging about?" Orestes nods. "She's stoked about being part of some superhero mission or something. Lisa's involved too. Sounds like they're doing well."

"Good for them."

---

[12] The events of *Time & Again* take place in parallel to this period of time, so check out that novel for context and to see what certain of our favorite heroes get up to off-screen! ~ Cape-Watcher Vogel

Vivienne's heat-addled mind drifts back to her recent visit to Cobalt City, and specifically Ruby's blessedly air-conditioned penthouse. It feels like a dream, and one she awoke from rather abruptly and rudely when the private plane let her back off at SeaTac into a boiling pot of water. Ruby's people had to restrain her to keep her from climbing back up the airstairs.

"Maybe I'll take a shower," Angel says.

"A shower sounds good," Orestes says.

Vivienne rolls her eyes. "We're out of cold water."

Orestes raises an eyebrow. "You mean hot water."

"I said what I said." She leans back from the foggy screen. "I'm gonna pee before you two hog my shower *again*."

"Hey, whoa, I didn't say—" Orestes says, face red from more than the heat.

Angel gives him a look that says the shower sex was implied.

Vivienne does her business in the bathroom and runs water to splash on her face. She turns it on cold, but it's still only tepid. At least there's a ceiling fan in here and no windows, so it's a little cooler than out in the main apartment. Unfortunately, there *is* a mirror: cracked several times, including one long seam diagonally up through the middle. She's put off telling the building management about it for years now, and not because she hates looking at herself. (She does, but that's not the point.)

No, those cracks are important because they splinter Azazel's power. Since the demon lord aided her in overcoming the Yellow Sign five months ago, his whispers have grown louder and more frequent. *Insistent.* As he sees it, Vivienne owes him, or at least she'll ask for his help again. And why wouldn't he think that? He has infinite time and patience, and she's only one mortal woman who makes questionable moral choices.

Sure enough, when she looks up from splashing the lukewarm water on her cheeks, she's not alone in the mirror, but it isn't the Many-Mouthed Devourer.

"My darling avenger," Loki says. "Long time, no reflection."

She can only see the god in the mirror under the crack, which cuts off the top half of their face, but she would recognize that grin anywhere. That and the immaculate green suit embroidered with shifting black and yellow patterns that seem to sway and dance whenever you aren't looking at them directly, and sometimes when you are. All of it is quintessentially Loki, the god of mischief.

"Hey."

Vivienne casually looks over her shoulder, but of course the god isn't actually standing there. As far as she knows, Loki can't leave whatever dimension they abide in, though she doesn't know enough about magic to explain why. Ruby could, and she and Loki have some kind of understanding and even a nexus or something in her building that lets the god manifest physically in this plane of existence.

Which doesn't explain what they're doing haunting her bathroom mirror.

"You're wondering what brings me here," Loki says.

"If this is a booty call, can we do it in the shower? Heat wave, you know."

"Delightful as that would be, my dark Valkyrie," Loki says, "I'm afraid I've come on business, not pleasure. I seek a boon of you."

"A favor?" Vivienne quirks an eyebrow. "I assume this is the kind of ask that has barbs?"

"Why would you make such assumptions, oh mistress of well-deserved retribution." Not a question, because they both know the answer. "This boon concerns a certain fiery enchantress of our mutual acquaintance, and I'm given to understand you've repaired your bond—"

Of course. "What's Ruby done now?"

Loki's grin widens slightly. "It is what she has not done, and that is fully care for herself. Powerful as her mystic arts are, there are certain attacks they are ill-suited for—"

"Just spit it out, Lie-smith."

"Lady Killingsworth has been wounded." Loki raises their hands to forestall Vivienne's outburst. "Fear not—she will recover, but it will take time. She used magic beyond what any mortal should be able to control without the assistance of a deity, and it has left her empty. She will recover her energies, but my concern is what will happen the next time she suffers such an attack."[13]

---

[13] Loki is referring to Ruby's wounding in *Time & Again!* ~ Once and Future Editor Vogel

Vivienne eases her clenched fists open and takes note of the bloody moons her nails have sunk into her palms. "What sort of attack?" she asks, trying to keep her voice level.

Loki looks as though they've tasted something sour. "Mortal firearms," they say with distaste. "Lady Killingsworth was not prepared with suitable defensive spells, but she channeled enough power to halt the projectiles regardless."

Vivienne isn't sure what that means, but it sounds like a lot of strain. "And you don't need me to heal her. You want me to protect her. She needs something bulletproof—or *someone*."

"Quite."

Vivienne nods. "I've got a few ideas."

"Then we've an accord." Loki's image starts to blur. "I shall take my leave then—"

"Wait," Vivienne says. "And what do I get in exchange for this favor?"

Loki has become a green cloud with two gleaming amber eyes. "What, you'll not aid our mutual beloved out of affection." Again, not a question.

Vivienne would, but she's not just dealing with Ruby—she's dealing with a literal god of mischief, and unless she closes the deal, Loki will find some way to exploit it in the future. Maybe Ruby doesn't mind being in debt to a prophesied destroyer of the world, but Vivienne is already full up of cosmic entities with a claim on her soul.

"Is this you showing care, god of mischief?" Vivienne asks.

That gives Loki pause, though when they answer, it is with the same cool aloofness with which they say basically everything. "Perhaps. But no one will ever believe you."

"Fair enough," Vivienne says. "So. About that favor?"

"Very well," Loki says. "Ask, and it shall be done."

Vivienne isn't sure what to ask for. Mostly, she just wants Loki out of her hair, unless it's grasping it while she's on her knees ... y'know, this isn't the time. Besides, she has a better direction to send Loki's attentions. "I have this ... friend. Big fan of all things Norse. I want you to call upon him and ... assist him in his hour of need. Mostly because it will be hilarious."

Loki considers. "For you or for me?"

"Oh, definitely both."

The god of mischief chuckles. "Done."

Loki disperses, leaving a faint green sheen to the mirror, which makes Vivienne grimace. She pulls out a bottle of Windex and the bathroom roll of paper towels and gets to work. In the process, pain blooms in her wrist when she gets too close to the crack, and a faint trickle of blood flows down her forearm. Crap. If the kids see this, they'll think she's hurting herself. They'll be right, of course—getting in bed with Loki is tantamount to self-harm, but if it's for Ruby ...

And siccing Loki on Tony will be just punishment for ghosting her all these months. He's such a Norse fanboy, surely he'd appreciate hanging out with an actual Norse god. The *worst* Norse god, but still. If there's one man who needs a little chaos infused into his staid life, it's Tony DeSantes.

More important, however, is Ruby.

Trust, but verify.

Vivienne fishes her phone out of her bra and calls Jaccob. A quick consult confirms everything the Lie-smith said. Not a little bit of her wants to drop everything and rush off to Cobalt City, but if they give up the search now, who knows how much progress they'll lose. Plus, she and Ruby are a little rocky, and the last thing the supervillain sorceress media mogul likes is to be smothered. What if she wakes up and realizes Vivienne has been sitting in her sick room watching over her, and without her full makeup? That could be apocalyptic.

No, she needs another solution. A bulletproof one.

"Hey, A!" she shouts out the bathroom door. "Got a job for you."

Also, she'll send some flowers.

# CHAPTER TWENTY: TAKE ME TO CHURCH

Despite its stereotype as a godless refuge for heathens, Seattle is home to a staggering number of faith communities, from century-old Christian churches to Synagogues to Mosques to Buddhist temples to a truly massive LDS church that just appeared in the Roosevelt neighborhood one day, as though by magic. By and large, Vivienne's never bothered with such places—she knows a number of gods and wants nothing to do with most of them—with one marked exception. Which, lovely as it is, might be the primary reason she avoids organized religion.

Our Lady of the Lake is a Catholic enclave nestled off 35th Avenue in Maple Leaf, about five or ten minutes north of the Devil's Due and not too far from her childhood home. The most striking aspect of the complex visually is a fountain out front over which stands a spire a little like a miniature Space Needle. The statue nestled beneath its curling foundations is not of Jesus but, in the Catholic tradition, depicts the Virgin Mary. It's quite the sight for tourists and people casually speeding along 35th to get to the Fred Meyer up on Lake City alike.

For Vivienne, the statue and tower are nostalgic, and not really in a good way. She did, after all, spend a good portion of her childhood going to school here, so she walked past the statue almost every day. Her memories of that time are blurry, but they involved a lot of angry nuns and Hail Marys. Vivienne has distanced herself so far from her upbringing that she uses "Lucifer" and "Lilith" the way other people use "God" or "Jesus," but she can still repeat that prayer by rote.

"Hail Mary, full of grace—" she murmurs, then looks away when a couple parishioners give her a quizzical look. A church isn't exactly where you expect a recovering gothpunk to hang out.

But Orestes was right. There's power in this place—the weight of decades of fervent worship, adoration, and not a little frustration—and some of it feels familiar, and she means that very literally. Athena or Carmen or whatever her name really is left her mark on this place, when she was a girl and also more recently. It seemed like a wild goose chase when the kid recommended it, but now that she's here, Vivienne knows it wasn't wasted effort.

That, and a familiar emotional signature she can't ignore.

Vivienne heads right into the sanctuary, heedless of the curious looks. The familiar worship hall is full of pews and iconography. American Catholicism might not be *the* most ostentatious version of Christianity, but it's still Catholicism, and even the relatively spare Pacific Northwest variant has still got it going on. Everywhere she looks, there's ornate carvings of saints, scenes embellished from a much-translated holy book, and a suspiciously cut Jesus who never skips core training. The statue of the Virgin Mary is just as, if not more, prominent, and the fact that the faith organizes at least somewhat around a female figure is probably what kept Vivienne from burning it down when she was a troubled tween.

"Athena!" Vivienne says when she steps into the sanctuary, but immediately knows it isn't her. She winces and murmurs apologies and makes her way swiftly up to the front, where she kneels next to the woman in the black dress, who she's pretty sure no one else can see. "What are you doing here? I thought you had, y'know, moved on."

"You never liked this place," the spirit of Charisma Cain says, her hands clasped. "Neither you nor Carmen."

"And yet," Vivienne says, careful to whisper, and not just because of the disapproving nuns glaring at her suspiciously. "Here you are. Where neither of us would think to look for you."

"I'm always with you, mija," she says. "You didn't realize that?"

"Like ... always?" Vivienne pictures some particularly compromising moments since the Fearworld expedition. "Even in the bathroom?"

Charisma quirks her lips in distaste, and it's reassuring to know Vivienne can still annoy her mother, even when she's a ghost.

"Why is that?" Charisma basks in the light of the chapel as though absorbing some sort of holy calm Vivienne has always found elusive. "Why don't you like it here? This is a place of peace. Of welcome."

"Yeah, well, not for us socialist trash pandas," she says. "Or Jesus, for that matter. Most American 'Christians' would insist the Second Coming be deported. Or executed all over again."

"Shh!" says one of the nuns near the altar.

Apparently, she's whispering to herself too loudly.

Charisma seems displeased by her smarm, but the expression she gives Vivienne is one of long-suffering patience. She used to look at her like that in life, but only very occasionally. After the dementia got her, only on those rare occasions when she fully recognized Vivienne. The memory strikes Vivienne with an unexpected pang.

Vivienne lowers her voice to seem more like praying. "The sisters would probably have some stern words about my abortion, too." She means it as a flippant, off-hand joke, but that comment makes Charisma stare at Vivienne with unexpected intensity. "What?"

"You were never the best-behaved girl, mija," Charisma says. "But what abortion?"

"My ... you know." Vivienne bites her lip. "Do we have to talk about this in front of the nuns?"

"What? Abortion?"

At first, Vivienne feels sad. She thought dying cleared her mother of Athena's gaslighting bullshit, but for Charisma to forget about something like that? It's not like Vivienne talks about it a lot—she's pretty sure Orestes and Angel and most of her present friends don't even know about it. She never even told Tony, who had a pretty vested interest. Only three people know: Vivienne, Andre, and her mother, and she's dead. Only apparently, she doesn't ...

"You know, twenty years ago, when Tony and I—"

She trails off. Her mother is staring at her extremely intently, and Vivienne isn't sure why. Is she upset? Vivienne stopped being a good Catholic girl when she was thirteen. Surely Charisma wasn't expecting her to keep it up during her gothpunk phase, let alone as Lady Vengeance, poster girl for counterculture and women's liberation in a very "uppercut men in the balls" sort of way. If anything, having an abortion when she was twenty-two just made sense. They're not going to have this fight all over again ... Wait. Did they ever fight about it in the first place? Vivienne can't remember.

"Keep going," Charisma says, in that infuriatingly patient way of hers.

"What?" Vivienne asks too loudly, earning curious glances from fellow churchgoers.

"Did we ever fight about it? Did you keep it from me?"

"No," Vivienne says. "Even if I tried, you ... You're psychic. You'd know. You—" She furrows her brow. "I can't remember."

"Can't, or won't?"

"Can't. The memory isn't there. I felt it. Being pregnant. I remember feeling it. But—"

"But you don't remember it ending."

"No, but it must have, right?" Vivienne asks. "Because if it didn't, then—"

Charisma nods slightly.

"Fuck." Vivienne blinks rapidly. "You mean, Angel ... she—?"

Charisma nods.

It makes a sort of sense, though it still blows Vivienne's mind. "She's my ... and Tony's—?" She closes her eyes. "She's *my* daughter. Not Carmen's. *Mine*."

Again, Charisma nods.

She tries to keep it together. Mostly, it feels like her brain is going to implode if she lets herself think about it for even a second. Twenty years of a lie she didn't even know was a lie. It just seems too big. Too massive to wrap her head around.

Lady Vengeance has faced eldritch horrors and dark gods, but unexpected motherhood is scarier than any of them. This ... this will take a while to process.

"Fuck," Vivienne says, drawing stern glances and shushing from the nuns. She moderates her voice. "You couldn't have told me this before? And don't give me that 'I can only tell you when you're ready to face it' bullshit. I think I was ready to handle this."

"I told you, I can only tell you when you're ready to face it." Charisma sighs. "And you know my memory is coming back slowly, mija. It wasn't until I saw him that I remembered."

"Oh, bullshit. If you're haunting me, you saw him like four months ago!"

"And my *my*, how that greasy pendejo has become a fine, handsome man."

"*Jesus*, Mamá!" Another set of stern warnings. "How long have you been sitting on this information? I told him that we ... fuck, this is getting really complicated."

"Do you really want to be with him, mija?"

Vivienne sighs. "No. I haven't changed my mind. But—"

"You don't need to be with the father to have a daughter," Charisma says. "I didn't have either of your fathers. Though that was Carmen's fault as well."

"Of course." Vivienne bites her lip hard. "You could have told me literally yesterday, before I sent her to Cobalt City."

"And risked you telling her impulsively and regretting it?"

"True. So ... How do we do this? Do I tell her? Do you? Please say you do it."

Charisma smiles distantly. "I think it has to be you."

"I was afraid you'd say that." Vivienne pulls out her phone, then thinks better of it. This isn't the sort of thing you tell someone over text. "I sent her to protect Ruby. I'll tell her when she gets back."

Charisma nods, though there's a distant sadness in her face, like she's waiting for the other shoe to drop and has braced for impact.

Then it drops, and the impact is shattering.

"Athena, she—" Vivienne closes her hands into fists. "Carmen did this. That's what you said before. Her mind-fuck thing."

"Mija, language."

"No, fuck that." Vivienne stands before she tears the pew from the floor. Energy is flowing through and around her limbs, and she doesn't even care who sees. "This ... this is the most fucking horrific thing she has ever done to me. Not only did she fucking steal my daughter, but she made me think I aborted her. I mean, what the *fuck*."

Charisma Cain doesn't answer, because she's gone—evaporated into tiny motes of light in the vague shape of a person.

A number of the sisters are hissing urgent whispers at Vivienne, and there are a couple of well-dressed gentlemen who read immediately as security to her coming down the aisle. Catholic ushers, man—they don't fuck around. And while Vivienne might be an anti-religious punk, she doesn't want to add "burned down a church" to her sordid list of accomplishments.

"Yeah, yeah, I'm going," she says. "Don't touch me."

She does, however, cast a glance back at the statue of the Virgin Mary up at the altar. If it were Jesus, she'd probably have a few choice profanities to utter, but in the face of that beatific and ultimately sorrowful expression, all her overflowing rage cools to a simmer. Mary doesn't fuck around, and neither will Vivienne.

"I'm going," she says, trembling. "And my sister and I are going to have fucking *words*."

~

Marcus Orestes wasn't raised in a religious household, and he can count on one hand the number of times he's been to a church service. But his dads instilled in him a great respect for people of genuine faith and the moral character to be just, kind, and good to others, which has always seemed to him like what Christianity is all about.

Still, leaning against the battered old Cain jeep outside Our Lady of the Lake isn't the most comfortable of experiences. Sure, a lot of the people going into or out of the church ignore him or even smile at him, but a Black man with dreadlocks loitering on the street corner inevitably draws an increasing number of suspicious looks. Maple Leaf is a pretty white neighborhood in a pretty white city, and white people pretty much always get nervous in the presence of non-white people. He's used to it, having grown up in Magnolia, but that doesn't make him like it. Not one bit.

Maybe he should wait in the car, rather than leaning against it? Is that more suspicious or less?

Vivienne emerges from the church before either some angry white lady comes to yell at Orestes, or the cops show up. She looks no happier to be here than he feels, but there's a grim determination to the set of her jaw that pulls him up short. She makes a beeline for the jeep.

"You good?" he asks as she approaches.

She nods. "Get in."

They climb into the jeep. He takes the driver's seat, as Vivienne doesn't seem to like driving ... not cars, anyway. But they'd look pretty silly stacked up on her motorcycle, and Orestes has higher standards than riding in a sidecar. His dads raised him with progressive perspectives on gender roles—i.e., that they're bullshit—but he does have *some* pride. Also, Vivienne is terrifying behind the handlebars of a motorcycle. In the passenger seat of the jeep, she sits back, arms crossed, expression troubled, jaw clenched almost hard enough to crack her teeth. It happened.

"So." Orestes takes a breath. "You figured it out about Angel, huh?"

"Fuck!" Vivienne does a literal doubletake and shatters the passenger-side window with her head. "Ow, fuck."

"You okay?" He extends a hand to her. "Do you need me to—?"

"Yeah, I'm fine, what do you mean, *figured it out* about Angel?" Vivienne demands.

Orestes sighs. "You know, that omniscience thing I have going."

"Fuck, the thing I hate, right." Vivienne looses a massive sigh and slumps down in her seat. "You just saw into the future or the past or something and know this big thing about us, but you didn't tell either of us. Unless—oh shit." She glares at him. "Did you tell Angel?"

Orestes winces. "Okay, one thing at a time. I ... um, this is embarrassing."

"Spit it out, kid."

"It wasn't my Godsight. Well, I mean, not really. That just confirmed my suspicions."

"What?" Vivienne glowers.

"I, um, I had this head-canon," Orestes says. "And I wasn't the only one, okay? It's a minor fringe theory in the fandom. That they were setting up a major reveal in a future story arc."

"You mean from our fucking comics," Vivienne says. "You're saying there are a bunch of pasty losers in their mom's basements speculating that Angel's my daughter. With Tony."

"That is an unfair stereotype," Orestes says. "But I always thought, you know, the ages were plausible, and that you two were so alike."

"How the fuck so?"

Orestes purses his lips. "Sure, you dress different, but she's just as moody and angsty as you, and she's like one day away from a full goth downward spiral. You argue the same way. You're both hard on Mr. DeSantes, but you love him. And Athena is after both of you. Also—" He hesitates.

"Also?"

"Well, you've never shown even the slightest romantic interest in each other," Orestes says. "And I mean ... it's not like you won't go after straight girls half your age."

He expects her to object, but instead, she just nods. "Go on."

"And you ... you love each other. You fight all the time, but when it comes to it, you've got her back, and she's got yours."

"Okay, okay, fine," Vivienne says. "But our powers are totally different."

"Are they, though?" Orestes asks. "You both absorb emotional energy and empower yourself. You just have different preferences."

"All right, *ugh*." She crosses her arms. "And you didn't tell us your suspicions because—?"

"They were just head-canon—and even after my upgrade, I wasn't *sure*," Orestes says. "Besides, I figured maybe you, y'know, already knew and were keeping it a secret or something."

"Kid." Vivienne gives Orestes a cool look. "Do I look like I could keep a secret like that?"

"You faked your death and hid out for years—*twice*."

She nods, conceding the point. "And Angel ... yeah, that girl can keep secrets."

"Agreed."

"But not in this case?"

"If you're asking if she knows, I don't think so."

"Don't suppose you want to be the one to tell her?"

"Oh sure, I'll just go tell my girlfriend that you're her mother."

"Well, you *are* her boyfriend." Vivienne considers. "I guess I'm supposed to have an opinion about that."

"Do you?"

212

"Depends." Now she looks at him very directly, purple eyes flickering. "Those times you've almost kissed me. Were you trying to kiss me?"

"V." Orestes regards her evenly.

"In my defense, you *are* really cute."

He smiles faintly. "That's not appropriate ... uh, Mom?"

"Ooh. Don't love that."

"You're right, that's weird."

The two of them sitting there are attracting some attention, and Orestes's internal timer for when the cops show up to arrest him for being Black in a "nice" neighborhood is ticking down. He puts the car in drive and pulls out onto 35th Avenue. "Do we have a lead?"

"Head up to 125th," Vivienne says.

"Did Athena leave a trail to Lake City or something?"

"No, there's this great dim sum place, and you and I need to talk." Vivienne smiles grimly. "I have a theory about how to kick this investigation up a notch."

She pulls out her phone.

# CHAPTER TWENTY-ONE: WE ARE NEVER EVER GETTING BACK TOGETHER

The morning of August 30th, Alaska Airlines Flight 587 sets down at SeaTac in the middle of a wall of smoky fog like something out of a Silent Hill game. Descending into that umber murk felt like sliding into a hot tub full of unfiltered water that no one noticed has been tainted by rotting leaves for the past month, which have now dissolved into a filthy grime. Getting off the plane isn't much better, as the saturated humidity of Seattle is nothing compared to the relative paradise of San Francisco.

Antonio DeSantes hasn't flown coach in years—hasn't even been a passenger in a plane since he was twenty—so this has been a novel experience. But fuel for a combat-ready fighter craft isn't cheap, and neither are grassroots revolutions. So if he has to slum it to maintain the movement's coffers and his own cover, then so be it. It's kind of nostalgic, in a way, flying commercial under an alias. He's wearing decent but upscale street clothes and sunglasses.

The first strange thing is seeing Vivienne Cain waiting for him at Arrivals. And she's wearing a dress: black, of course, but nothing ostentatious. Cotton jersey, off-shoulder, flattering, showing off her tattoos nicely. Particularly the two birds tattooed on her upper chest: one raven, one wren. Fitting. Honestly, that's how he recognizes her, considering she's also wearing big clunky sunglasses and a wide-brimmed white sunhat. Like a movie star or adult film actress going for a vaguely incognito look.

They greet each other with air kisses, playing out the pantomime of jet-setting celebrities who don't want to be recognized. She smells of gardenia, jasmine, honeysuckle, and something else. A complex perfume, and not the sort of thing he'd expect her to wear. She usually smells like sweat, whiskey, and/or sex, depending. But this is nice.

"Didn't expect to see you, Viviana," he says. "I like that scent you're wearing."

"It's from Sucreabeille," she says. "It's called Chloroform."

"Once a goth, always a goth," Tony says. "Must be important if you're here to meet me."

"I said it was, didn't I?" She looks around briefly. "No suspiciously young groupies?"

"If you mean Henrietta and Maria, they still work for me," he says. "They're back in Colorado, administering my last months of office."

"Sure, you haven't called me in five months, and let's talk about other girls."

"You brought them up. And they're nearly thirty."

"Could've fooled me. Ugh." Vivienne pulls a face. "I spoke too soon."

He looks over at a couple of sorority girls who have blushingly approached him.

"Um, are you—y'know?" one of them asks.

"Maybe," he says.

"He isn't," Vivienne says, a little annoyed, but the girls ignore her.

"Can I, um, have your autograph?" the other girl asks. "Sign my boarding pass?"

Tony can practically hear Vivienne rolling her eyes. "Sure."

He signs "Pedro Pascal," winks at them, and holds a finger up to his lips to keep the secret. They seem convinced. They head off to the gates, buzzing with excited gossip and giggles.

"You done?" Vivienne asks. "Shit, I thought the Ravenettes were bad."

"Viviana."

"It's fine," she says. "Let's go."

~

Apparently, she didn't mean to go far, as they grab a corner booth at a local roast house called Sharps, where Vivienne

216

proceeds to order the most ridiculous drink on the menu—something called a Skinny Bitch—despite it being just after noon. It falls to Tony to obtain a cornbread appetizer to soak some of it up, as well as an Old Fashioned for himself. She responds to all his questions and attempts at small talk with stoic denial until their drinks arrive, which includes a demonstration of the waitress pouring vodka, cranberry, and grapefruit over what looks like a glass of cotton candy, which dissolves under the alcohol in a swirl of sweet clouds. A glowing ice cube tops off the display.

"Impressive." Tony sniffs at his Old Fashioned. "Now—"

Vivienne cuts him off with a raised finger, drains about half her magical drink, and waves to the waitress. "Scratch Manhattan. And keep 'em coming."

"It's gonna be like that, is it?" Tony's Old Fashioned is pretty great: smoky and savory and excellently balanced. He's not sure if they distill their own proprietary whiskey on-site or partner up with a local distillery, but either way, it's excellent.

"You got a problem with that?" Vivienne's red-wine eyes shoot him a challenge.

"Eat some of the cornbread. I won't eat the whole thing."

"You're back on carbs, Mr. Abs-for-Days? Oh wait, that's Jaccob."

Tony doesn't rise to the barb. She's anxious, and he knows her well enough to recognize the signs. He pulls out his phone but hesitates. "What is it, Viviana?"

"Hang on." She finishes her cotton-candy drink and stares at the sparsely populated dining room, saying nothing until the waitress reappears and mixes a Manhattan at the table for her. Vivienne drinks about half of it. "More of these, please."

Tony's familiar with the "get drunk" strategy from Vivienne, though that only narrows down her dire news so much. This has historically been her strategy with almost everything—that or sudden overwhelming violence. And while he isn't afraid of her—he physically can't be—he doesn't want to provoke a conflict that might trigger Ruby's curse and make his heart explode. That wouldn't be ideal.

And so he sits back, content to wait. If whatever she's got to say is as critical as she implied on the phone, she would have blurted it out at Arrivals. If she's got to build up to it, that's fine.

Just in case, though, he sends a text.

Their food arrives: a steak and fries for her, a well-balanced salad for him, served in an upside-down beer stein that the waitress slowly draws up and off, allowing it to spread through the shallow bowl. Quite an entertaining display.

"Maybe I should have ordered that," Vivienne says, at least until she takes a bite of the steak. "Never mind. This is perfect." She waves for another scratch Manhattan, which will be her third.

It's an interesting tactical consideration Miss Killingsworth has set for him: how to interact with Vivienne without doing anything that the curse might perceive as hostile or harmful. There's no chance she'll provoke him into an attack, thanks to the brain surgery that seared the fear response out of his amygdala, allowing for a more analytical, proactive means of approaching her. He knows it frustrates Vivienne to no end that he doesn't fear her, the possibility of her possession, or anything else. The whole situation gives him an opportunity to test the limits of the curse, which might be useful information. For instance, does the fiery way their interactions tend to dissolve count as an attack? If he inflicts emotional harm on her, will that trigger the curse? Not that he wants to, of course.

"Tony," she says. "You're staring at me with that hunter expression of yours."

"My what?"

"You know, the way you look at a mark. When you're figuring out how best to kick their ass. Or kill them. It's creepy."

"I'm not a psychopath, if that's what you're asking."

"Sounds like what a psychopath would say." Vivienne occupies herself cutting her steak into tiny pieces. Stalling. "You sure your surgery didn't burn out your emotions entirely?"

"You tell me," he says. "You're the empath."

"Oh, I think we both know how you feel about me."

"And that is?"

"Complicated."

"True."

His phone buzzes, and he glances at it surreptitiously as Vivienne drizzles a healthy supply of ketchup on her fries. He reads his texts, then starts a timer.

~

Tony has decided to wait, and he waits for a long time.

After their early dinner at Sharps, Vivienne drives the clanky jeep up into Seattle proper, specifically the Ballard neighborhood, where they bounce around to several bars and distilleries. Vivienne seems to be trying to limit herself to one or two drinks at each stop, perhaps in an attempt to keep within her impressive tolerance, though Tony has been keeping track, and she's up around twelve at this point. Perhaps she summoned him to Seattle to tell him she has liver cancer? Unlikely.

He orders IPAs at each stop, not because he particularly likes them—he doesn't—but because they're easy to nurse. He also insists Vivienne drinks a glass of water for at least every two drinks, and to his surprise, she does. That in itself is probably the most remarkable part of the day so far.

The smoke dome gripping Seattle only deepens during the day, not letting up and easing their breathing. People are talking about the long-overdue rainstorm that'll wash all the smoke away, and while rain would be on brand for Seattle, it hasn't rained in two months. Seems unlikely.

After three solid hours of bar hopping and drinking, Tony finds himself wandering through the Seattle Aquarium with Vivienne. He thought initially it was just an attempt to get out of the sun, and her awkward, taciturn manner lends some credence to that view. The Seattle Aquarium is clearly targeted to a younger audience, with lots of displays and hands-on activities for kids, but Vivienne somehow manages to not seem annoyed. She drags Tony along to the various wings, where she looks at each tank for about ten or fifteen seconds, longer with the octopus, and moves on. Tony follows silently.

"So," she says. "Did you hear about the aquarium ghost?"

Tony raises an eyebrow.

"Apparently, a while ago, the fish kept disappearing in one of the tanks. Like there one day, gone the next. And they couldn't figure out what it was. Didn't feed them enough? Water toxicity? No, they balanced everything out, and the fish kept disappearing."

"Hmm."

Vivienne looks a little amused. "They finally set up cameras, and it turns out the octopus figured out how to get out of its enclosure. It would wait until closing, then climb out, pull itself across to the nearest fish tank, eat *all* the fish, then head back to its tank. All before opening the next morning."

"Fascinating," Tony says.

He had, in point of fact, heard this story, but it's good to see Vivienne enthusiastic about something. Her energy has been off all day, and it's not just the alcohol. The dress, the sunhat, the various stops along the way ... Maybe she *is* dying, and she's still working up the courage to tell him. Either way, he's content to wait.

They head out of the aquarium and bum around the waterfront for a while, which is an interesting experience, because Tony hasn't really been down here since the viaduct came down. The smoke dome that has captured Seattle for a month keeps too many tourists off the street, and it's a little like breathing in the ash from a volcano, but Tony is just too fascinated by Vivienne's behavior to mind. She leads them into the Miner's Landing museums full of old-timey arcade games and animatronics, the many stalls selling knick-knacks for tourists, and seems both disappointed and relieved that the nineteenth-century carousel is closed for the day. He has to remind her he doesn't like shellfish to stop her from forcing them to stop at Ivar's Acres of Clams.

They end up on the Seattle Great Wheel, which opened in 2012, a good ten years since Tony last spent much time in the city. He's never been on this particular ride, and he's not a fan of Ferris wheels in general. Too isolated. No easy escape routes. You're a sitting duck for any assassin who might be following, waiting for the right moment. At least the Great Wheel compartments are fully enclosed, like small pods floating through the late afternoon, as the sun dips toward the Olympics. Through the smoky fog, it looks like a perfect circle of blood-red.

Tony glances over at Vivienne sitting across from him, her sunhat on the bench beside her. Her gaze is locked on the sun with the sort of intensity that only comes from a determination to blind oneself. He remembers when Lyle Prather made national news glancing up at the eclipse, no doubt causing damage to his retinas. If not for those sunglasses and the thick smoke, Vivienne would have to start developing a new set of powers to compensate for her diminished vision.

"What is it?" he asks for the second time.

"Huh?" Vivienne stirs like she forgot he was there. Not like she was alone, but more like he has interrupted a very important train of thought that is lagging behind schedule.

"Why did you call me here?" Tony asks. "You said there was an emergency. That it concerned Angel. But it's just you and me. No Angel. What's really going on?"

Vivienne stares at him for a dozen seconds, then frowns and adjusts her sunglasses. She stands halfway and shifts to sit next to him. "Just enjoy the moment, Tony, *fuck.*"

He's about to protest when she leans against him. Despite spending at this point an entire afternoon together, they haven't actually touched. Her body is warm, strong, and tense. She's definitely sitting on a secret, it's something big, and while she clearly wants to tell him, she hasn't yet found the right moment. It can't be that she's still utterly in love with him, because if there's a more romantic moment than the height of a Ferris wheel at sunset, smoke or no, he's not sure what it is.

"You're not dying, are you?" Tony asks.

"What? No such luck, pendejo."

"Bien."

Tony puts his arm around her, holding her close, and Vivienne offers no objections. She inclines her head against his shoulder. He's content to wait.

Though not too much longer.

~

The Theo chocolate factory in Fremont kicks them out around six p.m., after they've both taken the tour and sampled every single chocolate bar they make. Tony was most interested in the chocolate-making process, as this factory is one of the few independent, start-to-finish factories in America. Most chocolate is imported and repackaged, but not at Theo, which is committed to free trade and indie practices. Vivienne, unsurprisingly, preferred the free samples, of which she ate more than can possibly be healthy. The better to soak up the alcohol, he guesses.

"I always forget how much I like that place." Vivienne consults her phone. "We can grab a drink at Mischief or something, but we gotta make it fast. Our forge appointment is in an hour."

"Forge?" Tony raises an eyebrow.

"Yeah, there's a forge down in SoDo. They do corporate events and individual workshops. I signed us up to make Damascus rings. I mean, I figure that's—"

"Vale, basta, I give up," Tony says. "What's going on?"

Vivienne blinks at him. "What do you mean?"

They've paused outside the jeep, which is illegally parked in a load/unload zone on Phinney, but fortunately it's Sunday. Tony notices the jeep is cleaner than he's ever seen it, both inside and out. To his knowledge, Vivienne has never so much as driven through a carwash, much less actually vacuumed. She barely remembers to clean her apartment. If he had to guess, he would say the jeep has been professionally detailed. Also, is that a The Raven sticker on the bumper? All of this is suspicious as fuck.

He gestures expansively. "We've been on the longest date either of us has ever been on—"

"That is not true," Vivienne says. "Ruby is very thorough as a date planner."

"I'm sure," Tony says. "But that too. All of this, you apparently planned. You even made an appointment at the local forge. To make rings? Why?"

"I remembered you like making things," Vivienne says. "So sue me."

"No, why *today*?" Tony asks. "What are you trying to tell me? What can be *this* bad?"

Vivienne pauses, her entire body going rigid. "Fuck."

Not a good sign.

Will Tony have to attack her? Is she under some kind of mind control? Or maybe this is an imposter? No, she acts like and *feels* too much like Vivienne. If he attacks her, that'll trigger the curse and his heart will explode. At least he'll have an answer if this is really her, but that's a very faint silver lining to being dead. At least the smoke has kept the street sparsely populated, so not a lot of people are around to see their confrontation and his potential death by catastrophic heart failure.

222

"Just tell me," he says. "Whatever it is, I promise I won't be angry."

"Sure." She trembles. "You say that *now*."

"Viviana."

"Angel is our daughter!" Vivienne squeezes her jaw so tight he hears her teeth grinding. "Yours and mine! Not Athena's! Mine."

The words hang between them like crackling fire, so bright and hot and sharp that Tony can't pay attention to anything else. Seattle has receded into dark, smoky gloom. Distantly, he hears a clap of thunder and realizes the pressure has dropped. Maybe that rain is coming after all.

"Say something," Vivienne says, her voice trembling with uncharacteristic weakness.

She's afraid, Tony realizes. He has rarely known her to be afraid, let alone show it. It draws him to her, her vulnerability. He wants to take her in his arms and reassure her, and maybe she would even let him. But they aren't there yet. If you asked him before today, he wouldn't have been sure they would ever be there again. But now ...

"Makes sense," he says.

Vivienne blinks at him for a full thirty seconds before she replies. "What?"

"I said it makes sense."

His cheek explodes in pain where Vivienne slaps him. Okay, he deserved that.

"Athena's memory manipulation powers," Tony says.

"You ... how long have you known about that?"

"I worked it out in ... 2008?" Tony shrugs. "Explains the gaps in my memory. I—"

"You impossible asshole!" She winds back for another strike, but he puts up an arm to block. "You knew Athena could do that, and you never told me?"

"I thought you were dead at the time," Tony says.

"No you fucking *didn't*."

"True. I didn't." He inclines his head. "And I didn't think Athena was dead either."

"You—" Vivienne bites her lip. "Okay, how much do you know about this? Did you ... did you already know? About—"

"That you're Angel's mother?" Tony shakes his head. "That didn't even occur to me. But it makes sense." He holds up a hand to stay her as her expression turns murderous again. "Athena is a murderous angry god. Of course she stole our child."

"Our ... okay, we'll circle back to this 'angry god' thing, but first things first." Vivienne takes a deep breath to steady herself. "You're okay with this? About Angel being yours and mine—?"

"Viviana." He reaches out to touch her cheek, and she doesn't flinch away. "I was deeply in love with you. I wanted to be with you. Having a child with you—" He shakes his head. "That would have been the happiest moment of my life."

"Yeah." Vivienne shivers. "Fuck, maybe it was. That's why Athena had to take it."

Tony sets his jaw. "Puta."

"Agreed." Vivienne rubs her arms. It's gotten a little chilly despite the smoke. "So—"

"Who else knows?" Tony asks.

"Besides you and me?" Vivienne considers. "Orestes—he figured it out on his own. Apparently some comic book geek fuckery, but I'm sure the Godsight was involved. Probably some of the sisters at Our Lady of the Lake. Oh, and my mom."

Tony frowns. "Your mother ... is dead, isn't she?"

"Long story. Too much to get into now."

"So you haven't told her," Tony says. "Angel, I mean."

"No." Vivienne winces. "I got no idea how she'll react. I was hoping you might. Um. Tell her."

"I could." Tony purses his lips. "But it might be better coming from you."

"How do you figure?"

"You have a closer relationship with her," he says.

"Bullshit."

Tony shakes his head. "I've been working on building up our connection for years, but you—you've been part of her life much longer. She trusts you."

"Have you ever met your daughter?"

"*Our* daughter."

"Our. Right." Vivienne nods. "The thing is, I don't know how to be a mother. That's the thing I'm least qualified for. If I can't even talk to my kid, how am I supposed to do this?"

"Well, you're out of time."

"Huh?"

Tony pulls out his phone. "I texted Angel from the roast house. I estimate she averages about five hundred miles an hour, and it's three-thousand miles from here to Cobalt City, so—"

His six-hour timer is down to about thirty seconds, give or take.

"You're shitting me." Vivienne glares. "This is just like you. Force me into something I don't want to do because of math. Fuck you, Tony."

"Hey, all you told me was my daughter was in trouble," he says.

"*Our* daughter."

He can't help but smile a little.

"Fucking Tony."

His estimation wasn't too far off, it seems, as the smoke above ripples and parts to admit a streaking form in a white jumpsuit with a pink energy trail. Angel has clearly been decelerating for a while, but she still smashes down onto the sidewalk hard enough to put a small crater in the concrete. She's wearing her racetrack-like helmet as well as a backpack—one of the bags Tony designed for her to survive high-velocity air travel. The pink power lines on her suit slowly fade, smoke stirring around them and wisping away to nothing.

"Okay, I'm here," she says. "Where's the fire?"

She stares at the two of them—at Tony standing impassively and Vivienne grumbling a series of curses that can't even be repeated in print—and acquires a confused expression.

"Um?" she says.

"Hey ... A," Vivienne says. "How was your trip?"

"Oh my God, Ruby Killingsworth is awesome!" Angel brightens. "She lives in this massive tower but also has this ginormous mansion with a hedge maze and a pool and like any number of fountains. Also, we're recording an album together, and she's gonna send me on a tour with actual MerMeg to screw up Prather's chances at re-election because he woke her up early or something. I don't know why she makes decisions, but when she does, they're major. Also? She has a personal three-star chef and finally fed me enough, and there weren't even that many future terrorists with guns, and it was such a good vacation—" She looks from one to the other and trails off. "What?"

"Viviana," Tony says.

"Don't rush me."

"Viviana, just tell her."

"Tell me what?" Angel blinks at them. "You guys are being weird."

"A—Angel," Vivienne says. "You know how Athena is alive, or at least still active?"

"Yeah?" Angel raises an eyebrow. "You found her? Tell me you found her. I've so been looking forward to punting her right in the—"

"She has memory manipulation powers," Vivienne says. "That's her core power set."

"Okay?" Angel pulls up short. "So?"

"She's used those powers on us," Tony says. "All of us."

Vivienne shoots him a look. "Stop helping."

Angel furrows her brow. "I'm confused. So she what, made you forget something? Like where she's hiding out? I mentioned wanting to—?"

"I'm your mother," Vivienne says.

Angel's words cut off and she blinks at them both. Then she smiles broadly. "Ha! Yeah, right."

"It's true, mija," Tony says.

"Okay, Dad." Angel only laughs harder. "OMG, you had me fly across the country to tell me you two sleep together sometimes? Lol, I *know*." She looks around, her smile spreading wider than is quite healthy. "Where are the cameras? Is this a TikTok challenge? Is Marcus hiding in the bushes recording this?" She turns to the bushes near the entrance to the chocolate factory and calls out with marked desperation. "Marcus? Babe? You can come out now!"

"A—" Vivienne reaches for her hand.

"No." Angel wrenches her hand out of Vivienne's reach. "No, don't touch me, thanks." She looks at Tony, and now her eyes are dangerous. "This is a prank, right? Dad? Please tell me it's a prank."

Tony has spent the last years doing everything he can to be there for his daughter. He abandoned her for the first sixteen years of her life, which, come to think of it, was probably a result of the memory manipulation. Athena had let him remember Angel as a baby, but not her birth—which would have included Vivienne, presumably—and he'd always thought his daughter had perished in the attack on Seattle, only one more reason to hate Vivienne. And somehow, he didn't *really* remember her until 2017, when she and Vivienne fought the Aphid.[14] And since then, he's been trying to make up for lost time.

But Angel always seemed to remember *him*, so maybe Athena didn't wipe her memory the same way? She would have been just a baby the last time they saw each other, but apparently Angel retained some memory of him. But if that's the case, wouldn't she remember her mother, too? Wouldn't she—?

Oh. Tony realizes that's why Angel's trying to deny all this. Because it sounds right to her, even if she wasn't consciously aware of it. She embraced the accepted history and went along with it, believing Athena was her mother, but deep down, she knows. She *knows* this is true, and that realization only reinforces Tony's own belief.

"Oh mija," he says. "Lo siento mucho."

Angel looks away from Vivienne, whom she has fixed with a death glare for the last few seconds, and looks to Tony. "So you're saying this is real? She's really my mother. Her. Not Athena. *Her.*"

"That's right," Vivienne says. "You were just a baby. It's not your—" She trails off.

"Not my fault?" Angel crosses her arms. "Is that all you're going to say on the subject?"

"I'm sorry?" It's unclear if Vivienne is asking for clarification or trying out an apology as a response. Either way, it doesn't even remotely work.

"How ... how dare you?" Angel asks, as though she's honestly surprised. "You are unbelievable. Both of you. Bad enough that *you* neglect me almost my whole life, and you blast me with your powers a bunch, oh, and almost get me killed dozens of times, but now you've been my mother this whole time and you what, just never mentioned it?"

---

[14] He means the "first" adventure of Lady Vengeance and A-Girl in *Libations for the Dead*, not counting their appearances in other works. Memory warping powers are weird. ~ Continuity Cop Vogel

"Our memories were erased, mija," Tony says, helpfully. "Just like yours were."

"Zip it, Boomer. You don't get to—oh God." Angel makes a horrified face. "All those times you made those passes at Marcus? Ugh, do you literally have no shame, you psychopath? I thought fucking your daughter's boyfriend was just a porn thing. I didn't think you'd actually *do* it."

"Hey," Vivienne says.

"Shut up. I'm talking now." Angel grasps her forehead. "Shit, does Marcus know?"

"I don't see how he could," Tony says.

"Yes," Vivienne says, drawing a curious look.

"Right." Angel takes a deep breath, and her pink aura deepens to an angry rose color. "I will deal with you. Don't think I won't. But right now? I need to talk to Marcus."

Vivienne reaches for her. "A, don't—"

"*You* don't." Angel whirls on them, holding up one finger. "I'm a whole adult with my own life, and you need to not make me fly across the country for bullshit reasons that could have been a text message. Ugh, I can't believe I'm missing rehearsal for this shit. And I was going to bake cookies with freaking *Stardust* afterward. I could be eating those right now." Her eyes flash. "Right. *Now*."

"Mija," Tony says.

"Oh, and thanks for wishing me happy birthday, Dad and ... Mom. *Ugh*."

Angel takes off with enough force to put a crater in the sidewalk. Tony thought she was past the "collateral property damage" phase of learning to use her powers, but apparently, bad habits die hard. Especially when your whole world is turned upside down.

Vivienne is staring at the crater with sincere remorse and not a little trepidation.

Tony clears his throat. "Did you actually—?"

She speaks without looking at him. "Sleep with Marcus? Of course not. I have limits."

"Oh yeah?"

She glowers at him, then looks away. "She's not going to ... kill him, is she?"

Tony shrugs. "She's your daughter."

"Is that a yes or a no?"

He shrugs again.

"They're stronger than we ever were," Vivienne says. "They'll figure it out."

"Will they, though?" Athena asks.

Before Vivienne can even react, Tony turns with explosive speed, sending a razor feather out of his suit sleeve in the same fluid movement. The blade hits nothing but air until it chips off the brick of the chocolate factory and disappears into the bushes.

"Amusing."

There Athena stands in all her golden majesty, her mantle floating around her, though obviously not physically, per the knife throw. Whether the fearsword in Vivienne's hands would actually strike her is unclear, but she clearly isn't here to fight. She looks young and beautiful and vibrant as ever, but Tony knows it's an illusion. How much about her always has been?

A lot, he suspects.

"Time for a villain monologue, huh?" Vivienne asks, face illuminated by her purple fearsword. "We're not interested."

"Oh, I think you'll find you *are*," Athena says. "I'm here to offer you an invitation."

Vivienne almost attacks her right then, but Tony holds up a hand to stay her. "We're listening."

"I'm not," Vivienne says, but she backs down anyway.

"Now that the truth is out in the open," Athena says. "I propose a ... family reunion, of sorts. With Antonio's brain and your little Goblin Queen's magic, it's only a matter of time until you track me down, and if we're going to finish this, we should do it *right*. All of you, versus all of me."

"All two of you, you mean?" Tony asks. "Or is it three?"

Athena just smiles. "I'd say we should reunite at the tower—for old time's sake—but I know you'll negotiate a venue as far from civilians as possible, so let's just cut to the chase. But let's make it *scenic*. Snoqualmie Falls. I shall await you there—in our special place, Tony."

Tony glances at Vivienne, but if she has any reaction to that, she keeps it carefully hidden.

"When?" Vivienne asks. "Or are you just going to wait around for us to show up and kick your ass?"

Athena laughs. "You'll need time to prepare, so let us say, the eve of the New Year. A perfect time to leave old business behind. To find a new, fresh path."

"Sounds good to me," Vivienne says. "We'll even show up early. Leave plenty of time for champagne."

"Wonderful." Athena raises her arms, invoking swirling, cold power from below her, as though channeling the force of some hell dimension. *The very one she visited as a goddess*, Tony thinks. "Bring whoever you want, whatever powers you want, only come with your full force and fury. And let us put an end to this."

"An end," Tony says. "Vale."

"Leave your earrings at home, bitch," Vivienne says.

Athena laughs once more—a sound underpinned by distant echoes of a thousand other voices, crying out in mirth and sorrow. "Soon," she says, even as her visage fades into the smoke.

The Seattle evening deepens. There's that distant sound of thunder again. It's reassuring. It promises pain and relief in equal measure. The road is set. The path clear.

"So ... what now?" Vivienne asks.

Tony lets the silence linger for a long time, then nods. "You said rings. At the forge."

"I did," Vivienne says. "Damascus rings."

"Real Damascus or—?"

"The modern technique we call Damascus," Vivienne says. "Forging multiple kinds of steel together to produce patterns. See, I listen. Sometimes."

"You binged *Forged in Fire*."

"In my defense, Doug Marcaida is extremely hot."

"He is."

She looks up at him, her eyes damp. "So ... we actually doing this?"

"They're not engagement rings, right?"

"*Fuck* no, I'm not marrying you."

"We're not getting back together?"

"Nope. Never ever."

Tony nods. "Let's go forge some rings."

It starts to rain.

# CHAPTER TWENTY-TWO: YOU CALL ME A BITCH LIKE IT'S A BAD THING

---

The next two and a half months pass in a wild mess of shouting, snark, and studiously ignoring one another. As one might expect.

Caught in the middle of it all, Orestes does what he can to keep the peace. When Angel appeared at the window of their apartment on Capitol Hill, he could tell from her expression that something had gone down, and she didn't even have to lay into him about her stupid father or disappointing aunt/mother for Orestes to know what it had been. There were a few sharp words for him, of course, but it became clear very quickly that Angel considered Orestes her ally in all this, and she eventually broke down crying that night. Which, hard as it was, suggested progress. Orestes just held her and listened and did his best to support her.

Clearly, Angel doesn't want to see Vivienne, and the feeling seems to be mutual. Aside from that day at the church, he hasn't seen Vivienne most of the fall outside occasional check-ins at the Devil's Due, and then she disappeared entirely toward the end of October. Wherever she is, she isn't dead, because she keeps texting back, and Tony would probably make some major move if he has reason to believe she's in trouble. Historically speaking, she was probably whisked away on some romantic adventure with Ruby Killingsworth.[15] Lucky or cursed, hard to say.

---

[15] See the forthcoming *Femmes Fatale 3: Bad Romance*! Said romantic misadventure, set between late October and Christmas 2020, happens

Mediating all this tension between Angel, Tony, and especially Vivienne has been quite the headache, though. Oh, and the political fate of the United States. He's felt notably less anxious since he came back to life—something about constructing a new body out of thin air alters brain chemistry—but the cold war tension among those three tells him that he isn't as cured as he thought he was. And now it's the middle of November, and he wonders where all the time went.

Apparently, Vivienne's back, which he discovered when she called a meeting at her apartment.

The rain outside the window comes down in soft, reassuring waves. After a season of so little precipitation, the downpour is welcome.

A t-shirt lands on his face, jarring him out of his reverie.

"Hey!" Angel leans out the bathroom door, curling iron in her hair. "Would you get up? My dad said 0800 sharp."

The clock says 7:30, Saturday, November 14th.

"Five more minutes?" Orestes asks. "I can get ready fast."

"We're not flying there," Angel says. "It's raining."

"I don't mind the rain."

"Well, I don't want to drop you when you're all slippery. Plus, I'm doing my hair."

"Um?"

"I don't want helmet hair."

"Okay."

Orestes opens his phone and scans the push notifications. Ever since Prather was crushed a couple weeks ago, the news has been pretty much entirely democratic jubilation and optimism. According to most news outlets, the guy who won—Martin Crane—has the charisma of a zucchini, but Prather caused himself and his Republicans so much damage over the last four years that a turnip would have unseated him, and a zucchini is an objectively superior vegetable. Crane simply has the capacity for self-awareness and empathy, and really, that's all it takes after four years of chaos, pain, and stupidity.

---

concurrently with this and the next two chapters.

The country's getting back on track. And surely this would never happen again, right?

Right?

Orestes is deeply relieved, but something gnaws at him. A worry about getting complacent. He doesn't know what will happen. He can't see past a point. All he has to do now is get past that point.

Angel sweeps back into the room, looking gorgeous and perfect as ever, especially in just her pink underwear. "Okay," she says, holding up a pink top and a red one. "Which?"

"I don't have my glasses. Come closer."

"We both know you don't need glasses anymore." She rolls her eyes and does so anyway, and he makes a daring grab for her midriff. "Hey now, don't change the subject."

She doesn't pull away, though, and only edges a little closer when he kisses her on the hip. Then a little inside, then a little further.

"Hey, nuh-uh." With a sigh, Angel pulls out of his reach. She tosses the red top into the haphazard pile of clothes in the closet and shrugs into the pink one. "Get your butt up, Marcus Orestes. We're going to that briefing, and we are going to look so fab that my aunt has an embolism."

"You mean—?"

"My mom, right." Angel sets her jaw. "Four minutes, but I'm calling the Uber now. Get dressed."

Orestes lies back in the bed, listening to the rain as he watches Angel pull on her jeans. He wishes it could be like this for longer. Forever, if possible. He wishes that what he's already seen doesn't happen, even if he knows it will. It might be possible to avoid it, though. Maybe.

~

"A!" Yumi exclaims, as they head into the lobby of Vivienne's apartment complex.

"Oh, thank *God.*"

The hyperactive ninja girl bounds away from a haggard-looking receptionist to embrace Angel with obvious joy. Orestes can't help but share in the feeling of relief ... at least until Yumi hugs him, too, and he feels the tension fairly vibrating all through her wiry body.

"What's wrong?" he asks, prompting Angel to raise an eyebrow.

"What, is Justice 2.0 psychic now?" Yumi grins, but it's weak—a front. "It's nothing. Lisa and I had ... um—"

"A fight?" Angel suggests.

"A disagreement," Yumi says. "She found out I was back in my dad's good graces and have my trust fund again."

"And that's not a good thing?" Angel asks.

"Well ... considering I spent half a year just not mentioning it, yeah. Also, she's suspicious about what I had to do to get my card unlocked. Ooh, I love your hair, A."

"Thanks."

"What *did* you have to do?" Orestes asks.

"Nothing!" Yumi says. "Nothing much. It's ... look, you know which apartment is V's right? I've never been here, and the receptionist is being less than helpful."

"She's not under her own name," Orestes says. "Hang on."

The lobby is still decorated for Halloween with spiderwebs, pumpkins, the whole thing. A couple of guys in black are currently in the process of replacing these with Thanksgiving decorations. Orestes heads over to the desk, where he halfway expects to find Jessie, the receptionist he first met two years ago, but she quit this summer, and instead it's a person with sharp features whose nametag says "Qaren, they/them." Karen with a Q? More like Quran? Best not to chance it.

"Hey," he says, flashing them a smile. "I'm here to see my friend. In apartment 221?"

Qaren types something in the computer but hesitates over the Enter key and gives Orestes a dubious look. They've got a pastel goth thing going, which may be a leftover Halloween costume or may just be their cute aesthetic. He has no frame of reference. "Name?" they ask.

"Marcus," he says. "She's expecting me."

"I mean your friend's name."

"Oh. It's Christina." He leans in closer to whisper. "Christina Ricci."

"Who?" Yumi says behind him.

Angel shrugs.

234

Qaren, on the other hand, brightens suddenly. "Oh! Her. She's awesome." They throw back their colorful hair and laugh. "Head on up. I'll buzz you in."

"Thanks?" Orestes wasn't expecting that, but he'll take it.

"What was that about?" Angel asks. "Did V make a friend or something?"

"Dude, your aunt *is* awesome," Yumi says. Then, when they both stare at her: "What?"

~

When they get up to apartment 221, Tony and Vivienne are already at her cluttered dining room table, poring over notes and sketches. He has plugged a device into her TV, which currently displays a series of maps, charts, and arcane and occult symbology. Orestes recognizes some of those symbols, from truly ancient memories his death and resurrection dredged up. This gives him confidence that bringing Tony in was the right call.

Even spending most of his time fomenting rebellion and leading anti-fascist efforts in San Francisco, he's been here off and on over the autumn, and he and Vivienne have kept up virtually to share data and bounce ideas around. He was in the Bay Area during the election earlier this week, bracing for protests and crackdowns, but Prather's whole bloated fascist regime collapsed with the wheeze of a deflating balloon, and now he's back to give this action briefing.

And not a moment too soon: Angel needs something to set her mind to, having just finished up her commitments to Ruby Killingsworth's anti-Prather music tour. According to Angel, Ruby's campaign to overthrow the Prat Hat menace seems to be based more on her loathing for the man than any democratic or civic responsibility. Orestes isn't so sure. He has only met Ruby a couple times, mostly in passing, but he suspects that beneath her uncaring, high-functioning sociopathic façade, she has a heart of— well, if not gold, at least something lustrous and valuable. Platinum, maybe.

Not, of course, that he would ever say such a thing out loud.

"Good," Tony says. "Everyone's here."

Vivienne gives them a weary wave. She looks like she hasn't slept in days, which might be a hangover, or might be withdrawals. Either way, she perks up a little when Yumi stutters and stammers out profuse thanks for inviting her.

"—anything you need, I'm here, I swear, literally anything," Yumi is saying.

"Relax, kid," she says. "We're none of us morning people."

"Sorry, it's just that it's eleven for me. Oh, I brought donuts, who wants donuts? I'm on a diet so—"

Orestes pays more attention to Angel, who isn't quite giving Vivienne a death stare, but it's definitely a serious wounding stare.

"A." Whether because she's trying to seem approachable or because it's eight in the morning, Vivienne has a big glass of orange juice rather than a bottle of Jack.

Angel doesn't acknowledge her but instead raises her chin.

Vivienne sighs and sips some of her drink.

"You owe me twenty bucks, by the way," Yumi says to Angel.

"Give it a minute," Angel replies. "Could be half vodka."

They were betting on whether she'd be drunk at the briefing? Things are worse than he thought.

After coffee, donuts, and orange juice are distributed, the five of them sit around Vivienne's battered kitchen table. It's centrally located and a relatively public place, so the chances of being attacked are low, and they've all been there except, apparently, Yumi. The main disadvantages are the size of the unit—which can barely handle five warm bodies at a push—and the parking situation in Belltown, but even sandwiched between Downtown and Seattle Center, it's surprisingly not too bad.

Of all of them, it's Angel who speaks first.

"Do we really have to be here?" She shoots a glare at Vivienne that makes it clear what she means. Two and a half months later, and she's not over it.

"Mija, we need to share information," Tony says.

"Do we? I figured you'd just share it when it was convenient."

"Angel," Vivienne says. "I'm sorry, okay? Can we just—?"

"*I'm* sorry, *no*, we can't," Angel says. "You invited us here. To this meeting that could have been an email. So you just get to deal with it, Boomer."

236

"I was born in 1978," Vivienne says. "That's Gen-X. It was literally my forty-second birthday a week ago. Not that you came to my party."

"The drunken pity party?" Angel flips her perfect hair and smirks. "Pass."

"Joke's on you," Vivienne says. "I don't need a party to drink."

"Or to feel sorry for yourself."

"Ladies," Tony says.

"Shut up!" they say in surprising unison.

"Can we focus?" Orestes asks. "We've all done a lot of work here, and no one wants to drag this out."

They both look at him sharply, and at first it looks like Vivienne will argue, but that would only invite another barb from Angel. She nods. "Fine. Go on, Tony."

"Why are they so aggro?" Yumi asks Orestes quietly. "This is like, a new level of hate."

Orestes bites his tongue. That's not really his story to tell, and now isn't the right time anyway.

"Ishtar challenged us on a field of her choosing." Tony brings up a map of the greater Seattle area on Vivienne's TV and zooms in on the Snoqualmie region. "She chose Snoqualmie Falls. She and I *do* have a place there, one could argue: The Salish Lodge."

He pulls up a picture of a scenic hotel beside a waterfall: a classic and probably extremely expensive spot, especially if you book the riverside rooms. But what a view.

"Why does that hotel look familiar?" Angel asks.

"It's the hotel they used for *Twin Peaks*," Vivienne says. When no one shows any sign of recognition, she sighs. "It was one of my favorite TV shows back in the nineties."

"Oh!" Yumi says. "I've stayed there before! They do this honey waterfall thing. It's amazing."

"I thought you were vegan," Orestes says.

"I mean, not about *honey*."

"We only stayed there once," Tony says, as though they never interrupted him. "For our honeymoon. But other than that, I wouldn't call it *special*."

Yumi snerks. "Skill issue."

Vivienne glowers. "Not sure we need those details."

Angel pulls a face. "Yeah, Dad, *jeez*."

"We think she has a haven there," Vivienne says.

Yumi looks confused, Angel annoyed, so Orestes pipes up. "What's a haven?"

"Gods can't exist in our dimension—not directly," Tony explains. "They need an avatar to anchor their being or, barring that, a focus point. An area of space specially prepared to overlap the mortal coil and ... the immortal one. Like the floors of Ruby Killingsworth's tower that allow Loki to manifest. Do I have that right?"

"More or less." Vivienne shrugs. "Sounds like you know more about magic than I do."

"I read," Tony says.

"Back up." Yumi blinks rapidly. "Loki? Like ... *Loki*, Loki?"

"He means from Norse mythology," Vivienne says. "Loki, the god of mischief, prophesied to bring about the end of the world, but mostly they're just an annoying troll. Hot, though."

Tony clears his throat.

"It's not mythology if it's real," Angel says with a huff.

"All myths are based on some degree of truth," Tony says. "Loki is real, as is Thor."

"Oh, Loki is definitely real," Yumi says. "I saw her once. She was *real* hot."

"It's they, technically," Vivienne says. "You see what you want to see."

"How many?" Orestes asks. "How many gods, I mean?"

"Who knows." Vivienne shrugs. "Maybe all of them. The only one that really matters right now is this one." She holds up a picture of a ceramic fertility idol. "Ishtar. Goddess of love, fertility, wisdom, and war."

"That's ... an interesting combo of deific interests," Yumi says.

"More common than you'd think," Tony says.

"Ancient Mesopotamia had it going on," Orestes says, because his inner mythology nerd can't resist. "Though really, Ishtar? That's her Babylonian name, right? Why not Inanna?"

"Why not Athena?" Vivienne asks, her tone cold.

"Or Carmen," Angel says, which makes Vivienne glare at her.

If Tony feels the barb, he shows no sign. "Because that is what she called herself." Tony touches several images on the screen, pulling them up. How he made Vivienne's LCD TV a touchscreen,

238

who can say. He's the tech hero, after all. "It is possible the same entity has empowered cults to Astarte, Aphrodite, and even the Virgin Mary. We simply do not know. But we can respect her chosen name."

"So progressive," Vivienne says. "This woman literally fucked up our lives, but let's not disrespect her or anything."

"I'm sure you'll do plenty of that," Angel says. "Old people don't understand chosen names."

Vivienne bristles. "You know what—"

"What is with you two?" Yumi asks. "You're bitching at each other even more than usual. Did something happen?" Everyone stares at her. "*What?*"

For a long moment, it seems like no one will speak. When Orestes opens his mouth, Angel shoots him a glance and raises her hand. She takes a deep breath.

"She's my mother, okay?" Angel says. "Not my aunt. My *mom.*"

"She ... she is?" Yumi looks at Vivienne. "You are?"

Vivienne nods. "Apparently so."

"That's so cool!" Yumi squeals. "Since when?"

"Since she was born?" Vivienne glowers at her orange juice, as if wishing it *were* half-vodka.

"No, I mean, like, since when have you known?" Yumi asks. "Were you keeping it a secret for some big reveal or something?"

"Thank you," Orestes says. "I knew I wasn't the only one."

"Our memories were erased," Angel says.

Vivienne nods in agreement.

"So cool!" Yumi says again. "I mean, obviously it sucks, and we should kick the ass of whoever or whatever did this to you, but you've gotta admit, it's an amazing plot twist!"

"I think you'll find that we don't," Vivienne says.

"Yeah, what's so cool about it?" Angel asks. "Instead of a neglectful aunt, I have a neglectful mom. And instead of an undead mother figure, it's a crazy psycho bitch who stole me as a child."

"Okay, but ... this is *legendary,*" Yumi says. "Congratulations!"

It's the wrong thing to say. The tension has only grown between Angel and Vivienne, and as much as Orestes hoped Yumi's enthusiasm would make things better, it seems to have had the opposite effect. The gloves come off, and they start arguing immediately, slinging insults and barbs at each other. It's the same old thing: Vivienne is pissed about Angel's jabs and snark, and Angel is furious at Vivienne keeping this secret from her, even though both of them are actually angry at Athena, not each other.

Eventually, Orestes gets up and drifts to the balcony. From here, he can see the monorail track about fifty feet to the north and the fire station across the street to the east. It's hardly the most ideal locale, but there's something comfortable about it. He's spent a lot of time here, usually in one nonsense situation or another, and slept on that couch more times than he can count. It feels like a big change is coming, though, and he's not sure anything will ever be the same.

The Godsight activates, and he sees more figures on the still darkened street, heading about their business on this nice-ish November morning. A tour bus shaped like a boat and decorated with a duck motif rolls by, with dozens of tourists waving duck calls. A few unhoused people asking for change. A three-legged white and black dog, which bounds to sniff at a guy standing there, looking up at the apartment ...

Wait.

Orestes focuses on the figure: a short man dressed in a ragged coat, his skin drawn and gray as if with sickness. He's not a future projection, but he's there now, just below them on the street. Could just be another drug addict or weirdo, but there's something about him. And not just because when the dog raises its leg to pee on the man's shoes, he doesn't even notice. He stares up at the balcony—at Orestes—and while his red Prat Hat shadows his face, his wild, bloodshot gaze fixes so directly on Orestes, it might as well be targeting software.

"Guys," Orestes says, but everyone is fighting too loudly to listen. "Guys—"

Abruptly the ragged man kicks the yelping dog aside and leaps, bony fingers outstretched. He clears at least ten feet with just that initial leap, and his fingers stick to the concrete of the building like adhesive. He crawls rapidly up the wall in total defiance of gravity, and Orestes finally catches sight of his face and, even more importantly, his long, dripping tongue.

"Guys—!" Orestes starts to cry, but the Aphid spits sticky vomit in his face, snuffing out his warning. He staggers back

240

through the sliding glass door, and his attacker follows right behind, clambering up onto the balcony like his namesake.

~

Orestes's cry draws Angel's attention, and no matter how irritated she is in the presence of her so-called mother, seeing her literal nightmare come scrambling through the door to the balcony makes that all go away pretty goddamn *fast*. The world slows around her as the hideous Aphid crawls into the apartment on all fours, his huge tongue lolling out of a too-wide smile full of broken teeth.

"Fantastic, Angel—just wonderful," Ruby Killingsworth said to her once, a couple weeks ago, as Angel stared at her phone in disbelief after the Detroit concert with MerMeg. Ruby looked fabulous as ever, of course, and had a celebratory Bellini in hand. "Whatever could be the matter, dear?"

"Oh, Miss Killingsworth, it's just—" Angel remembers showing her the phone, on which she'd called up a news story about the death of one Stefan Spencer in a maximum-security prison in Washington State. "I just ... that's the supervillain I told you about. Remember?"

"Is it? Fancy." Ruby skimmed the story. "It says here he swallowed his own prodigiously long tongue. How embarrassing. The only worse way to die would be on the toilet, I suppose."

"Yeah—" Angel recalled being surprised at Ruby's response. "You, um, didn't—"

"Have anything to do with said poor incel's demise?" Ruby laughed. "Don't ask silly questions, darling. I can barely remember his name, and that's all the way across the country."

"True." Angel nodded.

But pointedly, Ruby hadn't answered the question.

Just now, the creature that comes crawling in from the patio is barely recognizable as a human. His skin is gray and contracted, his limbs bending at impossible angles, and his features have shrunk so much his head seems too big for his face. And despite the furious, hungry light burning in his gaze, those bloodshot eyes don't seem even remotely alive.

Like when Injustice attacked them.

Why is she hesitating? Angel should be up and attacking. She should do something. But she's paralyzed in sudden terror.

Unsurprisingly, Yumi is the first to react. She hurdles the table and charges forward, Muramasa cutting a fiery swath through the air as it flies to her hand, but Vivienne tackles her abruptly aside. The live grenade that the Aphid hurled flies through the space where she was, narrowly skipping over Vivienne's back, and right into Angel's lap. That wakes her up, the way only catching a live explosive can.

"Dammit," she says. "I liked this top!"

She holds the grenade against her chest as though cradling a treasured heirloom, and it explodes dully against her, the damage contained in her hands. It was a fragmentation grenade, so the shrapnel tickles a little and, more importantly, shreds the ever-loving fuck out of her cute pink top. Good thing she's got on one of her father's patented enhanced harnesses underneath, which she got used to wearing as a sports bra some years ago. Being abruptly topless was *not* in her plans for today.

At least Vivienne tackled Yumi before she did something crazy like try to cut the grenade in half.

His hands and smile both spread wide, the Aphid has pulled out two more grenades, but Tony is already moving. Even with no suit, he's a force to be reckoned with, and he lands a push-kick into the Aphid's chest, which thwarts his forward movement and sends him into the bar between kitchen and living room. The grenades tumble out of his hands, and Tony shoves a cook pot over one of them.

"Orestes!" he shouts.

Angel looks up, startled.

The gross exfoliant mask hardens and crumbles away into unpleasantly warm ash, which flakes off Marcus's face. Then he throws as much power as he can against the other grenade, creating a bubble of force around it. The thing explodes, making him wince, but the containing bubble limits the effect to a very pretty, localized firework.

"A!" Vivienne shouts. "Stop hesitating and get rid of him!"

"Don't tell me what to—" Angel sees the vest full of flashing explosives on the Aphid, and it cuts her off. Heedless of her tattered clothes, she launches herself at him.

He's fast, no matter what his current status, but she's been practicing in the years since they last fought. She hits him dead on center mass and tackles him backward out the balcony door. His arms snap against the door jamb and the door itself, which shatters with the force, but the crunch of his bones is so satisfying. She carries him out, under the monorail, and then shoots up into the sky, trying for as much altitude as possible, as fast as possible.

"Heh," says the Aphid, in that recognizable decrepit voice, only worse. The words aren't really his. "Really thought you were safe from me, did you, false daughter?"

"You're not my real mom," Angel says. "And as for you, SS, you'll wish you'd stayed dead."

"Oh, he did," Athena says through the Aphid's mouth.

Too late, Angel realizes that the creature she's hauling into the sky is cold and brittle, like a collection of sticks wrapped in only slightly defrosted meat that's been freezer burned to hell and back. Stefan hasn't said anything himself, because he's not here. It's just Athena—*Ishtar*—puppetting his body.

"See you soon," the goddess says.

"As if!"

With a mighty shove, Angel ejects the explosive corpse, which tumbles out over the water far below, only to explode about twenty feet from her. The shockwave makes her wince and tumble back for a second before she regains her bearings. Which is when she hears the secondary explosion far below—in the apartment building she just came from.

Oh no.

Angel projects herself down at incredible, spiraling speed. If the Aphid dropped off more explosives before she got him out of there ...

Sure enough, that side of Vivienne's apartment building pours smoke into the air. An explosion has ripped the corner off, including both her apartment and the one above. Every window on the block is shattered, and the blast scattered rubble through the street.

"Marcus!" She lands inside the blackened remnants of Vivienne's apartment, which seems empty. Did the explosives vaporize them? "Dad? Mom—" She says it before she even thinks, then winces. This is no time to get annoyed. "Hey! Anyone?"

"Mija," comes Tony's voice, and Angel looks around desperately.

She peers out over the balcony and sees Tony waving to her from the street level. He seems to have escaped with just a few soot stains on his suit. Yumi is there too, coughing but okay. They seem to be directing traffic and evacuation efforts.

Angel lands next to them and throws her arms around her father. "Marcus? V?"

"Getting bystanders out," he says. "That young man of yours is exceptional at manipulating relative gravity."

"They're fine," Yumi says. "They're fine, A."

The two hug, and Angel can finally relax.

Vivienne appears out of the smoke and shadow. "I'm not getting my security deposit back, huh?"

Tony's jaw is set hard enough to cut glass.

# CHAPTER TWENTY-THREE: HURT

In point of fact, not only does Vivienne not get her security deposit back, but they also terminate her lease, effective immediately, no discussion. And as long as she's lived in that crappy apartment—as much of herself she's imbued into the wood and concrete—Vivienne entirely understands.

Still sucks.

It's when a hungover Vivienne stumbles into Fred Meyer and sees the Thanksgiving products replaced with Christmas products that she realizes time is still moving in the real world, and it's late December now. She picks up her usual: a dozen donuts, several bottles of bottom-shelf bourbon, and a five-pound bag of oranges, because you can't get scurvy before fighting the big bad. Also one fancy chocolate bar. She has to go through three cards to find one that won't get declined, and settles, unfortunately, on the debit card. She only has so much money left in her account.

It seemed ridiculous, when Athena slash Ishtar slash Carmen slash whatever-the-fuck gave them four whole months before this final climactic confrontation, but now she gets it. This was all intentional. Athena gave them this much time to expedite the deterioration. The isolation. She crashed with Ruby for a while—even went to a wedding—but that didn't really solve the problem. They had a big fight, the way they always do, and now that she's back, it's time to focus. That's what she tells herself anyway.

She hasn't been back to the Devil's Due in a month, because the last thing she wants is her evil undead sister sending a besotted suicide bomber zombie there and destroying it yet again. Andre can handle it, and honestly, Vivienne should have bequeathed it to him years ago. If she never comes back, that can only be good for him.

Angel barely talks to her. If they fought Athena right when Angel first learned the truth, that would have been bad enough, but given time for it all to sink in, their relationship is practically nonexistent at this point. And Orestes has chosen Angel's side, which, well, Vivienne can't blame him for. They still texted periodically until about two weeks ago, but Vivienne put a stop to that because it was starting to feel like cheating on Angel, and she doesn't want to put Orestes in that position. He's got his work cut out for him as-is.

Tony is barely in town, and just looking at him gives her all kinds of unpleasant feelings, including longing, disgust, and regret. Their communications these days are limited to tactical assessments and exchanging information, and as much as she wants sex, she wants equally to push him away. They've spent some time together in meat space occasionally, but not for at least a week. Wherever he is, he isn't in her bed, and she can't even say she's upset about that.

Vivienne could text Ruby again, but after their misadventures, maybe it's best to spend some time apart. Besides, Ruby's busy with her own stuff in Cobalt City. Something to do with Jaccob. But even on those occasions when they do talk, Vivienne can't bring herself to tell Ruby what's happening. At best, the woman would just do her thing: sweep in and fix everything, then be so irresistibly smug in a way Vivienne finds both adorable and infuriating. No bet.

Athena wants to strip her communities and support networks. Her sister knows her and knows she's too stubborn to reach out for help when she needs it. But Vivienne feels the weight of all her fuckups and mistakes, and it's on her to set it right. The others are part of this battle, too, but she needs to stay away from them for their own good and hers. She needs to do this alone.

With one exception.

"Got what you needed?" Yumi asks, standing by the bike parked outside.

"Yep." The bags get stuffed into the riding compartments with a crinkle of plastic. "Also, this." Vivienne hands over the chocolate bar. "Happy birthday."

"What? Really?" Yumi blinks. "And it's not even milk chocolate."

"Super dark. Like ninety-seven percent. Let's ... or you could just eat it now."

Yumi has already torn it open and takes a bite. "Mmm!"

"Good?" Vivienne asks. "I wouldn't think that much cacao—"

"It barely tastes like chocolate," Yumi says between bites. "But it's sooo good."

"You're easy to please."

"Not really?" Yumi flushes. "I mean, um—"

"I know what you meant."

Yumi didn't get to come into Fred Meyer, ostensibly because Lake City is a shady place to park, but really because Vivienne doesn't want Yumi to see how pathetic her shopping list has become.

Vivienne swings up onto her bike, which is low on gas, of course. "Let's go."

Yumi climbs on the back and wraps her arms around Vivienne's waist, which is more comforting than she wants to admit. Especially when Yumi leans her head against Vivienne's shoulder as they make their way down 35th. There's a storm coming. She can see the clouds on the horizon.

The girl is literally half her age. That's got to be a violation of some sort of dating math, right? But still, Vivienne is so deprived of physical touch at this point that she'll take what she can get. So long as she doesn't ...

~

Vivienne wakes up with a splitting headache, staring at the poster of Elvira on her bedroom ceiling. The next thing she sees is Yumi snuggled up next to her, head against her shoulder.

"Fuck," Vivienne groans.

The previous night is a wet blur. It was Yumi's twenty-first birthday, and Vivienne vaguely remembers a discussion about "legal age" for drinking, and it turns out Yumi is a complete and total lightweight. Vivienne, on the other hand ... Before this fall, she hadn't blacked out drinking more than half a dozen times in years, but it's like every other night now. Including last night.

Yumi stirs. "Hey," she says, laying her hand on Vivienne's back. "You okay?"

"No." Vivienne rubs her head. She has underwear on, which is a good sign. "Did we—?"

"You don't remember, huh?" Yumi also has a shirt on. The black one with the white letters that say "baby girl" on the front. That's not necessarily a good sign.

"No, I *don't*—" Vivienne climbs out of the bed and gropes around for something to put on. She settles for her leather jacket. "Sorry. I didn't mean to. I mean, you're a kid, and—"

"Okay, first of all." Yumi bunches the blankets up around her chest. "I'm a grown-ass adult, not a kid. Stop treating me like a child." The way she's pouting is one-hundred percent precocious goth girl.

"Yumi, I'm forty-two, and you're twenty-one. I suck at math, but that sounds like exactly double your age."

"So?" Yumi asks.

"So I'm old enough to be your mother. I *am* your best friend's mother."

"Well, Angel isn't my *best* friend. She's top five, though."

"You know what I mean!" Vivienne slumps down on the only other chair in the room, which goes with her mostly disused desk. Even when she was a kid, she rarely did her homework here. "Just ... tell me what happened last night. Please."

Yumi seems about to snark again, but she restrains the impulse. "Nothing," she says, with a tinge of disappointment. "I wanted a drink, you made me a drink, then you kept drinking, for like a *really* long time, and you started crying, and I held you until you fell asleep. That's it."

"Okay." So that's worse. Vivienne almost wishes they *had* had sex. Or at least fooled around. Even that amount of shame would feel better than letting someone see her *cry*. "Sorry about that."

"Hey." Yumi scoots across the bed closer to Vivienne, though she doesn't actually touch her. "Don't apologize for your feelings. We're all under a lot of stress. You especially."

It's funny, but Vivienne feels a little like when she's talking with Wren and they bring up a really good point, one that should have been obvious. Something about intense trauma and depression always seems to blind Vivienne to things that are staring her right in the face the whole time.

"What?" Yumi asks. "Am I really that off-putting? Like, you're that horrified to sleep with me?"

"Huh? No, it's not—" Vivienne stops herself. "You're just—"

*You're me,* she thinks but doesn't say.

"A kid?" Yumi sighs. "Look, V. I really like you. And it's not just some stupid teenage crush. If you aren't ready, that's okay. I'll wait."

It's raining very heavily outside, and Vivienne focuses on the sound of the precipitation on the roof. A branch swats against the window, trying to intrude as surely as her thoughts. The Cain house is their last retreat, because of the powerful wards against intrusion. Vivienne invited Angel and Orestes to stay there, too, but unsurprisingly, her daughter declined. Vivienne seems to be Athena's primary target anyway, and she's safe here—from outside threats. Not sure she'd be safe anywhere from *choices.*

"Don't you have a girlfriend?" Vivienne asks. Not that it has stopped her before, obviously. Sleeping with people in committed relationships used to be her preference, honestly.

"You're on my hall pass list," Yumi says.

"Your what?"

"You know, the five celebrities you and your partner agree you can sleep with, and it isn't really cheating?" Yumi brightens.

"And this is a real thing?" Vivienne asks. "Sounds like cheating."

"It's mostly a joke—you know, a way to talk about fantasies and stuff? Anyway, my list is you, Megan Fox, Jennifer Lawrence, Jaccob Stevens—"

"Wait, Jaccob Stevens?" Vivienne blinks at her. "He's even older than I am."

"Sploosh. I would ride that silver fox into *orbit.*"

"Not a bad choice, I guess. He's a prodigiously giving lover."

"Lucky!" Yumi grins.

"I noticed you had lots of women on that list—"

"Pansexuality is a spectrum."

"Don't I know it," Vivienne says. "All of them older than you."

"What can I say? I like my girls a little bit older."

Goddammit, Yumi. "Still sounds like cheating."

"Oh, Lisa has a list, too. Mostly athletes. Two tennis stars. She's got a type." Yumi shrugs. "Who's on your list?"

"I've slept with all my celebrity crushes."

"Seriously?" Yumi blinks. "Wow."

"Not as fulfilling as it seems." Vivienne shrugs, making her joints crackle. "Don't meet your heroes. They always disappoint you."

"You don't." Yumi takes her hand, but Vivienne pulls away.

"Stop," Vivienne says, light-hearted and half-serious. "You've had a front-row seat to how much of a mess my life is. You're in the fucking splash zone. Not like that, but you get it."

"Totally. And I'm still here."

Yumi touches her cheek, and this time Vivienne doesn't pull away. Yumi's crimson eyes are full of determination and fire, and Vivienne needs a little reassurance. Even if it is wrong.

"I'm good to wait," Yumi says. "As long as it takes."

Vivienne isn't sure what to say to that, so she says nothing. At first, it seems like Yumi might kiss her, and she isn't sure she'd stop her. In fact, she *knows* she won't. But Yumi stops herself. She touches her forehead to Vivienne's, but that's as far as it goes.

"Okay," Yumi says. "I'm gonna go make breakfast."

"Okay." Vivienne swallows the lump in her throat. "There should be some eggs—"

"I'll figure it out. You go back to bed if you want. You look exhausted."

"Rude."

"Still gorgeous, though."

"Cheeky."

Yumi gives her a sly smile and pads lightly out of the room.

Vivienne only realizes she's appreciating her backside in retrospect, and she groans at the realization. She flops back on the bed.

"The fuck is wrong with me?" she asks no one.

"*You can use this,*" comes the answer.

Suddenly, Vivienne is no longer alone in the room, or maybe he was there the whole time. Has he ever been far from reach? His voice is as deep as rolling thunder, and it takes her a second to realize he isn't just the storm raging outside.

"Same answer as before," Vivienne says. "Fuck off."

"*Think, Vengeance.*" Seated in her desk chair, Azazel folds one leg over his lap in a surprising and unsettlingly human gesture and grins at her with a dozen mouths in a way that is very much not. *"The girl-child is besotted with you. Desire is a weakness. One that can be exploited."*

"She's a grown-ass adult," Vivienne says. "And we're not doing that."

*"You, empathic projector, object to manipulating the emotions of others?"*

The Many-Mouthed Devourer has a point there. Vivienne's entire power set is based on fucking with people's feelings, just in a very literal way. But Yumi has precious little for Vivienne to absorb. She's fearless, for one thing. Not like Tony, with his burned-out amygdala, but Yumi has such a strong base of self-confidence that nothing will shake her. Well-earned, because have you seen that girl fight?

"Okay," Vivienne says. "Say we play this your way. Why her? I have dozens of caped friends."

*"Dozens?"* Azazel asks, with several sly grins.

"You know what I mean."

Their relationship really has evolved, Vivienne realizes. When she first heard his whispers, she was drawn to Azazel, and when she saw him for what he was, it left her so terrified and revolted that she practically had a nervous breakdown whenever he so much as spoke to her, let alone showed up. Now they can just have witty banter in her bedroom like it's cool.

*"It is not the girl herself, but the blade she wields."*

Azazel's hands shape an illusion in the air, and Vivienne sees the red katana, Muramasa, spinning lazily through the air like a pick-up in a PlayStation-era action game. It's almost worth laughing, but she wouldn't want to offend the cosmic horror in her bedroom. Or worse, make him try to be clever.

"What about it?" Vivienne asks, but she knows the answer.

*"The souldrinking sword can bind many foes—humans, monsters, even gods."*

"So you want Yumi to, what, kill my sister? Let me borrow her sword?"

*"Neither,"* Azazel says. *"You do not want what I want."*

"And what is it you want?" Vivienne asks.

*"You know what I want."*

"Yeah, but I want to hear you say it, General Halitosis."

Azazel never rises to her antagonism, which is quite annoying. Does he just not understand the references? Probably. It throws her off her trash-talk game.

"*I want you.*" The demon stands, or maybe levitates, spreading its mouth-ridden arms wide. "*You will call upon me, in your hour of need. You will welcome my aid and my succor. You will be mine, and I will be in you. All will be well, and all things will be as they must.*"

"Hmm. Yeah, hard pass."

Azazel seems exactly as bothered by her defiance as ever, which is not at all. "*Humans exist to be ruled. You fear choice. You evade responsibility. You lack conviction. And so all your efforts will fail, and you will call upon me. Because you cannot do what is necessary. Because you are weak.*"

"You're wrong," she says, but they both know she isn't nearly as certain as she sounds.

"*I have never lied to you, Vengeance, and I never will. You will be mine, and this world will be ours. It is a kindness.*"

He melts away, his body diffusing into the shadows in the room, cast by the lightning outside and the glow of her black-shaded lamp. Those mocking grins are the last to disappear, bouncing around like those of a dozen Cheshire Cats. Vivienne wants nothing more than to blast them away with some leftover fear energy, but all she'll damage is her own room. The only way she can defeat Azazel is to deny him what he wants, and that's her.

"I won't," Vivienne says. "I won't be yours. I will do this without you."

She can still hear Azazel's laughter, though it might just be her imagination. Which it rarely is.

"*Veee!*" comes a cry from below. "The kitchen is on fire! Help!"

Girl can fight—can't cook.

"One second," Vivienne says.

She closes her hands into fists.

Let's do this.

# CHAPTER TWENTY-FOUR: I AM NOT A WOMAN, I'M A GOD

———

Christmas.

When she was a kid, bouncing from foster home to narrowly veiled prison, Christmas was Angel's favorite holiday. She always tried to stick it out at any particular home until December 25th, in the hopes that she might get a present.

It didn't always happen. Sometimes she was locked in the kids' room for being naughty—for stealing extra food, or mouthing off to the foster parents, or scrapping with the other kids—and sometimes they just forgot to give her a present entirely. But there were good foster homes, too, and those she mostly remembered because they gave her presents. They were always the sort of presents that would disappoint normal kids (socks, a notebook for the spring semester, calendars of dogs and cats), but for a little girl who had nothing and no one, they were precious.

Her favorite socks she got as a present when she was thirteen, though they don't really fit and they're full of holes. They're wool, and they're warm.

"Okay," Marcus is saying into the phone. "Okay, yeah. Merry Christmas to you, too."

"Was that V?" Angel asks, staring out the window of their apartment at the dreary Seattle night. It doesn't snow often in Seattle, and almost never on actual Christmas.

"Yeah," he says. "She asked about you, but I said you were busy."

Angel nods absently. The last person she wants to talk to is Vivienne, and the second-to-last person she wants to talk to is her father. It's ironic, as she's wanted a family all her life, and now that she finally has one, and it's Christmas Eve, she can't stand to be in the same room with any of them.

Adulthood *sucks*.

Under the cloud cover, Seattle seems to be poised, braced, and waiting for something. The news babbling on the TV doesn't help. Politically, there's some hope, even as Prather has been struggling to hold onto power. Maybe it's domestic terrorist attacks that they're braced for, and Angel and Orestes have been dealing with angry Prat Hats assembling in the streets to go about some delinquency. It's apparently worse down in Portland, birthplace of white supremacist street gangs, which is where her father has been, cracking skulls and fighting for freedom, and *why* is she thinking about Tony frickin' *DeSantes* right now?

Once this whole business with the evil goddess that possessed her fake mother and altered her memories or whatever is done, Angel wants to get away. Pack Marcus into his dads' Prius and just drive in some direction until it's just the two of them and they're together and away from all this nonsense.

Which is when Marcus comes into the room and tosses her pink duffel bag on the bed next to her. "All right, pick out some clothes."

Angel blinks at him, and at the bag, which she squishes between her fingers. "What, were you reading my mind?"

"What?"

"Nothing." She's been wondering if his evolved Godsight turned him psychic or something. His energy powers don't damage electronics anymore. He's still anxious, but it's under control. Why not his precognitive powers too? "Where are we going?"

His reply is firm and confident. Deliberate. "We're going on a date."

"A date?" Angel holds up the bag. "You don't usually pack a change of clothes for a date."

"It's an overnight date. I booked us a hotel room."

"On Christmas Eve?"

"It was expensive, but apparently the manager is a fan." He sits on the bed next to her, the better to pack his own overnight bag. "Not sure on the dress code, but probably a little nice. Business casual, maybe? Do I own a tie—?"

"That's ... That is so incredibly sweet." Angel gives Marcus a curious look. "What made you think to do that?"

"Oh, you know, you just seemed ... I thought it'd be good to get out of the house. Apartment."

"So you booked us a romantic getaway. On Christmas Eve."

"It's not too bad," he says. "A lot of people are home with, uh, family, so—"

"Are you gonna ask me to marry you?"

Maybe she spoke too soon about the electronic disruption effect, because as soon as she says that, the lights flicker, and the TV spontaneously switches through channels.

"That's, um," Marcus says. "I mean—"

"Relax, dummy." Angel takes his hand. "I'm gonna say yes."

"You are? I mean, good. That's a relief."

"You didn't think I would?" Angel asks. "I already said yes before. Remember?"

"I distinctly remember you didn't actually."

"I was thinking it."

"You were *thinking* it."

"Yes."

"But you didn't actually say it."

"I guess not?"

Marcus nods. "Well, to be fair, I disintegrated like five minutes later."

"And I'm not letting you get away again." Angel wraps her arms around his neck and kisses him. "We're in this together, Marcus Orestes. Okay?"

"You got it, Angel Cain-DeSantes," he says, then immediately winces. "Sorry."

"It's okay." She kisses him again. "When we get married, I'm totally taking your name, though. Angel Orestes. That works, right?"

"I mean ... that's not too old-fashioned?"

"Oh, it's a total old person move, but can you blame me? With parents like mine?"

"Not even remotely." Marcus's arms tense around her, then he eases back and holds her hands. "We don't have to do this, you know."

"What, fight my fake mother alongside my real one?" Angel asks. "Pretty sure we do, actually. Something like the fate of the world or some such BS rests upon it?"

He smiles gently. "Something like that."

That's the end of the conversation, she knows, but she's hesitant to let him go. Instead, she insists on more kisses and pulls him down onto the bed for a little fooling around before Marcus finally pulls away, laughing. "Hey, hey, save it for the honeymoon."

"Honeymoon?" Angel asks. "Marcus Orestes, what have you done?"

He gives her an impish smile. "Pack a change of clothes, and let's go."

Oh, she does. Mostly lingerie, but those are clothes, right?

~

The Salish Lodge is a classy hotel, intended for wealthy travelers, high spenders, splurge vacationers, and honeymooners.

Marcus and Angel aren't any of those, though not for want of trying. Angel gets plenty of residuals from endorsement deals and the Supergroup biopic—enough to afford their cushy apartment in Downtown—and she's had to fend off would-be job offers with a stick since the concert tour with MerMeg that lost Prather every single swing state. But Tony stressed the need to keep a low profile, so as not to attract attention from Athena or her agents, so they show up at the Salish in nondescript but decent clothes and ask for the reservation under their preferred pseudonym: Mark Angel.

As Marcus interacts with the receptionist, plying his slick adorkability, Angel idly consults a flier for spa services and admires the warm winter hunting lodge décor—Christmasy without being denominational. The interior is mostly rich burnished wood and smooth real stone floor, with brick-housed fireplaces and landscape art on the walls. Apparently they used this hotel as the set or maybe just inspiration for a TV show that Vivienne really liked back in the nineties? She can certainly see why. It has that unique Pacific Northwest darkness vibe to it, and while she doesn't personally go in for the gloomy goth thing, she can appreciate the aesthetic.

Which makes her think, unpleasantly, of her mother.

The gall. The absolute, unfettered *bullshit*. Yeah, okay, both Vivienne and Tony had their memories erased—they *claim*—but one of them should have figured this out, right? Some genius engineer and investigator her dad turned out to be, and her mom ... Angel has to correct herself. That woman is her aunt, or just V. It doesn't matter whose body she came out of. She has no mother—none who matters, anyway.

She's getting too angry again. Pointedly relaxing her fingers around the banister, Angel practices the calming breathing exercises Dr. Fulton taught her. No sense causing property damage before they've even checked in. Though if Marcus takes any longer, she might break the bed. No promises.

Angel wanders over into the attached bar, with its misty views of the waterfall and forested hills. A wealthy couple is sipping coffee and having a spirited conversation about stocks of something, while their tween daughter slouches on the couch nearby, absorbed in her phone. She catches Angel's gaze, and her eyes widen slightly. "Are you?" she mouths, and Angel returns an upraised fist with her thumb outside, pointed upward. The letter A. The girl smiles widely and starts texting furiously, but Angel dips out before she can snap a picture.

Not, however, before she picks up smells that make her mouth water and remind her that she's only eaten eight thousand calories today, which is not nearly enough.

She's suddenly very hungry for something else, though.

"Ready?" Marcus asks, keycards in hand.

Angel nods eagerly. Positively famished.

~

The sex takes about half an hour, and they lie naked and entangled in the luxurious bed, gazing out the window into the cold Northwest evening.

The only ding against their stay is that it's raining cats and dogs outside, prohibiting a stroll along any of the romantic vistas. But even then, their room has a balcony with a full view of the waterfall, and all the mysterious cold mist rising from its base as the rain falls. The sound of the rain is hypnotic and nostalgic, and Angel could lie here forever.

She must have fallen asleep, because when Marcus eventually gets up, she stirs and murmurs a vague protest. She hasn't been sleeping well for months.

"Go back to sleep," he says, kissing her temple.

"Mrff," she says, very sensibly. "Where ... you—?"

"Bathroom," he says.

She nods. It makes sense, as he didn't commandeer the bathroom as soon as they arrived like normal. They had important business, as she recalls. And much as she'd like to do a little more of that business, she's really tired, and her stomach feels a little lurchy. She paws at him, trying to pull him back anyway.

"Sleep," he says.

"Hmff," she says. "Don't ... wanna—"

She's asleep before she finishes arguing the point.

~

Orestes stands over Angel for a while. He admires the way the moonlight plays in her hair and the curve of her cheek and how adorable and fantastic she is, of course, but mostly he's just happy she's getting some sleep. This whole thing with Vivienne "I'm your mother" Cain has been hard on her, even more than she's let on. They've had conversation after fight after argument after louder fight about it, and he's not even the source of Angel's distress.

He's pretty sure she's mostly forgiven him for not saying anything, though he'll probably never hear the end of it his whole life. Sure, he knew the truth about their secret connection beforehand, though maybe "knew" is the wrong word. He had a strong suspicion, even before he met them in real life, because of a lot of contextual evidence from the comics, and because it just seemed like the way the story would go. They're so much alike, Angel and Vivienne, that Orestes always kind of just assumed it would come out when it came out. And it did.

It's not like the way these sorts of things go in the comics, where it's a big earth-shattering reveal that recontextualizes everything. Or maybe it has. Orestes can't say. He's not either of them. Regardless, all he can really see is the fallout, and that hasn't been good for either Angel or Vivienne. They barely talk, and Orestes knows it's mostly Angel who refuses to interact with her apparent mother. She understands, logically, that there was some mental fuckery going on—that Athena or the goddess within her gaslit everyone with her powers—but understanding and accepting the facts are different processes. Mentally, she gets it. Emotionally, though? Angel's never been the most emotionally stable ... which is yet another thing she and Vivienne have in common. The best thing Orestes can do is be there for her.

The second-best thing is what he's going to do tonight.

Orestes steps out onto the balcony despite the drizzling rain, most of which gets blocked by the balcony above. He leans on the rail, contemplating the waterfall and the mist rising around its base. He feels a little guilty, as he's keeping yet another secret from Angel, but this is the only way it can go down.

He lessens his personal gravity, vaults over the railing, and floats down toward the mist.

There, deep within, he sees what his Godsight has been suggesting to him all night: a golden light that transcends human vitality or power. A *divine* light.

A voice speaks in his mind. In his soul. *"Come to me, my beloved—"*

With one last thought of Angel, Orestes does just that.

~

Angel starts awake, her stomach churning, and she practically flies to the bathroom to empty herself of the last remnant of the multiple orders of surf and turf they splurged on at dinner. Her super metabolism means most of it is already digested, but there's enough to remind her unpleasantly of the taste. Still, it was worth it, and thanks to the credit line Ruby Killingsworth extended her after their very profitable concert tour, it doesn't break the bank. It is, apparently, very important to Tia Roja that Angel be "properly" fed. She's still figuring out exactly what that means, but turns out it's a *lot*.

Not that she can tell Vivienne about the arrangement. Something tells her that her aunt—her *mother*—won't take it well. She doesn't care about upsetting Vivienne, of course, but no reason to make life complicated for Tia Roja. It's nice to have an adult in her life who's actually supportive. For once.

Angel shoves the whole "fuck, you're my *mother*" thing aside. The last thing she wants to do on their vacation is spend it thinking about that whole mess. She'll just get angry and break everything. Or she'll start crying and never stop. Maybe both.

When she's done emptying herself, she roots through Marcus's canvas toiletries bag, which is larger than hers. That boy is extremely fastidious. Hair product, cologne, deodorant, ah, there, a little bottle of mouthwash. He has literally everything, and she has periodically considered not bringing a purse altogether. Maybe lipstick and mascara, and that's it. He always calls her beautiful regardless—because bless him, he thinks she wears makeup for *him*—and she's getting to the point where she doesn't care what others think of her. A-Girl is a made-up image, and fewer people recognize her when she "forgets" to put on her face.

Maybe, after this is all over, she and Marcus can get away from the superhero thing for a while—go on a real *vacation*, where no one will know them, and they can just be together. Just the two of them. Leave all the politics behind, the family drama, the endless social media nonsense, and just *rest*. Maybe she'll get lucky in more ways than one, and goddamn Vivienne Cain will drink herself to death and ...

"No, no," she whispers. "Not that again. Just stop thinking about her. *Ugh.*"

Easier said than done.

"Marcus, you awake?" she asks. "Babe?"

She finds the bed empty. She really needs a good cuddle and/or other things right now, and Marcus excels at snuggling and/or other things. But he's not in the chair or at the desk. Did he step out for some reason?

The bathroom was warm, almost muggy, so the comparatively frigid hotel room makes Angel shiver. The sliding glass door onto the balcony stands half-open, allowing mist to creep in and crawl across the floor. Did they leave that open? Is he out on the balcony?

"Marcus?"

She pushes outside, and finds the world full of freezing mist, like she's suddenly plunged head-first into a snowdrift. Winter in the Pacific Northwest can get really cold, sure, but this is a level of frigidity that you typically only get in an ice bath dunk tank. Angel has crashed into walk-in refrigerators more temperate, and it makes her instinctively want to find somewhere warmer. She could go back into the room, maybe take a hot shower, but the icy tendrils of mist have crept inside there as well.

There. She feels a spot of warmth in the mist of the fog—down near the waterfall. Not at its base, exactly, but at its core. If the majestic Snoqualmie Falls were a living, breathing thing, the broiling center she senses would be a pit of vitality in its gut. The center of its gravity and being.

And Angel recognizes that warm, blue energy. She would know Marcus's energy anywhere.

She climbs over the rail and flies off into the teeth-chattering mist.

Standing on the balcony alone was cold and disorienting enough, but once she's in the mist, Angel loses all sense of direction. There is no up or down, only the discombobulating mist soaking into her skin and sapping the warmth from her body. She should have put on some clothes, but too late now. The best she can do is push through the mist toward that beating heart of warmth.

"I'm coming, Marcus," she says, drifting that way. "Wait for me."

At the heart of the mist, behind the waterfall, there's a space. It's a larger space than should be able to exist there, suggesting that it isn't strictly physically connected to the mortal coil. The extra-dimensional space is partly magical, and Angel doesn't know much about magic. It looks like a temple, a little bit like that one city carved into the canyon wall in Jordan ... Petra, is it? That seems right. But this is older. Truly ancient.

Ishtar, in Athena's withered body.

Looking at her is strange, like two very different images superimposed over one another. There's her mother's body, which looks like the withered mummy she fought in the Nevada desert: talon-like nails, desiccated flesh pulled tight to yellowed bones, bandages and everything. And under and in the same place as that is a feminine figure that is the brightest, most beautiful thing Angel has ever seen.

The revealed goddess Ishtar is a being of pure light, and looking at her is like staring directly at the sun: blinding and fascinating. She can't turn away, though, as seeing is loving, and Angel has never loved anyone or anything like she does Ishtar. She almost loses herself in that divine visage, but the longer she looks, the dimmer it becomes. There are shadowy streaks—black, filmy haze that spreads across Ishtar's brightness—and they grow more noticeable the longer she stares. What is that?

"Please." The goddess speaks, and the sweet sadness of her voice stirs Angel from her fugue. "Hearken to me, Tammuz. Do not abandon me again."

Who does she mean?

Marcus has been standing there the whole time, not twelve inches from her, but Angel didn't see him at first. Now, however, when she looks at him, she sees a masculine figure juxtaposed onto him, just as Ishtar in-dwells and subsumes Athena. His god is less bright than Ishtar—less powerful, maybe?—but he has no shadowy spots. His is a warm, constant blue light. He disagrees with Ishtar, and Angel's heart breaks just listening to the hum of their shared sorrow.

"I have returned to you," Ishtar says. "As it has always been, as it will be again."

*What do you mean?* Angel wants to ask but can't. She has no voice in this exchange between gods. She pushes forward and only manages half a step. Her hand falls short of Marcus's arm.

"Why?" Marcus asks, though it isn't his voice. It's the god that dwells within him. The god who gives him his powers—who gave Justice his powers—and every iteration of him on and on back into history. "Why must you pursue me? Why can you not leave me be?"

"Because you are mine, my beloved husband," the goddess says. "It has ever been such. I have walked the darkest of paths, given everything and sacrificed all that I hold dear, simply to have you once more." She cups his chin. "I will do it again, as many times as it takes."

Oh *hell* no.

With all her strength, Angel pushes herself to take another step. Pushing against Ishtar's power is like trying to move the earth itself, and by rights it should crush her. But energy flows into her—Marcus's power—and it lets her interpose herself between her mother and her fiancé. Whatever divine bullshit she's got in her back pocket, Angel can take it.

"Look, lady," Angel says. "Marcus Orestes is *my* man, not yours. I don't know what messy drama you have with this god of his, but sounds like he's over you too."

Ishtar turns her attention to Angel, and it's a good thing she's fully stocked with power, because just that glare would have smote her dead. "It is not in the nature of gods to change," Ishtar says, eyes blazing with fury. "How dare you demand such a thing?"

Angel tries to reply, but her mouth won't work. Nor can she breathe. It's all she can do to keep her heart beating. If not for Marcus's hand on her arm, she would already have collapsed.

"My love," Tammuz says. "Have *you* not changed? What are these shadows upon you?"

"This?" The goddess looks away, but her anger remains. She lifts one hand, which courses with rippling black, like blood running through divine veins. "The taint of humanity. I have spent too long among them, and they have corrupted what I once was. Which is why I must have you, husband—that you might purify me once more."

Ishtar tries to reach for Marcus, but he draws back, just out of her reach—closer to Angel. His hand finds hers, and she feels his power flowing into her, and hers into him.

Ishtar's wrath is profound, shaking the mountain all around her. "You choose betrayal," she says. "You choose *her*."

"Damn right he does," Angel says.

Ishtar's anger ebbs somewhat, replaced with disgust and, surprisingly, sadness. "This is the path you have chosen, then. We will meet again in this place in seven days. And we will see."

Marcus nods in agreement. "We will see."

Angel, by contrast, does *not* agree. "Hold the fuck up, you Mesopotamian homewrecker—"

But Ishtar is already gone. If this was some sort of sanctuary, it isn't that now. Just a narrow cave in the rock, where teenagers might dare each other to climb and make out where no one can see.

"Dammit," Angel says. "What *was* that?"

Marcus says nothing, only takes her in his arms and floats them back to their room. It isn't flying—not exactly—but more just shaping gravity to move him. Angel thinks her flight could be that effortless, with enough practice. But that's what happens when you're playing avatar for an ancient deity. Cheat codes.

The mist has dispersed, driven away in the rain. They're soaking wet when they get back to the balcony, like they just went for a midnight swim the way only superheroes can. There they stand for a moment, gazing down at the waterfall, saying nothing. Then ...

"Ai!" Angel swats Marcus on the shoulder, nearly knocking him over. His eyes flutter, and he pulls himself together. "What were you thinking, cabrón?"

"I wasn't?" Marcus tries.

Angel crosses her arms. "You're always thinking, you nerd."

Marcus shrugs. "I thought we could learn something from her, and we did."

Angel is no more convinced than before. "Maybe. But you still shouldn't fly off alone in the middle of the night. Remember what happened last time?"[16]

"That was you, not me."

"And did it work out well for me?"

"It did not."

"I still have the scar from the missile."

"It's a sexy scar."

"Don't change the subject."

"Sorry." Marcus touches her hand. "Make it up to you?"

He goes to kiss her, but Angel turns her face. "Not while I'm all vomity and gross."

"Vomity?" he asks. "Why?"

"Because my nasty, undead, fake-ass mother trying to steal my fiancé?" Angel waves away the question. "Ugh. I need a shower."

"Oh," Marcus says, disappointed.

Angel rolls her eyes. "Tonto, make it up to me in *there*."

"*Oh*," he says.

For a pseudo-omniscient avatar of an ancient god, Marcus Orestes sucks at reading the room.

---

[16] She's referring to the events of *Fallen Angel*. ~ Eagle-Eyed Editor Vogel

# CHAPTER TWENTY-FIVE: JUDGMENT DAY

Through the scope, Antonio "The Raven" DeSantes scrutinizes the crowd gathered at Snoqualmie Falls to celebrate New Years Eve. The rain works to their advantage in this respect, limiting the time people are willing to spend outdoors. It's mostly just a few stupid teenagers and twenty somethings doing TikTok dances or taking blurry photos of the waterfall. Most of the festivities will take place inside the Salish Lodge or other establishments in the nearby town, and that keeps them away from the battle.

The few civilians willing to brave the rain also reduces the already miniscule chance that anyone will detect his sniper post some one hundred yards along the mountain, obscured by vegetation and his own patented cloaking technology. After the attack of 2001, he put the massive war chest of Supergroup's funds to good use developing this tech, even if he only carried a personal cloak out of Valhalla after the Valentine's Day attack. Of the leadership team at Supergroup, only Athena agreed with him about the need to develop assassination tech and protocols.

*Athena.*

The Raven checks the chamber and action on his rifle. It's a good weapon, the Barrett M82, aka the "Light Fifty," so-called for being light enough to carry while firing a 50-caliber cartridge at speed and velocity sufficient to disable a tank, if well aimed. He's fired basically every model, from the eighties original to the bullpup model, but his undeniable favorite is this one: the M107A1, with its titanium body, attached muzzle brake, and suppressor. He could upgrade to the XM500, but the classics are classic for a reason, and this one has sentimental value. It was a present from H and M for his fortieth birthday and even has its name—Gungnir—engraved on the casing, which was a nice touch. The Raven has bulls-eyed targets at upwards of one mile with this very gun. Putting a round into Ishtar's undead avatar at the length of a football field will be no problem.

They're fighting a literal goddess, but The Raven isn't afraid. After all, he physically can't be.

"Report," he says into the throat mic. "A? O?"

His earpiece hums. "We're in position," Orestes says. "You see us, R?"

"Confirmed."

The Raven can see his daughter and her boyfriend at the railing overlooking the waterfall. Probably no one will recognize them, except Ishtar herself, but she's expecting them, so why try to surprise her. Orestes wears the black duster The Raven got him for Christmas for exactly this operation, as well as a ridiculous, wide-brimmed, black hat Lady Vengeance ordered him online. Allegedly it's a fishing hat, and it keeps the rain out of his face, but it makes him look like some kind of urban fantasy cosplayer. A-Girl is hiding in plain sight in a white A-Girl brand jacket that obscures her white costume with the pink powerlines barely at all, but it makes her also look like a cosplayer. Can you cosplay yourself? Vivienne would know. She's always been a weeb.

"V, report," The Raven says.

"Shit." Her husky voice murmurs. "This isn't some elaborate scheme to shoot me, is it, Tony?"

"Codenames in the field."

"Look, I call Ruby 'R'—like fuck I'm going to call you 'R' too."

"R2?" Orestes asks. "Like Star Wars?"

Lady Vengeance chuckles. "He is practically a robot."

"R2-T2?" Orestes suggests.

"A *sexbot.*"

"Gross," A-Girl puts in.

"Sorry I asked," Orestes says.

The Raven sighs. "Go radio silent."

"Ooh, scold me, Daddy," Lady Vengeance quips.

A-Girl makes a gagging noise over the comms. "I'm gonna throw up over the waterfall."

"Sorry about this, Mr. De—I mean, T. Er, R," Orestes says, fumbling through the names.

"I could just shoot myself," The Raven says.

"Oh, would you?" Lady Vengeance asks.

He sighs.

The Raven can't see Lady Vengeance, but that's okay. She's famous and/or infamous enough that no one's going to fail to recognize her. Not that hiding from Ishtar is going to do much good, but if the tourists have a reason to congregate, that'll mess up his firing solution. Unless she was here with him in his sniper perch, hidden behind the runic wards and anti-magic cloak he called in favors to set up. Though if she were, he probably wouldn't be focusing on the task at hand.

There was some disagreement about the plan. Surprisingly, Vivienne was his most vociferous supporter, arguing that if he could put a high-caliber round through Athena's head and end it, that was for the best, but Orestes had argued that one can't kill a goddess that way. The best they would do is destroy her avatar, but that wouldn't solve anything. Angel was very quiet during that discussion, he recalls, and just went along with whatever they decided. She's still shaky, and he'll have to keep an eye on her. It wouldn't be out of character for her to go rogue and do something highly questionable.

Like mother, like daughter.

It's been surprisingly easy, reconciling with that truth. After her initial awkward attempts to test out a domestic life with him—something that obviously wasn't going to happen—Vivienne went back to her status quo: equal parts contempt and desire, looking to fight and fuck in equal measure, and Tony has been happy enough to oblige. There's something new between them, though. Last night, as she shuddered and moaned in his arms, Tony felt it again: a closer intimacy than they'd had for twenty years. They are no longer hunter and hunted, but both victims—both survivors.

He thinks she's forgiven him, as much as someone who calls herself "Lady Vengeance" can. And even more surprising, he's forgiven her, too.

Angel, on the other hand ... Tony isn't sure she'll ever forgive him, much less Vivienne. The revelation has triggered her abandonment complex something fierce, and she's not only refused to go to therapy, but she's retreated from all of them except Orestes over the past month. Which isn't ideal, but at least she has a good, steadfast source of strength. Tony hates relying on anyone—so much that he practically invented a brain surgery procedure to let him operate on himself—but if anyone is worthy of his trust, it's Marcus Orestes. Angel is a survivor, just like Vivienne and himself, and much as he wants to hold her in his arms and never let her go, he recognizes she needs space.

Over the long term ... Well, they don't have the time to sort through all that, which was definitely Ishtar/Athena's plan. They can't let her get in their heads any more than she already has. Once the threat is defeated, they'll spend all the necessary time in therapy to work it through. And knowing their preferences in terms of therapist, he will personally make Wren Fulton a millionaire with those bills. They'll have all the fights Vivienne and Angel and he need to have, like any family. That's what they are: a *family*, no matter how messy and fucked up and complicated. And it's what they always have been, no matter how a gaslighting goddess wants to mess with them.

It's thin, but it'll have to be enough.

The crowd starts clearing entirely as the sun goes down and the chill of the Pacific Northwest arrives in full force. The Salish Lodge and the Falls remain lit up, through a combination of Christmas lights and spotlights, making it pretty decent if not ideal for a battlefield. The Raven shifts, flexing his sore muscles beyond the camping exercises he's practiced all day. In his line of work, patience is king, but he's not getting any younger.

"Visual?" he asks.

Orestes is the first to speak. Very reliable. "No sign of Ishtar."

"You mean Athena," Lady Vengeance says, through some background noise.

"The target," The Raven corrects them. "And are you drinking at the bar?"

"What else am I supposed to do all evening?"

"Ugh," A-Girl says.

"Just stay vigilant," The Raven says. "Report in at the first sign. Over."

There's something about this. It's not just the involvement of not one but *two* wild cards in the last of the Cain women, who are both notorious for making the best concocted plan go entirely FUBAR. Nor is it the fragile strategy based on his best research—

read, shaky and dubious. No, there's something more. Tony DeSantes has always had a kind of sixth sense for impending peril.

"It'll be fine," Vivienne said to him last night, as they lay spent and entwined with each other. "I can tell you're nervous."

"I don't get nervous," he said. "I surgically can't."

"Yeah, well." She kissed him. "You still look it."

He wanted to tell her he loved her, but he didn't. They agreed.

Why is he thinking of this? What's this feeling in his chest?

He feels it and doesn't have time to react.

"There's something—" he starts, but that's as far as he gets, because Athena is kissing him.

She's here. Her well-muscled body, perfectly proportioned like a goddess of myth. Her fearsome gaze, impossible to ignore or deny. The smell of her, like everything he's ever wanted—or been led to *believe* he wanted. A creature of pure light and love and *desire*.

The runes all around them flare and dissolve, entirely overwhelmed by her divine presence. The anti-magic tech doesn't even activate.

As they kiss, her body changes: skin rotting away and atrophied muscles shrinking against yellowed bone. She grows lighter and less substantial, and colder than cold. It's like kissing a corpse, and not just that, but one that has decayed and skeletonized for years. Decades, even. She saps the warmth from his body and replaces it with her will.

"R?" comes a voice. Orestes's, he thinks. "Are you okay? Report?"

He struggles to control his vocal cords, but they won't respond.

"Dad?" A-Girl asks.

The Raven looks up at his captor, unable to do anything but obey her will.

"Answer them," Ishtar says.

"All good here," The Raven says, regardless of what he wants to say. "Over."

"Okay. Over," Orestes says.

"Whatever, *Dad*," A-Girl says.

Lady Vengeance doesn't comment.

"This was your plan? Lure me out and shoot me?" Ishtar smiles with Athena's rotted face. "Humans. Never fail to disappoint."

The Raven couldn't argue even if he wanted to, and he doesn't.

"Well. Get back in position." Ishtar touches him on the brow and his mind empties. "You're not done yet, poor man."

~

"Whatever, *Dad*." Angel sticks out her tongue as she leans against the rail over the waterfall. "This is a frickin' stupid plan, you know that, right?"

Orestes sighs. "We're doing the best we can with what we've got. Short of calling in reinforcements—"

"Like Tia Roja?" Angel asks. "Like I suggested? Like a billion times?"

"Yeah, well," Orestes says. "V wasn't lying when she said Miss Killingsworth couldn't participate in this fight. It's too risky, especially if she calls on Loki to assist."

He's giving a true assessment, but he shouldn't have mentioned Vivienne. It makes Angel dig in her heels all the harder. "Would that be so bad?" Angel presses.

"We don't know how Ishtar is operating in the mortal coil," Orestes says. "What if Loki takes control of whatever magic she's using? You really want to free a god of chaos?"

"Tia Roja trusts him." Angel's just being stubborn now, the way she gets sometimes.

"No one trusts them," Orestes says. "Especially not Miss Killingsworth."

"Fine," Angel says. "I bet she could kick Athena's ass, evil goddess or no."

"She's not evil," Orestes says before he thinks, and immediately regrets it.

"What, because you almost cheated on me with her?"

That's mostly a joke, and they both know it, but Orestes can hear the kernel of uncertainty underneath. Ever since the revelation about her real mother, Angel's been holding on by a thread. She may look fully put together—as beautiful and stylish as ever, even if she's sort of in disguise—but she's been irritable, fragile, and apt to snap over the smallest thing. Orestes knows he's a major part of that thread, but it doesn't mean Angel won't turn on him, too.

"She's ... sick," Orestes says. "She's a goddess of love, fertility, wisdom, and war, and it's mostly been that last one for millennia.

270

She's been trapped in a series of human avatars for so long, human emotions have messed her up."

"What does that mean?"

How to explain this? "Human emotions ... they're like an infection for divine entities. Gods serve particular purposes. Vibes, if you will. Humans are much more complex. We can hold two contradictory thoughts at the same time. Gods ... they can't do that. They don't know how to handle human emotions."

"So what, feeling sad makes them evil?"

"Kind of," Orestes says. "What you call 'evil' is just a logical consequence of having too much power and too little emotional intelligence. Ishtar barely remembers what it is to be a god."

"And you do? Or, well, um, *Justice* does?"

"Tammuz the shepherd," Orestes says. "He's an agriculture god, actually."

"You're shitting me." A-Girl raises an eyebrow. "The mighty Justice and Kid Justice get their powers from a farm god?"

"Shepherd," Orestes corrects her. "But generally, yeah. He's a god of plenty. Of caring for others. To each according to their need. You can see how that translates into justice—"

"Okay, yeah, I get it, I get it." Angel grins, and it's the most dazzling smile. "You don't have to go all Che Guevara on me."

"Martin Luther King Jr., actually, but who's counting."

That makes her laugh, and Orestes smiles. They're going to make it, he realizes. And that isn't just wishful thinking. The Godsight tells him that it's all going to work out. Not how, exactly, but there's a happy ending here. For the two of them, for Vivienne and Tony, for everyone.

He *hopes* that isn't just wishful thinking.

~

Teasing one finger around the brim of her third tumbler, which is mostly watered-down bourbon and a maraschino cherry, Vivienne hits send with her other forefinger.

V: *I'm drunk and bored and waiting at a bar for a fight that might not show up*

V: *entertain me*

271

No reply for a minute, and she's about to give up when the three dots appear. Ruby is typing.

R: *I shan't.*

Vivienne smirks and texts back immediately. She's on her best behavior, so she even fixes the autocorrect before she sends it. Because, believe it or not, she can be an adult.

V: *come on*

The response comes quick enough that it must have been prepared in advance. Which is hardly a surprise. Ruby Killingsworth is the kind of woman who always has a plan and is prepared for anything in exactly the way Vivienne is not.

R: *I'm at the opera league party surrounded by people who think party hats are an appropriate fashion accessory, and I am surviving by drinking mediocre champagne, all because a certain dark-haired vigilante decided she'd rather get drunk alone at a bar and wait for a fight that may not show up than to fly out here to spend New Year's Eve with me.*

R: *I shan't.*

Vivienne scoffs at that, which the bespectacled dude sitting next to her with his own smoked Old Fashioned seems to have taken as an invitation to smile over at her. He's her type: tall, semi-muscular, bearded, glasses, nerdy. Married. He's wearing a stainless-steel wedding ring with a leaf motif. Adorable. And she can tell that he is attracted to her. She could probably have him, if she wanted, but surprisingly, she doesn't. Call it growth. Instead, they exchange a toast, and she goes back to her phone.

V: *c'mon you know you want to*

R: *For your information, I had more than enough of you at Christmas, and I do not require any further flirtatious banter, thank you.*

V: *because Tony's here?*

R: *No comment.*

V: *that's a comment, though*

That bit of snark doesn't get a reply, as Vivienne expected. Tony's always been a sore spot for Ruby, especially the last year or so. I mean, she did put not one but two curses on him in an attempt to keep him away from Vivienne. She really shouldn't dare Ruby to put a third on him, but that fourth Old Fashioned is getting smoked behind the bar, so ...

V: *if it makes you feel better, your curse really cuts down on our play*

R: *...*

V: *does it*
V: *make you feel better*
R: *It does not.*
V: *seriously, that man is a terrible bottom*
R: *That seems unlikely.*

That makes Vivienne snerk again, but fortunately, the cute glasses guy finished his drink and headed off with his extremely beautiful wife, who looks like she runs marathons and builds houses in Uganda. She's definitely out of his league, but Vivienne can tell they're married based on the matching rings and how they feel about each other, which is so sweet she's tempted to switch to straight bourbon. They head off into the hotel proper, arm in arm, casually bantering in the manner of people who've known and loved each other for twenty years. Sometimes, that's exactly what Vivienne wants. Not the wedding ring or the banter, but the hot wife with the overdeveloped quads.

V: *you ever think about getting married*

There's no reply for a long time, and Vivienne thinks she's made a tactical error in even asking that question. How many times has Ruby let slip her utter contempt for the institution of marriage and reduced respect for any woman who voluntarily binds herself in shackles just because they have a diamond on them? They literally went to a wedding together. She knows the answer. She knows ...

R: *In general, or you, specifically?*
Vivienne blinks.
V: *the answers are different*
V: *???*
R: *I said no such thing.*
V: *yeah but*
V: *you kinda did*
No reply there, unsurprisingly.

Vivienne knows she's pushing it, but either she's drunker than she thought, or Ruby is feeling particularly lonely and honest. Does she get this way at New Years? She doesn't have enough frame of reference. But she'd like to. Ruby isn't the most difficult person she's ever tried to romance, but she's quite prickly, extremely proud, and has little patience for most people. Vivienne isn't sure what the Goblin Queen sees in her, sometimes. The sex, obviously, but if it was just that, they would have broken up long ago. They certainly wouldn't have gotten over Valentine's Day.

One more thing to try.

V: *tony and I are over btw*

Vivienne looks up at the mirror, which is full of couples and families out in the restaurant behind her, mostly looking extremely happy. It's a festive time of year. Heck, even Orestes and Angel look happy, posing as civilians out there in the rain. And while there's no ring, Vivienne has strong suspicions that a certain question has come up between the two of them. She's happy for them, even though Angel still needs space. And so does she, when it comes down to it.

R: *Is he dead?*

Vivienne smiles wanly.

R: *Impotent? I hear that happens to lots of guys.*

V: *we agreed*

R: *And whose idea was it? Yours or his?*

V: *mine*

V: *call it a new years resolution*

R: *What does that mean, exactly? No more of this "love of my life" thing? Or have you chosen celibacy entirely?*

V: *did you just put quotes in a text*

R: *Answer the question, Vengeance.*

Vivienne takes a deep breath, tries to focus, and does her best to convince herself that isn't Ruby's way of proposing to her.

V: *we're over*

V: *no more sex and stuff*

R: *Really.*

V: *not after last night, anyway*

R: *Of course.*

Vivienne doesn't have to be psychic or even on the same planet as Ruby to know she doesn't believe her. And why should she? Vivienne's been addicted to plenty of things, and it's tough to believe an addict under any circumstances, let alone that they've quit cold turkey. And hasn't Vivienne said this kind of thing before? To Ruby? Probably.

V: *ill prove it to you*

V: *this year, you'll get a whole new me*

R: *Sure, Vengeance.*

Vivienne is searching for the appropriate grinning gif to send when all the windows explode.

# CHAPTER TWENTY-SIX: GODDESS

The first sign that something has gone wrong is the lights dimming all around them. At least, that's what it looks like to mortal eyes. With his Godsight, Marcus Orestes can tell that the festive lights haven't changed, but that another entity is absorbing multiple spectra of light in order to remain unseen by the human eye. He becomes aware of her just before she shimmers into visibility, within arm's reach of where he and Angel stand at the railing.

The second sign that something is wrong is the 50-caliber round that smashes into Angel even as she starts bending at the knees to lunge at the radiant goddess. Thanks to super strength and durability, Angel may look petite, but she weighs nearly three hundred pounds and can tank anti-materiel rounds from much bigger guns if she manages to brace for them at least a *little*. Instead, caught by surprise even as she's gearing up to attack Ishtar, she spirals off over the parking lot, hurled like a ragdoll by the force of the high-velocity round. She'll be fine, and she'll recover her momentum, but the delay is just long enough for Ishtar to reach for Orestes's face, enveloping it in her hands from above like an angel. At her touch, all his power flows from him into her, through Athena's power. She stoops to kiss him.

"My love," Ishtar says. "You have come for me—"

Her lips almost touch his brow when a pink streak of energy explodes into Ishtar with such force and speed that the resulting sonic boom shatters every window in the hotel, parking lot, and probably in the nearby city, and the shockwave makes the whole hotel shake. Orestes tumbles to the ground, deafened by the impact, and blinks as he watches cars in the parking lot floating up into the air like casually discarded toys. The world sounds like a distant echo through the ringing in his ears.

"—cus!" A-Girl is shouting. "*Marcus!*"

There she stands over him, hands locked with Ishtar's own, straining with all her strength against the goddess. For her part, Ishtar hardly seems bothered. In fact, she smiles madly with her beautiful face superimposed over Athena's rotting visage.

"You are nothing to me, child," Ishtar says. "I thought you understood that."

Suddenly, Ishtar twists A-Girl's hands over, making her yelp in pain, and hurls her over the railing toward the waterfall below with such force that A-Girl sends up a geyser of water before the sound even reaches Orestes's ears.

He stumbles up, hands crackling with blue lightning, and faces Ishtar.

"You would strike me, Tammuz?" she asks. "After you came for me in the underworld?"

"No," he says. "We can still resolve this peacefully."

Ishtar doesn't seem to believe that any more than Orestes himself.

A crimson blur cuts out of folded light—a combination of Lady Vengeance's best spell work and a piece of Raven tech—and Muramasa appears, cutting at Ishtar's neck. A regular sword won't even scratch her, of course, but an ancient, cursed, soul-drinking sword of legend? There's a chance. And if she can imprison Ishtar's spirit in her sword, she can end this right here, right now.

Orestes didn't want it to come to this. Yumi has only killed one person with that sword—the Melting Woman—and he knows how hard just that one death weighed on her. But Vivienne convinced her, somehow, and if The Raven is compromised, Lady Vengeance is MIA, and A-Girl can't defeat Ishtar, then Muramasa is their best and only chance.

*I'm sorry, Yumi*, Orestes thinks.

But at the pivotal moment, Muramasa hesitates, and Ishtar moves as the katana cleaves a crimson swath through the air, just shy of her throat. She's moving faster than normal humans can comprehend, and Marcus realizes it's because she's leeched some of Yumi's power. Oh no.

Then Ishtar shoots out a hand and seizes Muramasa by the throat, only to hold her dangling helplessly at arm's length. Even with Athena's statuesque proportions, super strength, and leverage that defies physics, that feat should be impossible considering how fast Muramasa can move. And yet the goddess casually plucks her out of the air as easily as a lazy bumblebee drunk on nectar.

"This was your plan?" Ishtar asks. "Send your new handmaids to defeat me? Tammuz, *really*."

Ishtar raises her other hand wide to her side, fingers flexing into a claw, and catches A-Girl by the throat. She wasn't there before, and suddenly she appears, along with a rush of air that nearly upends the nearby tree. It's like Ishtar summoned A-Girl into her hand, like Yumi calling Muramasa, and arrested her charge with just a straight arm. It doesn't seem possible that she'd know exactly where and how to catch her, until Orestes realizes that Ishtar must have Godsight too. She is, after all, a goddess.

For her part, A-Girl twists and thrashes in Athena's hand, batting at her withered wrist and forearm. Muramasa hangs there like a terrified kitten, the bit of exposed flesh under her mask turning purple from lack of oxygen. Her body trembles with pain and terror.

"Why must you flee, my love?" Ishtar twists Athena's withered face with anger. "Have I not forgiven your infidelities? Why must you anger me so?"

"I told you no," Orestes says. "No means no."

"It is not your choice, my love," Ishtar says. "We are destined to be together for all time. That is the pact we made when I chose you."

"Times change," Orestes says. "Let them go. End this."

"There is no end."

His Godsight activates, and he twitches aside even as a 50-caliber round tears through the air right where his head was, leaving a line of pain across his cheek. The round slams into Ishtar's shoulder, twisting her torso halfway around on her pelvis with a violent crackle of bones and withered flesh. For half a second, she looks hurt, but when she turns back around, her eyes blaze with fury.

"Treacherous monkey," she says, and Orestes knows she means The Raven. She must be controlling him, and he expected Orestes to dodge that shot so it would hit her. He hopes.

Her gaze burns into Orestes. "I'll be back for you."

Then she hurls Muramasa at Orestes, sending her over the railing, and fires herself spiraling upward, dragging A-Girl in her wake.

~

It takes Vivienne a second to shake off the shock of the explosion, and she's almost glad it splintered her senses. Feeling the emotional cacophony of the chaos around her is enough to overwhelm her, making her giddy and clumsy. Her body seems intact, at least relatively speaking, but her phone is cracked in several pieces. She looks at her bloodied palm, where pieces of screen protector have cut into her flesh, and at the purple flames swirling around her limb. Maybe drinking in the bar before a fight was a bad idea, but the sudden explosive attack has elicited so much terror that she's boiling over with absorbed energy, even with the tipsy haze.

Two women in black and gray armor appear out of the smoke, one with an assault rifle, the other with a katana. Their eyes glow crimson, and they obviously look ready to fight, but no sooner do they arrive than their masks retract, revealing their light brown faces and dark eyes.

"Tranquilo," Henrietta says. "Estamos aquí para ayudarte."

"Stay calm, we're here to help." Maria says, in rapid succession. "Come with us." Her gaze meets Vivienne's, and she nods.

At least this part of the plan is going okay. H and M will load these people into Valhalla exfiltration vehicles. Distant sirens say local cops and firefighters are on their way, and Vivienne briefly wonders if they should have trusted the authorities with the plan. But no, they all agreed on this point. Not only are cops untrustworthy as fuck, but their organization is leaky as a colander. They'd take care of this themselves.

She hopes they made the right decision.

The sound of loud crying draws her attention, and she locks gazes with a young mother comforting her infant while her husband coughs and retches onto the floor. They were just eating a perfectly serviceable meal at a booth twenty feet away. They didn't ask for this, and Vivienne couldn't have prevented this. But she can damn sure get them some vengeance.

That's her name, after all.

"Don't worry, kid." She opens her dimensional pocket and slips on her Pentagonal Hex. With hardly a flicker of will, she sends magic running up and down her body, replacing her torn and soot-streaked jeans and blouse with her black and purple costume. The black leather jacket stays. "I got this."

Whether the little family can hear her, or which of them she was talking to, Lady Vengeance strides out of the shattered sliding glass door, claw blazing with power.

Outside, everything has gone seriously sideways. The area is a chaotic mess of splintered boards, rubble, leaves, and tangled branches, sent scattering by the multiple explosions that have gone off at the Falls overlook. A dozen overlapping car alarms sound from the nearby parking lot, and dust shrouds the area like fog. The rune traps and anti-magic Raven tech all seem to have done Jack and his shitty brother, considering the widespread destruction.

She has to correct that assessment as she approaches the twisted railing over the waterfall, where she sees Orestes sweating and straining to use his diminished power to float a thrashing Muramasa over the Falls. So clearly the traps they designed for Ishtar have had an effect, but on the wrong target.

Who would have thought a goddess would be such a powerful magic-user?

Her, that's who. But did they listen? *Nooo.*

"Hang on, kid," Lady Vengeance says. "I'm coming—"

Orestes looks over at her, his face a mask of effort. "V, look out!"

A 50-caliber round caves in a car parked just behind Lady Vengeance, rocking it back on its wheels. She blinks at the damage, then glances down the canyon below. Ishtar must have got to The Raven, and he must be fighting her enchantment to have made himself miss by just a fraction. Though whether it's out of concern for her or not wanting his heart to explode from Ruby's curse, she can't really say. Nor does it matter. The point is he *missed.*

"It's fine," she says through clenched teeth, pushing through her nerves. "Let me."

She molds fear energy into a crackling purple whip and lashes out to entangle Muramasa's ankle. The weapon bites into her flesh, scalding the leather boots, but it's better than falling to her death. A tug of the line draws the young woman toward the railing, where she collapses into Lady Vengeance's arms. She starts to pull away, but Muramasa's wiry arms tighten around her.

"Oh my god," Muramasa is saying. "Oh my god, oh my god, oh—"

"It's okay. Hey, it's okay." She pats the back of Muramasa's head and holds her trembling frame. She looks at Orestes. "What the fuck happened here?"

The kid slumps down next to the railing, exhausted. "Everything's fucked."

"I can see that. I—"

Orestes knocks her over just in time to dodge another 50-caliber round, which cuts through her hair and punches through a white van behind her. Okay, *that* time, he didn't seem to be trying to miss. They crouch behind the twisted railing, putting as much cover between them and The Raven's sniper nest as possible. Another shot detonates into the ledge, sending stone shards flying, but it doesn't hit them.

"Fucking Tony," Lady Vengeance grumbles under her breath.

"A bit late ... for regrets," Orestes says, his voice weak and thin.

She'd laugh, but it's hardly time for jokes, not with Muramasa panicking.

"No, no, no," Muramasa says, coughing and clutching the sides of her head. "I can't ... I can't ... I tried to do what you asked, but I just can't. I'm sorry. I'm so sorry! I've fucked it all up and now you're going to leave me and—"

"Hang on." Lady Vengeance pulls Yumi's helmet off and puts her hands around her face. "I got this. Just ... hang on."

She taps into Muramasa's emotions and draws the fear out of her, calming her tremors and quieting her sobs. Her racing pulse slows, and her breathing calms down. Lady Vengeance presses her forehead to hers, allowing her touch to soothe her.

"There." Lady Vengeance backs off, so as not to drain too much. "You good?"

Blearily, Yumi looks up at her through wet eyes and nods. "Thanks. That ... that's a thing."

"Yeah."

Absorbing people's fears seems like a great power to have. Fear won't be a hindrance on the battlefield, and the tougher and more terrifying an enemy, the more power created, and the more power she can absorb, until she has all the power she needs to defeat said enemy. In theory, anyway. If she could metabolize the energy perfectly, one for one, literally nothing could ever defeat her.

But Lady Vivienne is many things, and none of them perfect. At her best, she can manage like ten or fifteen percent, so she has to come fully prepared with all the fear and anxiety she can absorb from a week at the bar and in traffic, or a multi-hour airplane trip. Which is what she came to today with. Her batteries are full, and she's going to use every bit of it.

"V—" Yumi clings tighter. "I love you."

Lady Vengeance smiles crookedly. "I know."

She definitely took too much. Yumi sags into a kind of restful catatonia, fit to be evacuated. She'll be fine. Eventually. But for now, Lady Vengeance and Orestes are all that's left.

"What now?" Orestes asks. His energy is building back up—too slowly, but hey.

A cry of pain and rage filters down from the smoky clouds above, and Lady Vengeance looks up, her heart leaping. Angel is up there, and she needs help.

"Now—" Lady Vengeance's eyes turn black as purple energy sweeps along her skin, cloaking her in lamellar armor. "You take care of Tony and fix whatever his shit is." A single purple energy wing sprouts from her back. A blade appears in her opposite hand, and her claw crackles with power. "I go save my daughter."

And with a beat of her one mighty wing, she soars up into the sky.

~

A-Girl comes back to herself at the edge of the troposphere, or is she in the stratosphere? Higher? She can't tell for sure, but she's gasping for breath, and ice collects on her exposed skin. Definitely at least in the death zone. She's been curious how her body would manage at high altitudes, ever since Marcus started on his alpine documentaries kick. She's been meaning to fly to the top of Everest one of these days. Good to know her powers can handle the diminished pressure, even if her lungs feel like they're going to explode.

It takes an application of super strength to open her frozen-shut eyelids, and her eyeballs nearly explode out of their sockets. Her pink energy aura flickers dimly, probably preserving her in some way. She floats in the thin air and cold, head over heels, listless and seemingly unaffected by gravity. She's not high enough to be in orbit, is she? What did Ishtar do to her? And where is she?

A-Girl doesn't have long to wonder, because the double goddess—burning with an aura of golden radiance—comes hurtling toward her like a missile. A-Girl tries to dodge, but her body feels sluggish and weak. Best she can do is turn a direct hit into a glancing blow. Rather than tackle her, Ishtar clips A-Girl and sends her spiraling back in an uncontrolled spinning tumble. A-Girl arrests her flight, but not before she slams into a metallic object hard enough to dent it and bruise herself. When her vision finally centers again, she recognizes the StarCom logo.

One of Jaccob Stevens's communication satellites? What are the odds?

Athena crushes her into the satellite, knocking it spiraling off-course with a disconsolate sputter A-Girl feels more than hears. She barely hears anything, come to think of it. The air is so thin, there's nowhere for the sound to go. And yet, when Ishtar speaks without moving Athena's lips, A-Girl hears her loud and clear in her head.

"*It comes to this, false daughter,*" the goddess says, riding A-Girl and the satellite like this is some kind of MMA fight in low orbit. "*Now you know you are neither blood of my blood nor flesh of my flesh, and it has destroyed you. Where have you gone? Your strength? Your fire? Wasted! On a mortal man. A farmer!*"

A-Girl doesn't know what that's all about, but she has to focus on dodging Athena's fist lashing out at her face. The double goddess puts a hole through the satellite, sending sparks and a viscous substance pouring into space, then leaps back. A-Girl has about a second to react before the spark catches in the fuel reserve, and the satellite explodes under her. She tumbles into the atmosphere, blown in that direction by the force. Now gravity has a hold on her, and she plummets back toward the Earth.

*"I expected more, even from the spawn of this corpse's cursed sister."*

And above her blazes a golden field of light, shaped like a predatory raptor, with a goddess at its center. It's Athena's body, and it's burning up under the force of that much divine power and upon re-entry. But the virulent rage in that body is like nothing A-Girl has ever seen or even dreamed of in her worst nightmares. Does she hate her so much?

*"Pathetic!"* Ishtar screams in her mind. *"You can't even fight back."*

A-Girl crosses her arms, and Athena smashes into her like a battering ram, driving them both toward the ground far below, albeit closer than before. A-Girl isn't quite falling at terminal velocity, but if she doesn't fight back, she's going to put a fresh crater in the Pacific Northwest. And can she really survive an impact like that?

She's not gonna find out.

This time when Ishtar sends Athena snapping down at her, A-Girl twists aside, grabs her arm, and hurls her with her own momentum. It's a judo throw Kujikawa-sensei taught her, and Yumi has been only too happy to demonstrate however much A-Girl asks. A-Girl wouldn't have bothered with the technique if Yumi hadn't used it to kick her ass on more than one occasion during sparring.

"If you're ever overpowered—not like that'll happen," she remembers Yumi saying with an impish grin. "Use your opponent's strength against them."

She then put A-Girl through the wall, quite memorably.

Ishtar/Athena is taken off-guard just as A-Girl was then, and she goes flying wildly, below A-Girl. Shame there was no convenient mountain range to direct her flight into. A-Girl rights herself, swooping up with pink fire flaring, and Athena does the same. They come to the same level, circling around one another at thirty or forty feet. They're still high enough that they only share the space with clouds and the occasional airplane. One of which A-Girl sees in the distance. Approaching.

*"I will defeat you now,"* the goddess says in her mind. *"Prepare yourself—"*

"Why?" A-Girl asks, shouting to be heard over the whipping winds.

That gives Athena/Ishtar pause, specifically the Athena part. The ruined body hesitates, as though it doesn't want to attack A-Girl and is looking for an excuse to stand down. *"Why?"*

"Yeah, frickin' *why?*" A-Girl throws her arms wide. "Why do all this? Why pretend you're my mother? Why trick my father? Why—" She wets her lips. "Why convince V she had aborted me? That's really fucked up, even for an evil goddess. 'Because it's evil' is a pretty shitty excuse."

Ishtar considers. *"You deserve nothing but misery. All of you."*

"See, that's something an evil goddess would say," A-Girl says. "But you're not, are you? Marcus says you're not. He still believes in you."

*"Tammuz—"* This time it's Ishtar's turn to hesitate, but only for a second. Athena's withered face twists into an ugly caricature so fiercely that rotted tendons snap, and her jaw slips to the side. *"How dare you. He deserves better. And I will give him better."*

"Obsessive much?"

The goddess snarls.

"You're lonely, aren't you," A-Girl says. "You've spent centuries chasing a dude who wants nothing more to do with you. Cringe. Just think of all the friends you could have made in that time. All the people who could have loved you? But instead, you chose to be alone. What a loser."

*"Like you?"*

"Bitch, I'm adored by *millions*," A-Girl says. "And I have a good man who loves me—"

*"That is meaningless—"*

"Excuse me, I'm talking." Angel puts her hands on her hips. "I have a father who loves me—he's kind of shit at being a dad, but he's trying his best. I have friends who love me, no matter how you terrorize them. I have a kick-ass aunt who's a billionaire, and she loves me like *crazy*."

*"And your mother?"*

"That's—" A-Girl shivers. "That's none of your fucking business, you gaslighting monster."

The goddess smiles, which is especially gruesome. *"Let us end this, then."*

286

"Yeah." A-Girl cocks her fists. "Let's fucking *go*."

~

"Hey!" Orestes shouts at a couple cowering beside the path below the falls, sort of hidden behind a boulder. "Go to the hotel, look for two women in armor—they'll get you out."

"Women in armor?" one of the dudes asks. "What?"

Orestes doesn't have time to discuss, so he channels a little burst of blue electricity around his hand to serve as a visual aid.

"Oh my god, it's Kid Justice!" says the other dude. "You're awesome, bro!"

"Okay?" He hurries on, leaving the two to head up the path on their own.

It's a short hike from the entrance to the Salish Lodge down to the base of the waterfall, and Orestes is barely breathing hard despite running the whole way. All that working out has paid off. His heart is still thundering in his ears, but that has more to do with the barely controlled sociopath with a high-powered, anti-materiel rifle in a sniper's nest above the water.

Is he really going to do this? This is a terrible idea.

But what choice does he really have?

Orestes taps into the gravity around himself and springs into the air. The flight up to the sniper's nest is a quick one, and he arrives in a crackling storm of lightning as the fundamental laws of the universe bend and crackle at his will. Since his resurrection, he's taken to calling his powerset "Forces," because that's what he can control, and because it's his all-time favorite anime song, obviously. He's such a nerd, it's going to get him shot one of these days. Possibly today.

"Chill, Mr. DeSantes. Just be cool."

He didn't arrive subtly, because his powers aren't subtle, but faster than you'd expect from a dude in his late forties, The Raven levels his rifle at Orestes. At this short range, Orestes isn't sure he can stop a shot from that rifle. Maybe he should have thought this through a little better.

"Hey, hey!" Orestes puts his hands up. "It's me. Don't shoot."

"That pendeja made me shoot my own daughter," The Raven says, his voice like broken glass. "You think I won't shoot you, Bill?"

Orestes's comics fanboy powers beat his Godsight to the punch here. The Raven thinks he's William Broaddus. Orestes's father. *Justice*. Shit.

"If I'm Justice," Orestes says, keeping his tone conciliatory and calm. "That rifle won't touch me. And I would have taken you down already."

"Correct," The Raven says. "Unless you're trying to talk me down, which is entirely within Justice's pattern of behavior."

"Think it through," Orestes says. "You're seeing an illusion. Ath—" He winces. Best not to mention The Raven's ex. "Ishtar used her power on you."

"I figured that part out," The Raven says. "When I tried to shoot Miss Deathbringer, and I nearly went into cardiac arrest. Spoiled my aim."

"Miss Death—?"

Orestes's geekdom works overtime. Miss Deathbringer is a minor villain from the Supergroup rogue's gallery. Weapon generation. Regeneration. Goth aesthetic. Yeah, it makes sense that Ishtar would make Lady Vengeance look like her, especially because it would make sure The Raven achieved a kill shot right away. To keep her from getting back up.

Moreover, she was part of the attack that killed Supergroup. Is that ... the scenario Ishtar put in The Raven's mind? Oh god.

"You nearly had a heart attack when you shot at her?"

"Spoiled my aim." The Raven nods slightly, but he keeps Orestes covered with the rifle.

Bad ass. Good reminder not to piss off his future father-in-law.

"Okay, okay," Orestes says. "Retributive biofeedback isn't in her power set."

"Correct," The Raven says.

"But it *is* part of Miss Killingsworth's death curse."

"Ruby—" The Raven considers. "I nearly killed Vivienne. That tracks."

Orestes nods. "So if she wasn't who she appeared to be—"

"You're not either. Based on the similarity in power set, you're Marcus Orestes, unless Justice produced yet another undisclosed lovechild who has only appeared just now."

"That seems contrived. Even for a cape story."

"It does." The Raven lowers the rifle. "Sorry, son."

"No problem." His approval fills Orestes with a warm tingle that has nothing to do with his pseudo-divine powers. "I can try to remove her spell, if you want?"

The Raven nods curtly. "Get me back in the fight. On the correct side, this time."

"You got it, Dad."

"Don't push it."

"Yes, sir."

~

Lady Vengeance's lungs deflate and her body shivers as she rises through the thinning air. She can't fly at the speed of sound, and her very human body isn't cut out for operating at these high altitudes. As such, the best she can do is sweat and heave and watch the battle unfold as she desperately tries to get up there to help.

A-Girl and Athena/Ishtar circle around each other at high speeds like dog-fighting jets, only to slam into each other with enough force to knock orbiting meteors out of the sky. She's already had to dodge the flaming wreckage of a StarCom satellite, which Jaccob is not gonna be happy about. Not that she can call him or anyone else, her phone having been destroyed in Ishtar's initial attack. She'll apologize to him later. She's on her own, and that's fine. Her daughter needs her, and she's going to rise to the challenge.

Eventually.

Slow and steady.

"Fuck," she grumbles, under her hard-to-catch breath.

She's feeling her age in more ways than one. Twenty years ago, she'd already be up there, helping A-Girl against the horrible divine cancer in her sister's corpse, but her powers have practically atrophied since then. She can scare people, sure, create weapons and armor out of fear energy, and even shapeshift sometimes, but that's about it.

What if she had spent the intervening two plus decades developing her abilities? Perfecting her craft, instead of drinking herself into a blackout stupor half the time? Learning more magic? Ruby has already taught her more magic than she ever controlled with any confidence. She could have worked out, even while in hiding? It never seemed important, but just now, looking up at her daughter fighting for her life against a literal goddess, Lady Vengeance is full of regret.

"I'm sorry, mija."

Alongside her, Charisma Cain's spirit appears, tenuous and weak, fading from this world even as she tries to whisper a last message.

"What are you talking about?" Lady Vengeance asks. "¿Mamá? ¿Qué pasa?"

"She was in me for so long," the spirit says, her voice mournful. "I should have seen it, but I've only just realized ... only two ways—"

"What? Spit it out?"

Charisma is flickering in and out of existence, her voice broken up as though by static. "She needs ... a new avatar—"

"What do you mean?" Lady Vengeance demands. "¿Mamá? ¡Mamá!"

Charisma Cain musters the last of her power and force to grasp her daughter by the arms and whisper in her ear. "There are only two ways ... Two ways to take a new avatar. Birth ... or death."

Oh shit.

Only then does Lady Vengeance see what Ishtar is doing. It all falls into place. The memory warping about Angel's birth, the gaslighting about her parentage, the attacks by the Aphid and Nemesis and that face-shifting weirdo in Nevada ... She's manipulated the game board and choreographed this exact scenario. She tried in the desert, but A-Girl didn't cooperate. No, she needed something bigger. She needed the truth. She needed to break Angel, to push her over the edge.

All this time, in her lazy, drunk, narcissistic fugue, Vivienne thought this was about *her*. About some petty revenge between sisters fighting over some dick. But no. She wants Angel.

290

Or more specifically, she wants Angel's *body*.

That's it. If Athena had been Angel's mother, Ishtar could have passed to her, the way she passed from Charisma to Carmen. But Tony knocked up Vivienne instead, and Ishtar couldn't have that. She probably tried, over and over, but this became the plan. Fuck, did she engineer the attack on Supergroup? How far back does it go?

It doesn't matter. Lady Vengeance has to get up there. Has to stop A-Girl before ...

A flash of golden light dazzles her, and she's abruptly spinning uncontrolled through the air until strong hands catch her with a jolt. Lady Vengeance breathes easier for a second, until she recognizes that cold, hard grasp of hands like bony claws. And more importantly, her fear energy drains out of her, the way only Athena's leeching power can.

Fuck.

"V!" A-Girl shouts.

She's streaking toward them, leaving behind a trail of pink trending toward red. She's bruised and battered and furious and so beautiful. They could have been happy together. A family.

"*Hello, sister*," Ishtar says in her mind. "*Are you ready to witness your greatest failure?*"

"No," Vivienne says. "Angel, don't—"

Which is when Athena's hand plunges into her chest, Ishtar's hand super-imposed within it. The corpse's hand is old and withered, shrouded in poorly fitted, yellowing bandages, and even as it tears through, it collapses like brittle cardboard against Lady Vengeance's black leathers, and she feels only the tiniest of scratches.

Ishtar's hand, on the other hand, flows through and right into her heart.

Athena's power pulls the warmth and energy out of Vivienne, it suddenly feels like there's an elephant sitting on her chest, and her whole body goes numb.

The last thing Vivienne hears as her senses fade out is A-Girl's scream.

~

Again.

It happened *again.*

"*Good riddance.*" The goddess casually tosses aside Lady Vengeance's limp body.

Someone is screaming, and A-Girl realizes it's her.

Not again.

"*You do not deserve love,*" Ishtar says.

That's it. It's too much. It's just too much.

A-Girl isn't thinking anymore.

Not *again.*

Her power aura turns vivid, vibrant red, like fresh blood sprayed across snow. All the rage she has felt for months—for over a year—all of it fountains up inside her, coloring her powers to match. Her body hardens like coal crushed to diamond, all condensed into a single, red-hot point of fury.

She's just a human woman—just a girl, really—but in that moment, she will kill a *god.*

It's over in a heartbeat. Even as Vivienne's broken body tumbles down, A-Girl flings herself like a bullet train into the golden heart of Ishtar's power and punches through her chest. Cleaves her withered body asunder with her bare hands. She cries out in anger and pain and sorrow, wrenching her arms wide and hurling the two halves in different directions. Blackened blood showers her—in her eyes, in her mouth, all over her skin—and she screams.

"Thank you," she thinks she hears, and it might be the first time she's ever heard Athena's real, unadulterated voice. Just a faint whisper on the cold wind.

Then it's just the spirit of an ancient goddess floating before her, impossibly beautiful and pure and eternal. She smiles at A-Girl as she encloses her heart-shaped face in her hands.

Wordless, she kisses Angel on the lips.

She has come home.

~

Orestes and Tony stand on the overlook by the Salish Lodge, watching as H and M evacuate the last of the revelers. Those sirens have turned into flashing lights and then emergency vehicles. The authorities are on site, collecting statements. They're going to come hassle Orestes in a second, but he doesn't care. He's staring up into the sky, where a crimson streak of light intersected with and destroyed a golden heart, popping it like a balloon.

"What happened?" Tony asks. "Can you tell?"

Orestes can. But he doesn't want to believe what the Godsight is telling him.

Yumi appears, still clad neck down in her dusty, torn costume. She hasn't bothered to put her mask back on, or maybe she lost it somewhere. Seems like she's past caring about her secret identity. She grabs Orestes's arm. "V? Where's V?"

That, he doesn't know. He can't see her. He can't feel her.

It's the same with Angel.

"Brace for impact," he says.

"What do you—?" Yumi says, but her body is already reacting. A crimson light trace dances through the air as Muramasa tumbles into her hand.

Tony has closed his mask and raised his rifle.

Abruptly the air shatters, as A-Girl lands on one knee and one hand, caving a crater into the parking lot and sending cars flying among a storm of crimson lightning. People run in all directions, screaming in terror as cars crash on top of each other and siren wails fall away to disconsolate whines. Golden hair swirling, she looks up from her crater and offers the three who stand against her a winning smile.

"I've come for you, my love," Ishtar says through A-Girl's lips. "As I always will."

The Raven starts firing.

Ishtar moves faster than should be possible. Angel *can* move that fast, but she never has, as far as Orestes remembers. She hurls herself at them without any wind-up or bracing, and she's covered half of the space between, crackling with crimson lightning, before the Godsight even activates. He sees the world in slow motion— her rippling, wiry muscles, her manic smile, the malevolent obsession in her eyes—and only his own divine powers allow him to flinch.

The high-powered rifle goes off, its muzzle contracting as an explosion of gunpowder and force sends a round capable of denting a tank toward Angel. She dodges it easily, as it just floats through the air past her like a balloon. Angel grasps the hot barrel, wrenches the rifle from The Raven's hands hard and fast enough to break his fingers, and hurls it over the waterfall.

Her powers working on full blast, Yumi moves sluggishly, and her sword slides past Angel harmlessly. That strike goes faster than the human eye, but Ishtar is faster. She knocks the weapon harmlessly up into the air, punches Yumi in the chest hard enough to send her flying with the sound of cracking ribs, and finally closes her arms around Orestes. She feels so much like Angel, but also alien—wrong in a way he can't really explain. But also horribly familiar.

*"Finally,"* she says in his mind. *"Finally, we can be together. Once you are punished."*

She begins to squeeze.

# CHAPTER TWENTY-SEVEN: TEETH

*"Vengeance."*

The word wakes Vivienne—just a little. The world is mostly dark, though she can dimly see the ground far below. She's falling, or perhaps floating. It doesn't matter. She has failed.

Purple light flickers around her, as her fearwing splinters apart, leaving shards of glassy feathers like tears trailing in her wake. That and her blood, which seems to float through the air, weightless in a way she, personally, is very much *not.*

Maybe this is what she deserves. Every time anyone in her life needed her, she's let them down. Even the good times, they were all just building to this moment. Caught up in the schemes of gods, overconfident, sloppy. So *sloppy.* A drunken fuckup. An abject failure.

Why did she survive her fucked-up childhood—the shit with the Agents of Awesome and Supergroup—fifteen years in hiding— all of it? If she had died, none of this would have happened, right? Only because she stubbornly clung to life was any of this possible. If she hadn't fucked Tony that night during the riots, when everything was falling apart ... If she had just left well enough alone, the goddess could have had whatever she wanted, and she never had to be involved.

What has she struggled for all this time?

Not that it matters much anymore. She's dead, or soon to be. Whatever Ishtar did to her, she can't have much longer to live, and even if she survives that, falling from a mile in the sky is definitely going to finish the job.

She's such a fuckup.

"Are you afraid?" he asks.

She is.

Vivienne likes to pretend to be free of fear. To have grown beyond it—to be so used to it that it doesn't faze her. But just now, staring down the barrel of her utter failure and not only her own personal doom but the death of everyone she has ever loved ... or worse, the same thing that happened to her. That they'll live out their lives never knowing the truth until some insane ancient goddess decides she warrants revelation, and then only for her own benefit—not Vivienne's. To spend her whole life as a tool for a cosmic horror that doesn't give a shit about her, but only about herself.

And like always before, she reacts to fear in her quintessential way.

With rage.

"Fuck," she manages to murmur through chapped, broken lips.

"*Yes.*"

"*Fuck.*"

Her heart beats, hard enough to bruise the inside of her crushed chest, and she clings to that pain. That tells her she's alive.

"*Rage,*" the voice says.

"Yes."

This won't fucking stand. She's not going out like this. Even if it kills her, she's going to crush that piece of crap goddess, if it's the last thing she does. And she hopes it is.

"*But at what cost—?*" A tiny little voice seems to ask, but she doesn't listen.

Fuck the cost.

"I need the power," she says. "Give me the power ... to save her."

"*And what will you give in return?*"

"Whatever it takes."

"*Your terms—*" The Many-Mouthed Devourer is pleased. "*Are acceptable.*"

The sky abruptly grows darker, clouds swirling and shot through with purple lightning. Rain scythes like knives around her, but she floats between the raindrops. She alights upon the swell of the wind, and the flutter of wings brushes her cheek. The gnashing of teeth fills her ears.

"*I have waited long,*" the demon says. "*You have traveled a long and lonely path, but I have ever walked at your side. I am yours, and you are mine. I am your shadow. Your darkest self. Your true self.*"

"Yes."

Vivienne extends her arms, falling from heaven like a broken angel, but still alive. Still pulsing with rage. With hatred. With need.

With *hunger.*

"*Call to me,*" the demon says. "*Name me. Claim my power and give yourself to me. Loose your chains and burn your dread. Ravage and tear the earth asunder. Together, we will annihilate your foes and scour this world to ash. Call upon your doom and die.*"

Whatever it takes. *Yes.*

"Come to me, Azazel, the Many-Mouthed Devourer," Vivienne says, feeling the darkness swirl around her. The demon's power and presence suffuses her, and it lends her words mounting power. "Dwell within me and grant me power. Destroy my foes. Shatter this world and any who *dare* claim it from me. From *us.*"

He embraces her, and his touch is as sweet and horrid as when he first came to her. Her life is a petty thing to offer beside what he can do. What he wishes to do. What they will do. Together.

Briefly, she has a doubt. What would Ruby think?

Silly Vivienne. She'll *love* the new her.

Purple light flares around her, her armor and wing pulling themselves back together. *Wings.*

Whatever it takes.

"*Call my name!*" the demon says, triumphant. "*Scream your defiance to the heavens!*"

With the last breath left in her body, she cries out, and the voice is not just hers.

"*VENGEANCE!*"

It is done.

~

Ishtar holds Orestes like a spurned lover, crushing him slowly and mercilessly in her arms, even as she whispers soothing words in an ancient tongue no one living has even heard, much less speaks. She cannot drain his power anymore—without Athena, she seems to have lost that ability—but it takes all of his divine force to keep Angel's impossible strength from crushing every bone in his body.

Tony lies crumpled, wincing as he tries to move his ruined hands and broken body. Yumi is god-knows where, if she's even alive. Ishtar just batted her into orbit for all he knows. And he—he isn't strong enough to resist her.

"Do not worry, my love," she says. "I will find you a new body. Once I pulverize this one in front of my host's eyes. With her own hands. So she learns her place."

Orestes can only choke and sputter. His world is shrinking, waves of crackling pain closing in on an increasingly narrow field of vision. He isn't even trying to fight Ishtar anymore. He just wants to talk to Angel—just once more. Or, barring that, at least see some of her in her body's eyes. But there's only Ishtar—only love twisted to obsession, fertility turned cancerous, and endless, hopeless war. Only the darkest perversion of all those things Ishtar once was, only to be twisted and tainted by humanity.

Then a blast of power separates them, making Ishtar/Angel stagger back, and a figure slams into the ground between them. At first, she seems to be cloaked entirely in purple fire, but her wings open like the petals of a flower—all *eight* of them—and standing within ...

"V?" he asks, panting.

The purple-armored form turns to Orestes, and he sees that she is cradling Yumi's broken body. Even the sight of his friend in such obvious distress isn't enough to tear his Godsight away from Vivienne's face. From her jet-black eyes, utterly devoid of emotion, empathy, and anything remotely human. He can see the demon inside her and knows his Godsight wasn't lying to him.

"I'll heal her," he says, and accepts Yumi's huddled form.

When Vengeance speaks, it isn't only Vivienne's voice. "You do that." Her tone is frigid.

"Kick her ass," Orestes says.

Vengeance grins.

Golden power flares, but Vengeance bats the attack aside with a flutter of her mighty wings. She turns and waggles one armored finger at Ishtar in Angel's body, which half-crouches, clutching its middle in obvious pain. Ishtar's golden gaze glares up at this new opponent, and the hatred oozing from her is almost a palpable thing.

"What is this?" the goddess inside Angel asks with her voice. "What have you done?"

"Oh, Great Ishtar." Vengeance unfurls her purple wings, resplendent in her power. "You've had your fun, but playtime is over. Get the hell out of my daughter."

"I have waited too long for this," Ishtar says. "Too long to let an interloper interfere!"

"Interloper?" Vengeance shrugs her broad shoulders. "I merely fulfill my purpose, fallen goddess, as all things must. You have strayed from your path, and that I find ... anathema."

With a hideous scream, Angel launches herself at Vengeance, who drags her spiraling up into the sky. There they fight, sending blasts of energy and waves of force that batter down upon the Earth like thunder.

Orestes pours the last dregs of his power into Yumi, who coughs her way awake.

"What?" she asks, as he turns to Tony and heals him next. "What ... happened—?"

Orestes isn't sure how to answer that question. "I have to go."

"Go?" Yumi asks. "Go where?"

That, he can't explain either. There isn't enough time.

He's seen this all with his Godsight, even if his power is almost spent now. There's only one way through, and he has to follow the course. He strides toward the twisted railing, mostly destroyed during the battle. He closes his eyes, waiting for the moment.

~

They clash, and it is like the thunderous eruption of shattering stone. Light and dark strive, neither able to conquer the other. Cracks rip through the stone and concrete underfoot, and the skies bleed red, sunset or no. And why not? Today, a demon prince strives with an ancient goddess, and the Earth trembles.

And even more, their chosen avatars are mother and daughter, and the bond between them—full of anger and hate and fear and love and need and sorrow—is more powerful than either.

Ishtar's golden radiance spreads out behind Angel like a raptor's wings—or, perhaps, a heart—then contracts into a storm of lances, which hurl themselves at Vengeance, but she flies around and past them, and none strike her. To her is given the heavenly grace of a fallen angel, for that is the power for which she has bargained.

"No!" Ishtar cries in Angel's voice, the words in the ancient dialect of Sumer. The words spoken when she was an even older goddess—when she bore the name Inanna. "This is not our pact. This is not how it should be."

Lances, spears, and arrows of purest golden light sail toward Vengeance from all angles, but inky black power shot through with purple veins absorbs them one and all. The goddess snarls in frustration, summoning a golden spear to one hand and a reaving axe to the other.

"Oh, foolish child, blinded by love," Vengeance says, in those same words of archaic Uruk, before the Akkadian conquest. "When you descended into the darkness that is mine, heartbroken and alone, did you think you would emerge unscathed?"

The goddess strikes with the fury and form of a lion, pouncing upon the devil harrying her. She slashes through Vengeance's wings, cutting deep furrows through purple energy that shatters like glass. But the devil rakes her own claw across Angel's body, tearing costume, flesh, and soul with infernal power. Ishtar feels the wound, deeper and more painful than even Tammuz's rejection.

That darkness. That cold. She has felt it only once before, in the depths of the world below. She has all but forgotten that suffering, which by contrast was almost a paradise, but the devil's curse reminds her. Vengeance lashes out at her with hatred and dread and fear, and Ishtar cannot endure. This is a battle she cannot win.

But even as she is love, so too is she *war*. She cannot be defeated.

Until she is.

They paint the sky with fire. Steel clashes and shivers to splinters that disintegrate amongst the clouds. Spears of light like shooting stars streak into the darkness around Vengeance and disappear, swallowed up and absorbed. No matter the attack, Vengeance cannot fall. Indeed, she only flies faster, produces more armor, and shines all the brighter. She is beautiful and terrible and inevitable.

300

Ishtar feels the rain upon her face and wishes Tammuz were here with her. His is the power to call upon the lightning, and it has served the justices well as they have endured through the ages. He gives to her and she to him, and together there is nothing they could not do. They two could defeat this monstrosity—this thing that should not be. But she burned away the last of their bond when she tried to claim him against his will. In her victory, she sowed the seeds of her fall. In striving to have all she wanted, she betrayed herself, and now she will suffer for it.

The longer the fight goes on, the less energy Ishtar has. Angel DeSantes's body is young and strong and nigh invulnerable, but the battle she waged with her family took a great deal of strength. By the time Ishtar took possession of her, Angel was all but spent. By contrast, Vengeance holds herself in reserve, absorbing all the hate and violence Ishtar hurls her way. It only seems to make her grow stronger. If Ishtar could land a blow upon the devil's avatar, that would be one thing, but the feararmor is impenetrably thick. All the damage she inflicts upon it fades away with the next attack. The devil has an inexhaustible supply of power, it seems. All the fear in all the world.

The end, when it comes, is swift.

Ishtar in Angel's body takes a daring, wild lunge at Vengeance, but the devil-woman flinches aside and embraces her instead. It surprises Ishtar such that she barely feels the woman sinking the claws of her infernal gauntlet into Angel's stomach, piercing right through her mighty strength.

"You made a mistake, Queen of Heaven, when you abandoned Athena—and her power." Vengeance twists the claw deeper, making A-Girl's body go taut with pain. "If you were still her, you could take my power. You could take my memories—my strength—all the things that empower me. But I—" She plunges her bare hand into Ishtar's head, fingers going right through her flesh and bone and brain as though intangible. "I will take all the vile, disgusting things within you. Your fear. Your dread. Your rage. Your hate." Now Vengeance grins madly. "Call it a gift."

And even as it is spoken, so is it done.

The darkness peels away from Ishtar—centuries of the accumulated filth of humanity—and flows into Vengeance. She sees people in chains, hurling themselves into the sea. She sees bombs falling on families. Emaciated bodies lined up for summary execution. She sees mushroom clouds. Starving children. Faces full of hate, mouths full of blood, guts full of maggots. Pits of rotting human flesh. She watches a parade of goosestepping soldiers flying swastikas, wearing white hoods, wearing red ballcaps. A wellspring of the deepest, darkest depravities of humanity, over and over and over again.

Wading through an endless flood of atrocities would shatter the strongest of human minds and corrupt the greatest of mortal souls. Ishtar has all this darkness inside her, and it has tainted her beyond rationality and her original purpose. No human could ever absorb millennia of malice, but Vengeance is no mere human. Not anymore. Never again.

Instead, the darkness fuels her. She is humanity's darkness. She is dread. She is doom. She is fear. She is hunger. She is the end of dreams. She consumes all. She *is* all.

Ishtar never stood a chance.

Vivienne Cain floats down toward the waterfall, cradling Angel's torn body in her arms. That's what anyone would see, if they chanced to look. And many are watching: patrons of the Lodge, New Years revelers, police, firefighters, and their family. Tony is shouting something, but neither of them can hear it.

*No,* Vivienne thinks. *This isn't what we agreed.*

But Azazel does not and has never cared what she wants.

The abyss yawns beneath them: a hole in reality only those with the sight of gods can see. And within, a world of fragmented mirrors reflects a thousand terrible truths. Every mirror an insight into the sins and mistakes of the viewer. Every mirror a mocking grin.

Gently, Angel reaches up to touch her mother's face, chapped fingers brushing her cheek.

"She will survive," the goddess says, voice weak as the thinnest breeze. "As the flower greets the spring, I will pass the winter and be reborn. So long as love and light endure, *she* shall return."

"Oh." Vengeance's smile is almost motherly. "I know."

And she spreads her hands, letting the goddess in Angel's body fall into the Fearworld.

Blue lightning crackles, and Vengeance sees Orestes flying toward her. No, not toward her, but toward the portal to the

Fearworld. He catches Angel, enfolds her in his arms, and they fall together into that world where lies cannot abide. Where the horrible, devastating truth lurks on every surface.

As the hole in reality seals between them, she flashes Orestes one last smile.

One with too many teeth.

# ABOUT THE AUTHOR

The author of some 25 novels and counting, Erik Scott de Bie is a speculative fiction writer whose favored genres include fantasy, sci-fi, horror, and superheroes, and especially pieces that mix all of the above. He is also a known quantity in the gaming industry, being an author and/or editor of a number of major releases for *Dungeons & Dragons*, *Pathfinder*, *Iron Kingdoms*, the Cthulhu Mythos, and others. He is best known for his Shadowbane series set in the Forgotten Realms, his World of Ruin post-apocalyptic fantasy series, and his contributions to the Dungeon Scrawlers livestream community, of which he is a founding member. He lives in Seattle with his wife and their menagerie of pets. Find him online at erikscottdebie.com.

www.ingramcontent.com/pod-product-compliance
Lightning Source LLC
Chambersburg PA
CBHW051939220626
47052CB00004B/713

* 9 7 8 1 9 4 8 2 8 0 4 8 8 *